# CITY IN RUINS

## ALSO BY DON WINSLOW

# CITY
## IN
## RUINS

### A Novel

## Don Winslow

*wm*

WILLIAM MORROW

*An Imprint of HarperCollinsPublishers*

CITY IN RUINS. Copyright © 2024 by Samburu, Inc. All rights reserved. Printed in the United States of America. No part of this book may be used or reproduced in any manner whatsoever without written permission except in the case of brief quotations embodied in critical articles and reviews. For information, address HarperCollins Publishers, 195 Broadway, New York, NY 10007.

HarperCollins books may be purchased for educational, business, or sales promotional use. For information, please email the Special Markets Department at SPsales@harpercollins.com.

FIRST EDITION

*Designed by Kyle O'Brien*

*Art credits include: Virrage Images/Shutterstock; Miune/Shutterstock*
*schmaelterphoto/Shutterstock; davemattera/Shutterstock; Martins Vanags/Shutterstock*

Library of Congress Cataloging-in-Publication Data has been applied for.

ISBN 978-0-06-307947-2

24 25 26 27 28 LBC 5 4 3 2 1

*To Shane Salerno, who did everything he said he would.*
*What a ride, huh? Thank you, brother.*

*And to end as we began—to Jean and Thomas, the how and the why.*

So, couldn't they die on the plains of Troy?
So, couldn't they stay defeated in defeat?

Virgil

*The Aeneid*

Book VII

# CITY IN RUINS

# PROLOGUE

**D**ANNY RYAN WATCHES THE BUILDING come down.

It seems to shiver like a shot animal, then is perfectly still for just an instant, as if it can't bring itself to acknowledge its death, and then falls down on itself. All that's left of where the old casino once stood is a tower of dust rising into the air, like a cheesy trick from some lounge-act magician writ large.

"Implosion," they call it, Danny thinks.

Collapse from the inside.

Aren't they all, Danny thinks.

Most of them, anyway.

The cancer that killed his wife, the depression that destroyed his love, the moral rot that took his soul.

All implosion, all from the inside.

He leans on the cane because his leg is still weak, still stiff, still throbs as a reminder of . . .

Collapse.

He watches the dust rise, a mushroom cloud, a dirty gray-brown against the clear blue desert sky.

Slowly it fades and then disappears.

Nothing now.

How I fought, he thinks, what I gave for this . . .

Nothing.

This dust.

He turns away and limps through his city.

His city in ruins.

# PART ONE

# Ian's Birthday Party

## Las Vegas
## June 1997

But devout Aeneas now—the last rites performed and the grave-mound piled high . . . sets sail on his journey . . .

Virgil
*The Aeneid*
Book VII

# ONE

**D**ANNY'S DISCONTENT.

Looking down at the Las Vegas Strip from his office window, he wonders why.

Less than ten years ago, he thinks, he was fleeing Rhode Island in an old car with an eighteen-month-old son, a senile father, and everything he owned jammed in the back. Now he's a partner in two hotels on the Strip, lives in a freakin' mansion, owns a cabin up in Utah and drives a new car every year that the company pays for.

Danny Ryan is a multimillionaire, which he finds as amusing as it is surreal. He never dreamed—hell, nobody who knew him back in the day ever dreamed—that he'd ever have a net worth beyond his next paycheck, much less be considered a "mogul," a major power player in the major power game that is Las Vegas.

Whoever doesn't believe that life is funny, Danny thinks, doesn't get the joke.

He can easily remember when he had twenty bucks in his jeans pocket and he thought he was rich. Now the clip he keeps in one of his tailor-made suits usually has a thousand or more in it as walking-around money. Danny can recall when it was a big deal when he and Terri could afford to go out for Chinese on a Friday night. Now he "dines" at Michelin-starred restaurants more than he wants to, which partially accounts for the shelf developing at his waistline.

When asked if he's watching his weight, he usually answers that yes, he's watching it slide over his belt, the bonus ten pounds he's gained from living a mostly sedentary life at a desk.

His mother has tried to get him into tennis, but he feels stupid chasing a ball around just to whack it and have it come right back at him, and he doesn't play golf because for one thing it's as boring as shit, and for another, he associates the game with doctors, lawyers, and stockbrokers, and he's not any of those.

The old Danny used to sneer at those types, looked down at those effete businessmen from beneath. He'd jam his toque down over his shaggy hair, climb into his old peacoat, grab his brown-bag lunch with pride and a chip on his shoulder, and go to work on the Providence docks, a Springsteen kind of guy. Now he listens to *Darkness* on a Pioneer stereo system that ran him a bill and a half.

But he still prefers a cheeseburger to Kobe beef, good fish-and-chips (impossible to get in Vegas at any price) to Chilean sea bass. And on the rare occasion when he has to fly anywhere, he goes commercial instead of taking the corporate jet.

(He does, however, fly first class.)

His reluctance to use the company's Learjet pisses his son off no end. Danny gets it—what ten-year-old doesn't want to fly on a private jet? Danny has promised Ian that the next vacation they go on of any distance, they'll do it. But he'll feel guilty about it.

"Dan is a chowderhead," his partner Dom Rinaldi said one time, meaning that he's an old New England, practical—well, *cheap*—guy . . . for whom any kind of physical indulgence is deeply suspect.

Danny deflected the issue. "Try getting a decent bowl of chowder here. Not that milky baby puke they serve, but *real* chowder in the clear broth."

"You employ five executive chefs," Dom said. "They'll make you chowder from the foreskins of virgin Peruvian frogs if you tell them to."

Sure, but Danny won't do that. He wants his chefs spending their time making the guests anything *they* want.

That's where the money comes from.

He gets up, stands by the window—tinted to combat the relentless Las Vegas sun—and looks down at the Lavinia Hotel.

The old Lavinia, Danny thinks, the last of the hotels from the fifties building boom—a relic, a remnant, barely hanging on. Its long-gone heyday was the era of the Rat Pack, wiseguys and showgirls, counting room skim and dirty money.

If those walls could talk, Danny thinks, they'd take the Fifth.

Now it's on the market.

Danny's company, Tara, already owns the two adjacent properties to the south, including the one he's standing in. A rival group, Winegard, has the casinos to the north. Whoever ends up with the Lavinia will control the most prestigious location left on the Strip, and Las Vegas is a prestige kind of town.

Vern Winegard has the purchase all but sewed up, Danny knows. Probably for the best, probably not wise for Tara to expand too quickly. Still, it *is* the only space left on the Strip, and . . .

He buzzes Gloria in the outer office. "I'm going to the gym."

"Do you need directions?"

"Funny."

"Do you remember that you have a lunch with Mr. Winegard and Mr. Levine?"

"I do now," Danny says, although he wishes he didn't. "What time?"

"Twelve thirty," Gloria says. "At the club."

Even though Danny doesn't play golf or tennis, he's a member of the Las Vegas Country Club, because, as his mother instructed him, it's pretty much mandatory for doing business.

"You have to be seen there," Madeleine said.

"Why?"

"Because it's old Las Vegas."

"I'm *not* old Las Vegas," Danny said.

"But I am," she said, "and like it or not, to do business in this town, you have to do it with old Las Vegas."

Danny joined the club.

"And the bouncy castle will be delivered by three," Gloria says.

"The bouncy castle."

"For Ian's birthday party?" Gloria says. "You do remember that Ian's party is this evening."

"I remember," Danny says. "I just didn't know about a bouncy castle."

"I ordered it," Gloria says. "You can't have a kid's birthday party without a bouncy castle."

"You can't?"

"It's expected."

Well then, Danny thinks, if it's expected . . . A horrifying thought hits him. "Do I have to assemble it?"

"The guys will inflate it."

"What guys?"

"The bouncy castle guys," Gloria says, getting impatient. "Really, Dan, all you have to do is show up and be nice to the other parents."

Danny is sure this is true. The ruthlessly efficient Gloria has teamed up with his equally methodical mother to plan this party, and the two of them together are a terrifying combination. If Gloria and Madeleine ran the world—as they think they should—there would be full employment and no wars, famine, pestilence or plague, and everyone would always be on time.

As for being nice to the guests, Danny's always nice, affable, even charming. But he does have a justified reputation for sneaking off at parties, even his own. All of a sudden someone notices his absence, and he's found in a back room by himself, or wandering around outside, and on more than one occasion, when a party has gone late into the night, he has simply gone to bed.

Danny hates parties. Hates schmoozing, small talk, finger food, standing around and all that shit. It's tough, because socializing is a big part of his job. He pulls it off, he's good at it, but it's his least favorite thing.

When the Shores opened, just two years ago after three years in construction, the company threw an opening-night extravaganza, but no one can remember seeing Danny there.

He didn't give one of the several speeches, he didn't appear in any of the photographs, and the legend started that Danny Ryan didn't even attend the opening of his own hotel.

He did—he just stayed in the background.

"Ian's going to be ten," he says now. "Isn't that too old for a bouncy castle?"

"You're never too old," Gloria says, "for a bouncy castle."

Danny clicks off and stares out the window again.

You've changed, he thinks.

It's not just the excess pounds, the slicked-back Pat Riley haircut, the suits from Brioni instead of Sears, cuff links instead of buttons. Before Las Vegas, you wore suits only at weddings and funerals. (Given the hard facts about New England in those days, there were more of the latter than of the former.) It's not just that you have folding money in your pocket, that you can pay for a meal without worrying about the tab, or that a tailor will come to your office with a tape measure and swatches.

It's the fact that you like it.

But there's this sense of . . .

Discontent.

Why? he wonders. You have more money than you can spend. Is it just greed? What was it the guy in that dumb movie—his name was like some lizard or something—said: "Greed is good"?

Fuck that.

Danny knows himself. With all his faults, his sins—and they are legion—greed isn't one of them. He used to joke with Terri that he could live in his car and she'd retort, "Have a good time."

So what is it? What do you want?

Permanence? Stability?

Things you've never had.

But you have them now.

He thinks of the beautiful hotel he built, the Shores.

Maybe it's the beauty you want. Some beauty in this life. Because you've sure as hell had the ugly.

A wife dead from cancer, a child left without a mother.

Friends killed.

And the people *you* killed.

But you did it. You built something beautiful.

So it's more than that, Danny thinks.

Be honest with yourself—you want more money because money is power and power is safety. And you can never be safe enough.

Not in this world.

# TWO

**D**ANNY HAS LUNCH ONCE A month with his two biggest competitors. Vern Winegard and Barry Levine.

It was Barry's idea, and it's a good one. He owns three mega-hotels on the east side of the Strip across from the Tara properties. There are other casino owners, of course, but these three form the nexus of power in Las Vegas. As such, they have shared interests and common problems.

The biggest one now is a looming federal investigation.

Congress has created the Gambling Impact Study Commission to investigate the effects of the gaming industry on Americans.

Danny knows the numbers.

Gaming is a trillion-dollar business, grossing over six times more money than all other forms of entertainment combined. Last year, players lost over $16 billion, $7 billion right here in Las Vegas.

The idea is gaining steam that gambling isn't just a habit, or even a vice, but an illness, an addiction.

When gambling was illegal, it was organized crime's breadbasket, by far its biggest profit center after Prohibition and bootlegging ended. Whether it was the numbers racket hawked on every street corner, or the race wire, the sports books, or backroom poker, blackjack and roulette games, the mob raked in vast amounts of money.

The politicians saw that and of course wanted their taste. So what once was a private vice became a civic virtue as state and local governments muscled in on the numbers with their own lotteries. Still, Nevada was about the only place that a gambler could legally play table games or bet sports book, so Las Vegas, Reno and Tahoe pretty much had a monopoly.

Then the Native American reservations figured they had a loophole and started opening their casinos. States, particularly New Jersey with Atlantic City, started doing the same thing and gambling proliferated.

Now anyone can just get in a car to go lose the rent or mortgage money. Some social reformers are likening gambling to crack cocaine. So now there's going to be a congressional investigation.

Danny's cynical about the motives, suspicious that it's just them trying to stick their noses into the trough. Some of the Democrats are already floating the idea of a 4 percent federal tax on gambling profits.

For Danny, the tax isn't the worst of it.

As it stands, the bill will give the commission full subpoena power to hold hearings, call witnesses under the penalty of perjury, demand records and tax returns, look into shadow corporations and silent partners.

Like me, Danny thinks.

The investigation could blow the Tara Group to bits.

Force me out of the business.

Maybe even put me in jail.

I'd lose everything.

This subpoena threat isn't just an annoyance or another problem—it's a survival issue.

"A *disease*?" Vern asks. "*Cancer* is a disease. *Polio* is a disease."

Polio? Danny thinks. Who the hell remembers polio? But he says, "We can't be seen to be fighting this. It's a bad look."

"Danny's right," Barry says. "We have to do what the alcohol industry has done, big tobacco—"

Vern won't let it go. "You show me the craps table that's given anyone cancer."

"We put out some PSAs about gambling responsibly," Barry says, "we stick brochures for Gamblers Anonymous in the rooms, we fund some studies on gambling addiction."

Danny says, "We can issue our mea culpas, throw some money along the lines that Barry suggested, fine. But we can't let this commission go on a fishing expedition into our businesses. We have to shut down the subpoena power. That's the line in the sand, as it were."

No one disagrees. Danny knows that neither of them wants their financial laundry aired in public. Those sheets wouldn't be squeaky clean.

"Here's the problem," Danny says. "We've only been donating money to the GOP—"

"They're on our side," Vern says.

"Right," Danny says. "So the Democrats see us as the enemy. They'll come after us with a vengeance."

"So you want to give money to our enemies," Vern says.

"I want to hedge our bets," Danny says. "Keep giving to the GOP, but get some quiet money to the Dems, too."

"Bribes," Vern says.

"Never entered my mind," Danny says. "I'm talking about campaign contributions."

"You think we can persuade the Dems to accept money from us?" Vern asks.

"You think you can persuade a dog to accept a bone?" Barry asks. "The issue is how we start making nice."

Danny hesitates, then says, "I invited Dave Neal to the party tonight."

Dave Neal, a major player in the Democratic Party who holds no official position and is therefore free to maneuver. The word is if you want to get to the highest level of the Democratic Party, you could go through Neal.

"You think you might have talked to us about that first?" Vern asks.

No, Danny thinks, because you would have objected. It was one of those permission/forgiveness things. "I'm talking to you now. If you don't think I should make an approach, I won't. He comes to the party, he eats and drinks, he goes back to the hotel—"

"At this level," says Barry, "a comped suite and a blow job aren't going to do it. These guys are going to expect some real money."

"We'll ante up," Danny says. "Cost of doing business."

There's no disagreement—the other two men agree that they'll come up with money.

Then Vern asks, "Dan, are wives invited to this thing tonight?"

"Of course."

"I didn't know if they were, and mine's nagging me," Vern says. "You don't have to worry about that, you lucky prick."

Danny notices Barry wince.

It was an insensitive remark—everyone knows that Danny is a widower. But Danny doesn't think that Vern meant any harm or offense—it was just Vern being Vern.

Danny doesn't dislike Vern Winegard, although he knows a lot of people who do. The man has the social graces of a rock. He's abrasive, generally disagreeable and arrogant. Still, there's something to like about him. Danny isn't sure exactly what, some vulnerability under all that posturing. And although Winegard is a sharp businessman, Danny has never heard of his cheating anyone.

But he feels this little stab in his chest. Once again, Terri won't be there to see her son's birthday.

But the meeting went well, Danny thinks. I got what I wanted, what I needed.

If money will kill this subpoena thing, great.

If not, I'll have to find something else.

He glances at his watch.

He just has time to make his next appointment.

# THREE

D ANNY WAKES TO TENDRILS OF sable hair on a slender neck, musky perfume, beads of sweat on bare shoulders even in the chill of his air-conditioned bedroom.

"Did you sleep?" Eden asks.

"I dozed off," Danny says. "Dozed," bullshit, he thinks, starting to come to. You dropped off like you were dead, a short but deep postcoital sleep. "What time is it?"

Eden Landau lifts her wrist and looks at her watch. It's funny, it's the one thing she never takes off. "Four fifteen."

"Shit."

"What?"

"Ian's party."

"I thought it wasn't until six thirty," she says.

"It isn't," Danny says. "But, you know, things to do."

She rolls over to face him. "You're allowed pleasure, Dan. Even sleep."

Yeah, Danny has heard this before, from other people. It's easy to say, it's even rational, but it doesn't acknowledge the reality of his life. He's responsible for two hotels, hundreds of millions of dollars, thousands of employees, tens of thousands of guests. And the business isn't exactly nine-to-five—there are famously no clocks in casinos and the problems are twenty-four seven.

"You of all people know I take time for pleasure," he says.

True, she thinks.

Mondays, Wednesdays and Fridays, two o'clock sharp.

Actually, it works for her. Fits perfectly into her routine, because she's on a Tuesday/Thursday teaching schedule, with one night class on Wednesdays. Dr. Eden: Psych 101, General Psychology; Psych 416, Cognitive Psych; and Psych 441, Abnormal Psych.

She sees clients late afternoons or evenings, and sometimes wonders what they'd think if they knew that she just got out of bed from one of these matinees. The thought makes her chuckle.

"What?" Danny asks.

"Nothing."

"You laugh at nothing a lot?" Danny asks. "Maybe you should see a shrink."

"I do," she says. "Professional requirement. And 'shrink' is derogatory. Try 'therapist.'"

"You sure you don't want to come to the party?" he asks.

"I have clients tonight. And besides . . ."

She lets it trail. They both know the deal. It's Eden who wants to keep their relationship a secret.

"Why?" Danny asked once.

"I just don't want all that."

"All what?"

"All that comes with being Dan Ryan's girlfriend," Eden said. "The spotlight, the media . . . First of all, the notoriety would hurt my work. My students wouldn't take me as seriously, and neither would my clients. Second, I'm an introvert. If you think you hate parties, Dan, I *hate* parties. The faculty dos that I have to go to, I arrive late and leave early. Third, and no offense, casinos depress the hell out of me. The sense of desperation is soul-killing. I don't think I've even been on the Strip in two years."

Truth be told, it's one of the things that attracts him about her, that she's the exact opposite of most of the women he meets in Las Vegas. Eden doesn't want the glitz, the gourmet dinners, the parties, the shows, the presents, the glamour, the fame.

None of it.

She put it succinctly. "What I want is to be treated nicely. Some good sex, some good conversation, I'm good."

Dan checks those boxes. He's considerate, sensitive, with an old-school sense of chivalry that just borders on paternalistic sexism but doesn't cross the line. He's good in bed and he's postcoitally articulate, even though he's clueless about books.

Eden reads a lot. George Eliot, the Brontës, Mary Shelley. Lately she's been on a Jane Austen kick. In fact, for her next vacation she already booked one of those tours of Austen country, and will go blissfully alone.

She's tried to get Dan interested in literature outside of business books.

"You should read *Gatsby*," she said one time.

"Why is that?"

Because it's you, she thought, but said, "I just think you'd like it."

Eden knows a little about his past. Anyone who ever waited at a super-market checkout counter does—his affair with movie star Diane Carson was tabloid fodder. And when Diane Carson committed suicide after he left her, the media went nuts for a while.

They called Dan a gangster, a mobster. There were allegations that he'd been a drug trafficker and a murderer.

None of that squares with the man she knows.

The Dan Ryan she knows is kind, gentle and caring.

But she's sufficiently self-aware and trained to know that she enjoys the frisson of danger, of disrespectability that comes with his reputation, whether true or not. She was raised in an utterly respectable, normal background, so of course she'd find the difference attractive.

Eden feels a little guilty about it, knows she's flirting with immorality. What if the stories about Dan are true? What if even some of them have a basis in reality? Is it still right for her to be literally in bed with him?

An open question that she's unwilling at this point to answer.

Dan's affair with Diane Carson was six years ago, but Eden thinks that he really loved that woman. Even now, there's an air of sadness to him. She knows he's a widower, too, so maybe that's it.

They met on a fundraising walk for breast cancer, each of them engaging to walk twenty miles a day for three days. Dan got his rich friends and colleagues to sponsor him and God knows how much money he raised.

But he walked, she thought, when he could have easily just written a check.

She said so to him. "You're committed."

"I am," he said. "My wife. My . . . *late* wife."

Which made her feel like shit.

"And you?" he asked.

"My mother."

"I'm sorry."

He asked her about herself.

"I'm a walking stereotype," Eden said. "A Jewish girl from the Upper West Side who went to Barnard and became a psychotherapist."

"What's a New York psychiatrist—"

"Psychologist—"

"*Psychologist*—doing in Las Vegas?"

"The university offered me a tenure-track position," she said. "When my New York friends ask me the same question, I tell them that I hate snow. And you? What's your story?"

"I'm in the gaming industry."

"In Las Vegas? You're kidding!"

He held his hand up. "The truth. By the way, I'm Dan—"

"I was joking with you," she said. "Everyone knows who Dan Ryan is. Even I do, and I don't even gamble."

That was on the first day's walk. It took him until day three, after a good ten miles, to ask her out.

What surprised her was that he was so bad at it.

For a man who'd had an affair with a movie star, one of the most beautiful women in the world, a billionaire casino owner who had access to all kinds of gorgeous women, he was incredibly awkward.

"I was wondering if . . . I mean, if you don't want to, I get it . . . no hard feelings . . . but I thought . . . you know . . . maybe I could take you to dinner or something sometime."

"No."

"Right. Got it. No problem. Sorry to—"

"Don't be sorry," she said. "I just don't want to go *out* with you. If you'd like to come over and bring dinner . . ."

"I can have one of my chefs—"

"Takeout," she said. "Boston Market. I love their meatloaf."

"Boston Market," he said. "Meatloaf."

"I have next Thursday night free. Do you?"

"I'll make it free."

"And, Dan," she said, "this is just between us, okay?"

"You're ashamed of me already?"

"I just don't want my name in the gossip columns."

Eden stuck to that. The occasional dinner, fine; the three-times-a-week matinees, fine. Beyond that, no. She wants a quiet life. She wants Danny on the down-low.

"So I'm basically a booty call," Danny said one afternoon.

She laughed at him. "You're not allowed to be the woman in this relationship. Let me ask you, is the sex good?"

"Great."

"Is the companionship good?"

"Again, great."

"Then why do you want to mess it up?"

"You never think about marriage?"

"I had a marriage," she said. "I didn't like it."

Her ex-husband, Frank, was a good guy. Faithful, nice, but so needy. And the neediness made him controlling. He resented the evenings she spent with patients, the alone time she wanted with her books. He wanted her to go out to too many dinners with his law firm partners, tables at which she had nothing to say and less to hear.

The offer from Las Vegas came at the right time.

A clean break, a reason to leave both Frank and New York. She knew he was probably relieved, although he would never say so. But she wasn't the wife he needed.

To her immense surprise, Eden likes Las Vegas. She had thought it would be her rebound location, a pit stop to heal from her failed five-year marriage before moving on to a place with more culture.

But she's found that she likes the sun and the heat, likes to lie out by the pool at her condo complex and read. Likes the ease of living there as opposed to the endless competition that is New York—the fights for space, for cabs, a seat on the subway, a cup of coffee, everything.

She drives to her office on campus and has a designated parking spot. Same with the covered parking structure at the medical building where she sees her clients. Same with the condo.

It's easy.

So is grocery shopping, always a hassle in New York, especially in the snow and sleet. Ditto going to the pharmacy, the dry cleaner, all the mundane errands that took up so much time in New York.

Which lets her focus on the important things.

Her students, her patients.

Eden cares about her students—she wants them to learn, to succeed. She cares about her patients—she wants them to get well, be happy. She wants to bring all her intelligence, education and skills to bear to achieve these things, and the ease of living here allows her the energy to do that.

The students are pretty much the same; so are the patients. The neuroses, the insecurities, the traumas, the same steady drumbeat (heartbeat?) of human pain. There are a few local Las Vegas twists—the gambling addicts, the high-end call girl—but those are about the only infusions of the casino world in Eden's life.

Well, except for Dan.

Her New York friends ask her, "What about the museums? What about the theater?"

She tells them that they have museums and theater in Las Vegas, and let's be honest, the struggles of working and living in New York left them with little time to go to exhibits and plays anyway.

Aren't you lonely? they ask.

Well, not anymore, she thinks.

The arrangement (Can you call it a relationship? she asks herself. I suppose so) is perfect. They give each other affection, sex, companionship, laughs.

But now he wants me to come to his son's birthday party? Where all of power Las Vegas will be present? Talk about jumping into the deep end . . . But knowing Dan—he probably doesn't really want me to come, he just doesn't want to hurt my feelings by not inviting me.

"Dan," she says, "I don't feel like you're hiding me. I want to be hidden."

"Got it."

"Does that hurt your feelings?"

"No."

Danny has loved two women in his life, and they both died young.

His wife, Terri—Ian's mother—the breast cancer had been unforgiving, unrelenting, capricious and cruel.

Danny left her comatose and dying in the hospital.

Never had a chance to say goodbye.

The second woman was Diane.

In an earlier era, Diane Carson would have been called a goddess of the golden screen or something like that. In her own time she was a movie star, the stereotypical sex symbol that everyone loved but who could never love herself.

Danny loved her.

It was his one blazing affair as they trotted out their love for the world to see, a feast for the tabloids, the clicking of camera shutters the leitmotif of their life together.

It was too much.

Their different worlds pulled them apart, *ripped* them apart. Her fame couldn't tolerate his secrets; his secrets couldn't abide her fame. But in the end, it was a secret of hers, a deeply held shame, that destroyed them.

Danny left, thinking he had saved her by going.

She overdosed, the tragic Hollywood ending.

So the last thing that Danny wants now is love.

But he's always been a one-woman man, he doesn't have the desire or the time to "chase tail," even of the professional sort, and he needs a routine.

So the afternoons with Eden work.

Eden is great.

Drop-dead gorgeous—lush black hair, full lips, dazzling eyes, a figure out of an old noir movie. She's funny, full of wit and charm, and in bed, well . . . One time, shortly after they first went to bed, she offered him the *spécialité de la maison,* and it was certainly special.

Now Danny hops out of bed and gets into the shower. He's in there for maybe a minute, then comes out and gets dressed.

Typical Dan, Eden thinks. Always efficient, no wasted time.

"You're sure about the party?" he asks.

"I am."

"There'll be a taco bar."

"Tempting."

"And a bouncy castle."

"A combination with immense potential," she says. "But . . ."

"I'll lay off," Danny says. "Monday?"

"But of course."

He kisses her and leaves.

# FOUR

I T SEEMS LIKE HALF THE town is there.

Spread out on Madeleine's broad lawn, sipping wine, munching on the catered food, exchanging gossip.

When Gloria had insisted that all Ian's schoolmates and all their parents had to be invited, Danny didn't realize that meant most of the movers and shakers in Las Vegas.

I should have, he thinks now. Ian goes to The Meadows, where all the major players send their kids. And most of them accepted the invitation— some to accompany their children; others because they were afraid to turn down an invite from Madeleine McKay and Dan Ryan; the rest out of curiosity.

Then there are some friends, partners and senior employees of Tara, their spouses and significant others.

Danny doesn't even want to know how much this event is costing—the liquor, the food, the band, the freakin' bouncy castle, where, as Gloria predicted, a gang of kids—Ian included—are jumping up and down, screaming and laughing.

Danny remembers his own childhood birthdays, which mostly consisted of his father forgetting it was his birthday. He thinks it was maybe his ninth birthday when he filched a dollar from Marty's pocket, went to the drugstore and bought a Coke, a candy bar, two comic books, and sat on the sidewalk savoring them.

It was, he thinks now, one of the best birthdays of his life.

Madeleine interrupts his reverie. Walking up behind his shoulder, she says, "Ian seems to be having a good time."

"Why not?" Danny asks.

"And his dad?"

"Wonderful," Danny says. "I live for parties."

"Sarcasm only works for gay men and stand-up comedians," Madeleine says. "It doesn't suit you—you're too earnest."

My mother, Danny thinks, the product of a Barstow trailer park, has evolved lately to making regal pronouncements of this sort. *Sarcasm is for gay men, only salesmen wear plaid, women over thirty must always wear bras* . . . She watches far too much BBC.

And she does look regal in a loose white dress that a Greek goddess might wear, her red hair swept into an updo, her makeup subtle and perfect as always.

Now she says, "All the mothers seem to have shown up."

Danny knows what's coming next, so tries to cut it off. "Except Ian's?"

"He needs a mother," Madeleine says.

"No, he doesn't," Danny says. "He has you."

Ian was an infant when Teresa died, so he doesn't remember her. He's had his grandmother, and Danny thinks bringing in another woman now would only confuse the boy. It would be an intrusion into what has become a surprisingly stable life. He has a mother *figure*, Danny thinks, who's literally an angel. Perfect in the boy's imagination. No real woman could live up to that.

"But what do *you* have?" Madeleine asks.

"I'm fine."

"You must have needs."

"If you think I'm discussing my sex life with—"

"The nuns did a job on *you*," Madeleine says. "You should go mingle."

For professional and personal reasons, Madeleine thinks. If there is an eligible single man in Las Vegas, her son is it. Rich, successful, handsome—he could have his choice. A man his age should have a wife to absorb some of the social responsibilities—serve on charitable committees, charm important business associates, that sort of thing.

But since Diane . . .

She was a catastrophe.

A sweet, beautiful, wonderful, warmhearted mess, a broken soul past fixing. And Danny, sweet, soft Danny, loved her with all his heart, in a way he hadn't loved since Teresa.

Poor Danny, so star-crossed in love.

# FIVE

**D**ANNY MINGLES.

 Doesn't like it, but does it.

Talks shop and sports with the casino executives, children and school with the wives, accepts compliments on the home ("Well, it's my mother's, not mine"), the food, the party in general.

He checks in with Gloria.

"The juggling show will start at seven thirty," she tells him.

Ian, God bless him, had insisted *no magicians, no clowns.* So instead there'll be jugglers.

"The cake at eight," Gloria says. "Then the fireworks."

"What about the elephants?" Danny asks. "The gladiator fights and the human sacrifices?"

"Funny," Gloria says. "The fireworks will cue the guests to leave and then you can give Ian your presents."

Danny had held firm on this issue—no gifts from the guests. Instead, a contribution to St. Jude's or Sunrise Children's Hospital in Ian's name. Ian totally got it ("That's a great idea, Dad"), which made Danny so proud of the kid.

Of course, Ian is hardly deprived. He has everything a kid could need or want, and Danny's gift to him is an expensive mountain bike that Ian's been bugging him about.

It's good, though. It will get him away from the damn video games and they can use it up in Utah. That's his other gift. A full week away, just the two of them. A road trip, biking and hiking, camping out, eating trash in diners and drive-through fast-food places.

Ten-year-old-boy heaven.

Danny heaven, too, he thinks, at least the junk-food part.

"You'd better get me a mountain bike, too," Danny says. "And a guide to the best biking trails."

"They're both on the way," Gloria says.

Of course they are, Danny thinks.

He spots Jimmy Mac standing by one of the serving tables.

Jimmy MacNeese, his childhood friend, longtime wheelman and right hand. If Danny's old crew had been Italian instead of Irish, Jimmy would have been the consigliere.

Now he lives in San Diego, where he owns three successful car dealerships. His broad, freckled face is fuller now, his always pudgy body a little more so. His smile is the same, though—big, wide and bright.

"Nice party, Danny," he says.

The two men embrace.

"Thanks for sending the plane," Jimmy says. "That was a treat. The boys about pissed themselves."

"Where *are* the boys?" Danny asks. Jimmy's sons must be, what, fourteen and twelve now?

"I think they're at the taco table," Jimmy says. "A taco table, Danny?"

"You know what I like about tacos?" Danny asks. "They're their own plate."

"You didn't need to send the plane," Jimmy says. "We could have driven. It's what, four or five hours?"

"It can be a tough drive, though."

Danny had sent the corporate jet to bring Jimmy and his family in for the party. Also old Bernie Hughes, who, like Jimmy, had decided to settle in California and not follow Danny to Las Vegas.

Sending the jet was a gift to Jimmy, but there was another reason. The feds keep a weather eye on who comes in and out of McCarran International Airport on commercial flights, and Danny didn't want any of his old crew to be spotted. So Jimmy, his family and Bernie had come in on the Learjet; a car picked them up on the landing strip and whisked them straight to the party.

"Did Angie come?" Danny asks. He's fond of Jimmy's wife. They've known each other since high school, and Angie has been a great wife and mother. Danny suspects that she was the one who wanted them to stay in San Diego, but he doesn't hold it against her.

He misses Jimmy—his friendship, his easygoing humor, his counsel. But the man has a right to live his own life and he's done well.

"She's wandering around somewhere," Jimmy says. "Are you kidding? A chance to get away from me and the kids, drink some wine, eat some food she didn't have to cook?"

"I arranged a suite at the Shores," Danny says. "On the VIP floor. Everything's comped."

"You didn't have to do that."

"I know," Danny says. "Stay as long as you want. Make a vacation of it."

"A night or two," Jimmy says. "I gotta get back. Business, you know how it is."

Danny knows.

"Well, if Angie and the kids want to stay longer, we can fly them back," Danny says. Jimmy won't do it, though, won't want to take advantage. "How did Bernie do on the plane?"

Jimmy laughs. "Bitched the whole way about how much it was probably costing. He ate the muffins, though."

"Because they were free," Danny says.

They both laugh. Bernie, the old accountant, was the longtime money handler for the Irish mob in Providence, first for Danny's father, then for John Murphy, then for Danny. Came out to California when Danny went there and decided to stay—largely, Danny thought, because he so liked the complimentary breakfasts at the Residence Inn.

Still lives there in a one-bedroom that Danny pays for.

Danny and Jimmy look at each other, and there's that moment of recognition—recognition of all they've been through together. Their childhoods, the jobs they did, the war they fought, the friends they lost, the lives they took.

And the big score. The armed robbery of a cartel money cache—forty million dollars.

Danny used his cut to buy into Tara.

Jimmy bought a car dealership.

He's rich, a millionaire, but doesn't have Danny's kind of wealth. Danny tried to get him to invest in Tara, but Jimmy was too cautious.

Jimmy isn't the envious type, he just isn't. He's too good-natured to be anything but happy for Danny's success. Jimmy Mac is like that, has always been content with what he has.

Danny's not so sure about Angie—maybe there's a little resentment there—and he makes a note to find a moment to sit down with them and (again) offer a piece of his Tara holdings at a favorable price.

"I'd better mingle," Danny says. "Stick around after the fireworks, there's sort of a private family party."

"Yeah, we brought something for Ian."

"You weren't supposed to bring gifts."

"Nothing big," Jimmy says. "One of them Super Soakers."

"He'll love that."

"You go mingle," Jimmy says.

Danny goes and looks for Bernie. The old man isn't hard to spot—tall, stooped, saturnine, his head of white hair like a layer of fresh snow.

As the story goes, Meyer Lansky once said that Bernie Hughes was the only Irishman who could do math, and tried to hire him away. But Bernie wouldn't leave Providence.

"Bernie, thanks for coming," Danny says.

"Thanks for having me."

"Trip okay?"

"Lovely, thank you."

Bernie's clearly aging but sharp, and Danny still consults him on money matters. His financial world is infinitely more complicated than it was in the old days, but the basics are still the basics.

"Two plus two is four," Bernie has said. "Two million plus two million is four million. It doesn't change."

The partners in the Tara Group are scrupulously honest and immaculate in their bookkeeping, which Bernie appreciates. Still, he looks at the books, and *tcch*es at some of the expenses he thinks superfluous or extravagant. Bernie will never get Las Vegas, and Danny doesn't want him to. He needs that old-fashioned New England frugal perspective. One of Bernie's favorite sayings is: "A dollar saved is not a dollar earned. It's a dollar *ten* earned, with the interest." So he'll be appalled at the luxurious room Danny's reserved for him, but pleased that his breakfast will be delivered at seven sharp, according to Danny's instructions.

Danny repeats his invitation to the private family party and sees the flash of concern in Bernie's eyes.

"It's early," Danny says. "Ten at the latest."

Bernie looks relieved.

That's all the old crew who came in on the plane.

The rest live in Las Vegas.

DANNY FINDS THE Democratic Party operative by a table serving prime rib sliders.

"Great party, Dan," Neal says. "Thanks for inviting me."

"Thanks for coming."

Dave Neal is a pleasant-looking man with a friendly face and chestnut hair. In his forties, he stands about five-ten and is just a little stocky.

"You want the cook's tour?" Danny asks.

"Sounds great."

Danny walks him around the grounds of the ranch. "This used to belong to a guy named Manny Maniscalco, who was sort of the cheap lingerie king of America. He and my mother were married for a few years, then divorced, but she came back to take care of him when he was dying, and he left the place to her. Along with millions of dollars. Coals to Newcastle, because she was already wealthy in her own right. Investments."

Danny tells him the story, but he has a feeling that Neal already knows all about Madeleine and her top-level connections on Wall Street and Capitol Hill. He strikes Danny as a guy who does his homework.

"I crashed here when I came to Las Vegas," Danny says. "Thought I'd stay a few weeks until I found a house. That was six years ago. I don't know—inertia, I guess. And my son is very close to his grandmother."

"It's nice for both of them," Neal says. "But you didn't walk me away from the other guests to talk about your domestic situation."

"No," Danny says. "We're very concerned about this Gambling Impact Study Commission."

"You should be," Neal says. "You guys give millions to the GOP."

"They're pro-business," Danny says.

"I know who you are, Dan," Neal says. "You come from a blue-collar factory town. You may be a millionaire now, but by instinct and inclination, you're still a working-class guy at heart. We're not your enemy."

"A four percent tax?"

"How many billions did the gaming industry make last year?" Neal asks. "Some of it from people who can't afford it. You can't chip in a little to help them out? But the issue is negotiable."

Danny hears that as Neal opening the door.

"What about subpoena power?" Danny asks. "Is that negotiable?"

"Can we cut through the shit here?" Neal asks.

"Please."

"We know you own a big piece of Tara," Neal says.

"I'm just an employee," Dan says.

On paper, Tara is owned by two real estate guys from Missouri—Dom Rinaldi and Jerry Kush—and Danny is the operations manager.

"An aggressive committee will expose that fiction," Neal says. "The Bush administration didn't want to know. The word came down from on high that Dan Ryan was a no-fly zone. Something murky involving an operation against a drug cartel that was funding left-wing insurgents in Central America? But that protection is off now, Dan. You have enemies. There are a couple of congressmen who are dying to get on that committee and chop you down at the knees."

"Well, you cut through the shit all right," Danny says.

Neal leans against a paddock fence and turns around to look back at the estate. "You strike me as a decent guy. We don't care about your past. We don't want to see you get hurt in this."

"So, cutting through the shit," Danny says, "what's the price tag?"

Neal says, "If the Las Vegas gaming industry were to contribute, say, an even million, it would go a long way to tell us that you're not our enemies."

"That's doable," Danny says.

"But it has to be done right," Neal says. "We can't be seen accepting a big donation from the casino industry. And of course it has to be done legally."

"Of course," Danny says. "What if there was a lunch, a fundraiser hosted by a prominent local Democrat?"

"There is such a thing in Las Vegas?"

"We can dig one up," Danny says. "Maybe half the money gets donated at that lunch. The other half goes from individuals to the Democratic National Committee?"

"That would work."

Danny moves on to the next sensitive issue. It's risky. "You must have expenses, too, Dave."

Neal shrugs.

But the gesture is a yes, not a no.

"When you go back to the hotel tonight," Danny says, "there will be $250,000 in chips in your room safe. You can take them or not. What you do with them is up to you. You can gamble with them or just cash them in."

"I'm not much of a gambler," Neal says.

"If the chips aren't there in the morning," Danny says, "I'll know we have a deal. I want your word. No subpoenas."

"You can trust us."

"No offense," Danny says, "but you need to know this—if you fuck me, there will be consequences."

"There always are."

"True that," Danny says. "You should try the tacos, they're great."

He drops Neal back at the party and then returns to mingling.

Vern Winegard comes up to him. "How did it go?"

"A mil and a quarter."

"Why am I not surprised?"

The only surprise, Danny thinks, is how cheap it was.

But he still wants insurance and makes a note to call Monica Cantrell, the town's most exclusive madam, to arrange to have a girl at the fundraising lunch. And a camera is already in place in Neal's room to capture him taking the chips from the safe.

Trust?

Trust is children waiting for Santa Claus.

# SIX

A PLATE OF FOOD IN HAND, Danny walks to the stables that used to house the Thoroughbred horses before Madeleine gave them up. Part of the building has been converted to a one-bedroom apartment with a small living-room-cum-kitchen and a bathroom.

Danny knocks on the door.

A minute later, Ned Egan opens it.

Seeing Ned makes Danny smile—his fireplug body, Popeye forearms, pug face—he looked the role of Marty Ryan's chief enforcer. The story goes that Marty rescued the boy from an abusive father, and Ned returned from the sea to become his devoted bodyguard, a role he served for Danny later.

The whole New England underworld used to be scared shitless of Ned Egan, and it was right to be thusly constipated.

Ned was a stone killer.

That was then, Danny thinks.

After Marty's death and Danny's withdrawal from that world, Ned had nothing to do and nowhere to go, so Danny brought him to Las Vegas and had the apartment built for him. Ned wanted to go to some SRO hotel downtown, but such a thing didn't really exist in Las Vegas. Danny was afraid Ned would get too lonely, so he virtually ordered Ned to move in, with the excuse that Madeleine and Ian needed the protection.

"You didn't come to the party," Danny says, going in.

Ned shrugs. Never comfortable in social situations anyway, he was concerned his presence would be an issue. People might ask *Who is that guy?* and the answer could be a problem.

"I brought you a plate," Danny says.

"Thank you."

Ned's getting older (Aren't we all? Danny thinks), in his fifties now, and isn't what he was (Who is? Danny thinks). Danny arranged a special satellite feed to bring in Red Sox games, and Ned spends most of his summer days watching the games, like he used to do with Marty.

Ian comes by to visit and Madeleine has Ned over for lunch or dinner about once a week, although what they have to talk about is a mystery to Danny. He's offered to bring Ned down to the Strip, but the man has no interest. Danny's also offered to arrange for female companionship, but Ned isn't interested in that, either.

He seems content to live a quiet life.

Danny knows beyond the shadow of a doubt that in the unlikely event that Ian or Madeleine *was* in any danger, Ned would lay his life down for them without a moment's hesitation.

"Some prime rib," Danny says, setting the plate on the counter. "Barbecued chicken, potato salad, a slice of cake."

He didn't bring any tacos, knowing they'd just annoy the old chowderhead. Native New Englanders tend to like their food neatly separated. Into meat and potatoes.

"Very thoughtful of you," Ned says.

Danny hears the drone of the television. "Sox winning?"

"Until they get into the bullpen," Ned says.

He's in shirtsleeves but wears the shoulder-holstered .38 like he always does. It's an appendage, Danny thinks.

"We're having a private gathering at the house later," Danny says. "Ian would love it if you came."

"I got him a present. A Sox cap."

"Time the boy learned the important things in life," Danny says.

There are three religions in Rhode Island, he thinks. Irish Catholicism, Italian Catholicism, and the Boston Red Sox. And like being Catholic, no matter how old you get or far away you go, the Red Sox never really leave you. So when Danny lived in Providence, he was a devout Sox fan; when he lived in the shadow of Dodger Stadium, a devout Sox fan. Nothing has changed in Las Vegas.

Being Catholic and a Sox fan both have to do with faith and suffering.

A lot of suffering.

Both are highly masochistic.

Danny was only half joking in what he said about the important things in life, because loyalty is one of the most important things, and being a Sox fan teaches you loyalty through loss.

Anyone who lived through that horrible moment in 1986 knows that. Danny can still feel the pain, the gut punch of watching that ball . . .

"Does Ian come over and watch games with you?" Danny asks.

"Sometimes."

Danny didn't know that. "He'll love the cap. See you later?"

Ned nods.


KEVIN COOMBS THROWS up on the lawn.

Just a few feet from the table where they're serving seafood crepes. So the shrimp come up fairly undigested.

"Ooops," Kevin says. He looks and smiles likes it's really funny, like he just pulled some highly comedic party prank.

Danny's not laughing.

He looks over to Kevin's best friend, Sean South, with an expression that unmistakably says: *Get him out of here.*

Sean grabs him by the elbow, but Kevin jerks his arm away. "Fuck off."

People notice. One of the female guests turns away as if she might retch herself.

Kevin's been out west almost ten years now but has made no concession from his East Coast punk roots. His brown hair is long and shaggy and he's wearing an outrageous Hawaiian shirt that looks like it came straight from the closet floor over a pair of ripped jeans and high-top Keds. He'd be wearing his black leather jacket, except even Kevin Coombs isn't going to do that in Las Vegas in June. He wipes his mouth with his hand and looks up to see Danny staring pure murder at him.

"Oh, no." Kevin grins. "I've upset the boss."

"C'mon, Kev," Sean says.

"'C'mon, Kev,' my skinny Irish ass," Kevin says. He looks back at Danny. "Sorry, Danny, am I *embarrassing* you?"

Yeah, and not for the first time.

Used to be Kevin Coombs was feared, for good reason. He and Sean, collectively known as the Altar Boys, were an efficient team, whether it was boosts, hijacks, or canceling reservations.

Kevin was always a loose cannon, but when there was a job to do, he straightened out, was there, and there strong.

Now he's a drunk.

When he's not doing coke.

Kevin's literally blown through a million dollars. The money he made off the big drug job—gone. The money he made off the movie investment Danny put him into—gone. The money he made out of his small piece of Tara—gone.

Booze, drugs, women and gambling.

The Fearsome Foursome.

He lives in Las Vegas, for Chrissakes, where all of the above are inescapable. That's not saying that you have to do them, it's just saying that they're always there if you want them, and Kevin always wants them.

Kevin has caused problems before—a scene with a blackjack dealer on the floor, a drunken fight on the sidewalk, bringing three hookers into the restaurant and demanding a table.

So Kevin wasn't invited to the party.

Sean, he's different, he's the serious one. With his red hair, he looks like something out of an Irish Spring commercial, but he's made the transition to serious businessman. Took his money and started a food wholesale business supplying the casinos. Danny has thrown him hundreds of thousands in contracts, and Sean pays him back by delivering a good product at a fair price.

Sean has given Kevin a well-paying job, but Kevin is the millstone around his neck. Kevin is going to drag him down, because he's always causing a problem that requires Sean's attention, Sean's help, Sean's money.

Sean won't cut him loose, though.

They're like brothers.

And now Kev is causing a scene at Danny Ryan's son's birthday party, in front of half the power players in town, bawling, "Why wasn't I invited? I'm not good enough for your highfalutin friends, Danny?! I'm embarrassing you?!"

"You're embarrassing yourself," Danny says.

"I've known Ian since he was a baby," Kevin says, drunken tears coming into his eyes. "Since we took him in a freakin' car when you were running away from Rhode Island. I was *there*. I remember that. I guess you forgot, huh?"

Danny doesn't respond.

But this is a problem.

Back in the day, this is the kind of talk that could get someone clipped. Hell, if Pasco Ferri were here, it *could* get Kevin clipped.

"I remember a lot of things," Kevin says. "I remember where you got the cash to start your big freakin' business. I remember when you didn't *own* casinos, you rob—"

Sean hits him, a solid shot at the base of the jaw that drops Kev cold.

Then he picks him up.

Danny walks over, speaks into Sean's ear. "Get him out."

"I will, Danny."

"I mean out of *town*, Sean."

Two security guys come up and help Sean drag Kevin out to his car.

Danny looks at the stunned guests and says, "My apologies. I'm afraid the man was over-refreshed."

It gets a weak, awkward laugh.

But Vern Winegard laughs loudly. "'Over-refreshed.' That's a good one."

"We use it at the hotels to tactfully describe drunks on the floor," Danny says.

"It's good, I might steal it," Vern says. It's ninety-something degrees out and he's wearing his trademark black—a black polo over black jeans. Something about being a Raiders fan, if Danny remembers right. Winegard has even talked about bringing the team to Las Vegas someday.

"Who *was* that guy?" Vern asks.

"A disgruntled former employee," Danny says.

A bunch of people are standing around, eavesdropping on a conversation between the two giants.

"What I've learned, Dan?" Vern says. "Once an employee is disgruntled, you can never gruntle him again."

"That's funny, Vern."

Danny nods to Dawn, a tall blond lady with legs longer than a lonely road. To the common speculation that she married Vern more for his money than his looks, he commonly responds, "We use the assets we have."

"Hi, Dawn," Danny says.

"Lovely party, Dan."

"It was until a minute ago," Danny says.

"We all have that friend," Dawn says.

"Is Bryce here?" Danny asks.

"Checking out the girls," Vern says. "You remember fifteen."

"I do," Danny says.

"He was made captain of the lacrosse team," Vern says.

"That's great," Danny says. Lacrosse? They play lacrosse in Las Vegas? He always thought of it as something prep school kids in Connecticut did. But he can see it. Bryce is a big, husky kid—confident and cocky like his dad, but fortunately he inherited more of his mother's looks. Bryce is Vern's pride and joy, the light of his life. Maybe because he's everything that Vern wasn't—team captain, homecoming king sort of kid.

Vern's not ready to let the embarrassing incident go. It gives him a little edge and he's going to take advantage of it. "That guy seemed to know you pretty well. He mentioned something about Ian as a baby? Leaving Rhode Island or something?"

Despite himself, Danny flushes. Feels the heat coming to his cheeks, and there's nothing he can do about it.

He's pissed.

Dawn looks uncomfortable. Men play rough, sure, but one thing you don't do is bring kids into it. "Vern . . ."

"No, I'm just asking," Vern says.

Dog with a bone.

"Who knows what drunks are talking about?" Danny says.

People are listening. Trying to look like they're not, but doing a shitty job of it.

Vern should let it go.

That's what he should do.

He doesn't. For some reason that he will never be able to explain, he laughs again, lifts his glass and says, "Dan Ryan. Man of mystery."

Bringing it all back.

All the rumors, the whispers, the innuendos.

Bringing Danny's past into his kid's birthday party.

Danny walks away.

# SEVEN

**D**ANNY STANDS IN THE KITCHEN and watches Madeleine stick candles into a cake.

They're in the house, standing in the kitchen, getting ready for the private party.

"Another cake?" Danny asks.

"That was a public cake," Madeleine says. "This is a private cake. Anyway, I made it."

"You *made* it?" Danny asks. He's never seen his mother make anything other than toast, and that on the cook's day off.

"I'm a woman of mystery."

"You heard about that?" Danny asks.

"Everyone heard about it," Madeleine says. "Don't let Vernon Winegard get to you."

"What's his problem?"

"That he wakes up every morning wondering why people don't like him," Madeleine says. "And he's jealous of you."

"For what?"

"Really?" Madeleine asks. "He's Dick Nixon and you're Jack Kennedy."

"Whatever that means," Danny says.

"You know perfectly well what it means," Madeleine says. "Listen, I've known Winegard since he opened his first grind joint. I knew him in the days he was snorting coke and balling cocktail waitresses. Don't get in the mud with him. Give him his space, let him stew in his own torment. He's nothing to you. It's that Kevin Coombs you should worry about."

"He's gone," Danny says. "And I'll have a word with the security company."

"I already fired them," Madeleine said. "I asked them why someone who wasn't invited to my home gained access to my home, and they had no answer."

That's Madeleine, Danny thinks. Either you perform or you don't, and if you don't, you're dismissed. A string of exiled lovers could attest to that.

"Anyway," she says, "the party was a success."

She's right, Danny thinks. People loved the food; the jugglers were great and the fireworks fantastic. As Gloria predicted (planned?), most of the guests dutifully departed after the pyrotechnic finale, leaving just family and close friends now gathered in the living room.

Danny goes in.

He looks around.

His son is there, of course, sweaty and overstimulated from an evening of a bouncy castle, swimming pool, sugar, general running around and excitement. Jimmy Mac, his wife and boys, Ned Egan, Bernie Hughes. Gloria is there. So is Dom with his wife and kids, Jerry with his family. Madeleine behind his shoulder, holding the cake as they all start to sing "Happy Birthday."

This is all that really matters, Danny thinks.

These people, this *life* we've built together.

This good life.

# EIGHT

**I**T WASN'T ALWAYS.

When Danny left Rhode Island in the gray winter of 1988 ("Left" being a euphemism, he thinks now as he gets ready for bed—"fled," "chased out," "running for my life" are more accurate words), his life was in ruins.

Terri was dead—gone, anyway.

The Irish mob that had been the center of his life was destroyed, its members dead or in jail. Potential indictments—for drug trafficking, maybe murder—hung over his head like, if he had known the term, the sword of Damocles.

He was a fugitive—running from the Mafia, from the feds—but without the advantage of being alone. He had an infant son and an almost senile father to care for. And a crew, or what was left of it anyway—Jimmy Mac, Ned Egan, the Altar Boys and Bernie Hughes—to look after.

So he made the journey out to California, the westward migration to the land of dreams, the land of reinvention. (If anyone needed reinvention, he thinks now, it was me.) Landed in San Diego and made a quiet life there tending bar and being a single father, with all the daily rituals that entailed.

He wasn't exactly happy, but he was content.

But they found him, they always do.

A fed (FBI? CIA?) tracked him down but instead of arresting him made him the proverbial offer that couldn't be refused. Hit a drug cartel's cash house, split the proceeds with Uncle Sam. (They needed the money for some kind of covert operation in Central America—Danny never asked, never cared.) All will be forgiven, all forgotten, go forth and sin no more.

Danny and his crew did it.

His share came to about ten.

Million.

Enough money to fade into the sunset, take his kid somewhere and live the American Dream.

Except you didn't do that, Danny thinks as he gets into bed.

You went to Hollywood.

Talk about the land of dreams.

What happened was that the Altar Boys were shaking down the production of a movie about the New England mob and people reached out to Danny to rein them in.

Danny bought into the movie.

Literally.

He invested eight mil.

And fell in love with the star.

Diane Carson.

It was crazy, it was wrong, it was ill-fated. They both knew this from the start, but they couldn't help themselves.

The people from their separate worlds didn't like it, especially when the tabloids ran with the "Gangster and the Moll" theme and they became a celebrity couple.

I had my past, Danny thinks, she had hers.

I could live with mine; she couldn't.

One night in bed she confessed to him, told him about her brother who had come into her bed, had sex with her—be honest—made love to her. The same brother who later murdered her husband (God, how the tabloids loved that) and was serving life in a Kansas prison.

And threatened to tell the world.

It would have destroyed her, professionally and personally.

So Danny reached out to people in his world and had the problem taken care of—the brother got knifed in the yard. But the price was high—Danny had to leave Diane.

He lied to her, told her he had nothing to do with it and then lied again—said he didn't love her—and then left her.

She overdosed that night.

Fatally.

Danny has to live with that.

Didn't do it well at first, went out and got drunk for weeks, then sobered up and found his way back to Las Vegas, where he had left his son with his mother.

Used his film profits to invest in the Tara Group.

Off the books.

Pasco Ferri and a few of his "associates," Danny's mother, Madeleine, several of her hedge-fund connections, and a couple of young and hungry real estate guys—Dom Rinaldi and Jerry Kush—who wanted to get in on the big game. They put together $75 million to purchase an old casino at a bargain-basement price.

The Scheherazade had been built in the third wave of construction in the mid-sixties.

The first wave, of course, was the Flamingo in 1946, Bugsy Siegel's dream that cost him his life when he overspent the mob's money and probably skimmed off the construction costs. Legend has it that Lucky Luciano's and Siegel's old friend Meyer Lansky gave the order, and Danny has heard that his own old friend Pasco Ferri also signed off on the hit.

But the wiseguys soon learned that Siegel had made the right bet on Las Vegas. Mob money flowed in during the fifties, financing the big boom with the Sands, the Sahara, the Riviera, the Dunes, the Hacienda, the Tropicana, the Royal Nevada and the Stardust, basically creating the Strip.

Then the big Teamster money came in the sixties and built the Aladdin, Circus Circus, Caesars Palace and the Scheherazade.

When the Tara Group bought the place, it was in the red.

The casino had always struggled. Located at the southern edge of the Strip, it had waited for the town to develop down to it. But by the time it finally did, the hotel was old and outdated, unable to compete with the huge theme hotels that were offering circuses, pirate ship battles and volcanic eruptions.

For another thing, no one could pronounce, much less spell, Scheherazade. It had a cheesy Arabian Nights theme replete with belly dancers and guys walking around in what looked to Danny like towels. Tara didn't have the capital to redo the entire theme, so they quickly renamed the casino Casablanca and got busy trying to turn it around.

Most of Las Vegas was laughing at the newcomer Tara Group for getting suckered into buying the place.

Danny wasn't laughing. He had invested all he had into the hotel and couldn't let it fail. Sitting his fellow investors down in his mother's living room, he asked, "What do we have that the mega-hotels don't?"

"Nothing," Dom Rinaldi said.

Danny shook his head. "Our size."

"You mean the lack of it," Jerry Kush said.

"That's exactly what I mean," Danny said. "We have just under a thousand rooms. The mega-hotels average three thousand."

Dom said, "And you see this as a strength because . . ."

"You think that we're in the gambling business," Danny said, "but we're not. We're in the service business."

Because every casino offers pretty much the same thing as far as the gaming is concerned. Sure, you can tighten or loosen the slot payoffs a little, maybe raise or lower stakes at the table games, but what really sets you apart is the service.

"What we can offer," Danny said, "is superior service. *Personal* service. We turn our perceived weakness into a strength. You're not just one of thousands coming to Casablanca—you're a personal guest. You're not grist for a gambling mill, you're a human being."

He'd run his numbers.

Every year the percentage of profit the casinos make through gaming declines and the percentage of profit they make from the rooms and the food rises. People want to gamble, sure, but they also want to have great meals and a beautiful room to go back to.

"They want spectacle," Jerry said.

"They can walk down the street, stand on the sidewalk and see the pirate battle, the volcano going off," Danny said. "Then they come back to us—stay in our rooms, eat our meals, play our games. Let our competition pay for our guests' entertainment."

The partners liked that idea—drafting off the deep-pockets guys. Let the mega-hotels spend millions imitating Disney World, Danny told them—we'll do things that cost us little or nothing.

Like making sure the staff calls every guest by name. That they smile, ask if there's anything they can do to improve the guests' stay—not just at the hotel but in Las Vegas as a whole. Ask if they need suggestions, directions, show tickets, dinner reservations. Be proactive about it.

"How much would it cost," he asked, "to provide concierge service for every guest, not just the high rollers? To make every guest feel like a VIP?"

Instead of paying "pirates" and acrobats, Danny added more parking valets to get the guests inside faster, more desk staff to reduce the check-in time. He hired more cooks and waitstaff to make sure that the room-service breakfast reached the guests' rooms quickly and hot. He brought in more cleaners so that each one could spend more time making each room not just clean but immaculate.

Small things that cost very little but meant a lot. A handwritten note from the cleaner addressing the guest by name to ask if everything was in order. A quick phone call from the same person who checked you in making sure that you were enjoying your experience. A personal greeting every time the guest came back through the door.

Danny trained managers to stroll through the dining room at breakfast, recognize a guest who had come back for a second or third stay, pick up the tab and say, "This one's on me."

"What does it cost us for a couple of eggs, toast and coffee?" Danny asked. "A buck, buck-fifty? How much do we make when that guy comes back again?"

Keeping a customer, Danny said, is a lot cheaper than acquiring one.

All the managerial staff had a small budget for that kind of thing—buy the guest a drink, slip her a few tokens to play some slots, maybe even a couple of tickets to a hot show.

Danny and his people got rid of the tacky *I Dream of Jeannie* uniforms and Madeleine supervised a classy retro look straight out of Bogart and Bergman as well as a remodel of the lobby that made it resemble Rick's Café Americain.

Casablanca was in the black within two years.

It surprised everyone.

What also surprised everyone—Danny included—was how hands-on he was during the process. He was supposed to have been an investor, a silent partner in a business fronted by Rinaldi and Kush, his financial stake, like Pasco Ferri's, hidden inside a maze of corporate screens.

Because the Nevada Gaming Control Board wasn't going to let Danny Ryan own a casino.

Having spent years getting organized crime out of Las Vegas, the feds, the corporations and the NGCB weren't going to let it sneak back in, and the board made the determination that Danny had "known mob associates."

For instance, Pasco Ferri, the former boss of the New England syndicate, now in retirement in Florida.

Danny's lawyers argued his cause.

"There isn't a single fact linking Mr. Ryan to organized crime," the lead attorney said. "Not an arrest, not an indictment, never mind a conviction. All you have are rumors and a few articles in the tabloids. Mr. Ryan attended a couple of beach parties—clambakes—hosted by Mr. Ferri. If attending a party thrown by a mobster was a criterion for disqualification, half your board couldn't *serve* on your board."

His lawyers knew it wouldn't play. All the NGCB needed to ban ownership was the *appearance* of impropriety. The appeal was an effort to keep Danny out of the dreaded Black Book, which would have prevented him from even entering a casino.

The tactic worked.

Danny was denied ownership but not employment. He received the crucial Key Employee gaming license that allowed him to work in casinos. His official title at Casablanca was director of hotel operations.

He was all of that.

Never a businessman, Danny took himself to school, staying up at night to read books on finance, management, customer service. He consulted with gaming experts, restaurateurs, chefs, hotel managers, stockbrokers—whoever he thought could teach him anything.

Danny became a constant presence at Casablanca. He was notorious for going at random into a vacant room, making a note like the toilet paper was pulled down instead of over the top as it should be, that there was dust on top of some molding, that the room temperature wasn't set right. But when he found everything perfect, he also made a note to find the cleaner and thank her, maybe slip her an extra tip or see about a raise.

He was in the casino's three restaurants, sampling the food, talking to the guests, asking the cooks and the servers what they needed to do their jobs better. He was on the casino floor, keeping an eye on the pit bosses, the dealers, the cocktail waitresses.

Danny was determined to run a clean operation. He'd made it a specific condition when Pasco invested in the company.

"I have no interest in getting back into the mob shit," Danny said.

"No one does," Pasco said. "There's no future in it."

So there was no skim at Casablanca—no cash leaving the counting room in bags to be delivered to bosses in Chicago, Kansas City or Providence. There was too much money to be made legitimately without risking it for stupid side hustles.

Danny also banned the rough stuff.

For the dealer caught stealing, there was only one punishment. Not a hammer shattering his fingers, like in the old days, but instant dismissal with a bad reference that would prevent him working anywhere in Las Vegas.

So Danny walked the floor of his first casino. When the staff saw him, the smiles became a little brighter, the postures straighter, the deals sharper. They all knew that whatever the ownership papers might show, this was Dan Ryan's place. He was in charge, he saw everything.

The details are the stuff of Danny's days now, and he worries about them constantly. His partners chide him about why he obsesses over whether a napkin is folded properly when he has hundreds of millions of dollars in properties to be concerned with.

Because that's where the millions come from, he tells them.

In Casablanca's early days, when they were trying to turn things around, the partners worried that Danny had his nose too close to the grindstone, that he couldn't see the big picture.

They were wrong.

As soon as Casablanca went into profit, Danny proposed a major strategic move. The property just to the north, an old casino called the Starlight, was going into a downward spiral.

"I think we should buy it," Danny said.

"Another turnaround project?" Dom asked. He thought about it for a few seconds and then said, "It's not such a bad idea."

But Danny didn't want to just spruce the place up. He thought that would be like the sixtyish woman who puts on thick pancake makeup—she can dim the lights as much as she wants, but the lines still show. Besides, he didn't want Tara to become known as the "turnaround company." He wanted it to be seen as something far more.

"I don't want to turn the Starlight around," Danny said. "I want to demolish it and build a new hotel."

"We're just in the black on Casablanca," Dom said. "Maybe this isn't the right time to expand."

"It might be the only time we have," Danny said. "If we don't move, Winegard will."

Vern Winegard was ambitious, Danny knew. He wanted to be *the* man in Las Vegas, and the Winegard Group already owned three big hotels on the Strip. If Vern acquired the Starlight, then only the old Lavinia would stand between his properties and Casablanca.

"We'd be cut off from any expansion to the north," Danny said.

Dom smiled. "I didn't know we were expanding to the north."

Danny shrugged and smiled back. He already knew that Dom would get on board. They were young gunners, good businessmen, and they didn't get into this to be small.

But they were also cautious, conservative.

His mother raised an eyebrow.

Over dinner at her place that night, she listened to his idea and then asked, "One hotel isn't enough?"

Danny looked right back at her. "No. It isn't."

And he knew what she was thinking. Her son, for so long void of anything that resembled ambition, who had always settled for mere survival, now wanted . . .

More.

Which surprised Danny a little. He never thought of himself as particularly ambitious, just as a guy trying to survive in a world that usually had other ideas. He'd already made far more money in his life than he'd ever thought he would—the last few million relatively honestly. His son would inherit money, his organization was legit, it's what he set out to do, it ought to have been enough.

But it wasn't.

"Enough" isn't really a concept in Las Vegas, an over-the-top town where too much isn't enough, success is *ex*cess, and more is always better.

You have a kingdom, Danny thought, but you want an empire.

"I'm all for it," Madeleine said.

Madeleine McKay knew a little about building empires. Trailer-park trash from Barstow, she came to Las Vegas to be a showgirl and parlayed her looks into a successful career as an investor, first gaining influence and then power.

She knew about wanting more.

Danny convened a meeting of the partners and introduced his plan for the Shores.

"The Shores?" Jerry asked. "We're in the desert."

"Exactly," Danny said. "You know what you get on a lot of beach vacations? Bad weather. A guy lays out a thousand bucks for a week on the beach and it rains. It's always sunny in the desert."

"We have sun," Jerry said. "We have sand. What we don't have is an ocean."

"We build one," Danny said.

He laid out his vision.

"You pull up to the hotel," Danny said. "What's the first thing you see out front, before you even get in? Waves. Surf. Beautiful blue water rolling in front of you. The valet takes your car and you walk along a palm-lined spit of sand across the water into the lobby, all done in blues and greens, the shades of the sea. There's a giant wall of water in front of you—beautiful fish in a thousand vibrant colors—and then suddenly you see . . ."

He paused for effect until Dom finally asked, "What? What do you see?"

"Sharks," Danny said.

"You mean animatronics?" Jerry asked.

"No, real sharks," Danny said. "Dangerous. Sexy. Risky. Like gambling. You're ready for action before you even check in."

He goes on to describe the rest of it.

Four different pools in the back, all surrounded by sand, just like the beach. One will be just for relaxation; another will be a gentle wave pool for the guests with kids; still another will have larger waves.

"We'll have boards available," Danny said. "And instructors. You can learn to surf. If you already know how, have at it—perfect waves, coming in sets of four, twenty-four seven. Surfer heaven."

The fourth pool, farthest to the back, will be in an enormous grotto. Big rocks, little caves hidden behind waterfalls. No kids allowed. Mom and Dad time.

"Think about it," Danny said. "Hawaii is a six-hour flight, and that's from the West Coast. Tahiti is nine hours. We can give people that experience with a maximum three-hour flying time, for a lot less money, with good weather guaranteed. *And* they can gamble."

Dom kicked in. "What's the biggest problem for parents coming to town? What to do with the kids when they want to do a little gambling. With this, they dump Bobby and Cindy at the kiddie pool—we have certified lifeguards and licensed babysitters—and they hit the machines and the tables."

"Which they can't do at Disney World," Danny said.

"What's the projected cost?" Jerry asked.

"Five hundred and fifty million," Danny said.

Several moments of shocked silence, and then Dom laughed. "So much for Dan being too focused on the small stuff."

You had some nerve, Danny thinks now.

The balls on you, huh?

Where the hell did you think you were going to get five hundred and fifty mil?

# NINE

H E REMEMBERS HIS MEETING WITH Pasco.

Danny offered to fly to Florida, but Pasco wanted to come to Las Vegas, "for old times' sake." They met at Piero's, an iconic Italian restaurant frequented by the Las Vegas cognoscenti, because Pasco couldn't be seen inside the casino. The irony that he couldn't set foot in a hotel that his money had helped turn around was obvious, but Pasco didn't mention it.

"So this is the 'new Las Vegas,'" he said. "I barely recognize the place. Frankie, the Rat Pack, Momo and them—they're all gone. Those days are over."

"I think so."

"No, it's a good thing," Pasco said. "It needed to happen. Your dad loved the old town, though. It's where he met your mother, you know."

Danny smiled. "I've heard the stories."

Madeleine had been married at the time—in what they'd now call an open marriage—to Manny Maniscalco. Marty Ryan had come into town on some business for Pasco, met Madeleine at a bar, and they started a blazing matinee affair. He knocked her up, which was too much for Manny, who sent his wife packing. She went to New York to have Danny, and a few months later dropped him off in Marty's arms in Providence. *"Here, you take him."*

Now Danny looked at Pasco. The mob boss had aged. Still deeply tanned, but his white hair had receded higher on his forehead and was thinner. The ropy muscles of his forearms still were strong, but under skin that looked like wrinkled paper.

"The old Scheherazade," Pasco said. "I owned a piece of it, did you know that?"

"No."

"Back in the day," Pasco said. "Me and a group of New England guys put some money in. Now I own a piece again. Life, huh?"

He sipped his iced tea and then took a bite of the linguine vongole. "What did you want to talk about, Danny? Why am I here?"

Danny told him about his idea for the Shores.

Pasco ate while he listened, never interrupting, and when Danny finished, he said, "Five hundred million? Nobody I know has that kind of escarole."

"I'm going to go to the banks."

"Banks don't like casinos."

"Things are changing," Danny said. "I think I can make the pitch."

Pasco looked at him for a long moment. With those famous pale eyes. The eyes, Danny knew, that were the last things more than a few guys saw in their lives. "So you want to go to the banks and put up the—what do you call it now?—Casablanca as collateral."

Danny nodded. "We could start a new company for the Shores, but I doubt the banks would go for that."

"So if your new project fails," Pasco said, "you lose your hotel *and* I lose my investment."

"Yes," Danny said. "But it's not going to fail."

"You know who else said that?" Pasco asked. "Benny Siegel."

"And he was right," Danny said. "The Flamingo turned into a big success. Started all of this."

"But he didn't live to see it."

"I will," Danny said.

"I'm not threatening you," Pasco said. "Those days are over, too. You fail, your problem is with the banks, not me."

"So you're saying you're okay with it?"

Pasco signaled the waiter and made a small circle with his index finger, ordering an espresso. "It will dilute my investment in the company."

"That's true, too," Danny said. "But you'll make a lot more money with the smaller share."

The age-old question, Danny thought. Is it better to have a large share of small or a small share of large? "Pasco, we can stay where we are and be small. We're all making money, it's fine. But do we always want to be small, always on the edge, when the Wall Street guys are in the center? We're talking generational wealth here, a chance to put the rackets behind us forever."

"So that's your real reason," Pasco said.

"I don't get you."

"You want to get clear of the dirty money."

Pasco's right, Danny thought. He'd considered it—dirty money, old mob money, criminal money makes up a significant share of the current company. But if we go to the banks to raise hundreds of millions, it's diluted. You put a spoonful of dirt in a glass of water, you have dirty water; you dump the same spoonful in the ocean, you don't even know it's there.

"Let me tell you something, young Ryan," Pasco said. "There is not and never has been any such thing as clean or dirty money. There's only money. If you think the Wall Street money is spotless, you have a lot to learn."

Danny knew better than to answer. He'd known Pasco all his life, known him when he was still the boss of New England, before he retired down to Florida. Knew that he still maintained connections with the heads of all the crime families nationwide, maybe even in Sicily. Knew, in any case, when to speak and when to be quiet.

Now he stayed quiet.

The espresso arrived. Pasco dropped in a cube of sugar and stirred. He tasted it, approved and then said, "We invested with you for a reason, Danny. To bring us out of the old days into the new. If this is you doing that, then *che Dio vi benedica*."

Danny didn't need God's blessing, he needed Pasco's. To go to the banks and dilute the mob's investment.

It wasn't easy.

Pasco was right—there was a lot of resistance in the New York investment banks to the gaming industry. Especially in Las Vegas, especially with Atlantic City opening right next door and casino gambling spreading onto every Native American reservation. It used to be that people had to fly to Las Vegas to gamble; now most people lived within a two-hour drive of a casino.

This will be the first casino-hotel, Danny argued, where the rooms, meals and entertainment will outearn the gaming. People will come to see the sharks, go to the beaches, ride the waves. In between they'll play the slots and sit down at the tables.

He didn't make these arguments himself, but through Dom and Jerry, who actually went out to the banks. Too risky for Danny to be out front, with the whiff of OC still around him, although fainter with every year.

And Dom and Jerry were great at it, with their earnest, clean-cut midwestern affect, their solid record of achievement, their no-nonsense, zero-bullshit, commonsense approach.

Madeleine opened the doors for them with her myriad connections to bankers, hedge-fund managers and stockbrokers, but when Dom and Jerry walked through those doors, they owned the room.

They killed.

They raised the five hundred mil, largely by Danny's prediction that the Shores would bring a 22 percent return on the investment.

Getting the funding was one thing. Getting the Shores built was another.

Danny was involved in every aspect of the construction, from the architectural design to the shape of the drawer handles in the rooms. It had to be done in a hurry, on time and on budget, and the other hotel owners watched and laughed and waited for the Tara Group to fall on its ass so they could laugh some more.

Nobody had ever seen anything like it because there *was* nothing like it.

You flew into McCarran airport in the desert, got in a car, and ten minutes later you were in Polynesia.

Without the humidity or the bugs.

Without a visa or a passport.

You walked the sandy causeway across the "ocean" out front. A gentle wave rolled at you, its spray cooling you off, and then you walked into the air-conditioned lobby and saw the sharks.

*Danny's* sharks.

God, he remembers, what it had taken to get the okay for the shark tank. How many commissions and boards they had to testify to, how many reports and impact studies they had to pay for, bureaucratic hoop after hoop.

Jump, Danny, jump.

They'd all wanted to give up. *"Danny, forget the freaking sharks. Just get some really big tropical fish and call it a day."*

It's my hotel, Danny thought, not a Chinese restaurant. No one is going to come to see fish. They'll come to see sharks.

Jerry suggested that they just hire lawyers, put them in wet suits and have them swim around the tank.

"Where do you even *buy* sharks?" Dom asked in the middle of all of it. "*Can* you even buy sharks? I mean, are there, like, shark rescue places looking for good homes?"

As it turned out, yes. Public aquariums had a surplus of sharks, and through them and some private suppliers, Tara was able to acquire four tiger sharks.

Danny gave three of them names—Fang, Jaws and Fin. He let Ian name the fourth. The kid thought for a while and then said, "Mark."

"Mark?"

"Mark the Shark," Ian said, as if it were obvious.

So Mark the Shark it was.

Danny remembers the night the Shores opened.

He was so nervous he thought he might throw up.

But it all went, well, swimmingly.

He stood quietly in the background while Dom and Jerry made speeches and took their bows and he didn't feel any resentment, just a quiet satisfaction and pride that he was instrumental in making this happen.

The first year of its existence, the Shores made $200 million. The hotel was full at 98 percent occupancy, as it has been since it opened.

The bankers were happy.

And Dan Ryan became a legend.

Because everyone in the business who mattered knew who was behind Dom Rinaldi and Jerry Kush, knew that as competent as they were, the driving force behind the Tara Group was Danny.

The other casino owners knew it.

The bankers knew it.

Vern Winegard knew it.

Hell, even the NGCB probably knew it, but turned a blind eye because Danny had created a huge moneymaker for Nevada gaming, one that brought in thousands of tourists and was spotlessly clean to boot.

No skim.

No wiseguys hanging out.

No violence.

The Shores was family-friendly.

Danny was insistent that his security staff keep the prostitutes out of the hotel, identifying even the classiest working girls and politely asking them to leave and not come back. He had undercover staff pose as single male customers, and if they were approached by a hooker, they quietly showed her the door.

The word got around. It was too much trouble and a waste of time to hustle at the Shores.

It cost Danny some customers who were looking for that kind of action, but he didn't care. He was filling his hotel with discriminating customers who were hitting the machines and the tables.

The Shores didn't return twenty-two points on investments.

It returned twenty-five.

No one was laughing anymore at Dan Ryan and his sharks.

So why aren't I happy? Danny thinks now, unable to sleep.

About one in the morning, Danny rolls over in bed, picks up the phone. And calls Dom.

"Did I wake you up?" Danny asks.

"No, I had to answer the phone," Dom says. "What's up?"

Danny tells him.

"I want to buy the Lavinia."

# TEN

*Providence, Rhode Island*
*1997*

**M**ARIE BOUCHARD ANSWERS THE PHONE and hears, "We got him."

"Got who?" she asks.

"Peter Moretti Jr."

Marie almost drops the Styrofoam cup of stale coffee in her left hand. "Where?!"

"Florida," Elaine says. "Pompano Beach. Broward County sheriff is holding him for us."

"Jesus Christ," Marie says. They've been looking for Peter Moretti Jr. for six years, since the night he murdered his own mother and his stepfather at their house in Narragansett.

For Marie, the chief prosecutor in the Rhode Island attorney general's office, this has been a quest, an obsession, an almost holy mission. It was a horrific crime. Moretti, a marine just home from Iraq, had practically decapitated Vinnie Calfo with a shotgun, then walked upstairs to the bedroom and laced his mother with a blast to the stomach and another to the head. "How did they find him?"

"Stoned out of his gourd in a 7-Eleven parking lot," Elaine says. "The clerk called the cops and they ran him. Bingo."

Better to be lucky than good, Marie thinks.

She took the case personally.

Was morally offended by it.

Matricide?

Killing your own mother?

Other than killing your own child—sadly, she's prosecuted those cases as well—she can't think of anything worse.

If Rhode Island had a death penalty, she'd go for it. As it is, she thinks she can get young Peter an LWOP—life without possibility of parole, which is better than the little bastard deserves.

He'll get that on Celia Moretti's murder, maybe less on Calfo's, who was the boss of what was left of the New England Mafia at the time of his sudden demise, and juries tend to be more forgiving on mob hits.

They consider them a professional hazard.

Doesn't matter, Marie thinks.

How many life sentences can you serve? Concurrent or consecutive, Peter Jr. is going away for the rest of his life.

She has him dead to rights.

Fingerprints, shoe prints in the blood, DNA everywhere.

And an eyewitness.

The crime had not exactly been the act of a criminal mastermind. Not only did Peter Jr. identify himself to the security guard at the gate, but video surveillance cameras also had him walking up to the house with a shotgun in his hand.

And it caught the license plate of the car, so within hours of the murder, RI State Police had picked up Tim Shea, a fellow marine, who confessed to driving Peter Jr. to the scene.

Faced with incontrovertible evidence and Marie's explanation that he was equally guilty of the two homicides, Tim pled out to twin accessory charges, carrying a term of ten years each in the Adult Correctional Institutions gray stone prison, where he still resides.

Doubtless, Marie thinks, holding a grudge against his old friend for leaving him holding the bag. That, and the offer of an early release, will be enough to get him to testify against Peter Jr., and his sworn statement describing the crime is on the record anyway.

Marie Bouchard doesn't lose trials.

She just doesn't.

For one thing, she only brings cases she knows she can win, as much for ethical reasons as for professional ones.

"If we're not confident that we can convince a jury," she has told her staff, "then we're not confident of our case. If we're not sure our suspect is guilty, we have no business taking that person to trial."

For another thing, she's thorough. Marie wants all the nails in the coffin before she picks up her hammer. But when she does, look out. Her cross-examinations are as efficient as they are vicious, prompting the legendary moment early in her career when a car thief who would thereafter always be known as "OK Johnson" just gave up during her cross and whined, "Okay, okay, I did it."

And juries love her.

Maybe because in this heavily Catholic state, she used to be a nun.

Marie comes from the mostly French Canadian mill town of Woonsocket, although by the time she made her appearance the mills had mostly gone south. She grew up speaking French as well as English, a devout girl who always imagined something different for herself than being a housewife in a home that would see unemployment, disappointment and despair. With limited possibilities, that meant the church, and because she was barred from becoming a priest, she joined the Sisters of Mercy.

Marie wanted to make a difference, and she thought that a nun could make a difference.

She was right, to an extent.

Enrolling in Salve Regina College, Marie got her teacher's certificate. She was great in the classroom and did make a difference for five classes of high school students.

Which was good but not enough.

So she took a leave of absence and went to law school at Providence College, got her degree, passed the bar on her first try, and then left the sisterhood.

It wasn't a loss of faith—Marie still retains her Catholic beliefs—it was the church hierarchy, specifically a bishop who thought she was getting a little too big for her wimple, especially when it came to the prosecution of a priest for molestation.

Given a choice between backing down and leaving the order, Marie chose door number two.

It was tough, being in the male-dominated, testosterone-driven attorney general's office, but Marie Bouchard was tough. It didn't hurt, she knew, that she was petite and pretty, so a little less threatening, but she was also sarcastic, funny, and just good.

She worked her way up to lead prosecutor.

Juries handed her verdict after verdict.

At first she was afraid that they would hold her leaving the church against her, but they seemed to like her, trust her, believe her. (Would a nun lie?) After a high-profile trial, a *Providence Journal* cartoonist drew a caricature, which still hangs on her office wall, of Marie questioning a witness while holding a ruler in her hand. She'd won so many cases the place became known as Mother Superior Court.

Marie Bouchard became a Rhode Island celebrity.

Attila the Nun.

Sister of No Mercy.

The only blot on her record has been her inability to bring the killer of Celia Moretti to justice.

And she's about to wipe that out.


PETER MORETTI JR. sits in a holding cell.

He's totally fucked up and just as totally fucked.

Jonesing at some cushy rehab in Malibu is one thing; doing it on the concrete floor of a cell is another. He's shaking, puking, aching, not thinking about his future, which is probably a good thing, seeing as he doesn't have one.

Because he's guilty as hell.

Not of one homicide but of two.

He doesn't feel so bad about killing Vinnie Calfo. After all, Calfo killed his father, shot him in a bathtub while he lay there helpless.

But his mother?

Yeah, Peter Jr. feels bad about that, even though his mother gave the nod to Calfo for the murder. She'd been fucking Vinnie for a while, Peter Jr. learned, blaming his father for his sister's suicide.

What a fucked-up family I come from, he thinks now, wrapping his arms around himself and rocking.

The memories are brutal.

Maybe not so much memories, really, because they seem like they're happening right now, over and over again. My mother's face, her pleading eyes, her coming at me. Her stomach ripped open, the stomach I came from, where she carried me, open now, guts spilling out as she slumps along the wall, staring, openmouthed.

He gets up, starts banging his head against the wall.

Harder and harder, trying to bash his brains in.

Or out.

The guards come running.

Grab him.

Wrestle him into a restraint chair.

Wish the Rhode Island cops would get there, take this whack job off their hands.

"BULLSHIT." MARIE SAYS. "He's setting up an insanity defense."

"You didn't fly up here with him," Elaine says. "Catatonic the whole way."

"It's an act."

Elaine shrugs and that gives Marie doubts. Elaine Wheeler is the best investigator she's ever worked with and she trusts her instincts. So maybe Peter Jr. is off his rocker now, maybe he's an addict *now*.

He wasn't *then*.

He was a decorated marine.

Compos mentis.

She looks through the window slot at Peter sitting in the interview room. His wrist cuffed to the table, his ankles shackled. Wearing the standard orange jumpsuit that would make Mother Teresa look guilty.

"You ready for this?" Elaine asks.

"I've been ready for six years."

She goes in.


PETER JR. DECLINED a lawyer.

Always a big mistake.

A rookie mistake that career criminals never make. They shut up and let their lawyers do the talking, which is basically: *Show us your evidence, see you at trial.*

Peter Jr. starts off like that. "There's nothing to talk about. I want to confess."

"Then there's a lot to talk about," Bonnie Dumanis says. The homicide cop looks across the table at him. "You have to walk us through the whole thing."

Bonnie's relatively new to the case, the detectives who originally caught it having retired.

Marie sits in the corner of the room, just watching.

"What do you want me to say?" Peter Jr. asks. "I did it."

And that's it, Marie thinks. Peter confesses, he pleads guilty, there'll be no trial. What there will be is a sentencing hearing, at which she intends to press for the max on both counts.

"Tell us about it," Bonnie says. "Let's start with you driving to the house. You went with the intent of murdering—"

Marie hears shouting in the hallway and then banging on the window.

*"Stop! Stop! Don't you ask him another question!"*

She gets up, opens the door and sees exactly the one thing she didn't want to see.

Bruce Bascombe.

Tall, rail thin, his white hair parted in the middle with this long skinny braided ponytail—which has always for some reason annoyed the hell out of Marie—trailing down his back. He wears a black suit, an open-neck blue shirt, and white tennis shoes.

Bruce Bascombe is the best criminal defense attorney in Rhode Island.

Maybe in New England.

Maybe the world.

"Marie," he says, "don't you ask my client another question."

"Your client? Since when?"

"Since now," Bruce says.

"He declined representation," Marie says.

"He's in no mental condition to make an informed decision," Bruce says. "In any case, I've been engaged to represent him."

"By whom?"

"You're not entitled to that information," Bruce says. "Now I want to speak with my client."

"I don't know that he's your client," Marie says. "I need to hear it from him."

"Well, let's go in and hear it, then."

They go into the room.

Bruce says, "Peter Jr., I'm attorney Bruce Bascombe. I've been engaged to represent you. Do you want me as your lawyer?"

"I don't want a lawyer," Peter Jr. says. "I just want to get this over with."

"See ya, Bruce," Marie says. "Bye-bye, now."

He smiles at her. "Marie, I'm shocked and appalled that you would conduct an official interview with a suspect in this obviously distressed condition. You and I both know that any judge will throw whatever you get here out with yesterday's newspaper. You'd be better off to have him represented."

"I can look after myself, thank you."

"I want a moment with Mr. Moretti."

"Peter," Marie asks, "do you want to speak with Mr. Bascombe?"

"Okay," Peter Jr. says.

Shit, Marie thinks.

"I'll require a room," Bruce says, "without cameras or recording equipment. Appearances to the contrary, this is not Stalinist Russia."

"You can stay here," Marie says. "We'll suspend the recording."

"I trust you, Marie."

"I'm thrilled."

She goes out with Bonnie.

Elaine says, "Junior is a junkie hanging around a 7-Eleven parking lot. Where does he get the money for Bruce Bascombe?"

"His sister inherited the Narragansett house," Bonnie says. "Maybe she put it up."

"Or he's doing it pro bono," Marie says. "It's a high-profile case. Bruce has never seen a camera he didn't love. He's worse than Jesse Jackson."

"You think Peter will go for him?" Elaine asks.

Marie shrugs. "It's a speed bump."

But she's worried.

# ELEVEN

**B**RUCE PULLS A CHAIR BESIDE Peter and sits down. "Peter, Pasco Ferri sent me. He feels bad about turning you away and wants to help you. Will you let me help you?"

"I'm guilty," Peter says.

"You literally don't know what 'guilty' means," Bruce says. "And I never want to hear you say that again. Now, I can't make any promises, there are no guarantees, but if you'll work with me, there's a very good chance that one day you'll walk away from all this. I *can* promise, and I do guarantee, that if you *don't* work with me, you'll spend the rest of your life behind bars. You're a young man, Peter, that's a long time."

"Uncle Pasco sent you?" Peter Jr. asks.

"That's right."

"Who's paying you?" Peter Jr. asks. "I don't have any money."

"We'll work all that out."

Peter Jr. waffles. "But I did it."

"Again," Bruce says, "in a legal sense, you don't know what you did or didn't do. Whatever it was or wasn't, you deserve the best defense available, and that's me."

"All right."

"All right, I represent you?" Bruce asks.

Peter Jr. nods.

"I need to hear you say it," Bruce says.

"You represent me."

Bruce stands up. "Here's what's going to happen. They're going to come back in the room to restart the interview. I'm going to tell them that you won't answer any further questions. They're going to charge you with two homicides, process you and take you to jail. No judge is going to release you on bond, so get your head straight that you're going to be in a cell until the trial is over. Do you get that?"

"Yes."

"Here's the most important thing," Bruce says. "From this moment on, you don't talk to anyone but me. Not to the detectives, not to the prosecutor, not to your cellmate—especially not to your cellmate. Do you understand?"

"I understand."

"Good," Bruce says. "And Peter? It's going to be all right."

Peter Jr. nods again.

Although he doesn't think so.

"Now, what did you tell them?"


MARIE SITS DOWN at a table across from Bruce.

"Okay," Bruce says, "tell me what you have."

"For starters," Marie says, "I have a confession."

"'I did it?'" Bruce asks. "What did he do? He didn't say. Could be anything. He robbed a liquor store, he stole a car, he wore white after Labor Day? 'I just want to confess.' Again, to what?"

"To the murders of Vinnie Calfo and Celia Moretti."

"Says you," Bruce says. "And even if you do somehow manage to sell that inference, I'll have it thrown out based on his mental condition. I'll make the case that it was coerced. Really, Marie, given your personal history, I'd expect you to be more compassionate."

"This is why you can't trust stereotypes," Marie says. "See, given your appearance, I'd expect you to be, I don't know, Cheyenne? Sioux? But not the old-line WASP you are."

"I don't want the Native American forgotten," Bruce says. "And my client was in no condition to make a statement."

"You're just trying to set up an insanity defense."

"There is a history of mental illness in the family," Bruce says. "His younger sister slashed her wrists. Anyway, I'm not pleading insanity. I'm going to get an acquittal."

Marie laughs.

"You've over-charged," Bruce says. "Murder one? Come on."

"It was premeditated," Marie says. "He went to the house with intent."

Timothy Shea will testify that he drove Peter to the house, that they brought a shotgun with the express purpose of killing Calfo and Moretti. He'll further testify to having seen Peter firing the shot that killed Calfo. He'll testify to hearing a second shot, and that he saw Peter, splattered with blood, running down the stairs from the room where Celia Moretti was killed.

Shea will testify that, in the car, Peter screamed, "What did I do?! *What did I do?!*" That they busted up the shotgun and threw it into the Harbor of Refuge before driving to . . .

Marie enjoys this bit: ". . . Pasco Ferri's summer house. What was that about, Bruce? Why did they go there? What did Peter and Pasco talk about? Did Peter tell him that he just killed Calfo and Moretti? I'll subpoena him and ask. And you can't represent Ferri—conflict of interest."

The expression on Bruce's face tells her that Pasco sent him to represent Peter.

Marie lays out the rest of the case.

She has his client at the scene, she has his client fleeing the scene, she has his client making a guilty admission. She has fingerprints, footprints and DNA. She has the security guard who will identify him. In short, she has Peter by the short and curlies.

"So if you want to make a deal, Bruce," she says, "this would be the time."

Marie thinks he does. She thinks Ferri sent him to shut this thing down. He doesn't want to go back and tell Pasco that there's going to be a trial and that he's going to be on the stand.

"Do you have an offer?" Bruce asks.

"If Peter pleads out to both charges," Marie says, "I'll drop the LWOP request."

"On a double homicide, what's the difference?" Bruce asks. "He still dies in prison."

"Exactly."

"That's harsh."

"Killing your mother is harsh."

"But irrelevant."

"A jury won't think so," Marie says.

"You're good," Bruce says. "Why don't you get off this recidivist factory treadmill and come work for me? Do some good in the world for a change."

"Locking up mobsters is enough good for me," Marie says.

"Is that what this is about?" Bruce asks. "If this weren't the Moretti family, would you be so rigid? This kid was never in the family business, he was a marine, for Chrissakes."

"Yeah, he's Al Pacino, right?"

"Drop to murder two on both counts, I'll plead him."

"Ten years?" Marie asks.

"On each count," Bruce says. "He serves twenty, he still has some kind of life left."

"What kind of life does Celia Moretti have left?" Marie asks.

"She had her husband killed," Bruce says. "Come on, murder two and we can both go home, put this thing to bed."

"Pasco Ferri will be so happy."

"So we have a deal?" Bruce asks.

"Here's the deal," Marie says. "Your client can plead guilty to two counts of murder one or take it to trial."

"Nuns," Bruce says.

"You bet your ass," Marie says.

You unreconstructed-hippie, wannabe-Indian, hipster-doofus, pigtail-wearing contrarian pain in the ass.

# TWELVE

CATHY PALUMBO IS ARGUING OVER the price of tuna.

"Five ninety-five a pound?" she asks. "I can't make money at five ninety-five a pound. I lose on every plate I sell."

"Raise your prices," Gig says.

"If I raise prices, I can't compete."

"What can I tell you? That's the price, Cathy."

"Bayside is selling it at four fifty," Cathy says.

"Then buy from them," Gig says.

"They won't sell to me," Cathy says. "And you know that."

John Giglione does know that. Everyone in the restaurant supply business knows that he had an exclusive deal with Chris Palumbo, and no one is going to try to come in and undersell him.

Just like everyone knows that Chris got John and a bunch of other guys to invest in a shipment of heroin that got busted. They all lost their money, and Chris, he just took off.

Some people think he jacked ten keys of the smack himself. Others allege that he's in the Witness Protection Program. A charitable few say he's dead. Whatever, he departed without facing up to his responsibilities, leaving his wife, Cathy, holding the bag. Half the wiseguys in New England have been chipping away at her ever since, getting their money back a little at a time.

No one knows this reality better than Cathy.

When her husband took a powder, he left her the restaurant, a strip club, a dry cleaner, an auto repair shop and some loan-shark money on the street. Some of Chris's old crew volunteered to collect on the loans and delivered pennies on the dollar to Cathy, the rest going into their own pockets.

What was she supposed to do?

She had no weight.

Cathy couldn't go to Peter Moretti, because it was Peter that Chris really fucked on the heroin deal, and the boss of the family had problems of his own. Then he got killed, and the new boss, Vinnie, couldn't have cared less.

Except to get his own money back.

"Let me explain something to you, Cathy," Vinnie told her. "Your no-good husband cost a lot of guys a lot of money. The businesses he left behind are what do you call it, encumbered."

Vinnie did nothing for her.

So Cathy got to work.

It was tough. As a mob wife, Cathy knew pretty much nothing except how to do her nails and her makeup, cook meals, tend house and "keep her pretty mouth shut except for blow jobs," which is how her husband described her role to her. In all fairness, she had to admit that she liked her life. The money was good, she had a nice home, Chris took care of his family. He had *gumars*, but which of those guys didn't, and at least he was discreet.

But now she works.

And for what?

The restaurant? Guys came into the seafood place on the shore, ran up huge bills and left without paying. They hit her with overcharges on everything from the table linens to the food costs, and she was a captive customer who couldn't go anywhere else.

Cathy knew a chunk of that money was going to Vinnie.

Then he got killed (good riddance to bad garbage), nobody took the top job, and it's been sheer chaos ever since.

A free-for-all.

Everyone and his dog feels free to take a bite out of Cathy.

The strip club? Forget it. The bartenders pour two of their own drinks for every one of hers, and the cost of the liquor is highway robbery. The girls are supposed to kick in half of what they make, but the doormen are taking a chunk of that in addition to the complimentary bj's and are passing none of it on to Cathy.

The dry cleaner? Yeah, she has a few customers who are civilians, but the bulk are connected joints that send their towels and linens at a cut-rate price they swear Chris negotiated, and half the time they don't pay *that*.

The auto repairs? They make her take good parts from the cars and replace them with aftermarket shit. They run stolen vehicles through the place and use it as a chop shop.

Chipping away, chipping away.

A dozen guys claim they got ripped off by Chris and they're just getting their money back.

With compounding interest, the motherfuckers.

Every day, Cathy thinks, I lose ground. The faster I run, the farther behind I get. She'd shut down every business, just close the doors and get a regular job, but they won't let her.

*Cathy, you gotta pay.*

They'll keep at it, squeezing every ounce of juice out of every business, stopping just short of bankrupting them so they can keep coming to the trough.

A few of these assholes have other ideas.

Like John Giglione. "Cathy, maybe we can work something out, you know what I mean."

Cathy stares at him. She's still a good-looking woman, still hot—a MILF, like the kids call it. She knows that her blue eyes are still startling, that her waist-length blond hair is a little young for her age, but it's sexy. Her body is still thin and trim. She knows what she has left to sell.

But John Giglione?

Gig?

He's not a *bad*-looking guy, if you go for the gray wavy-hair type, the sort of guy who calls himself a "silver fox." But he has the charisma of a subterranean rock, the heart of a shylock and no sense of humor whatsoever.

Say what you will about Chris, he was funny.

He made her laugh.

"You want me to fuck you for *tuna*?" she asks Gig. "What, do I just blow you for littlenecks? A hand job for calamari? If I want swordfish, I guess I have to let you fuck me up the ass. Hey, why not? You're doing it anyway."

"The mouth on you," Gig says. "You don't gotta be nasty."

I don't know, Cathy thinks. Maybe I should just give up. At least three of these jadrools have offered to marry her, take care of her; maybe she should just give in and let them do it.

Yeah right, she thinks. Just what I need, another wiseguy for a husband.

Fuck you, Chris, wherever you are.

She sighs. "How about we say five fifty. Maybe you use a little lube, you know."

"I'll use all the lube you want, baby."

Great. "So five fifty?"

Her son, Jake, goes predictably apeshit when he sees the bill. "Mom, this is too fucking much."

"No shit, huh?"

"How could you agree to this?"

He's a good kid, Cathy thinks. Adored his father, took his leaving hard, and then snapped out of it. Went to URI, but dropped out after three semesters because they couldn't afford the tuition and he wanted to help her. Jake does what he can, but there isn't a lot to be done. Chris's debtors are just going to bust the businesses, and that's that.

"Mom, we can't live with these prices," Jake says. "We can't be charging twelve bucks for a plate of tuna."

"What do you want me to do, Jake?"

"If Dad was here . . ."

That's his refrain lately, his mantra.

*If Dad was here, if Dad was here, if Dad was here . . .*

Jake has forgotten his hurt and resentment, and now he has turned Chris into some kind of hero, like he's off winning World War II or something, instead of just the guy who abandoned them.

It could be worse, she thinks.

Peter Moretti Jr. *killed* his mother.

Jake stays at it. "If Dad was here—"

"Well, he isn't here."

"If he was—"

Cathy snaps. Maybe it's the daily grind, the constant swimming upstream, the fact that she hasn't gotten laid in eight years. Maybe it's the fucking tuna, but she slams a pen on the desk and yells, "HE ISN'T!"

Jake looks surprised.

She isn't done. "Tell you what, Jake, you want your dad so bad, why don't you go find him?"

"Maybe I will."

"Be my guest."

"See if I don't!"

"Go for it!"

He walks out of the office.

Great, Cathy thinks, now I've lost my husband *and* my son.

Four ninety-five for tuna . . .

# THIRTEEN

WHAT CHRIS PALUMBO HATES ABOUT Nebraska—actually, about the *only* thing he hates about Nebraska—is the weather.

Winter in Nebraska was not meant for human beings. The temps can be subzero and the wind blasts down from the Arctic Circle with barely a tree to slow it down.

Living on the second floor of an old farmhouse, Chris hates getting out of bed on a winter morning, so he usually doesn't. Not early, anyway. He lingers under the heavy quilts that Laura makes and waits until *she* gets out of bed and cranks the thermostat up and the house warms.

Chris has decided that winter in Nebraska was made for buffaloes, not people. Even the freaking cows *die* out on the plains in January and February, and the other thing about winter in Nebraska is that it lasts forever. You'd think sometime in March, winter would just stop, but you'd think wrong. March comes in like a lion and goes out like a lion.

Spring is beautiful.

For the hour and a half it lasts.

Nebraska tends to go straight from winter to summer. Sometimes in a single afternoon. Chris literally was inside on a snowy morning, then walked out and it was eighty-three degrees. He took a nap and missed spring.

Now it's summer.

Summer sucks.

What's that old saying? Chris thinks as he sweats bullets twisting a wrench on the radiator of Laura's VW bug. "It's not the heat, it's the humidity"? It's the heat *and* the humidity, stupid. They go together. The soup and sandwich, the peanut butter and jelly, the Laurel and Hardy that are the misery of a July day in Malcolm, Nebraska.

And it's not like you can go inside to escape, because the old house has no air-conditioning. Laura never saw the need—"We have the breeze." "What breeze?" Chris asked. The wind that won't freaking quit in winter suddenly gives up in summer, leaving a stultifying stillness that sucks the air out of your lungs.

Still, Laura persists in a routine of "organic" solutions: opening and closing the drapes and shades, windows and screen doors, and a touching if frustrating faith in the two small electric fans that she strategically moves from window to window.

"They circulate the air," she says.

Yeah, Chris thinks, they circulate the hot air.

He's looking forward to autumn, which can last for days and even weeks before winter bullies it offstage. Autumn in Nebraska is beautiful: the air crisp and clean; the changing colors of the harvested fields vivid; the nights cool, great sleeping weather with the windows open.

But other than the weather, Chris likes his life here in the middle of the country and the middle of nowhere.

Who'd have thought?

He was driving across the flyover zone with a car full of cash from selling a load of smack in Minnesota when a flat tire intervened like fate and brought him into contact with Laura, who pulled over to offer help.

Chris ended up in a one-night stand that has now lasted . . .

Jesus, Chris thinks, can it have been eight years?

How did *that* happen?

He'd always intended to leave, to get up and go back to where he was living in Scottsdale or maybe even back to Rhode Island, now that both Peter Moretti and Vinnie Calfo are in the dirt.

It was probably safe to go back.

Without Peter, without Vinnie, and with Pasco playing bocce ball in Florida waiting to have a stroke, the New England family is the proverbial ship without a rudder, a canoe without a paddle, going in circles as it tries to navigate shit creek.

Yeah, but chaos can be dangerous. Without a chain of command, guys go freelance and do random, dangerous things.

Chris is happy to be out of it.

When he was Peter's consigliere, he used to fantasize about becoming boss, but who needs it? What with the feds, RICO and everyone and his brother turning rat.

Chris doesn't miss it, any of it.

Not the dinners, the parties, the endless tedious bullshit sessions with the guys, none of it.

He's perfectly happy under the quilt with Laura.

His wife, Cathy, was good in bed—actually, she was great in bed—but Laura is another order of things altogether. She takes sex very seriously, lifting it to a level that Chris didn't know even existed.

So Chris means to leave but can't seem to make himself do it. It's like Laura's pussy has a magnet in it, like she has some sort of spell on him.

Which is a good thing, because his job is basically fucking.

Chris hasn't exactly told her the truth about his financial situation, the fact that he has hundreds of thousands of dollars stashed first in the trunk of the car, later in various parts of the farm—the barn, the toolshed, the attic. He isn't really sure what he's squirreling the money away *for*—he just has this innate sense that you never tell the truth about money, and that if you can live for free, you should.

Laura doesn't seem to care that he has no interest in finding gainful employment, just as long as he gets the job done in the sack.

So they subsist on the acreage that Laura rents to the neighboring farmer and what she makes teaching yoga and selling her quilts, blankets, scarves, hats, mittens and the other creations she weaves and knits.

Sometimes—okay, rarely—she sells one of her artworks—weird collages made from old photos, bits of yarn, twigs and stones and shit. Chris doesn't know why anyone would buy that, but sometimes they do.

Go figure.

Chris contributes in other ways. He maintains the vehicles, drives into town to do the grocery shopping and cooks most of the meals, although this is more out of self-defense than anything. Otherwise Laura will serve some weird organic casserole that tastes like lawn clippings.

He likes going to town, teasing the store clerks, shooting the shit with the locals over coffee at the diner—although the coffee is total shit, weak and pale compared to the espressos he makes back at the house. And the locals like Chris, have stopped asking questions about who he is and where he came from and what he does. They know that his job is mainly screwing Laura, whose sexual appetite is an accepted fact, tolerated in this straitlaced Methodist town with gentle amusement.

There are worse jobs, Chris thinks as he finishes the last twist of the wrench and closes the hood.

Sometimes he feels guilty about deserting Cathy, but she's a smart, tough babe, and besides, he left her with thriving businesses that should take care of her quite well.

As they say, in the style to which she's become accustomed.

He misses his kids, but Jill is like her mom, and Jake—Jake has a good head on his shoulders.

Not like poor Peter Jr.

How fucked up is that? Chris thinks as he walks toward the house to get lunch. Peter getting arrested after all this time even made the papers in Nebraska, and now the kid's life is *over*.

Chris opens the screen door and walks into the kitchen. Laura made sun tea—never a problem in Nebraska in the summer—before she left for town to teach her class, and Chris pours some into a jelly jar as he takes out the stuff to make a bologna sandwich.

Vinnie had it coming, Chris thinks.

He never liked the guy.

And Celia.

She was a materialistic, nagging *strega* who made Peter's life miserable. That family, though—one kid kills herself and another kills his own mother.

Something in the blood, maybe.

Chris takes two slices of Wonder Bread—what they got in the little grocery—lays two pieces of bologna on them and slathers them with mustard. Then he sits down at the table to eat.

No, count your blessings, Chris thinks.

You got good kids, they got their heads on straight.

They'll be okay.

So will Cathy.

With her looks, her smarts and personality, she probably has another guy anyway.

Then Chris feels something he didn't expect, a sudden stab of jealousy, even anger, at the thought of some other guy banging his wife. It's not fair, he knows, but it's what he feels, and he has to make an effort to shake the image out of his head.

He gets up, puts the dish in the sink and decides to take a nap.

You'll need it for later, he thinks.

It'll be way too hot upstairs—an oven—so he goes into the living room and stretches out on the couch. If he lies real still and barely breathes, he can almost not feel the heat.

He's asleep in seconds.

# FOURTEEN

THE DREAM.

Danny explains his vision to the Tara Group board.

"Las Vegas has built replicas of things that exist," he says. "Pyramids, pirate ships, state fairs . . . Casablanca, the Shores. I want to build something that *doesn't* exist—a dream."

When we're inside a dream, he tells them, it feels as real as life, with the important exception that anything is possible. There is no time, no space, no linear continuum. We see people we know, people we don't, people who are alive, people who are dead. We see things that were, things that are, and things that could never be. And yet, there they are. We can see them, smell them, touch them, taste them, and yet they're ephemeral, as fleeting as a shadow that races across the sky.

"Most of the time we forget a dream as soon as it's over," he says. "Other times we remember it for the rest of our lives."

That's what he wants to build on the site of the Lavinia.

A 3,000-room hotel-casino of incomparable beauty and understated elegance, sleek and sexy with subtle colors, walls of shifting light and changing images, guest rooms of refined luxury, five-star restaurants, a theater that stages shows of daring and imaginative spectacle.

"You'll enter a dream," Danny says, "go to sleep in a dream, wake up in a dream, eat in a dream, see a dream. When you leave, you ask, 'Did that really happen? Or did I dream it?' And you come back again and again. You've had dreams like that, haven't you? Dreams that were so beautiful, so peaceful or exciting, so sensual that you wish you could dream them again? Now you can."

He can tell the room is edgy, uncertain, confused. But Danny's convinced that now is the time to expand.

Jerry asks, "What's the theme?"

"There is no theme," Danny says. "Just beauty."

The theme hotels worked well for years, Danny argues. The family experience, the re-creation of the Disney model in Las Vegas was a good idea. But times have changed. The internet revolution is changing the economy, the dot-com fortune holders want luxury and have the means to pay for it.

They demand an *experience*, one that caters to their tastes and their whims. Rooms that don't *have* art, but *are* art. They don't want to eat, they want to *dine*, and they want it to be an adventure. They don't want to go see a comic or singer perform something they can hear at home on their JVC stereo system, they want to be engaged in an immersive experience that they can't get anywhere else—a performance that speaks to their intelligence, to the innovative, entrepreneurial mindset that made them the money to get there.

"We can't build any more fake anythings," Danny says. "The idea is played out, tired. What are we going to put up? Bigger pyramids? London instead of Paris? A bigger beach with bigger waves? Once you've seen it, you've seen it. People get bored with it. You never get bored with dreams."

"Tell me this," Dom says. "Do people gamble in your dream?"

"Of course," Danny says. "Because nothing is real in a dream, there are no consequences. And the guests who are attracted to this kind of experience and have the disposable income to afford it will place larger bets and play the higher-stakes games. But the real money, the profit center, will come from the rooms and the meals."

Dom and Jerry are no fools. They're brilliant business structuralists who immediately see that Danny is pushing the Tara model to the breaking point, maybe beyond it. The exclusive customer base that he's proposing might be *too* exclusive, too small to compensate for the enormous cost of his vision.

And yet, as Missouri boys used to being looked down on as hicks from the flyover zone, they share Danny's underdog chip on his shoulder, so the idea of bucking the establishment and creating the best of the best is appealing, almost irresistible.

But there's a big problem. Well, there are a lot of problems, but this one is immediate and stops things before they can start.

"The Winegard Group," Jerry says, "is already in the late stages of buying the Lavinia property. It's all but a done deal."

"Meaning it's *not* a done deal," Danny says. "They're engaged, they're not married."

"How would Vern react to our interfering?" Jerry asks.

"Who cares?" Danny asks.

"I care," Jerry says. "The town will care. If we step in and steal the Lavinia from Winegard, we turn a cordial rivalry into a war."

"And if we don't," Danny says, "Vern gains control of the Strip and we start the long downhill slide to becoming irrelevant. Not only that, but the future of the town is at stake. Vern builds another gigantic grind joint, Las Vegas will become just another amusement park. It will fade into shabby schlock."

Madeleine's smile is wry. "So you're picturing yourself as a sort of city father? A savior? Dan Ryan to the rescue?"

"Hardly," Danny says. "I just don't see why we should resign ourselves to second place behind the Winegard Group."

"For the sake of argument," Jerry says, "let's say that we *can* talk George Stavros into selling to us instead of Vern. Where are we going to get the money? Do you have a guesstimate as to how much your dream is going to cost?"

Dan doesn't blink. "North of a billion."

"Billion?" Dom asks. "That's with a *b*?"

"Yeah," Danny says.

"That's insane," Jerry says. "The banks aren't going to fund us to the tune of a billion dollars. It's a nonstarter, Dan."

"Unless . . ." Dom says.

I've got him, Danny thinks. He's considering it. "Unless what, Dom?"

"We took the company public," Dom says.

"No," Danny says.

Tara is privately held. The people in this room make all the decisions. If they took the company public, the shareholders would control it.

"If you want to build this hotel," Dom says, "it's the only way to raise the capital and get the banks on board."

"We could lose control of our company," Danny says.

"We could," Dom says, "but it's doubtful. The present owners would retain enough stock to wield the balance of power, and we make sure we sell another big chunk to friends and allies to have the majority vote."

"It's risky," Danny says.

"And building a billion-dollar luxury hotel isn't?" Dom asks. "If we're going to do this—and I'm by no means convinced yet that we should—going public is the only way."

"It's a moot point," Jerry says. "Stavros is committed to Winegard. And from what I hear, his wife thinks Vern hung the moon."

"Okay, that's the first step," Danny says. "If we can convince Stavros to sell to us, can we build my hotel?"

"Will you go public?" Dom asks.

Danny doesn't like it, not at all.

But the Missouri boys know more than I do, he thinks. If they say it's the only way, then it's the only way. "Reluctantly."

"Who makes the approach to Stavros?" Jerry asks.

"I do," Danny says.

"Are you sure that's wise?"

"Stavros is a friend of a friend," Danny says. "I can talk to him."

"Okay," Dom says. "But the hotel, I don't like the name."

"The Dream?" Danny asks. "What's wrong with it?"

"It's too plain," Dom says. "Not classy enough. It doesn't have the cachet for what we're envisioning."

"I agree," Madeleine says.

"But that's what it is," Danny says. "A dream."

"Sure," Dom says. "I don't know, maybe if we put it in a different language. Something French or Italian."

"What's Italian for 'dream'?" Danny asks.

No one knows. Danny buzzes Gloria and asks her to find out. Thirty seconds later she calls back. "Il Sogno."

She spells it out.

"Same problem as Scheherazade," Jerry says. "No one will know how to pronounce it. They'll call it the Sog-no."

"No," Danny says, "it will have snob appeal. The people in the know will know how to pronounce it."

He tests the sound of it. *Sone-yo.*

"I love it," Danny says.

So the Dream becomes Il Sogno.

And Il Sogno becomes the dream.

But first they have to sell George Stavros.

# FIFTEEN

GEORGE STAVROS IS AS GREEK as olive oil.

That's what Pasco tells Danny over the phone. "I knew him even before he came to Vegas. The family is from Lowell, Massachusetts. There's a big Greek community there, worked in the mills. My old man did some boxing shows up there back in the day. His father had a diner, we'd see each other."

Stavros went off to World War II, then didn't want to come back to either the mills or the diner. His troop train had stopped in Vegas, he liked what he saw, so when he survived Iwo Jima and Okinawa, he decided to settle there.

Opened a restaurant, then another, then leveraged them both to buy a little hotel, and made a success of it. When the big building boom of the sixties came along, Stavros got in on it.

"Was he connected?" Danny asks.

"Loosely," Pasco says. "Not made, of course—he's Greek. But sure, everyone was looking to get in on Vegas, we needed fronts, Stavros was a smart guy, knew what he was doing."

"You owned a piece?"

"If memory serves," Pasco says. "So did your old man."

Like a salmon swimming upstream, Danny thinks. Back to the place I was spawned.

"Listen," Pasco says, "Stavros played ball. He tolerated a certain amount of skim, didn't complain, didn't open his mouth, let the girls work as long as they were discreet. Still does, what I hear. He bided his time—when all the federal shit came down, he bought out all the silent partners, owned the place whole. Made a mint."

"Now he wants to retire," Danny says.

"I know the feeling," Pasco says. "I've been trying to retire for years now, but with the clusterfuck up in Providence . . . If everyone is in charge, no one is in charge, you know what I mean?"

Danny knows what he means but couldn't care less about what's going on back in Providence. Earlier in his life he followed every nuance as a matter of survival. Now it seems trivial. What matters to him now is acquiring the Lavinia.

He's researched its history.

Built in 1958, it was of that classic generation of Las Vegas hotels that gave the city its swinging reputation. Sinatra and the rest of the Rat Pack played and gambled there, as did a lot of gangsters and movie stars. If you went to Las Vegas in the sixties, the Lavinia was a must, but it had started to fade by the end of the decade. Caesars Palace stole some of the luster, then Circus Circus, and the Lavinia became thought of as second-rate, a bargain whose value was mostly nostalgia.

Stavros resisted any changes, wouldn't sell it—even to Howard Hughes when he offered—but also wouldn't put up any real money to remodel. The hotel occupied sixty acres of prime Strip real estate and sat there like an elderly lady who refuses to leave her home, as the new hotels closed in on it from the north and the south.

Old Stavros knew what he was doing, though, Danny thinks. Knew that even if the value of the building itself declined, the worth of the location it sat on would only increase as space on the Strip grew more and more scarce. It was one of the last privately held hotels in town, and Stavros held on to it with a fierce, personal grip.

But Winegard has offered him an overvalued $100 million, and Stavros is finally ready to let go.

"How do I approach Stavros?" Danny asks.

"With *respect*," Pasco says. "He's old-school. No shuck and jive, no *cazzate*. He loves that hotel, it's like a child to him. You know how it got its name, right?"

"No, I just thought it was weird."

"Well, let me tell you a story . . ."

Danny's impatient. He doesn't need another story from the old days, what he needs is an edge to persuade Stavros to sell the hotel to him.

Pasco hears it, even over the phone. So he says, "Okay, you're in a hurry. I'll just tell you, don't go to Stavros empty-handed."

Gee, thanks, Pasco. "What can I bring a guy that's better than a hundred mil?"

"Well, that's the story I was going to tell you, you were too busy to hear," Pasco says.

Danny listens to the story.


GEORGE STAVROS CATCHES grief from his wife.

"Why are you going to meet with Dan Ryan?" she asks. "What's the point? We have a deal with Vern."

"The point is courtesy," Stavros says. He pours water into the briki, already filled with coffee, then peeks to see if Zina is looking. She's not, so he sneaks in two teaspoons of sugar to make it *glyko*, sweet, which he's not supposed to do because of the damn diabetes. "Ryan has been a good neighbor, I owe it to him to hear him out."

"What will Vern think?"

"He'll understand." Stavros stirs the mixture as it heats. He reaches down and adjusts the gas burner to low heat. "Who knows? Maybe Ryan isn't coming to make an offer. Maybe he's coming with another concern."

He stops stirring when the coffee is dissolved. That's the mistake that a lot of people make, they keep stirring. It's a matter of patience, of waiting until the foam, the *kaimaki*, comes to the top.

Zina won't let it go. Of course she won't, Stavros thinks, she's Zina. She hasn't let anything go in fifty-two years.

"What if Ryan makes a higher offer?" she asks.

"I won't accept it," Stavros says. "Vern made us a good deal, we said yes, end of story."

"Good," she says. "Did you put sugar in that coffee?"

"I have diabetes," Stavros says, because he won't lie to his wife. He watches the briki until the coffee just starts to boil, then takes it off the stove and turns off the burner.

He pours the coffee into a small cup and takes a sip.

The blend of bitter and sweet is exquisite.

A lot of people call this Turkish coffee, Stavros thinks, but that's ridiculous. Those barbarians couldn't invent the wheel, much less decent coffee. Almost every civilized thing came out of Greece.

"You couldn't have met him at the office?" Zina asks.

"I could have," Stavros says. "I'm not."

"When is he coming?"

"Any minute."

"Any *minute*?!" Zina says. "I guess you want me to put something out."

"I don't know."

"You don't know," Zina says. "What are we now, animals? I have some cookies, some cheese . . ."

"Not those diabetic cookies," Stavros says. "They taste like dirt."

"You know what really tastes like dirt?" she asks. "Death. Death tastes like dirt. Meet the man, give him a couple of cookies, send him on his way."

"This was my plan."

He has no intention of selling the Lavinia to Dan Ryan.

He's going to sell to Vern Winegard.

# SIXTEEN

**V**ERN WINEGARD IS A BIG man with bad skin.

The acne scars of his youth still mar his cheeks and, some say, his personality, which manages to be defensive and aggressive at the same time.

He'd laugh if someone had the balls to tell him this. He'd say that the acne that tortured his school years was the least of it, far more benign than his old man's belt, his mother's bottle and the murdering blight that, the same year he was born, killed all the apples in his native Apple Valley, California, kicking the desert town over the cliff into decline.

Vern would be the first to say that he's not a handsome man, wasn't a handsome youth, wasn't a handsome boy. Nor was he popular—one of those lonely, geeky boys in high school who was in the AV Club, rolling video machines, slide projectors and televisions into classrooms as the other boys smirked at him, the girls ignored him and the teachers underestimated him.

Everyone did.

His father mocked his endless "tinkering" in the little shed in the (mostly dirt) backyard. "What do you do out there, jerk off?"

"No."

"No," his father said. "You just play with your little toys."

Wires, gears, circuit boards.

"I should get you some *Playboys*," his father said. His son didn't want

*Playboy*s, he wanted wires, gears and circuit boards. He wanted a Phillips-head screwdriver, needle-nose pliers, a soldering iron. "You want that shit, buy it yourself."

Vern did.

What Vern did have—what everyone should have seen but overlooked—was a fierce, dogged ability to concentrate. He just put his head down and *worked*. First at the quintessential paper route, then as a busboy in a local diner; then he added a job as a pumper at a gas station out by the highway.

That bought him his tools, his gadgets. When he graduated from high school—his father didn't attend and Vern wished his mother hadn't either—it paid for his tuition at a technical school, where he got his certification in aeronautic electrical engineering.

Vern didn't actually want to fly, he wanted to make things fly. So when he looked up at the sky and saw one of those big, beautiful machines soar above him, he could think: *I made it do that.*

I made it fly.

He made good money, too, got himself a nice little apartment and a car, but he was still that lonely dweeb, that guy who did his job, did it well, and then went home to a frozen dinner, a little television, a lot of tinkering.

Vern worked his way from an airplane repair facility to an engineering design firm, and if any of the other employees had been asked if a Vern Winegard worked there, the answer would have been along the lines of *Yeah, I guess so.*

What none of them saw, what *none* of them saw, was that Vern was a motherfucking genius.

When he designed a special electrical circuit that could open and close the cargo door of a jet at the push of a button, then patented it and licensed it and sold it to every major aircraft manufacturer on a royalty basis, the general reaction was along the lines of *Vern? Vern Winegard? That guy?* Like when the cops find twelve dissected bodies in a bachelor's freezer and all the neighbors say what a quiet person he was.

Every time a cargo door opened or shut, Vern got paid.

He bought his own cargo plane and then a fleet of cargo planes, and within a few years Winegard Commercial Air was flying merchandise all over North America. When friends (funny, Vern had a few now) asked if he ever wanted to get into the passenger airline business, he would answer, "Are you kidding me? Boxes don't want legroom, coffee or one scotch too many. They never complain and you don't have to feed them."

Vern always preferred objects to people.

And why not?

Speaking of things, Vern developed a taste for the finer ones in life—Cuban cigars, fine wines, gourmet meals. The guy once content with a turkey TV dinner now took himself out to lunches in the best places that the Imperial Valley had to offer.

And cars—he bought himself Cadillacs and Corvettes, and it was in one of the latter that he drove to Las Vegas for the first time.

Which was a revelation, I-15 as the road to Damascus.

Vern was making millions from people pushing buttons. Every time someone pushed the button on a cargo door, money flowed into his hands. So he got to Vegas and what did he see?

Thousands of people pushing buttons, pulling levers—and every time they did it, other people made money.

Casino owners.

As an electrical engineer, Vern was awed at a system *engineered* to make people perform an activity at which they knew they would ultimately lose but did anyway. Vern looked around at the hotels and casinos and knew that they weren't built because the customers won. They lost and lost and kept pushing and pulling and Vern wanted in, so he took a few of his millions and bought a cheap joint on Fremont Street north of the Strip.

The place was a dump—the carpets stained and frayed, the wallpaper faded, the food bad (but cheap), the service indifferent . . . *and people kept coming anyway*. It didn't matter; the customers poured in to push the buttons, pull the levers and lose their money.

Vern put in more machines.

More people came.

Not the high rollers, not the whales who would risk millions at baccarat, not the Asians who would fly in for comped suites or the Arab oil sheikhs, but your average working-class man and woman, there for a guilty, naughty thrill and the chance, just the chance, to beat a system that had been grinding them down their whole lives. And when they lost, as they almost always did, they almost felt good, because it only confirmed their worldview that the game of life was rigged and the odds were stacked against them.

As, of course, the odds were.

Vern had a genius idea.

He gave them a better chance, "loosened" the slot machines to make them pay out more, and more often.

More people came and he made more money.

He made so much money he could forget about his father's swinging belt and the mother who jilted him for Jack and Johnny and a sad town of dead orchards.

And the acne scars.

What Vern found out was that *now* women wanted to fuck him. Not just the working girls (although legions of them did), but regular beautiful women with long legs, big racks and movie-star faces who were attracted to money and power. Now he didn't need *Playboy* magazines, he had actual Playboy Playmates and Penthouse Pets.

Vern would later admit that he went a little crazy in those years, when everyone was doing blow and balling their brains out, and he would confess that he fucked about everything that moved and maybe a few things that didn't.

He got tired of it.

Bored.

Married Dawn, a model at one of the auto shows, and settled down. Had a son they named Bryce.

Those were the last of the mob days, too, when Lefty and Tony the Ant still held sway, when the skim was flowing from the counting rooms to Chicago, Kansas City, Detroit and Milwaukee.

But not from Vern's joint.

The wiseguys came at him, but Vern engineered an arrangement. They stayed out of the gambling operation, but he would give them the food and linen supply contracts.

Yeah, okay. It was reasonable.

On Vern's part, it was a delaying action. He knew the OC days were about over, that a far bigger, better-engineered machine was coming in— the world of investment banks and corporations.

Vern bought another casino and then another. He put together a group of investors to create the Winegard Group, and demolished one of his hotels to build a new one on the north end of the Strip. Still a grind joint, but a bigger, better grind joint with a theme to bring Mom and Pop America in.

"What do people like?" he asked his partners.

Rides, he answered.

They like rides.

They'll stand all fucking day in the heat at Disneyland, Disney World or Six Flags to get strapped into a seat and get the shit scared out of them. Come out quivering and puking and get right back in line to do it again.

What else do Americans like?

Junk food.

The more fat, the more sugar, the better.

And games.

Anything at which they can win some cheap piece-of-shit prize, as long as they win something.

He called his new hotel State Fair and filled it with roller coasters and a lobby that looked like a midway, with food stands hawking hot dogs, cotton candy, doughboys, deep-fried candy bars. Carnival games like knocking down bottles, shooting squirt guns to move along model race horses, all that happy shit. He had barkers, stilt walkers, the cocktail waitresses dressed as farmers' daughters with a titillating air of innocence and a hint of promiscuity.

And slots.

So many slots.

He had poker tables, of course, blackjack, roulette, all the higher-end games, but the bulk of the space was given over to slot machines so people could push buttons, pull levers, and donate their money.

Vern knew his market.

So when the Winegard Group made another move south on the Strip, they built the Riverboat, which looked exactly like a giant paddle steamer, with a deep bass whistle that went off every hour, incessant banjo-playing on the deck, but top-flight country and western acts in the 2,000-seat theater in the basement.

America flocked to the Winegard hotels.

They were idealized versions of its best image of itself—Disney without the lines, carnivals without sleazy carnies. They were affordable and middle-class friendly, with no off-putting snob appeal; the food was familiar and cheap.

Vern Winegard was rapidly becoming the King of Las Vegas.

But just as he was completing the Riverboat, the new kid came into town. Dan Ryan and his Tara Group turned the failing Scheherazade into the successful Casablanca. Fair enough—the newcomers did a good job. But then they moved north and built the phenomenon that became the Shores.

So as the Winegard Group moved south, the Tara Group moved north, and now what stands between them is the empty space, the vacant lot that was the old Lavinia.

More than just a competition between two businesses, the rivalry displayed polar opposite visions.

It's a generalization, but basically the Winegard Group represents Middle America, the low rollers, the machine players attracted by a congenial, easy theme. Ryan's Tara Group represents the better-heeled, the high rollers, who come for luxurious rooms and gourmet meals and the table games.

Again, the age-old question—do you want more customers who spend less or fewer customers who spend more? Each group has its business model that works well for them.

Dan and Vern agree—they've talked about it many times—that the two visions are not so much conflicting as they are complementary, as between them they cover a wide spread of the market and bring more tourists into town. A guest at one of the Tara hotels might want a change of scene and spend a few hours at a Winegard joint; a Winegard customer might want to splurge a little and go into a Tara hotel.

Vern Winegard and Dom Rinaldi have appeared together at press conferences and promotional events, denying the rivalry that the media would love to stoke, with discipline and tact putting out the same message—there's room for both. There's *need* for both. They're friendly rivals, partners in greater Las Vegas.

Except Vern is about to be the dominant partner.

He's buying the Lavinia.

The Winegard Group is about to wrap a deal to purchase the space. It will put up a mega-hotel that will block Tara from further expansion and establish itself as the center of power on the Strip.

# SEVENTEEN

MARIE BOUCHARD SITS BY HERSELF in the bar at the Providence Bilt-more Hotel, nursing a scotch on the rocks with strict instructions to the bartender not to float the ice.

She needs the drink, she's getting ready for the trial of Peter Moretti Jr.

The whiskey feels good going down when Tony Sousa suddenly plops down on the stool next to hers. The lawyer is a short, trim man with curly white hair and a small, neat mustache. "Marie, Marie."

"Tony."

"I'll have what the lady's having," Tony says. "So, Marie, how's the prosecution business?"

Marie knows why he's here. "You saw my witness list."

"Pasco Ferri?"

"Peter Jr. went to talk to Ferri both before and after the murders," Marie says. "I have to call him."

"Your investigator took a sworn affidavit," Tony says. "Why not just have that read into the transcript?"

"It's not the same," Marie says. "And Bruce will demand a chance to cross."

"Maybe not," Tony says. "He might be willing to stipulate."

"Rhode Island." Marie shakes her head. "Ferri sent Bruce to plead the kid out so he won't have to testify. Save your breath, Tony, we both know that's what happened. Bruce didn't plead him, Ferri picks up the check anyway. Why? You want to hear my theory?"

"I'm here."

"Pasco feels guilty," Marie says. "Peter Jr. came to him. 'Vinnie Calfo killed my dad. What should I do?' Pasco went old-school on him, gave him the green light, the kid thinks he's Michael Corleone and goes to kill Vinnie. Gets carried away in the adrenaline rush and does his mother, too. Now Pasco's looking at the pearly gates opening for him and feels all guilty. Tries to save the kid he pushed through the door."

"He's an old man," Tony says. "He's not well. I can get a doctor's statement that he's too sick to travel. Bog you down for weeks, maybe you never get him."

"I'm calling him, Tony."

"Why do you want to make enemies, Marie?" Tony asks. "There are a lot of people who don't want to see you go on a fishing expedition with Pasco on the stand. You have a political future. Could have, anyway—"

"If I play ball."

"If you limit your field of inquiry," Tony says. "The jury already will know who Vinnie Calfo was, you don't have to make Pasco establish it. Just stick to what happened that night, get him on, get him off, you'll make friends."

"What makes you think I want friends?" Marie asks.

"Everyone needs friends," Tony says. "Even you. Pasco likes you, he respects you. If you promise to narrow your examination, I can produce him without a fight. Otherwise, strap yourself in."

Marie finishes her drink. "I'm not looking to relitigate every mob trial in New England. I'm not looking to paint Ferri into some corner and work him into a perjury trap. I just want his true testimony on what Peter Moretti Jr. said to him."

"I have your word."

"Would a nun lie?"

"They did in *Sound of Music*," Tony says.

"I can't sing a lick," Marie says.

Can't fly, either.

# EIGHTEEN

THE COOKIES—*MELOMAKARONA* MADE WITH HONEY, olive oil, walnuts and sugar—are delicious.

Danny makes sure to eat two, to show that he likes them. He doesn't really care for olives but eats one anyway so as not to be rude.

Stavros sits across the coffee table from him in the family living room. Zina met him at the door to greet him. He gave her the bouquet he brought, they made a minute of small talk, then she discreetly disappeared.

"That was some do at your place the other night," Stavros says.

"I'm glad you could come."

"Wouldn't have missed it," Stavros says. He takes another cookie. "You won't tell Zina."

"Your secrets are safe with me."

"Dan," Stavros says, "I don't want to waste my time or yours. If you're coming with an offer for the Lavinia, I've already accepted one from Vern. Thank you for your interest, I'm flattered, but that horse has left the barn."

"What if we make you a better offer?"

"Again, thank you," Stavros says. "But money isn't my problem in life. I've done well, thank God. My word means more to me than money. My answer still has to be a no."

So, Danny thinks, now I have to go where I didn't want to go. No, you don't have to, you could just get up, shake hands and forget about the whole thing. It's probably what you should do. Instead, he says, "Pasco Ferri asked me to give you his regards."

A shadow comes over Stavros's face. "How is Pasco?"

"He told me an old story."

The story goes back to the late fifties, when Stavros owned just his one little hotel. A small-time gangster named Benny Luna came to shake him down for protection money.

Stavros told him to go fuck himself.

Stavros and Zina had one child, a daughter they named Lavinia. A beautiful child with lush black hair so thick that Zina broke a pair of scissors one time trying to cut it.

She was the light of Stavros's life.

In those days, they lived in an apartment at the back of the hotel—frugal, saving money—and Lavinia, she just loved to be in the kitchen. Seven years old, she reveled in helping her mother cook, and sometimes she would get out of bed when her parents were asleep and sneak down to the kitchen to play at being the mommy.

The firebomb came through the kitchen window. It ignited the girl's thick black hair. By the time Stavros heard the screams, smelled the smoke, fought his way through the flames, it was too late.

"You ever notice Stavros never wears short sleeves?" Pasco asked Danny. "That's why. The scars."

Stavros and Zina never got over it.

Who would? Danny thinks.

They never had another child.

The police never caught the arsonist.

Because Pasco Ferri caught him first.

He and Marty Ryan drove Benny Luna out into the desert. Stavros was with them. They made Benny dig his own grave. Real deep. Not to lie down in, deep enough to stand. They tied him up and dropped him in. Then Marty poured the gasoline at Benny's feet.

Stavros tossed the match.

"I'm not telling this to blackmail you," Danny says. "The conversation ends here. I will observe that Pasco never asked you for anything in return. He's not asking now. He knows who you are, he knows that you'll do the right thing."

Danny stands up. "Thank you for your time. Please thank Zina for her hospitality. Our offer is a hundred million, the same as Vern's. We'll donate another ten million to fund the Lavinia Stavros Burn Unit at Children's Hospital. I can see myself out."

Danny walks into the harsh desert sunlight.

Stavros goes upstairs and finds Zina resting in the bedroom.

He tells her that he's going to sell the Lavinia to Dan Ryan.

# PART TWO

# The Powers of Hell

## Las Vegas
## 1997

If I cannot sway the Heavens, I'll wake the powers of Hell!

Virgil
*The Aeneid*
Book VII

# NINETEEN

**D** ANNY STARTS DOWN THE STEEP slope of rock.

It scares the shit out of him, but not as much as the sight of his ten-year-old son in front of him, racing down the trail at full speed, apparently fearless.

Or just ignorant, Danny thinks.

Kids don't know about life, they think they're indestructible.

But Danny has taken every precaution. The boy is armored like a medieval knight—helmet, shoulder pads, elbow and knee pads. He'd complained mightily, but Danny had held firm—no protective gear, no ride.

To avoid his son's self-righteous accusations of hypocrisy, Danny is similarly decked out and he feels ridiculous. But mostly hot. Maybe July wasn't the best time to take a dirt-biking vacation in southern Utah, but it's the time Danny has. And besides, dirty and sweaty is the name of the game on this trip, and Ian has been in boy bliss for the three days they've been out.

It's not just the biking. Ian loves that, of course, but it's also the alone time with Dad, something he doesn't get enough of.

It's been great.

They drove out of Las Vegas, up through Zion National Park, and spent the first night in their cabin in Duck Creek. They got up early, had a big breakfast of eggs, pancakes and bacon, and then drove up to Torrey to bike the Escalante trails. Dined that night on big greasy cheeseburgers and did the same thing the next day. Then they took the back roads to Moab to try the trails outside Arches National Park.

Danny and Ian haven't talked much while actually biking—it's too rigorous and Ian usually ranges ahead of Danny. But on the drives and over meals, Ian has been, in Danny's eyes anyway, surprisingly communicative.

He especially surprised Danny on the road east of Torrey when he suddenly asked, "What was Mom like?"

Danny thought for a few seconds and then said, "Funny. Tough. Strong. Very loving."

"I don't remember her."

"No, you couldn't," Danny said. "You were just a baby when she died."

"Of cancer, right?"

"Yes."

Ian was quiet for a minute, and then he asked, "If she had lived, do you think you guys would still be married?"

"No doubt. Why?"

Ian shrugged. "A lot of the kids at school . . . most of the kids at school . . . their parents are divorced."

"That's a shame."

"I guess, but . . ."

"At least they have two parents?" Danny asked.

"Something like that," Ian said.

"You got the short end of the stick," Danny said. "No question."

"Did you ever think about getting married again?"

"Maybe once."

"But then Diane died, right?" Ian asked.

Danny's surprised again. Ian was just old enough, then, to have maybe remembered Diane. "That's right."

"Did you love her?"

"I did."

"Like Mom?"

"I don't know," Danny said. "No, different, I guess. I don't think you love different people in the same way."

That seemed to satisfy the boy.

But the next day they took a lunch break on the trail—sandwiches and granola bars Danny had stuffed into a light backpack. They were sitting out on a ridge, other red ridges, deep canyons and tall spires displayed in front of them. It was a beautiful, vast open space, serene and almost spiritual.

Ian said, "Dad, the other day, at my party . . ."

He looked awkward, hesitant.

". . . what Uncle Kevin said."

"You weren't there."

"People have talked about it."

"What people?" Danny asked. "Who?"

He can hear himself getting defensive.

"Kids," Ian said.

"Uncle Kevin had too much to drink," Danny said. He had long dreaded this moment, had harbored some hope that it would never happen, but here it was, and he wanted to kick it down the road just a little longer.

"Yeah, I know," Ian said. "But he was saying something about us running from Rhode Island, about where you got your money . . . Some kids said their parents said you were some kind of gangster."

So there it is, Danny thought.

The moment's here.

I could duck it, but it's not fair to the kid. Not fair to me, either.

Every father wants his kid, especially a son, to look up to him. You want to be an example, you want him to think you're perfect. So it hurts like hell, it's scary, to admit that you're not. You don't want him to be disappointed in you.

But if you don't do that, Danny thinks, you set him up for disappointment, anyway. Maybe a worse one, because he's going to find out you're a fake, a liar. He'll wonder if anything you tell him is true.

So Danny said, "Ian, a long time ago, I did some things I'm not proud of. If that made me a gangster, yeah, I guess you can call me a gangster. But that was then. It's not now."

But isn't it? Danny thinks now as he careens down the slope. Didn't you just bring it all back, using something terrible Pasco and your father did to persuade George Stavros to sell you the hotel?

Would you ever tell your son about that?

Ian seemed to accept his explanation, but asked, "Did we really run from Rhode Island? I mean, why?"

"Some people wanted to kill me."

"Do they still want to kill you?"

He sounded concerned.

"No," Danny said. "Those days are over, Ian. I promise. You have nothing to worry about."

"Okay."

"If anything happens to me," Danny said, "it's going to be from falling off the freakin' bike."

Ian laughed.

Now Danny grips the handlebars and makes it to the bottom of the slope without breaking his neck, puts the bike into a skid and stops.

Ian stops, turns and smiles at him. "You made it!"

"You had doubts?!"

"Yeah!"

"That makes two of us!"

They bike Moab for two more days, staying in a modest hotel in town (Danny finds its lack of luxuries refreshing) and eating burgers or tacos in local restaurants or fast-food places. The last night, they're sitting in the car grubbing Taco Bell when Ian asks, "Is the plane coming tomorrow?"

"Yup." Danny has been as good as his word. While the flight from Moab to Las Vegas is ridiculously short, he promised Ian a ride in the corporate jet.

"Could it maybe not?" Ian asks.

"What do you mean?"

"I'm kind of enjoying the driving," Ian says. "Maybe we could just drive home?"

It's not ideal.

Danny needs to get back because just two days later, Tara will go public with its initial IPO. A huge moment, one that will decide whether he can realize his dream.

The last few weeks haven't gone exactly as expected.

In a good way.

Barry Levine's fundraising lunch went off perfectly, with a million dollars raised and a quiet quid pro quo that the 4 percent tax idea had been some kind of premature gaffe from an overeager ex-staffer and that there would be no subpoenas from the commission.

So Danny could breathe a little easier about that.

Likewise the fallout from George Stavros's announcement that he was selling the Lavinia to the Tara Group.

Winegard's reaction was surprisingly subdued. In response to reporters' questions, he answered that of course he was disappointed, but that George Stavros had more than earned the right to decide the terms of his disengagement. He wished the Tara Group luck and promised to be a good neighbor.

Danny had expected that kind of public response, but not what he heard about Vern's private reaction. He thought Winegard would go into a rage, but people who knew him well reported that it was more one of chagrin and that he had said, "The hospital wing. I should have thought of that."

So the fear of a war with the Winegard Group seemed to be unfounded.

The other pleasant surprise was the public reaction to news that Tara was going public. While Danny and the partners had thought it would be positive, they weren't prepared for the enthusiasm that erupted when they made their announcement.

The gaming media were particularly ebullient, citing Tara's record in turning around Casablanca and its amazing accomplishment with the Shores, citing its unprecedented profit margins in such a short period of time.

Banking and hedge-fund analyses were likewise positive, and Dom was saying that they could easily raise the price of the prospective shares while retaining a larger portion of the stock themselves.

It's all good news, but nevertheless, probably not the best moment for Danny to take a week away—he's been disciplined about not answering his cell phone, even in the areas out here where it actually worked—much less take an extra day.

But how often does a kid say he'd rather spend a long day in a car with his dad, grubbing at fast-food joints and gas stations, than flying in a private jet?

How often does your son want to go on a road trip with you?

"Yeah," Danny says, "I can call, tell the jet to stand down. Are you sure, though?"

"I'm sure."

Back at the motel, Danny makes the call canceling the jet. He and Ian watch junk television for a while, then go to sleep. In the morning they get up, have breakfast and get in the car for the drive home.

Danny follows the longer, slower roads—the scenic route—which takes about nine hours.

It's one of the best days of his life.

# TWENTY

REGINA MONETA, THE FBI SUBDIRECTOR for organized crime, flies into Las Vegas.

She's not coming to town to gamble, drink, catch a show or lay out in the sun. She's not here for a destination wedding, a bachelorette party, or a convention.

Reggie's here for a singular purpose.

To take down Danny Ryan.

His Tara Group might be the shining star of the gaming establishment and the financial world, the announcement of a new wing at a children's hospital might make him a beloved philanthropist in this town, his success with his casinos might make him a local darling, but to Reggie he's nothing more than a mobster, a jumped-up New England hood who thinks he's shucked off his past like a snake sheds its skin.

And maybe he has, Reggie thinks as she gets into a cab. Because what infuriates her most about Ryan is that he's gotten a pass. Maybe it's his powerful bitch of a mother pulling strings on Wall Street and in DC, maybe it's his murky relationship with the intelligence community over a favor he did them regarding a drug cartel, maybe it's his unfortunate but undeniable charisma, but the world seems to let Danny Boy Ryan get away with anything.

The Nevada Gaming Control Board has turned a blind eye to his OC connections, the same tabloid media that labeled him a gangster and a drug slinger when he was tapping that movie star (who, with delicious irony, died of an overdose) have developed selective amnesia, and now a congressional commission that might have ripped the protective cloak off Ryan's shoulders is simply going on a search-and-avoid mission.

Worst of all, her own bureau seems not to give a shit that Ryan probably murdered one of its own agents.

They all say it's ancient history, yesterday's news, but to Reggie, the shooting of Agent Phillip Jardine back in December 1988 is still an open wound. He was her friend and her lover—a good guy even though the bureau seems to have accepted unsubstantiated rumors that he was dirty, implicated in the theft of forty kilos of heroin.

So they've hushed it up, swept it under the carpet—as if Ryan leaving Phil dead on a winter beach didn't matter. The bureau's precious reputation was more important.

Reggie made subtle efforts to get Marie Bouchard to reopen the case, but the Rhode Island prosecutor evinced little interest, obsessed as she is with the sensational Peter Moretti Jr. trial.

Since killing Jardine, Ryan has gone from strength to strength.

Reggie has credible intelligence that Ryan and his crew staged a robbery of a cartel stash house and made off with $40 million in untraceable cash. She knows that he invested some of his share in a film that became a hit and doubtless made him more money. His affair with actress Diane Carson was on every television entertainment show and supermarket checkout counter. Danny Boy jilted her, she OD'd, and Ryan went off the radar for a while.

Then he reemerged as the silent partner in Tara, with no official standing but nevertheless in control, a reality that the NGCB refuses to acknowledge, much less act on.

Reggie watched in fury as Ryan acquired the old Scheherazade and made it into the success that was Casablanca, was even more outraged when he pulled off the economic miracle that was the Shores and became the toast of the town.

And now this?

Buying the Lavinia?

With plans to build a mega-hotel?

And go public?

No, Reggie thinks.

*No.*

Not if I have anything to do with it.

The problem is that she can't do anything overt. Ryan still has powerful protectors in DC who have given her a hands-off order.

Ryan, they've told her, is a no-fly zone.

We'll see about that, she thinks.

She doesn't have the cab take her to the FBI office, but to a hotel in the suburb of Henderson.

Jim Connelly is already in the lounge, sitting in an armchair by the window. He gets up when he sees Reggie come in. They're a study in contrasts—she short with a mid-forties thickness settling around the waist; he tall and uncommonly thin, a little stooped in his early sixties, his once-blond hair fading to a color that can only be described as yellow.

His blue eyes are bloodshot.

But they always are, Reggie thinks as she sits down across from him. Jim Connelly always looks like he just came from a long night of drinking, which isn't actually the case. She knows that he suffers from some sort of dry eye syndrome, which has been exacerbated by his years in the desert.

Once the Las Vegas resident agent in charge, he retired to take a big security job in the casino industry, as did a lot of retired FBI agents in the town. So now Connelly is the head of security for all the Winegard hotels, a big job that pays big money.

For which he owes Reggie Moneta.

She got him the RAC job as a setup for his cushy retirement, gave a glowing recommendation to the Winegard people, although the truth was that while Connelly did a competent job, he did exactly shit when it came to OC.

Not uncommon in Las Vegas.

Prior to the early eighties, the office here was a joke, Reggie thinks. The RACs put blinders on when it came to mob influence in the casinos, knowing that if they really worked the wiseguys they'd only make enemies in the town and shred the lines of their golden parachutes. Worse, the senators and congressmen who represented Nevada were firmly in the pocket of the gaming industry and used their power in DC to squelch any serious investigations of the casinos.

Joe Yablonsky changed that culture, going after the mob hard and effectively, and it was during his tenure that organized crime was pretty much chased out of town, with the notable exception of the strip joints. But he stepped on a lot of Las Vegas toes doing it, and when his retirement came, no one in Las Vegas or DC picked him up.

When Connelly came in, he took notice of Yablonsky's experience and didn't repeat it. His predecessor had wielded the broom that swept Chicago, Kansas City and Detroit out of town, and Connelly felt no need to pick it up. When he pulled the pin, the Winegard Group was happy to hire him. Now he turns his bloodshot eyes on Reggie and asks, "To what do I owe the pleasure?"

"Danny Ryan."

"Jesus, Reggie, are you ever going to give that up?"

"No," Reggie says. She gives Connelly a long look. "I thought Phil was a friend of yours."

She had cherry-picked Connelly deliberately out of the Boston office for the Las Vegas job for that very reason.

"He was," Connelly says.

"So you're just going to let Ryan collect the cash and prizes?" Reggie asks.

"What am I supposed to do?"

"Light a fire under your boss," Reggie says. "Christ, Ryan just stole the Lavinia out from under him, and Winegard is just going to take that lying down?"

"Apparently."

"No."

Connelly laughs. "What do you mean, no? He's my boss, I'm not his."

"He'll listen to you."

"You know who Vern Winegard listens to?" Connelly says. "Vern Winegard."

"So he has an ego, use it," Reggie says. "I also want the NGCB to start a Key Employee license investigation of Ryan."

Anyone who holds any major job in a casino has to have a Key Employee gaming license, which certifies that the employee has no serious criminal record, no ties to organized crime, and no known gambling or drug problem. Ryan, as the director of hotel operations of the Tara Group, has a KEL.

Dan Ryan is a power in this town, Connelly thinks, the Tara Group is a power. If I go against them and it gets back to them, there's no telling what they'd do. And if I try to tell Vern what he should do?

He'll fire my ass.

Connelly sits back in his chair. "I can't do what you're asking, Reggie."

"I got you this job," Reggie asks. "So this is how you repay me?"

"Ask me for anything else," Connelly says.

"I'm asking you for *this*."

Connelly doesn't want to be an ingrate, but the fact is that he doesn't work for Reggie Moneta anymore and there's nothing she can do to him. Or *for* him, for that matter. "Sorry, Reggie, no can do."

"I get it," Reggie says. "You have this nice life. House in the suburbs, four bedrooms, two and a half baths, pool."

Connelly doesn't say anything. What can he say? She's right.

"It can all go away," Reggie says. "You're an ungrateful, greedy prick, Jim. You're also a *careless*, ungrateful, greedy prick."

She opens her briefcase, takes out a thin folder and lays it on the little table in front of him. "An affidavit from a professional gambler named Stuart Alcesto. He's been counting cards at all the Winegard hotels and you've looked the other way in exchange for a cut. He got popped with a big load of coke and decided to trade you in."

Connelly doesn't read the affidavit. Doesn't need to. He already knows what's in it.

"So," Reggie says, "either you go to Winegard and the board to talk to them about Ryan, or I go to them to talk about you. You'll get fired, you'll lose your KE license, you'll be lucky to be pimping twenty-dollar whores in Atlantic City. Goodbye four bedrooms, goodbye two and a half baths, goodbye pool. It's going to be tough telling your wife, huh? So those are your two choices. I know which one I'd choose."

"Anything I can do to help you, Reggie," Connelly says, "you know I'll do."

"I do know that," Reggie says. "Thank you, Jimmy."

Reggie puts the file back in her briefcase and gets up. The sooner she can catch a flight out, the better.

She hates this town.

# TWENTY-ONE

JIM CONNELLY'S TOO SMART TO go directly to Vern and get hit by a shoot-the-messenger bullet. In a gossip-ridden city, he lets gossip do the work. Starting at State Fair, he says to the casino floor manager, "Man, that's some brutal shit Dan Ryan has been saying about Vern."

"What?"

"You didn't hear it?"

"No."

"What I heard," Connelly says, "is that Ryan said that he totally punked Vern. Made a chump out of him. You know, on the Lavinia sale."

He knows his man, knows this guy will spread it all over the hotel before the shift is over.

Connelly gets more vicious at the Riverboat. Over a drink with the security director, he says, "I can't believe what I heard about Dan Ryan. You know what I heard he said?"

He leans over and looks around like he wants to make sure he isn't overheard. Then he says, "I heard Ryan said that Vern 'lost face' over the Lavinia thing, except, given Vern's face, that would be a good thing."

"Jesus. He said that?"

"That's what I heard."

"Has Vern heard that?"

"I hope not."

The next day he makes a point to "bump into" Zina Stavros as she's coming out of her Women's Club meeting. They've known each other for years, so they make the usual small talk. Then Connelly asks, "Zina, can I ask you a question? What happened with the Lavinia sale? Vern thought he had a deal."

"I don't know," she says. "George just said that he changed his mind and didn't want to talk about it. You know how he is. Why?"

"People are talking."

"What are they saying?"

"You don't want to know."

"Tell me, Jim."

Connelly reluctantly tells her that the town is talking about how George got taken in by Dan Ryan, how he betrayed his old friend Vern, how he went back on his word.

"My husband is a man of his word," Zina says.

Connelly shrugs. Like, *Apparently not.*

Zina goes straight home and tells her husband what people are saying.

"I don't care what people say," George says. "Let them talk."

"But it's our good name," Zina says. "And you won't believe the horrible thing that Dan said about Vern. He said that he lost face, and that was probably a good thing."

"Where did you hear that?"

"It was all over the Women's Club."

"Clucking hens."

"Why, George?"

"Why what?" Although he knows very well.

"Why are you selling to Dan Ryan instead of Vern?" Zina asks.

George gets up from the high-top stool at the kitchen breakfast counter and goes to the refrigerator. As he browses for something to eat he asks, "How long have we been married?"

"You know it's fifty-seven years."

"And for fifty-seven years," George says, taking the half a tuna sand-wich wrapped in plastic, "it's worked out pretty well that I take care of the business and you take care of the house. Did I ask why you bought a blue sofa instead of a red one? Did I ask why the living room really needed a new carpet?"

"This isn't a carpet or a sofa."

He turns back to her. "Zina, believe me, trust me. There are some things that you don't want to know."

Like there are things he wishes he didn't remember.


VERN HEARS IT.

Walking the floor at State Fair, he hears a cocktail waitress say, ". . . lost face, which is no big loss."

The dealer laughs.

Vern stops. "What was that?"

"Nothing, Mr. Winegard." The waitress looks terrified.

"No, something was funny," Vern says. "I could use a laugh today. What was it?"

Because he's already heard about Ryan's remark.

It's all over town.

But hearing it on the floor of his own hotel . . .

"It was nothing, sir."

"Something about my face?" Vern asks. "Come on, you can tell me. I have a mirror in my bathroom."

Stricken, the waitress just stares at him.

The dealer looks down at his table.

Vern walks away for his weekly meeting with Jim Connelly.

Now he's pissed.

He's been on a slow burn anyway, since Stavros told him that he had changed his mind, but he tried to keep it on a business level. But it hurt, it stung. Losing the Lavinia killed his plans for expansion, put an end to his status as the King of Las Vegas. That crown was going to Dan Ryan, and Vern didn't like it one bit.

It's a truism of American life that no one really gets over high school. Either it was the summit of a person's life that he can never reach again, in which case the rest of his existence feels like a sad downhill slide, or it was a painful ordeal that he just wants to forget but can't.

Vern's a smart guy, he's aware that on some level he's always trying to compensate—maybe overcompensate—for being the kid with the acne, the "pizza face," the guy who never got the girl, who was never even considered for homecoming king.

He'd thought, with his millions of dollars, with the fact that a lot of the types who used to make fun of him—or worse, ignore him—now have to obey his orders, in fact, toady to his every whim, that he'd put it all behind him.

Yeah, except now it comes creeping back.

Dan Ryan—handsome, charismatic; in essence every team captain, quarterback, popular kid—is taking Vern's crown, reminding him that he was never that guy and will never be that guy.

At first it stung. Now it's settled into a dull ache, a gnawing at his gut.

Vern went to Stavros and argued his case. "You want a hospital wing? I'll build you a hospital wing. I'll build a whole hospital if you want."

"Now that Ryan offered it."

"We had a deal."

"The contracts weren't signed," Stavros said.

"Why?" Vern asks. "That's what I want to know."

"I like what he plans to do better," George said.

Of course you do, Vern thinks. Ryan's hotels are beautiful, elegant. Mine are blue-collar grind joints. His are for the cool kids, mine are for the AV types. I get it.

"What, this Dream?" Vern asked. "Come on."

But he couldn't budge him. Stubborn old man. So Vern was going to let it go. What else was he supposed to do?

Then he started hearing the rumors. About Ryan talking shit, making fun of him, gloating over his victory. Okay, Vern thought. Being honest, I'd probably have done the same thing myself.

But then the thing about his face.

He's heard all the fucking jokes before, lived with them since childhood, thought he had developed, as it were, a thick skin.

But coming from Ryan, after the Lavinia thing, it gets to him.

Fuck Ryan.

Fuck his dream.

"You heard all this shit Ryan's been saying?" he asks Connelly.

"I'd like to punch him in the mouth," Connelly says. When Vern doesn't answer, he says, "Or hit him where it really hurts."

"What do you mean?"

"Take the Lavinia back."

"That horse has left the barn," Vern says.

"Ryan's a gangster," Connelly says. "It took ten years to chase OC out of Vegas, and now we're going to let them take over again? You're the only one who can stop them."

"Dan's not a gangster," Vern says.

He's heard the rumors, everyone has. He heard what the drunk at Ryan's party said and regrets taunting him about it. The truth is that it's hard for any casino owner—almost all of them honest businessmen—to escape the old mob smear. Ryan's always behaved in a legit way, Vern thinks, and if he beat me to the Lavinia, it's still no reason to besmirch his reputation.

"You're too kind," Connelly says. "You're too much a gentleman. Come on, he was hooked up with Pasco Ferri. It was all over the tabloids a few years ago."

"Tabloids."

"Still," Connelly says, "who knows what kind of pressure he brought to bear on Stavros? Look, between you and me, the feds have their eye on Ryan."

"The hell you talking about?"

"If you decide to make a move on him," Connelly says, "you'd have allies."

"What allies?"

"Maybe feds."

"Quit being cute," Vern says. "You got something or you don't?"

Without giving her name, Connelly tells him about his meeting with Reggie Moneta.

He leaves a few things out.

"I don't know," Vern says. It's too late, anyway, he thinks. The Tara Group owns the property.

But then again, who owns the Tara Group?

# TWENTY-TWO

**I**T MIGHT HAVE ENDED THERE.

With Vern brooding and then letting it go. It might have ended there, if it hadn't been for the charity auction.

Danny doesn't want to go.

For several reasons.

One, he hates gala events. They're boring as hell and a waste of time. Rather than sit there for hours and bid on stuff he doesn't want and can't use, he could and would just write a check to the Rosa Blumenfeld Breast Cancer Research Fund.

Two, charity auctions don't make any sense to him. People donate things when it would be far more efficient to just give the cash. Is it really charity to buy something you want? And most of the people at the tables can afford to buy whatever it is they want, anyway. No, Danny thinks, they want to be *seen* giving, they want their generosity to be a competition, a philanthropic pissing contest, a display of one-upmanship.

Three, and most important, he knows Winegard will be there.

Usually no big deal—he's been to dozens of these affairs with Vern and they've both good-naturedly played the game of friendly rivalry, competing for items they're going to end up giving away. There's been a sort of ritual between them, each allowing the other to alternately win, while feigning

disappointment. It's become something of a set piece that the town antici-
pates and enjoys.

Now they're looking forward to something else.

Real enmity.

Danny's heard the gossip, too.

Dom came into the office the other morning and asked, "What the hell
did you say about Winegard?"

"Nothing."

"Not what I heard," Dom said. "I was getting in some racquetball and
the whole gym was saying you've been talking trash about Vern."

"Does that sound like me?"

"It doesn't," Dom said. "That's why I was so surprised. I mean, I know
you were pissed off about what he said at your party—"

"Fuck that."

"—but, Danny, making cracks about the guy's face?"

"What are you talking about?"

Jesus Christ, Danny thought as Dom filled him in. Somebody tells
somebody that somebody heard that I said something about Vern's face and
now, through repetition, it's become a fact. "I'll talk to him."

"I wouldn't," Dom said. "It might make things worse. I'd just let him
cool down."

Yeah, maybe, Danny thinks now.

Maybe I should talk to Vern directly, kill this thing, but I don't neces-
sarily want to do it in front of a big group of people who are hoping for some
kind of titillating confrontation.

"You have to go," Gloria says.

She's heard the gossip, too. Her freaking *hairdresser* was talking about it.
*"What did your boss say about Vern Winegard?" "Nothing. Mr. Ryan doesn't
speak like that." "Well, what I heard—" "I don't care what you heard."*

"I'm supposed to be in the background," Danny says.

But it's out there, Gloria thinks. And it's a problem. But if Dan dodges
this event, it will only add credence to the rumors.

"You're a high-ranking employee of the Tara Group," she says. "It's held at one of your hotels. You're expected to attend and you're expected to bid. And it's black tie, Danny."

"Even better."

"And better yet if you bring a date."

"*You* want to come as my date, Gloria?" Danny asks.

"What would my husband say?"

"Trust me, he'd be relieved."

Danny's met Trevor a few times and knows he'd be very happy to sit this one out at home with a beer and a ball game. But Tara has purchased five tables, so he's going to have to climb into a monkey suit and dutifully escort Gloria to the event.

"Do you know where your tux is?" Gloria asks.

"No, because you do."

"You don't need a date," Gloria says, "you need a wife."

"Maybe I can bid on one tonight."

"You don't have to bid," Gloria says. "You're the town's most eligible bachelor. You can have any woman you want."

I have the woman I want, Danny thinks.

And Eden won't go anywhere near the auction.

"It's exactly the kind of thing I don't want anything to do with," she said when he brought it up.

"What if they're auctioning a first-edition Jane Austen?"

"Are they?"

"Of course not."

"Then it's a hard no," Eden said. "But if you think you need to bring a date, feel free."

"I don't."

"All the ladies will be abuzz," Eden said.

# TWENTY-THREE

THE GALA IS JUST THAT.

Over-the-top, off-the-charts Las Vegas.

For one thing, the magician who has been selling out for two years at one of the Shores' theaters makes a Lamborghini disappear. The bright yellow Diablo-model roadster, valued at $250,000, was under a spotlight on the stage one second, and the next second it was . . .

Gone.

"How did he do that?" Ian asks. He looks handsomely miserable in his tux, secretly proud to be so dressed up in this sophisticated crowd.

"Magic," Danny says.

"Bullshit," says Ian.

"Language," says Madeleine. She looks properly elegant sitting next to her date, a respectable, fiftyish, closeted gay man who Danny thinks is a politician of some kind.

Over the applause, the magician announces, "The Lamborghini will only reappear at the end of the auction, when some lucky winner makes the highest bid!"

The crowd, Danny thinks, can be accurately described as "glittering," given the prevalence of sequined gowns, and there's enough cleavage to give an entire troop of Boy Scouts heart palpitations.

Danny goes back to his Cornish game hen, although why a miniature bird that's impossible to cut is considered gourmet food is beyond him. If you serve people chicken, they complain that you served them chicken, but if you serve them a tiny chicken and slap an English name on it, they don't feel mistreated.

"How's your Cornish game hen?" he asks Ian.

"Tastes like chicken."

Danny's really starting to love this kid. "Next dinner we host? Mac and cheese."

"Works for me," Ian says. "So are you going to get the Lambo?"

"No," Danny says.

For one thing, my dick still works, he thinks. For another, the plan is to let Vern win the car. Get into a bidding contest with him and then lose. Winegard has to come away from this evening feeling like he beat me at something.

"Come on, Dad," Ian says, "you can leave it in the garage until I'm sixteen."

"Yeah," Danny says, "when you're sixteen you're getting a used Honda. You know what ride *I* had when I was sixteen?"

He points at his thumb.

Ian looks at him blankly, Danny remembers that no one hitchhikes anymore, and he feels like a tool for playing the "when I was" card. Anyway, the driving thing is a long way off, thank God.

"I thought you were going to say a horse," Ian says. "Get it? You know, because you're old?"

"Funny. Funny kid."

"I think so." Ian smiles.

All the usual suspects are there—most of the hotel owners, the top executives, their wives and families, the event being held early in the evening so the kids could attend. Barry Levine is there with his wife and kids, Dom and Jerry with their families, Vern with Dawn and Bryce, who's almost as big as his father now.

Danny's eyes meet Vern's once or twice, as they're only four tables apart, but both men quickly look away.

It's no good, Danny thinks. It's time to get this over with. When Vern gets up, maybe to hit the men's room, Danny sees his chance. "I'll be back in a minute."

He catches up with Winegard in the lobby. "Vern, a word?"

Vern turns around. "You think maybe you've said enough words already?"

"I don't know what you've heard," Danny says. "I can only speak to what *I've* heard, and Vern, I didn't say any of those things."

"I have it on good authority."

"You know this town," Danny says. "It's a twenty-four seven game of telephone tag, and—"

"First you cut the legs out from under me on the Lavinia—"

"That was business." Yeah, it was business, Danny thinks. But be honest with yourself, you played dirty.

"Then you go around telling people that you punked me?" Vern asks. "That I'm your bitch?"

"I never said—"

"What *did* you say, then?"

"Nothing."

Vern doesn't respond. Danny sees that he's thinking it over, maybe even wants to believe him.

"I have nothing but respect for you," Danny says. "As a businessman, a father, a rival and, yes, a colleague."

Vern's face softens.

Then Danny fucks up. "And I'm sorry that—"

He stops, seeing from the look on Vern's face that it was a mistake to apologize.

"What are you sorry for?" Vern asks.

"That you heard all this ugly shit."

"Fuck you, Ryan," Vern says. "At least have the balls to say it to my ugly, pockmarked pizza face."

"Vern—"

"Stay away from me from now on," Vern says. "We got nothing to say to each other."

He walks away.

Several people turn their heads, but Danny knows that they saw and heard. It will be all over the ballroom in ten minutes. Dan Ryan tried to apologize to Vern Winegard and got it shoved in his face.

Great.

He goes back to his table and sits down.

"Everything come out all right?" Ian asks.

Ten-year-olds, Danny thinks.

They're all comedians.

# TWENTY-FOUR

THE AUCTION STARTS.

High-price, high-prestige items—a Patek Philippe watch, a Buccellati necklace, an Hermès bag, a ski trip to Aspen, a sailboat cruise from Tahiti to Bora Bora, a Kawasaki jet ski, a vintage MV Agusta 750 motorbike that Barry Levine snapped up at $175,000.

The Tara Group does its expected part—Madeleine buys one of the bags, Dom a ski trip, Danny makes the winning bid on a signed Carl Yastrzemski bat that he'll give to Ned.

The evening is a big success, raising a lot of money for cancer research.

Then the Lamborghini comes up.

The hosts make a meal of it, bringing the magician back onstage for the big reappearance, stoking the drama. Not that the audience needs it. By now the story of the confrontation in the lobby between Ryan and Winegard has circulated and their ritual competition for the biggest item needs no hyping.

Everyone's waiting for it.

The auctioneer reads the description—a 1997 Lamborghini VT Roadster, one of only two hundred made in the world, 5.7 liter, 485 horsepower V12 engine, five-speed transmission, can hit 202 miles per hour . . .

Danny doesn't really care, he's not much of a car guy. But Vern is—an engineer, an aeronautics guy, he has a collection of classic cars, so he's going to want this vehicle that's basically a land plane.

But now Danny wants it, too.

Not because he actually wants the car—he doesn't know what the hell he'd do with it—but because he has an idea.

The auctioneer starts the bidding at $50,000, a ridiculously low price, to stoke the fire.

Danny lifts his placard.

Sixty thousand.

Vern lifts his.

Seventy thousand.

There's a satisfied buzz in the crowd.

*It's on.*

Danny and Vern go back and forth. No one else bids—the crowd knows the game, knows that they're spectators in a tennis match, heads flipping between the two players.

The volleys are fast—immediate responses, no hesitations.

Eighty thousand, ninety thousand, a hundred thousand.

Just a warm-up, really—everyone knows the match is going into late sets.

A buck twenty to Ryan, a buck forty to Winegard.

*"Do I hear a hundred and fifty thousand?"*

Danny raises his placard.

Vern doesn't wait. "One sixty!"

Danny nods to the unasked request.

*"I have one-seventy, do I hear—"*

"One-eighty!" Vern yells.

It goes on like this, moving quickly toward the actual value of $250,000—Vern's bid. Which should be it, except Danny raises his placard and says, "Two seventy-five!"

The crowd ooohs.

Dom leans over to Danny. "What are you doing?"

"You'll see."

"I thought we wanted peace," Dom says. "You wanted Winegard to win."

"Three hundred!" Vern yells. He looks across the room at Danny. No pretense, no attempt to disguise the hatred.

Danny looks back and says, "Three twenty-five."

"Three fifty!"

A hundred grand over the actual value.

Danny knows that everyone is looking at him. He smiles and shrugs, says casually, "Four."

"Dan, what are you doing?" Dom asks.

Ian's staring at his dad, his mouth agape.

Madeleine looks across the table at him, her mouth in a tight, disciplined smile. But she doesn't say anything.

Vern raises his placard. "Four twenty-five."

It's not lost on anyone that Winegard has raised the bid by a lower factor. The volley is slowing as the match moves toward a close.

What Danny should do—what he knows he should do by the unspoken rules of the game—is raise by the same twenty-five, let Vern counter four seventy-five, and then get out.

Vern wins the pissing contest, Vern has the bigger dick.

Danny feels hundreds of eyes on him. Looking across the ballroom at Vern, he lifts his placard and says, "Five hundred thousand."

The room goes completely silent. All eyes turn on Vern. His face is flushed, his jaw tight, lips pressed into a snarl.

He stares back at Danny.

And sets his placard down.

"And the Lamborghini VT Roadster goes to Dan Ryan of the Tara Group!" the auctioneer says. "For five hundred thousand dollars! What a show of generosity! What a great day for cancer research!"

Vern turns to his wife. "That jerk. I just played him into paying half a mil for a car he'll never drive."

A drum roll, then . . .

The magician makes the car reappear. "Dan Ryan, come on up! Claim your prize!"

Danny walks up to applause. The auctioneer hands him the car keys and asks him to make a speech.

"I just want to thank everyone for coming," Danny says. "Thank you for your generosity. Together we'll find the cure. Thank you."

He steps down.

The crowd gets up, starts to work their way out.

"Dan, what the hell did you do?" Dom asks. "You humiliated the guy."

"You'll see."

Danny eases his way through the crowd and walks up to Vern, who's headed for the door with his family. "Vern, hold up."

"What do you want?"

Dawn and Bryce both look at Danny like they hate him.

Danny presses the keys into Vern's hand. "I want you to have the car. As a gift. For any offense that may have been caused. Call it a peace offering."

Vern drops the keys on the floor. "Fuck your peace."

He turns his back, walks off and leaves Danny standing there.

Looking like a fool.


"I DON'T KNOW what you were thinking," Madeleine says later, sitting in the living room.

"It was a peace offering," Danny says.

"You only gave him more reason to think that you actually said those things," Madeleine says. "As if you had a guilty conscience."

I'm an Irish Catholic, Danny thinks, I *always* have a guilty conscience, but the way I worked Stavros to get the hotel was wrong. I did a wrong thing to take Vern's hotel away from him.

Classic you, he thinks. You take a billion-dollar property from a guy and try to make up for it with a $250,000 car. No wonder he threw the keys in your face, or dropped them at your feet, whatever.

Danny knows that the town is talking about it.

The confrontation in the lobby.

The auction.

Vern rejecting his peace offering.

"He was jealous of you before," Madeleine says. "Now he hates you."

"Comforting words. Thanks."

"Would you prefer I lie to you?" Madeleine asks. "You wanted to have your cake and eat it, too. You wanted to make peace with Vern, but if you're being honest with yourself, you know that you also wanted to beat him. So you tried to do both and it didn't work."

She's right, Danny thinks.

"You've changed," Madeleine says. "The old Danny was always willing to come in second or below. That's not you anymore. The man you are now wants to win, and I, for one, am proud of you. You don't have to be ashamed of winning, Danny . . . or should I say Dan?"

Jesus, Danny thinks.

"You don't need Vern Winegard to love or even like you," Madeleine says. "Tara owns the Lavinia property now. Build your hotel. Build Il Sogno."

That's what Danny does.

He has the Lamborghini sold and the money donated to the cancer fund.

Then he goes to work fulfilling his dream.

# TWENTY-FIVE

JAKE PALUMBO IS THE PERFECT combination of his parents.

His father is, unusually, a red-headed Italian, his mother a blonde. Jake's hair is a blend of the two, going toward pale or red depending on how much time he spends in the sun. He has Chris's green eyes, Cathy's aquiline nose and thin lips.

He's a handsome young man, in good shape from his regular workouts, sensitive by nature, a trait that hard lives taught his parents to suppress. Jake has yet to absorb that toughening experience; he feels things acutely.

Has since he was a kid.

Jake was around twelve when he started to realize that his dad wasn't just a normal businessman but a member of the Mafia. This makes some mob sons boisterous and arrogant; it had the opposite effect on Jake, who became reserved, cautiously polite, careful not to take advantage of his father's status.

He didn't want to be that guy.

In that, he was a lot like his buddy, Peter Jr.—modest, self-effacing, a good student, popular with girls but not a player.

But Peter, he just lost his shit.

Jake could (barely) understand Peter killing Vinnie, but his own mother? Now the kid is going to trial and then probably to prison for the rest of his life.

It's sad.

Jake feels bad for him.

Both kids grew up knowing they'd eventually go into the family business. Peter Jr. wanted to do his marine thing first, but Jake had no such impulse. He was just going to get his diploma, go to work with his dad, one day take over.

Then his dad disappeared.

Just took off.

Abandoned them.

It broke Jake's heart because he idolized his father. He was strong, smart, funny, and if he was a gangster, okay, that's what guys of his generation did, but Chris had sat Jake down when he figured he was old enough to understand and explained that the whole mafioso thing was like a dinosaur that was going to die out, leaving other things behind.

Among those things were the family businesses. Sure, they had started with mob money and power, but they would eventually evolve into something legit. But if, occasionally, the family had to use some of its old muscle to protect their interests, well, that was life.

Jake was okay with this.

Still is.

Except now the family is in deep shit, and there is no muscle to set it straight. Guys like John Giglione are robbing them blind, disrespecting them, and there's nothing he can do about it.

His dad could.

But his dad isn't here.

So now Jake is out looking for him, which brings him face-to-face with the man on the other side of the screen in the prison visiting room. Jake didn't know where else to start. None of his father's other old friends are going to help him with the problem, because they *are* the problem.

So he came to see Joe Narducci, a man he remembers from childhood. Narducci is ten years deep in a twenty-five-year bit, and at age eighty-one, he's never coming out of this place.

Not vertical, anyway.

"Your dad?" Narducci says. "Sure, I knew him."

To Jake's young eyes, the man looks as ancient as time, or like one of those old buildings in Providence, abandoned, crumbling and about to fall down.

"Can you tell me anything about him?" Jake asks.

Narducci smiles, his small teeth yellow. "I can tell you everything about him. Your old man, back in the day, he was something. We all fought together against the Irish. It was a shame what happened to your father."

"What do you mean?" Jake asks, his heart beating faster. Does Narducci know something?

"Him getting shot in the tub like that," Narducci says. "Set up by his own wife."

Jake realizes that he's talking about Peter Moretti Sr. "Mr. Narducci, I'm Jake *Palumbo*. Chris Palumbo's son."

"I know that," the old man snaps. "How *is* your dad? Tell him I said hello."

Jake realizes that the visit will be useless. "I will."

But Narducci's eyes suddenly get sharp, sly. "I hear some people are giving your mom a problem. What are you going to do about that?"

"I'm trying to find my dad."

"What are you, in kindergarten?" Narducci asks. "You're a man now. The man of the family. It's up to you to do something."

Except I don't know what I can do, Jake thinks.

Kill John Giglione? I've never even been in a real fight, never mind killed someone. And even if I did, there are half a dozen others, and their crews.

"Look at that Peter Jr.," Narducci says. "He did the right thing. He's a chip off the old block."

"Peter's a good kid."

"*You're* a good kid," Narducci says. "I listen to you talk, I hear your old man. You have to make him proud now."

"Mr. Narducci, do you know where he is?"

"He's in the wind," Narducci says, fluttering his hand. "A leaf."

"Some people say he's in the program."

"Not your dad," Narducci says. "He's old-school. But have you talked to Paulie Moretti?"

"Why him?" Jake asks.

Narducci's eyes narrow. "I heard . . . he may have been told something."

"I don't think he'll talk to me."

"You don't know until you try," Narducci says. He straightens up to let Jake know the conversation is about over. "You were raised better than to come empty-handed."

"I brought some prosciutto," Jake said. "I gave it to the guard for you."

"Like I said, you're a good kid."

Yeah, Jake thinks, I'm a good kid.

Maybe that's the problem.

# TWENTY-SIX

PAM MORETTI ANSWERS THE DOOR.

Jake hasn't seen her in years. When he was an adolescent, she was a freakin' wet dream, the hottest chick any of them had ever seen. He used to fantasize about her.

She was also a legend, the woman who started the war between the Italians and the Irish when she left Paulie Moretti to be with Liam Brady. Now Brady's dead and she's back with Paulie.

And now it looks like she should put in some time on the treadmill, take some of that weight off. Her eyes are heavy-lidded, and even though it's only two in the afternoon, it looks like she's been drinking.

Or something.

To his surprise, she recognizes him. "Is that Jake Palumbo?"

"Yes, ma'am."

"*Ma'am*," she says. "You make me feel older than I am. You look just like your father. It's nice to see you, Jake."

"Nice to see you," Jake says. "Is Mr. Moretti in?"

She lowers her voice. "I think he's just getting up from his nap. Let me go see. Come on in."

Pam ushers him into the living room and leaves to go find her husband. Jake sits down on the couch. The room is unremarkable, as is the house, a basic one-story ranch ten blocks from the beach in Fort Lauderdale. There's the sofa, a couple of recliners, a big-screen television.

Jake had expected more of Paulie Moretti, the younger brother of the former boss. But he's kind of nothing since Peter was killed, just another wiseguy in a family without a leader.

Paulie comes into the living room looking disheveled, his hair uncombed, his eyes puffy from a heavy sleep. He has on a black T-shirt, jeans and black socks with no shoes. Plops down in one of the recliners and turns it to face Jake instead of the TV. "Chris Palumbo's son."

"Yes, sir."

"How *is* your old man?" Paulie asks. "That's right, you wouldn't know, none of us know. He don't call, he don't write . . ."

He's drunk, Jake thinks. Drunk or stoned.

"I loved your father, you know that?" Paulie says. "I *loved* the man."

Jake thinks Paulie might actually cry.

"Even after he fucked us over . . ." Paulie's voice drifts off, like a wisp of smoke wafting back into the past.

"Do you know what happened?" Jake asks.

Paulie tells him the story.

Chris had talked the family into making a heroin buy from the Mexicans—forty kilos. But, Chris being Chris, he had a twist to the deal—he sent a guy, Frankie Vecchio, to the Irish to talk them into hijacking the shipment. Then Chris set it up with the feds to bust the Irish, destroying them, winning the war. The fed, a guy named Jardine, was dirty, so all the H was going to find its way back to the family, but Danny Ryan stored away ten kilos that the feds didn't find.

"Your old man *did* find it," Paulie says. "He went to the stash house to grab it, but Ryan showed up. No problem, Chris had a crew waiting outside, but . . ."

"But what, sir?"

"Ryan," Paulie says, "had his own guys stationed outside *your* house. With orders to kill you, your sister and your mom unless he walked out with the heroin. What was your dad going to do?"

"He let Ryan go," Jake says.

"Because he loved you," Paulie says. "See you remember that. Anyway, Jardine turned up dead on a beach, your old man went into the wind, a lot of people lost money, end o' story."

Pam reappears.

Jake already knew that a lot of people lost money. They've been taking it out of his mother and him ever since. But he didn't know his dad had given over the drugs to save their lives, and he feels a flush of love for his old man. "I talked to Joe Narducci. He said you might have heard something. About where my dad might be."

"Let's have a drink," Paulie says. "You want a drink, kid?"

"I have to drive."

"No, you'll stay with us tonight," Pam says. "We have a spare room. Have a drink, it takes the sting out of life."

"Pam don't like it in Florida," Paulie says. "Me, one morning I get up in Providence, I'm scraping ice off the fucking windshield, I decide I'm done with that, I'm never shoveling snow again. We came down here."

"I wanted to go to Miami or West Palm," Pam says. "But Paulie said it was too expensive."

"The trust fund baby here," Paulie says.

"You know why old people move to Florida?" Pam asks. "Because when they die, they don't mind so much."

She fixes three tall gin and tonics and hands one to Jake. Then he sees her open a bottle of pills and drop one into her drink, then into Paulie's. She holds a pill up to Jake, her eyebrows raised to ask the question. "Valium. Pop one of these with your drink, you get through Thursday."

Except it's Friday, Jake thinks. But he doesn't want to offend them, he needs the information Paulie might have, and when in Fort Lauderdale . . . "Okay."

She drops the Valium into his glass. "Sweet dreams, young Jake."

# TWENTY-SEVEN

WHEN JAKE WAKES UP, HE'S not sure if Pam Moretti came to his bed or if he dreamed that. His head is fuzzy, his mouth feels like cotton. He gets up, brushes his teeth, splashes a little water on his face and walks out into the kitchen.

Paulie sits slumped on a high stool at the breakfast counter. "Coffee's in the pot. You want breakfast, it's served around eleven when Her Majesty gets up. You sleep okay?"

Jake wonders if it's a loaded question. "Yeah. You?"

"Like the dead," Paulie says. "I dreamed about my brother. You must remember him."

"I was pretty young, but sure."

"That prick Vinnie killed him in the bathtub, you believe that shit?" Paulie asks. "It was something, what my nephew did though, huh?"

"Except now he's going to spend the rest of his life in prison," Jake says.

"I dunno," says Paulie. "He's got him a pretty good lawyer. That hippie guy with the pigtail . . ."

"Bruce Bascombe," Jake says. "How's Peter Jr. going to pay for that?"

"Don't kid yourself," Paulie says. "You know who's picking up the check—the guy in Pompano."

Pasco Ferri, Jake thinks.

All right, good for him.

Pam appears in the doorway, wearing a blue silk robe loosely cinched around her waist. "Good morning, Jake."

"As I live and fucking breathe," Paulie says. "She arises. A little early for you, isn't it?"

"I slept well," Pam says, smiling at Jake.

Jake glances at Paulie. If he knows—if there's anything for him *to* know—his face doesn't show it. "Yesterday we were talking about how Joe Narducci said that you might know something."

"I hear Narducci has the Alzheimer's."

Jake says, "Mr. Moretti, I need your help. John Giglione and the others, they're bleeding us dry. I don't know how much more my mom can take. I need to find my father. Do you know where he is? Do you know if he's even alive?"

"Tell Jake what you heard," Pam says.

Paulie sighs. "You remember Joe Petrone? Used to have a fishing supply place out of Goshen? An old friend of your dad's?"

"No."

"No, I guess not, Joe is older than dirt," Paulie says. "Anyways, he's got one of them RVs he drives around the country, who knows why. He stops by here one day, tells me he saw your dad."

"When was this?" Jake asks, his heart speeding up.

"Couple of months ago," Paulie says. "Joe tells me he saw your old man in a bar in East Bumfuck, Nebraska. Maybe it was West Bumfuck, I don't know . . ."

"Did he talk to him?"

"No," Paulie says. "You just don't go up to a guy who's in the wind, because you might not walk away from that conversation. Anyways, Joe watches him leave, asks about him. Turns out this guy—Joe swears it was your dad—lives with some woman out in the boonies. The locals laugh that basically he fucks her for a living. Nice work if you can get it."

"Nice work if you can do it," Pam says.

Paulie doesn't react.

"How did Narducci hear about it?" Jake asks.

"I may have said something on the phone," Paulie says. "Or I dunno, maybe Phil said something. He could never keep his mouth shut."

"You think he'd talk to me?" Jake asks.

"If you have one of them, what do you call them, mediums," Paulie says. "Phil tapped out two weeks ago. Massive coronary. Behind the wheel. Thank God he didn't crash and kill someone."

So if this Phil had a mouth, Jake thinks, everyone knows. "I'd better be going."

"Stay a couple of days," Pam says. "Enjoy the beach."

"The kid said he needed to go."

"I'm going to make a Bloody," Pam says, looking at Jake. "You want one?"

"I really need to get going."

"Then go," Pam says. She's pissed.

Jake gets into his car and drives.

What am I supposed to do now, he thinks, cruise all around Nebraska until I bump into my dad?

He's not even sure where Nebraska is, although he has a sense that it's big. Of course, any state is big compared to Rhode Island. One thing is for sure: Giglione and the rest will be scouring Nebraska looking for Chris Palumbo. And not to talk about old times, either.

They'll be looking to kill him.

# TWENTY-EIGHT

PASCO FERRI KNOWS EXACTLY WHERE East Bumfuck is.

He got the real name of the town from Joe Petrone before the old man crashed his RV into a lighting pole.

Thank God I did, Pasco thinks.

The small town of Malcolm is a few miles northwest of Lincoln, Nebraska. If Petrone's story is true, Chris shouldn't be that hard to find.

He gives the job to Johnny Marks.

Johnny is one of those free-floaters who doesn't belong to any particular family but who does high-level jobs for all of them. He's professional, discreet and disciplined, just gets the job done with no fuss or muss. The last time Pasco used him was to go talk to Danny Ryan, give him the message to leave that Hollywood actress.

Which Danny did.

Now he needs him to go find Chris Palumbo.

Clean this mess up once and for all.

Because New England is a shit show.

Has been since the morning that Chris went off the reservation.

The leadership vacuum has been horrible.

Since Vinnie's death, no one has really stepped up to take the reins. Most guys don't want the job, given the history of its predecessors and that it's practically an invitation for the feds to fuck you with the RICO statutes.

Pasco used to sit in the big chair, but he retired and left it to Peter.

Or tried to retire, he thinks now.

Shit keeps coming up and the other families, the big families in New York and Chicago, keep coming to me to put out the fires.

Nobody wants to see the headlines.

It's bad for what's left of the business.

And now the families, especially New York, are pressuring him to fix New England. It's fucking chaos, like a car pulls into the circus ring and out tumble the clowns.

Like John Giglione.

Who now thinks he might want the corner office, but doesn't have the smarts or the muscle to really pull it off.

Still, Pasco thinks, a poor choice is better than no choice, and he was about to pour the oil on Giglione's forehead when the news came in that the long-lost Chris Palumbo had been found. And Giglione and the other bozos are going to go "take care of business."

Except they'll fuck it up, Pasco thinks. Oh, they might get it done, but in such a way that there will be more headlines. And that, combined with the Peter Jr. trial, would be catastrophic.

Hence the word from the big families.

You have to go back, Pasco, and take control again.

Fix New England.

Which is the last thing in the world Pasco wants. The doctors have given him three, four years, tops, and he don't want to spend them fixing anything—not roofs, not plumbing, not a decrepit crime family. But what is he supposed to do? If he wants those three, four years, he has to do *something*.

And what a clusterfuck the Moretti trial is going to be, Pasco thinks as he looks across the table at Johnny Marks. It has the potential to open up a lot of boxes that would be better left shut.

He had ordered Bascombe to shut the trial down, make whatever deal he could and plead Peter Jr. guilty, so the thing would go away with a day or two of media attention and no one—himself especially—would have to take the stand.

But Bascombe defied him on that, thinking that he could maybe even get the kid off. On a double homicide with a confession thrown in, Pasco don't see how, but he's letting the lawyer run with it.

Maybe, Pasco thinks, it has to do with what the doctors told me, maybe I'm thinking about that moment I meet Saint Peter and have to account for what I've done in this life. Sure, the priests say that Last Rites will cover it, but what if they're wrong? I've done some terrible things—most of them things I had to do—but terrible anyway.

One of them was what I did to that girl Cassandra. She was young—of course there were brides in the old country younger, but she was still young, and she never got over it, with all the drug and alcohol problems. Then she dies young, shot in the same bathtub with Peter Sr. She never opened her mouth in this world about what I did to her, but maybe she has in the next one, and maybe those charges will be waiting for me when I get there.

And then there's Peter Jr. He came to me to ask what he should do about Vinnie and his mother murdering his dad, and I did everything but push him through the door. Then when he came to me afterward, I turned him away.

So I owe the kid something.

A chance, anyway, at having some kind of a life.

One step at a time, Pasco thinks.

This whole thing started with Chris, so it could end with Chris. "I need you to get to our friend before the others do."

Marks says, "That shouldn't be a problem."

No, Pasco thinks, with Johnny Marks, it shouldn't be a problem.

Marks *fixes* problems.

# TWENTY-NINE

CHRIS PALUMBO DIDN'T SURVIVE THIS long in this life because he's stupid or unaware.

He spotted Joe Petrone in the bar.

Waited long enough for it not to be obvious and then got out of there.

Now he's worried.

It's not that he thinks that old Joe Petrone is a hit man out looking for him, it's just that Phil is a talker. Chris doesn't know that Phil recognized him, but can he take that chance?

You shouldn't, he tells himself as he walks along the field of harvested milo down toward the line of cottonwoods and the little creek.

Chris had never heard of milo before he got to Nebraska. Corn he knew, maybe wheat, but he never knew that milo existed or that it was some kind of sorghum, whatever the fuck that is.

The smart thing to do is to go.

Now.

But autumn in Nebraska is beautiful, the crisp air a welcome relief from the sweltering summer humidity. He dreads winter, but it seems a shame to leave in the fall.

Then there's Laura. What am I supposed to tell her? Or do I tell her anything? Maybe she just wakes up in the morning and I'm gone, like in some bad folk song. She'll understand, she'll find another guy.

But she's been good to you, Chris thinks.

Gives you a good life.

He reaches the cottonwood trees and sits down.

But . . .

There's always a "but," he thinks.

You're getting a little tired of it.

Good as Laura is in the sack, you're getting a little sick of "fuck or die." You could use a break, a little change. Face it, a little strange.

Back in Rhode Island, he had Cathy, but he also had *gumars*, because variety is the spice of life and all that happy crap. Laura, she has a lot of spices in her rack, but it's still the same drawer, and there are times now when he has to go to the videotape highlights to get the job done.

And sleep.

His dreams lately have been fucking weird.

Little visits to death.

One night he got into a conversation with his mother.

"I'm dead, you know," she said.

"No, I didn't know," Chris said. "What happened?"

"You. You broke my heart."

"Sorry about that," Chris said. "How's Cathy? You see her?"

"She has problems, like anyone else."

"She with another guy?" Chris asked.

"Not that I know of."

"Oh."

Another night he was sitting with Peter Moretti out on the deck of the Liffy, the oceanside bar where they'd hang out summers.

"If you ever go home, be careful," Peter said.

"Yeah, why's that?"

"These fucking women," Peter said, "you can't trust them. You hear what my Celia did to me? I gave that bitch everything, and she sent Vinnie to kill me. In the fucking bathtub, Chris."

"I heard you were with Cassie Murphy."

"Hey, what are you going to do?" Peter asked. He took a long pull of his beer and looked out over the water. "You just keep an eye out on Cathy, word to the wise."

"No, she's not like that."

Peter leaned across the table. "They're *all* like that."

That's when Chris woke up, felt Laura beside him.

Another night, he talked with another dead guy.

Sal Antonucci.

Big, tough, stone-killer Sal, who took a bullet as he walked out of his boyfriend's apartment. In the dream Sal was sitting downstairs at the kitchen table, eating donuts.

Dunkin' Donuts.

Glazed.

Sugar around his lips.

"I miss these," he said.

"They miss you," Chris said. "But, hey, you had a beautiful funeral."

Sal smiled. "Yeah? Did a lot of people come?"

"Are you kidding me?" Chris asked. "The place was packed. Standing room only."

Then Sal frowned. "Did anyone say anything about me being a *finook*?"

"No," Chris said. "It didn't come up."

"That's good."

"Of course," Chris said, "they buried you facedown."

Sal got up from the table.

"A joke," Chris said. "I was just busting balls. C'mon, Jesus, Sal, sit down, enjoy the donuts."

"I was a pitcher," Sal said, "not a catcher."

"Who the fuck cares anymore?"

But Sal left.

Weird fucking dreams, Chris thinks.

Maybe trying to tell me I should go back.

And face it, too, you're a little homesick.

Who'd have thought?

But it's true—you miss the ocean, miss the beaches, miss the food. If anyone in Nebraska makes a decent cannoli, they've kept it a secret from me, he thinks. And a clam cake? Forget it. Chowder? Ditto.

Yeah, like you can go back, he thinks.

If you're worried about them finding you here, just go back there. It would take about fifteen minutes for the word to get out and maybe another thirty to get you clipped.

But he wonders about his wife and he wonders about his kids.

How's Cathy doing?

How's Jill?

How's Jake?

He remembers how Cathy had laughed at him, given that funny wry look, when he said he wanted to name the baby Jacob, if it was a boy.

"Jake and Jill?" Cathy asked. "They what, go up the hill? Come tumbling down? He breaks his crown?"

"The fuck you talking about, crown?"

"It's a nursery rhyme. Jack and Jill?"

Chris didn't know.

But she relented and they called the boy Jacob and he's turned into a good kid. Smart, polite. Chris feels bad about what he did to him, abandoning him. But what was he supposed to do?

What am I supposed to do now? he asks himself.

Abandon someone else?

Maybe.

Go home? Face the music?

Maybe.

But maybe also means maybe not.

Maybe I stay here for the autumn. Just be extra careful, extra aware, tuck a piece under my jacket.

Wait until the snow falls and then decide.

# THIRTY

LAURA ALWAYS SAYS THAT SHE has intuition.

She can feel things.

She's psychic.

Maybe it's that, maybe it's just what a woman feels or a woman knows, but she can feel Chris slipping away from her.

Laura can tell in bed, when he's on top of her and closes his eyes and she knows that he's summoning some memory of another woman and she wishes he would just tell her because she doesn't mind, she could be that woman, she understands, she has a highlight reel of her own.

Maybe it would freshen things up.

Then maybe he'd stay.

Because she knows he's thinking of leaving.

Like the geese in autumn.

And maybe it's time.

She'll miss him, though, she'll be lonely.

It makes her sad, so after teaching her yoga class she doesn't go straight home but stops in the bar for a beer or maybe two. Which is where the universe gives her another message because a guy tries to pick her up.

He's cute, too.

A little old maybe, early sixties, she guesses, but with a full head of curly salt-and-pepper hair, a trim body, maybe five-ten or so, and he dresses well—a light brown suede jacket, blue twill shirt, khaki slacks over expensive-looking desert boots.

Not from here, but not a pheasant hunter, from the clothes.

Nice smile, too, clean, straight teeth.

She smiles back, and before she knows it, they're sitting in a booth, and three beers later she's spilling her guts to him. The dude's almost like, she doesn't know, a sexy priest or something.

One of those priests who, hopefully, fucks.

"You want to know what I think?" the guy asks when she finishes telling him about Chris. "Trust your instincts. You seem very intuitive to me. If you think he wants to leave, you're probably right."

He gets it, Laura thinks. He gets me. "What do you think? Should I try to make him stay?"

"You already know the answer to that," he says.

He's right, Laura thinks. I do. If there was a motel in town, she'd take him there right now. "I should let him go."

The guy just nods.

Turns out he's in Lincoln on business, had a free afternoon and decided to drive around the countryside a little.

"How long are you here?" Laura asks.

"Just tonight," he says. "But I'll be back a lot over the next few months. Is this where I'd find you, Laura?"

She tells him probably not, she's not much of a drinker.

But she tells him how to find her farm.


CHRIS FEELS IT before he hears it or sees it.

The presence of the other.

All prey have that sense. Sometimes it saves them; other times it's too late, an all-too-brief realization that life is over. Chris feels it as he gets into the car seat, behind the wheel, to go into town for groceries.

He slides his hand into his jacket for the gun, but it *is* too late.

A gun barrel presses into the back of his neck just below his skull and he knows that he's dead.

"Easy, Chris," Johnny Marks says. "Drive."

Halfway to town, Marks orders Chris to pull over.

"You can turn around," Marks says.

Chris turns and sees Johnny Marks. He feels like he's going to piss himself. In the movies, the tough guys go out tough, but this isn't a movie. He holds it in, though.

Just.

"The guy in Pompano sends his regards," Marks says.

"Just do it. Please." Chris is shaking. He can't hold himself together much longer.

"If I was going to kill you, would we be talking?" Marks says. "You know that's not how it works."

Chris does know that. The terror starts to recede a little and he can think.

"You have a nice life here," Marks says. "You have a good woman. Too bad you have to leave. Your old friends in Providence know where you are."

"Why is Pasco warning me?"

"He needs you to do something for him," Marks says.

THAT NIGHT. CHRIS and Laura have a farewell fuck. They both know what it is, so it's unnecessary when he says, "I'm leaving in the morning, first thing."

"I know."

"You've been great," Chris says. "This has been great. But I have to go home."

"After all this time," Laura says. "What does she have that I don't? Is she prettier than I am? Smarter?"

"No," Chris says. "I have responsibilities."

In the morning, before the sun comes up, Laura packs him a few ham sandwiches, a couple of apples, a bottle of grape juice.

"For the road," she says.

"You're too good to me," says Chris.

"I love you."

Laura watches him drive away.

She never hears from the cute guy in the bar.

# THIRTY-ONE

THE FIRST BATTLE IN THE homicide trial of Peter Moretti Jr. is fought without him.

A mano a mano between Bruce Bascombe and Marie Bouchard in a pretrial hearing on the admissibility of Peter Jr.'s confession.

"In the first place," Bascombe says, "my client wasn't represented by counsel when he made this bogus confession."

"Moretti was read his rights," Marie says. "He declined representation."

"He was in no mental condition to understand those rights," Bruce says, "much less to make an informed decision. He was suffering from extreme drug withdrawal—for which he received no treatment, by the way—and post-traumatic stress disorder."

"From what?" Marie asks.

"Witnessing the death of his mother."

Marie laughs out loud. "Your Honor, counsel is literally telling the old joke about the kid who murders his parents and then pleads for mercy on the basis that he's an orphan."

"Continue," the judge says.

Judge Frank Faella knows both of them well, has had them in his courtroom many times. Now he runs his fingers through his salt-and-pepper hair and leans back in his chair to watch the show.

"Arguing the merits—or lack thereof—of the alleged confession itself," Bruce says, "it was unclear to my client—and unclear to us now—what he was confessing to."

"How so?" Faella asks.

"Let's go to the videotape," Bruce says.

"Let's go to the transcript," Faella says.

"Fine," Bruce says. "It consists of two statements. First, 'There's nothing to talk about. I want to confess.' As I have already pointed out to Ms. Bouchard, confess to what? For all this disoriented young man knew, he might have been under arrest for drug possession, burglary, loitering . . .'"

"We made it very clear that—"

"Did you?" Bruce asks. "All I see on the record is Detective Dumanis saying, 'Then there's a lot to talk about. You have to walk us through the whole thing.' What 'whole thing'?"

"Obviously, the homicides," Marie says.

"Obvious to you, maybe," Bruce says. "But was it obvious to Peter? And I doubt that it would be obvious to a jury. Then there's the other statement—the only other statement—'What do you want me to say? I did it.' Same argument, Your Honor, same basic problem. It's vague."

"We were about to specify when Mr. Bascombe arrived and terminated the interview," Marie says.

"And thank God I did," Bruce says. "They'd have had him confessing to the Kennedy assassination next."

"Which one?" Marie asks.

"Probably both," Bruce says. "Your Honor, this so-called confession is impossibly vague, was coerced—"

"Coerced?!" Marie asks. "How?"

"A confused young man," Bascombe says, "probably suffering hallucinations as a result of heroin withdrawal, left unrepresented in a small room with intimidating detectives and prosecutors—"

"Oh, please," Marie says.

"Your Honor," Bruce says, "even if you do allow this 'confession' into evidence, I'll discredit it in front of the jury. I'll call constitutional experts, I'll call medical experts—"

"We'll rebut with experts of our own," Marie says.

"And the trial will last for months," Bruce says. "Let's try this case on the facts. Marie, if you're so confident you have the evidence, you don't need this piece of garbage."

Faella says, "I tend to agree. Marie, last whack?"

"It's a good confession," she says, knowing it sounds weak.

"I'm going to disallow," Faella says. "The confession will not be entered into evidence, and, Marie, I won't tolerate any sneaky efforts to refer to it and get it through the side door. Bruce would move for mistrial and I would grant."

Outside chambers, Marie says, "Round one, Bruce. Only round one."

"But you're already behind on points," Bruce says.


PETER JR. SITS at the table in the little meeting room at the Adult Correctional Institutions and waits for his lawyer to come in.

He's changed in the months since his arrest.

For one thing, he kicked his heroin jones lying fetal on the concrete floor of his cell. It was a nightmare, but now he's clean for the first time in years. And for the first time in years, since he pulled the trigger on Vinnie and his mother, his head is clear.

The door opens and Bruce Bascombe comes in and sits down.

"Your confession has been thrown out," he says.

"What does that mean?" Peter Jr. asks.

"It means it never happened," Bruce says. "Which it didn't."

Peter Jr. blows a sigh of relief. "Do you think I have a chance?"

"Are you religious, Peter?" Bruce asks.

"I'm a Catholic."

"Forget about all of that," Bruce says. "From now on you believe in one thing—me. 'I am the way, the truth and the life: no man cometh unto the

Father, but by me.' Which means that if you do everything I fucking say, and don't do anything I *don't* fucking say, you might have a chance. Otherwise, your world will always look pretty much the same as it looks right now. Do you understand?"

Peter Jr. understands.

He's done a lot of thinking sitting in a cell. He knows what he did. He knows what he did was horrible and wrong and that he deserves to be punished for it.

But he doesn't want to spend the rest of his life in a cell.

He'd kill himself first.

But I don't want to, he thinks.

Peter Moretti Jr. wants to live.

# THIRTY-TWO

**D**ANNY'S LIVING HIS DREAM.

Il Sogno.

Tara has set up a separate office in a nondescript warehouse on the city's edge to plan and design the hotel, and Danny spends most of his working hours there.

Driving architects, designers, and engineers batshit crazy.

Danny wants the main lobby to be constructed of LED walls on which the images are never the same, ever, twice. He wants the elevators to the rooms bathed in constantly shifting light. He wants the three residential towers of the hotel to sweep up in a graceful curve from the central building.

"What are you looking for?" one frustrated architect asked him. "Oz?"

"No," Danny said. "Oz has been done. I want something that hasn't been done."

The refrain "Dan, it's not possible" is standardly answered with the rejoinder "Anything is possible"; the oft-repeated phrase "We don't know how to do that" is met with his "We don't know how to do that *yet*."

They all think he's crazy, but the *really* crazy thing is that for the most part they find ways to meet his challenges; crazier yet, they secretly start to enjoy it. The ones that stay, anyway; a number quit, to which Danny's response is "We're better off without them."

The ones who stay—the Survivors, as Jerry has deemed them—work in the building like monks laboring on illuminated manuscripts, coming up with design after design, only to have them rejected with the mantra "We can do better."

They do.

The project moves forward.

For Danny, it's maybe the happiest time of his life. He's busy, engaged, immersed in creating something beautiful. From the wreckage of a life that has seen too much destruction, he's building something.

And finding balance.

He works long hours, but has stuck to a decision to be home for dinner every night, no exceptions. After Ian has gone to bed, Danny might go back to work, but he takes weekends off. Saturdays are Ian's day to choose whatever he wants the two of them to do—dirt biking, a movie, lunch, whatever. Sometimes the kid just wants to ride around, and Danny was thrilled when he asked to go to the warehouse to look at one of the many clay mock-ups of Il Sogno.

"It's really cool, Dad."

"You think so?"

"Yeah. *Really* cool."

Saturday nights are usually movie night. Danny, Ian and Madeleine—sometimes a close friend or two, sometimes Ned—sit in the screening room at the house and watch a film, eat popcorn and make ice cream sundaes, for which Danny will have to pay with more minutes on the treadmill, but he doesn't mind.

He misses Eden on weekends. They've discussed her coming to movie nights, but they're both ambivalent about it.

"Slippery slope, Dan," she said. "Next thing you know we're sliding headlong into a relationship."

"And that would be a bad thing?"

She shrugged. "I guess I'm thinking more about Ian."

"Me too."

"At his age," she said, "he'd attach . . . you know, charming and lovely as I am . . . and that wouldn't be fair until—"

"Until . . ."

"Unless," she said, "we took this to the next level. Whatever that would be. And I think we're good at the level we are right now."

Basically he thinks so, too.

He's happy with what they have.

So Danny's living the dream.

The attack comes out of nowhere.

# THIRTY-THREE

**D**ANNY'S AT THE WAREHOUSE, LOOKING at plans for the 1,800-seat the-ater, when Dom comes in.

"Something's happening with the stock," he says. "There's a move on it. People are buying it up."

"Isn't that a good thing?" Danny asks.

"Could be," Dom says. "Could also be a bad thing. Depends on who's doing the buying."

The answer comes with brutal speed.

Vern Winegard.

Vern and a number of his allies—individuals, hedge funds, banks—are snapping up Tara stock.

A hostile takeover.

Dom lays it out in stark terms. "Winegard couldn't buy the Lavinia, so he's buying the company that owns the Lavinia. Us. When he controls the majority of the stock, he'll control the board. Vote us out."

"Can he do that?" Danny asks.

"He's doing it," Dom answers. "We're a public company. Anyone can buy in."

Danny struggles to suppress a well of rage, fights off the urge to scream, *"I told you so! This is why I didn't want to take us public!"* But that would do no good—he can see that Dom is already distraught.

"We'll have to buy more stock," Danny says.

"We don't have the capital," Dom says. "The run is driving up the price. The only way we could get the cash to buy is to sell stock, which would defeat the purpose. Some of our allies are already selling out, profit taking."

"We're going to lose Tara," Danny says.

"Looks like it," Dom answers.

The reality is devastating. They'll lose not only the Lavinia property but also Casablanca and the Shores as well. Everything they've worked so hard to build will be gone, because they overreached and went public.

The dream is over, Danny thinks.

Before it can even begin.

Danny sits in the living room with Madeleine that night.

"I don't know what to do," Danny says. "Dom thinks we should get out now. Sell our stock and take the money."

"Wave the white flag," Madeleine says. "Is that what you want to do?"

"Of course not," Danny says. "But I don't know what options I have. We'll need tens, maybe hundreds of millions, and no one is going to lend us that. No one is going to invest against Winegard, not now."

Madeleine looks at her son, sitting there with his head literally in his hands. She remembers the first time she saw him as an adult, a mob gunman lying in a hospital bed with his hip shattered by a bullet.

He might be more broken now, she thinks.

You brought him back then, she thinks—the best doctors, surgeons, therapists—you have to bring him back now.

"First of all," she says, "you must be clear that you want to keep fighting because you want to build something, not out of some personal animus against Vern Winegard. If you fight just to not let him win, it's not worth it."

"I want to keep my company," Danny says. "I want to build my hotel."

"Second," she says, "you're right—no traditional funding source is going to come to your rescue."

"If you're thinking about Pasco and those people," Danny says, "forget it. Even they don't have this kind of money."

"Of course not," Madeleine says. "You need to approach Abe Stern."

Danny is gobsmacked.

*Abe Stern?*

The old man, head of the Stern Company, owns casinos in Lake Tahoe, riverboat casinos in a dozen states and a gigantic hotel chain—hundreds of properties—all around the world.

He's a multibillionaire.

Famously reclusive.

Just as famously, Abe Stern *hates* Las Vegas.

Absolutely refuses to do any business in the city. He had a hotel here back in the sixties, sold out and vowed never to come back.

"Abe Stern?" Danny asked. "Are you out of your mind?"

"I know Abe well," Madeleine says.

Of course you do, Danny thinks. You know *everybody*.

"I can get him to take a meeting," she says.

"We'd have to move fast."

Madeleine gets up and walks out. Comes back five minutes later and says, "He'll see you tonight. I suggest you take the company jet."

# THIRTY-FOUR

**D**ANNY SITS AT THE SHABBAT dinner.

He feels awkward; he's never been to one of these before.

Abe's grandson Josh had picked Danny up at the airstrip personally, which Danny thought was a positive sign. As was Josh's energy—friendly, open, enthusiastic.

Danny did his homework on the short flight and learned that Josh is a Harvard graduate with an MBA from Wharton. He came back to Lake Tahoe two years ago to help his grandfather run the business and was considered something of a wunderkind in the sophisticated use of data collection to drive business decisions.

Tall, athletic-looking, handsome, Josh is the heir apparent to run the Stern Company when Abe decides to pass the torch. Danny also learned that Josh's father—another Daniel—had died young from cancer when Josh was only ten, and that Abe had basically raised him.

Josh had practically bounded toward Danny, grabbed his bag and tossed it into the back of the Land Rover. Then they made the drive from the airstrip, past the town and up to the lakeside house that the family had lived in since the sixties.

"You must be a special guest," Josh said, "to be invited to Shabbat dinner."

"I didn't know I was."

"It's Friday," Josh said. "We're Jews."

He dug a yarmulke out of his jeans pocket and handed it to Danny. "You'll need this."

Danny said, "You picked me up personally for a reason."

"Sure," Josh said. "I wanted a few minutes alone with you. Look, Mr. Ryan—"

"Dan."

"Dan," said Josh. "Your reason for coming is obvious—you need an investor to fight off the hostile takeover from Winegard. We've been watching the stock carefully."

"Okay."

"Abe was impressed with your turnaround of the Casablanca," Josh said. "That's the basis of our business model—efficiency, intelligent use of resources, impeccable guest services. He thinks highly of the Tara Group."

"That's good to hear."

"But you need to know that Abe is seeing you only as a courtesy to your mother," Josh said. "He doesn't want a presence in Las Vegas. He's going to have you to dinner, meet with you privately afterward, and then tell you no."

Well, there it is, Danny thought. My only chance to save the company just went down the chute.

Then Josh said, "But I'm all for it. I think we absolutely should have a presence—a major presence—on the Strip. The data back me up. I think I can make the argument, but I don't know if I can make the sale. I love my grandfather, but that is one stubborn old man."

Now Danny sits at the dinner, the room softly lit with candles. The long table is full—adult children, grandchildren, nieces and nephews.

Danny's the only outsider.

He watches Abe Stern lift two loaves of bread and bestow a blessing.

Abe's voice is sonorous.

Strong.

Danny doesn't understand the words, but he senses that they are deeply felt, ancient and significant in a way that he can only guess.

*"Baruch atah Adonai, Eloheinu, melech ha'olam . . ."*

Abe's face is long—a high forehead, deep-set eyes, a strong jaw. His wispy hair is pure white, as is the stubble of beard. He looks every moment of his ninety-three years.

*". . . hamotzi lechem min ha'aretz."*

Abe sprinkles salt on the bread and then the loaves are passed down either side of the table, each person tearing a chunk from the loaf.

Danny mimics what he sees.

When the bread has been shared, the rest of the meal is served—something Danny learns is gefilte fish, followed by roast chicken, then a thick stew of meat, potatoes, beans and other vegetables.

The conversation is lively and unrestrained, and the nieces and nephews joyfully interrogate Danny—who he is, where he's from, what he does. Does he have a wife? Children? What does he think about President Clinton? The Middle East? Is he pro-Israeli? Pro-Palestinian? What does he think about the settler movement? Yankees or Dodgers, or is he a Red Sox fan?

The questions are interspersed with fierce debates on every subject as Abe sits back and says little. Danny knows that the old man is observing him, watching how he handles the questions, how he is with kids.

After a dessert of chocolate rugelach—Danny makes a mental note to get a recipe to serve in his restaurants—Abe suggests that they repair to his study.

Josh comes with them.

Abe sits behind his desk, Danny and Josh take armchairs.

Danny notes that the walls are lined with books. Glancing at the spines, he sees that they're mostly history and philosophy.

"I normally don't do business on Shabbat," Abe says, "but I understand that there's some urgency to this."

"I appreciate you making an exception," Danny says.

"I go way back with your people," Abe says. "Your father, Marty, and your father-in-*law*, John Murphy, were old friends and business associates."

Danny is shocked. "I didn't know that."

"We didn't advertise our connections back then," Abe says. "But in those days it was necessary to have . . . ambassadors . . . to the unions. And to the service trades. There were times when you couldn't acquire a napkin for the table without the cooperation of individuals who might now be viewed as undesirables. I never saw your people that way. To me, they were simply businessmen."

"I'm not my father," Danny says.

"This is what I've heard," Abe says. "As for your mother, Madeleine and I have known each other for donkey's years. We've exchanged stock tips, that sort of thing. To be clear, that was the extent of our relationship."

"I understand."

"So when she asked me to have a meeting with her son," Abe says, "even though it's Shabbat, I agreed. I like you. You're welcome in my home, any time. But I'm afraid that's as far as it goes—I can't help you in your fight with Winegard."

"With all respect, sir," Danny says, "you can. What you mean is that you won't."

"Yes, that is more accurate," Abe says. "I won't. My grandson disagrees, and judging from the tapping of his foot, I think he's about to tell us why. Joshua?"

Josh makes his case.

The Tara Group has an excellent record. It returns high profits. With proper data capture, the returns on the new project, Il Sogno, could be astronomical. Moreover, the Stern Company needs a presence, a prime location, on the Las Vegas Strip. It's a matter of prestige. While highly profitable and well thought of, the Stern properties are also considered somewhat pedestrian, middle class. A partnership in an exclusive, elegant hotel like Il Sogno would cast a luster on the entire company and all its holdings.

Abe says, "This middle class you disparage—"

"I didn't disparage them," Josh says.

"—has made us wealthy," Abe says. "Never forget, it's the ninety-nine percent who make the one percent. I'd be very careful about changing our branding in a way that would make them feel excluded."

Josh has his data ready.

He cites a number of hotel chains that have remained stuck to a mid-range branding and demographic and that are now on a downhill slide into second-rate reputations. He clicks off numbers about how much more profit there is to be had from fewer customers spending more money. He cites the advantages of vertical integration from the bottom to the top of the customer base.

"I'm not suggesting that we close doors on our current customer base," Josh says. "I'm suggesting that we open doors on new customers."

Abe looks at Danny. "This is the disadvantage of giving your progeny a good education. They use the acquired knowledge against you."

"But he's right," Danny says. "We learned a similar lesson at Tara."

"And now you're about to lose the company," Abe says. "So you have to come to me to bail you out. We would never have gone public, we never will. That was a terrible mistake, Daniel."

"I agree."

"You do?"

"Yes."

Abe seems to take that in.

"Zayde," Josh says, "this is a great opportunity. The synergy between our two companies—"

"Synergy," Abe says, looking at Danny. "Do you know what that even means?"

"No."

"Neither do I," Abe says. "But Josh does. He knows all kinds of words I don't understand. But he's made us a lot of money, I will admit. You said at dinner that you have a son?"

"Yes."

"Good luck with that." Abe stands up. "I wish you good luck with all your endeavors. But I can't help you. I simply won't do business in Las

Vegas. Josh will show you to your cottage and then take you to the airstrip in the morning. Shabbat Shalom."

It's over, Danny thinks. He gets up, shakes Abe's hand and thanks him for his time and hospitality.

Josh walks him outside to a guest cottage by the lake. "I'm sorry, Dan. I tried."

"I appreciate it."

Danny can't sleep that night. He just sits in a chair and looks at the moon out the window.

I've lost, he thinks.

Lost Il Sogno, the Shores, Casablanca—everything I've built.

Maybe it's for the best. Sell your stock, take the money and retire young. Stop feeling sorry for yourself, you're a multimillionaire. You used to have nothing.

He tells himself that, but he knows his heart is broken.

Then he sees a tall, stooped figure in the moonlight.

It's Abe Stern.

# THIRTY-FIVE

"OLD MEN DON'T SLEEP MUCH," Abe says. "Maybe it's because we know that soon we'll be getting too *much* sleep."

They're sitting in Adirondack chairs on the back lawn of the cottage, looking out at the lake.

"You don't sleep much, either," Abe says.

"I have a few things on my mind."

"I've built fortunes and lost them," Abe says. "Built them again. You will, too. You did something stupid, Winegard cut you off at the knees. Right now, your pride is hurt worse than anything."

"But what's my pride worth?" Danny asks.

"Dignity? Everything. Pride . . ." Abe lets it trail off, as if the answer is inconsequential.

A slight breeze wafts the water to lap on the shore.

"It's peaceful," Abe says. "You don't get that in Las Vegas."

"You didn't leave because of traffic noise," Danny says.

"No," Abe says. "Did Joshua mention to you his two great-uncles, Julius and Nathan?"

"No."

"No, why would he?" Abe says, more to himself than to Danny. "All he ever knew was that one was murdered and the other died in an asylum. Long before he was born. Do you have time for an old man's story?"

"Sure."

It was the mid-sixties, Abe tells him. He had his hotel on Fremont Street, was doing well.

He also had two younger brothers.

Julius and Nathan.

They were brilliant, probably geniuses. Problem was, they were *too* smart. Arrogant. Thought they could get away with anything and usually did.

Like cheating at cards.

They worked a long game.

Julius would get a job as a dealer. Play it straight for months. Then he'd slip a tiny mirror into the dealing shoe so he could see what the next card was going to be. Nathan would come in and play. Lose a little, win a little—legit—then leave the chips down. When the payoff was big enough, Julius would signal—through eye blinks—what the next card was going to be.

They'd hit big, Julius would wait a couple of weeks, then quit. Then they'd move up to Reno, or here to Tahoe, and do the same thing.

Then back to Vegas.

Switching back and forth as the dealer and the player. Different names, false IDs, disguises.

They made money hand over fist.

Problem was, they liked to spend it, too.

Booze, women, cars, suits, clothes.

Julius in particular, he was a clotheshorse. Loved the tailored suits, the silk shirts, the expensive shoes. Loved the pricey women, too, lavished them with gifts, put them on his arm and showed them off.

It got attention, it got noticed.

Abe tried to warn them. About both the cheating and the flaunting, but they wouldn't listen.

They were too smart.

At the time, there was a young Detroit capo named Alfred "Allie Boy" Licata, sent out to keep an eye on the family's interests, particularly its silent partnership in the old Moonglow Hotel. The Detroit family was taking skim out of that place in buckets, and insisted on having a monopoly on robbing the joint.

Julius and Nathan didn't agree.

Julius, he loved hitting the Moonglow.

Couldn't stay out of there.

Maybe it was because he hated Allie Boy and loved pissing on him in his own place. They'd gotten into some kind of a beef over a woman, had words, and you know how it is, sometimes that's all it takes to develop a permanent animosity.

Danny knows exactly how it is.

The brothers hit the Moonglow for fifty large with their dealer-player mirror scam and got away with it.

Should have stayed away.

But Julius couldn't help himself.

Went back to the blackjack tables there in a disguise and did his card-counting thing.

The people there weren't stupid, they caught on and Licata personally escorted him out with an invitation to never come back.

But Julius, he had a mouth on him. He called Licata every name in the book and a few he made up on his own. He cussed him out in English, Yiddish, Hebrew and a little Italian, even when they were beating the shit out of him.

Julius, he spat blood in Licata's face.

Licata even came to see Abe.

"You're good people," Licata told him. "Everyone respects you. I have to ask you, talk to your brothers, get them to knock it off."

Again, Abe tried to warn them. Stay away. Licata is bad business—a sadistic psycho.

"I'm not afraid of that guinea," Julius said.

"You should be," Abe said.

"Fuck him."

Even Nate told Julius not to go back, but no, Julius was too smart, too arrogant.

Back he went, in another disguise.

Got caught again.

Licata went back to Abe—tell your brothers to stay out of our hotels, or we're going to kill them.

Abe passed on the message.

"Then they're going to have to fucking kill us," Julius said.

"Why?" Abe asked. "Why are you doing this?"

Julius smiled. "Because."

Of course he went back.

Made a score and got away with it. But when he got back to the apartment, Nathan wasn't there. The phone rang.

*"You want your brother, come to . . ."*

Julius jumped in his car and drove to the warehouse on the outskirts of town. He knew it was a suicide mission, that they were using his brother as bait to get him, but he didn't care.

He was willing to die for his brother.

Julius walked into the fucking building and there was Nathan, naked, chained by the wrists from a steel beam, his toes just touching the concrete floor.

But he was alive.

"Let him go," Julius said to Licata. "I'm the one you want, right?"

"Right," Licata said.

He smiled, raised his gun and shot Nathan in the forehead.

"Jesus Christ," Danny says.

But that wasn't the worst part of the story.

Julius felt a whack on the back of his head, and when he woke up, he was naked and chained face-to-face to his dead brother.

They left him there for three days, as Nathan's body rotted, decomposed and bloated. Every few hours, someone would come and force water down Julius's throat, and sometimes Licata would come in, sit on a stool and smoke a cigarette as Julius begged to die. "Please kill me."

"I don't think so."

After three days, they unchained him and dumped him in the alley behind Abe's hotel. A waiter taking out the garbage found him.

By that time, Julius Stern was insane.

A bulging-eyed, drooling psychotic mumbling about being chained to his dead brother, a pathetic, incoherent wreck who would never be believed on a witness stand.

It took Abe weeks to get the story out of him, piece it together from the bits and snatches of screaming nightmares and rambling soliloquies.

Julius never recovered.

Abe took him to doctors, tried electroshock therapy, drugs, everything, but in the end had to commit him to a mental ward and the living death of heavy tranquilizers until finally, after twenty years, he passed away.

Nathan's body was never found.

Licata visited Abe one more time. "We think it would be better if you sell your hotel and leave town."

Abe agreed.

He never wanted to see Las Vegas again.

Now Danny understands Stern's refusal. "I'm sorry for your loss."

"It was a long time ago," Abe says.

"Whatever happened to Licata?"

"He became a pretty big wheel in Vegas," Abe says, "until the late eighties, when the feds chased the mobsters out. But do you know who he helped get into the casino business?"

Danny shakes his head.

Abe says, "Vernon Winegard."

"Vern's clean."

"Maybe now," Abe says. "But he still pays Licata points."

Jesus Christ, Danny thinks.

They sit silently for a minute.

Then Abe says, "When I turned you down, you accepted it with grace. And dignity. You didn't try to pull any of that mobster crap on me. The name Pasco Ferri never escaped your lips. If it had, we wouldn't be having this conversation."

Danny keeps his mouth shut, but feels his heart racing.

"I never thought I wanted revenge," Abe says. "I thought it was immoral, beneath me. Most of all, I wanted to protect my family from all that brutality, all that violence, that ugliness. I still do, do you understand?"

"Yes."

"When the market opens Monday, the Stern group will buy enough Tara stock to stop the takeover," Abe says. "You'll have the votes to control Tara. You and I will be partners."

"Thank you, Mr. Stern."

"One thing," Abe says. "Joshua will go with you. He'll move to Las Vegas to oversee our interests. He's a smart kid, smarter than you or me. He'll make you money."

"I know he will."

Abe gets out of the chair. It's a struggle. "The stupidest thing we ever do is get old. This hotel we're building, this dream of yours, I probably won't live to see it."

Danny stands up. "I'm sure you will."

"Promise me one thing," Abe says. "You'll take care of my grandson."

"I promise," Danny says. "Like my own family."

They shake hands.

# THIRTY-SIX

THE MEDIA ARE ALL OVER it.

Why wouldn't they be?

The news that the Stern Company has allied with the Tara Group is a game changer, a tectonic shift in the geography of the gaming world.

*"It may have been hostile, but in the end it wasn't a takeover,"* reads one article, *"and the Tara Group emerges stronger than ever as Vern Winegard's attack fails."*

Another read: *"This time it wasn't a Lamborghini or even the Lavinia but something much more valuable, as Winegard's bid to acquire the Tara Group fell short."*

Others had a different take.

*"The Stern Return"*

*"Hospitality and gaming giant the Stern Company rode in like the cavalry to rescue the Tara Group from Vern Winegard's hostile takeover. The move ended Abe Stern's long self-imposed exile from Las Vegas, bringing the hotel and casino behemoth south from his Lake Tahoe base to the desert at last. Inside sources say that Stern's grandson, Joshua Stern, will oversee the company's 40 percent share in the Tara Group. The move makes the Stern-Tara alliance by far the dominant force on the Strip, if not in the entire gaming world, as . . ."*

"You're gloating," Eden says.

"More like basking," says Danny, lying in bed. "I'm *basking.*"

Basking in relief, basking in victory.

It feels good to win.

"You gave up forty percent of your company," Eden says.

"But I still *control* my company," Danny says. "Anyway, it's not about the money."

"What's it about, then?"

"The dream."

"With a small *d* or a capital *D*?"

"Both, I guess," Danny says. "Same thing."

She's starting to fall in love with him.

But do not, do not, repeat *do not*, she thinks, let yourself fall in love with him.

Dan Ryan is in love with two dead women, whose memories you could never compete with. Two women who will never say the wrong thing, do the wrong thing, put on an extra pound, get cramps, have a red, runny nose, or get older.

Two women who can never disappoint.

It goes deeper than that.

Although she'd never say it to him, she knows that Danny is in love with his own sorrow, attached to the romance of his tragedies. They are *his* self-definition, whether he realizes it or not. He'll never let go of his sadness, he wouldn't know what to do.

Enough, Eden thinks.

You have a good relationship with the man. Friendly, affectionate, intimate in more than the sexual—well, as intimate as either of you is going to allow—mutually beneficial.

A symbiotic relationship, if you will.

You meet his needs, he meets yours.

Which is, of course, how people describe a good marriage, but Eden has no inclination in that direction. She knows that most women would, would want the money, the prestige, the power. The mansion, the country club, the committees.

I'd slash my wrists, Eden thinks.

She imagines the scene among the ladies who lunch. Reaching over her Cobb salad, grabbing a knife and severing her arteries. À la Julia Child, Dan Aykroyd in *Saturday Night Live*, spraying blood all over their thousand-dollar frocks while screaming, *I had to do it! You're boring the* shit *out of me!*

# THIRTY-SEVEN

V ERN SETS THE NEWSPAPER DOWN in disgust.

Who the hell thought that Ryan would have the balls to go to Abe Stern? Who the hell thought that Stern would ever agree to invest in Las Vegas?

"Ryan strong-armed him," Connelly says.

"How?" Vern asks. "How the hell could Dan Ryan strong-arm Abe Stern? It would be like Floyd Mayweather strong-arming Mike Tyson. Mayweather is a great fighter, but he doesn't have the weight. Neither does Ryan."

"Ryan has something on him," Connelly says. "Or he just threatened him. You know how these guys work."

"What guys?"

"Wiseguys."

"Are you on that again?" Vern asks.

"I'm telling you, Ryan had something on Stavros, that's how he flipped him on the Lavinia," Connelly says. "Abe Stern says for *thirty years* that he won't come to Vegas, Ryan goes up to see him *one night*, and now he's back? Come on."

"Even if it's true," Vern says, "what are we supposed to do about it? We don't have any proof."

"We go to the board," Connelly says, "get them to start an investigation, pull Ryan's license."

"They've already refused."

"There's someone on the board," Connelly says. "If this person was approached the right way . . ."

"We're getting down in the gutter with Ryan."

"It's the only way we're going to win this thing," Connelly says. "Or we might as well hang it up and let the bad guys win. It'll be like the bad old days, the mob running the town."

It's a game of dominoes, Vern thinks. If Ryan has mob connections through Ferri, then Dom Rinaldi and Jerry Kush have mob connections through Ryan. The board could pull their licenses, too, even force them to sell their hotels.

Tara will tumble.

I'll pick up the pieces.

"Make the approach."

"You're doing the right thing, Vern."

Long after Connelly leaves the office, Vern wonders if he *is* doing the right thing. He hates Ryan, but still doesn't quite believe that he's mobbed up. Or *still* mobbed up, because at some time or other he sure as shit was connected.

But we all have our pasts, Vern thinks, and it's risky business to be digging up Ryan's. No one in this business is completely clean. We all made our deals, all made our compromises. The best we can say is that we're mostly clean.

Now.

We're like Las Vegas itself.

We're mostly clean *now*.

Back then?

We did what we had to do to get into the business, to stay in the business. You start digging up Ryan's past, you're not the only one who can wield a shovel. Ryan might retaliate with an archaeological dig of his own.

You have skeletons buried in this dirt.

# THIRTY-EIGHT

J OSH LIKES LAS VEGAS.

"After all," he joked with Danny, "we're a desert people."

Josh is a triathlete, so the climate suits his training. He runs or bikes in the early morning, swims in the afternoon or evening. A guest at Madeleine's until he can find a place, he uses the pool and the gym, the steam bath or the sauna.

And works like a son of a bitch.

Danny's impressed.

Josh is in the office early and stays late, usually having lunch at his desk. When he's not there, he's on the properties, often with Danny, observing and learning all the details.

He spends a lot of his time putting his data collection apparatus into place, discovering what the average customer in each hotel spends, what they gamble on and how much, how many customers return to which hotels and why. His research is starting to show that Danny's argument that customers spend more on rooms, shows and meals than they do on gambling is correct.

When he's not working, he's training. When he's not training, he just basically hangs out, has dinner with the family, then maybe sits in the screening room with Danny, Ian and Madeleine and watches a movie.

He's teaching Ian how to play tennis.

Josh has very quickly become a member of the family.

Madeleine, of course, wants to set him up with a suitable young lady.

"That's not going to work," Danny said.

"Why not?"

"He's gay," Danny said.

"You chowderhead lunks think everyone is gay," Madeleine said.

"No," Danny said, "he told me he's gay."

It came up at lunch in Danny's office one day when Josh asked if there was a woman in Danny's life.

"Not really," Danny said, feeling a little guilty about Eden. "You?"

"Actually, I play for the other team," Josh said. When Danny looked blank, he added, "I'm gay."

"Oh."

"Oh." Josh laughed. "Hell of a reaction, Danny. Are you okay with it?"

"It's not for me to be okay with it," Danny said. "It's for you to be okay with it. Are you okay with it?"

"I'm more than okay with it," Josh said.

Danny was quiet for a few seconds, then asked, "Does Abe know?"

"He does."

Josh had been terrified to come out to his grandfather. He half expected to be disowned, disinherited. The financial consequences didn't scare him. He was educated, intelligent and creative, so he knew he could always make money, he'd be fine. But he loved his grandfather, loved his family, loved the business, and he didn't want to be banished.

He wanted to stay.

But not at the cost of living a lie.

So when he came home from college one summer he asked to see Abe in his study, alone.

"What's on your mind, Joshua?" Abe asked.

"Zayde, I'm gay," Josh said. "Homosexual."

"I know what gay means," Abe said. "You think, what, men started being with men last week? I know homosexuals."

"So what do you think?" Josh felt his voice tremble.

"I think that you're my grandson and that I love you," Abe said. "Am I overjoyed about this? No, I would like to see your children. Do I think any less of you? Also no. You're a fine person. I'm proud of you, I will always be proud."

"And if I were to bring a . . . significant other . . . to the house?" Josh asked.

"He would be welcome," Abe said. "If anyone in the family has a problem with it, they will also have a problem with me. And Joshua, as you know, no one in the family wants a problem with me. *Is* there such a person, this 'significant other'?"

"Not yet, not really."

"And are you being careful?"

"I'm not going to get pregnant, Zayde."

"Jokes, Joshua?"

"Of course I'm being careful."

Josh hasn't brought anyone to the family home, not yet. There have been lovers, there have been boyfriends, but no one he's wanted to introduce to his grandfather.

And now he's come out to Dan Ryan and is relieved and somewhat amused by his bland reaction. "Abe accepts me for who I am."

"Well, Abe's a good guy."

"He's the best person I know."

If Madeleine was surprised at Josh's sexual orientation, she recovered quickly. "In that case, I should set him up with a suitable young man."

"I think Josh can take care of himself," Danny said.

Josh thinks so, too, and politely declined Madeleine's offer of assistance in his love life. He's too busy for romance now anyway, absorbed in the business of taking the Tara Group to the next level and planning the funding and construction of Il Sogno.

"I love the concept," he's told Danny. "I think it could be extraordinary."

He goes to the bankers, the hedge-fund managers, the big players to get them to invest in the new hotel. His analytics, coupled with the Stern Company's weight, make a difference.

The word goes out that Josh Stern and Dan Ryan are a team to be reckoned with, a genuine new power in the industry.

One of their greatest collective strengths is that they argue.

Refining the design of Il Sogno, Josh's statistics sometimes clash with Danny's aesthetics.

For instance, the locations of elevators.

"You can't," Josh said, "let people move directly to the elevators without going through the slots."

"I want them to feel like valued guests," Danny said, "not manipulated targets."

"But we'll lose income capture."

"We'll gain it back in returning customers," Danny said.

They compromised—the traffic flow would take guests just past but not through the slot machines.

They debate about how much space should be allotted to poker tables, dice games and roulette. They argue about how much footage should be given over to retail stores and what those shops should be. They go round and round about lighting schemes, materials for walls vis-à-vis sound reduction, flooring materials for wear and tear.

As a result, both of them become firm believers in what Josh calls "the battleground of ideas"—they learn to check their egos at the door and let the best data, the best analysis and the best thinking win.

It makes them both better.

It makes Il Sogno better.

And amuses the hell out of Gloria.

"You two are the Abbott and Costello of the gaming industry," she told Josh. Seeing his blank look, she added, "No? Dean Martin and Jerry Lewis? No? Nothing? How about Jerry and George?"

"*Seinfeld*," Josh said.

"There you go," Gloria said. "The two of you would argue over the color of air."

"She brings up an interesting point, Dan," Josh said. "The circulation systems need to . . ."

Both Dom and Jerry become major Josh Stern fans—their new partner checks Dan's more extravagant impulses, brings serious financial security to the company and is an ever-cheerful, positive presence.

The person who maybe likes Josh the most is Bernie Hughes.

At Danny's request, the accountant has moved to Las Vegas to keep his weather eye on the numbers underlying the Tara-Stern partnership and also because Danny is worried about the old man's health and wants to keep him closer.

Bernie *loves* Josh. Loves his attention to detail, his conservative view of expenditures, and reserves for him the highest of praise: "The kid knows his numbers."

Yeah, the "kid" does, and wields them with a fluidity and imagination that serves Danny well. In the process, Danny and Josh become friends. So much so that Danny's a little sad when Josh tells him that he has found a place.

"You know you're welcome here," Danny says.

"I know," Josh says, "but you cramp my style."

"We're going to miss you," Danny says. "Ian's going to miss you."

"I won't be a stranger," Josh says, "and it's going to take a month or so to get the new condo together."

"Madeleine and Gloria will be happy to help."

"I'm a young gay man," Josh says. "I need their design help?"

"Then their brutal efficiency."

"That I could use," Josh says.

So Josh likes his life in Las Vegas. He's found a substitute family with the Ryans, is developing friendships around town, has a penthouse condo on the Strip. He bicycles to the office, runs trails outside of town. It would be nice to have a boyfriend—that would be the cherry on the sundae—but he doesn't have the time to go looking and has no taste for internet dating.

That will come, Josh thinks.

Every Friday he takes the company jet to Tahoe for Shabbat dinner and to see his grandfather.

So life is good.

For Josh.

For Tara.

For Danny.

And then—

# THIRTY-NINE

**D**ANNY DRIVES TO SUNSET PARK and pulls up alongside an unmarked car.

Ron Fahey is a lieutenant in the Organized Crime Bureau, Criminal Intelligence Section.

All the major casino operators have a guy or two in the police department. They're not dirty cops, they don't take bribes to turn a blind eye to crimes, but they're looking toward their post-retirement future, maybe a lucrative security or consulting job with one of the major gaming corporations.

Danny rolls down his window, and Fahey rolls down his.

"What is it?" Danny asks.

"I thought you should know," Fahey says, "an investigator from the board came around asking for the file on you."

Metro ISB has extensive files on every major player in Las Vegas.

Danny feels a stab of fear. "What's in it?"

"Old shit," Fahey says. "Ancient history, the usual. But, Dan, did you have lunch with Pasquale Ferri at Piero's?"

Shit, Danny thinks. It might be enough for the board to yank his license. "Do you know who on the board's behind it?"

"I'll see what I can find out."

It's Camilla Cooper.

Cammy to her family, friends and fans, of whom she has a lot, because Cammy Cooper is a star.

Tall, blond, blue-eyed, born-again Christian, mother of five, a former "Mrs. Las Vegas," she's a model—literally and figuratively—for the conservative, Second Amendment–boosting, anti-abortion, anti-gay-marriage "pro-family" crowd, which is a big one in Nevada.

She first made her public bones with something called the Promise Campaign, which called for teenage girls to take an oath to save themselves for marriage.

Cammy held rallies, at churches and even schools, that featured Christian rock bands, high energy and emotion, and she got thousands of girls to sign on. She talked about pregnancy, she talked about disease, she talked about morality, but she also talked, with the considerable influence of her stunning good looks, about the sexuality of abstinence—"It's just *better* in a committed, monogamous relationship."

Then, smiling seductively, she'd add, "Trust me, I know."

And she'd wink.

It was killer.

Sometimes the recipient of that wink was her husband, Jay, better known as Coop. Coop, as Cammy was happy to relate, was a "real man," a husband, a father, a hunter, and a former college football star with an almost imperceptible limp from the knee injury that kept him from the pros, who was doing very well, thank you, in the insurance business. Tall, handsome, Coop was the perfect foil, standing behind and slightly to the right, smiling, nodding, flushing with charming modesty when Cammy would allude to his qualities as a father and their more-than-satisfactory life in the bedroom.

Faced with criticism that the program was sexist in that it put the responsibility solely on girls, she expanded it to include boys, drawing thousands of horny adolescents to her rallies and getting them to come to the stage to take the oath.

The Promise Campaign launched Cammy's public career. She became a sought-after luncheon speaker, gave guest sermons at the mega-churches, started showing up on local television talk shows.

She broadened her scope.

Chastity to gun rights might not seem like a natural evolution, but Cammy sure made it seamless.

"The same liberals who are undermining our sexual morality," she preached, "also want to take away our guns. Well, I will not surrender my right to defend my home, my family and myself."

In a photo that became iconic, Cammy posed in an all-white jumpsuit, one long leg cocked, holster at her hip, blowing on the barrel of a Colt pistol.

To critics who expressed disappointment at the photo's raciness, Cammy responded, "There's no inherent contradiction between sexuality and Christianity. God gave us our bodies and wants us to enjoy them—within the sacred bonds of marriage."

The same seductive smile, with the same wink and the stage-whispered, "Just ask my husband."

Doubling down, Cammy, in conjunction with one of the mega-churches, launched the Behind Closed Doors Challenge, in which married couples would commit to have sex at least once a day for a month straight.

"We'll be tired," she said. "But we'll be smiling."

The BCDC—as it became known—was a huge hit.

"Have you ever noticed," Cammy asked at its conclusion, "how liberals are always miserable? Always whining about something? Worried about something else? Whereas conservatives are usually happy? Why is that? I think it's because we have our God, our families, our guns, our homes and our bodies that we treat as temples instead of gas station restrooms. I get up in the morning happy. I go to bed at night happy . . . So does my husband. We both sleep like babies."

Smile. Wink.

Coop Cooper blushed.

Cammy Cooper was pro-sexuality.

Well, heterosexuality.

Her next campaign was an all-out attack on gay rights, especially the dreaded specter of same-sex marriage. With Coop at her side, she'd proclaim, "It was Adam and Eve, not Adam and Steve," as if this were the funniest and most original one-liner since Henny Youngman said, "Take my wife, please."

"Marriage is a sacred contract between a man, a woman and God," she'd say into the television camera. "I will not have my marriage cheapened or degraded by a gross violation of that holy sacrament. If you agree with me, and I know you do, I want you to go right now and write your legislator, your congressman and tell him that you're pro-marriage and that you vote."

Cammy became a star.

She got her own TV show, and after one season it was nationally syndicated.

When appointed to the Nevada Gaming Control Board, she said, "I don't gamble much. Oh, maybe every now and then I buy a lottery ticket. But I know that gaming is a huge part of the Nevada economy. It creates thousands of jobs. I want Nevada gaming to be clean, free of the criminal influences that plagued it in the past. Under my watch, Las Vegas, Reno and Tahoe will be family-friendly."

But Cammy isn't going to be satisfied with a seat on the board. The word on the street is that she wants the governor's mansion.

And, Danny thinks, she's going to step on me to get there.

# FORTY

**D**ANNY TELLS HIS PARTNERS.

They need to know, because the threat isn't only to him. It could endanger all of them, even take down Tara, because if Cammy Cooper links him to organized crime, by association it also implicates Dom, Jerry and the Stern Company.

So he asks them to come to the house, gathers them in the living room, and tells them about Cooper's investigation.

"What did you ever do to Cammy Cooper?" Dom asks.

"Nothing," Danny says. "She needs a pelt to hang on the wall and mine will do."

"Does she have anything?" Jerry asks.

"She has my meeting with Pasco."

"Is that all?"

"That could be enough," Danny says. "Add to that the publicity from my time in Hollywood . . . it could be enough to pull my license."

It's the sword of Damocles that's hung over their necks since the beginning. They all knew that Pasco Ferri and some of his associates had money buried deep in Tara's funding; they knew that Danny had gone to him when it came to financing the Shores, had gone again to get his okay to go public. And while Ferri's share has been diluted to the point that it's almost nonexistent, the connection could still be lethal.

"Dan," Jerry says, "hard as this is to say, I'm afraid you're right."

Dom looks at Danny and nods. "I hate this, but we're going to have to ask you to resign as director of operations and sell your shares."

"That's outrageous," Madeleine says.

"What choice do we have, Madeleine?" Dom asks. "I'm sorry, but Dan's too big a risk."

Josh says, "Bullshit."

"What?" Jerry asks.

"I said bullshit," Josh says. "Dan made Tara what it is. It's his vision. You all knew who Danny was when you got into business with him. I'm not cutting him loose because things get a little tough."

"I'm cutting myself loose," Danny says. "I'll resign and sell out."

"I won't let you," Josh says. "It's this simple—if Dan goes, the Stern shares go with him. We'll sell, let Winegard buy you. Then we'll start a new company with Dan and run you all out of the business."

This is Josh? Danny thinks. Affable, carefree "tennis, anyone?" Josh?

"You want to talk to your grandfather about this first?" Dom asks.

"I don't need to," Josh says. "I have his complete authority on all matters regarding our partnership with Tara. You want to get on the phone with him, be my guest. But I can tell you what he's going to say: 'Talk to Joshua.'"

"What about the board?" Jerry asks.

"What about it?" Josh asks. "Dan, you don't have Stern's permission to resign. Good night, everyone."

They watch him walk up the stairs.

In the morning, at the breakfast table, Danny says, "You didn't have to do that."

Josh looks up from his scrambled eggs. "You Irish Catholics, you always want to be martyrs."

"Still . . ."

"You broke bread with us," Josh says. "You sat at our Shabbat table. You've welcomed me into your home. It means something."

"Billions of dollars?" Danny asks.

"My grandfather taught me," Josh says, "that money doesn't make character, but that character makes money. Always invest in character, he said. If the roles were reversed, you wouldn't have accepted Dom or Jerry's resignation."

He states it as a fact. There's no need to answer.

"If the Sterns were ever in trouble," Josh says, "Dan Ryan would stand by us. So what are we going to do about Mrs. Cooper? You know that Winegard is behind this."

"Do you think so?"

"Come on," Josh says. "Look at the timing. He tried a hostile takeover. That didn't work. This is his next play."

"He bought her."

"Of course he bought her," Josh says. "If she makes a gubernatorial run, she'll need the money. And she gets a Dan Ryan notch on that pistol of hers. It's a win-win for our Cammy."

"We can't prove it."

"No, we can't," Josh says. "We have to find something else. Cammy wants to dig up your past, we dig up hers. She can't be as clean as she looks."

"I thought you were Mr. By the Book," Danny says. "Mr. Clean."

"When the other side plays by the rules, I'll play by the rules," Josh says. "Until then, I'll play the game the way everyone else does."

Danny doesn't like it.

It's everything he's been working to get away from.

But as the safety warning goes, "Objects in the Rearview Mirror May Be Closer Than They Appear."

Yeah, Danny thinks.

And gaining.

# FORTY-ONE

ALFRED "ALLIE BOY" LICATA ALSO reads the newspapers.

"Allie Boy" is hardly a boy anymore, although the nickname has stuck from his days as a young Las Vegas hotshot. But he's in his sixties now, freezing his ass off in fucking Detroit, having been banned from the Nevada gaming world as an "undesirable."

But Abe fucking Stern is going back to Las Vegas, Licata thinks as he looks at the headlines and remembers what he did to Stern's brothers.

It gets him hard, thinking about those two brothers strung like cats over a clothesline, Julius squirming and moaning, his eyes getting crazier, the way his body jumped when they'd take a hose to blast the shit and the piss off him.

*Marone*, how that room smelled, though.

The body rotting, swelling up.

It was better than killing Julius, much better, sending his mind to a place of perpetual pain. That's the problem with torture: it usually ends, you can't keep it going forever, the guy dies too soon and then you have to find another one . . .

Licata has found plenty, though.

What's made him one of the most feared and hated guys in their world, which is a good thing.

Let them hate me, he thinks.

As long as they fear me, too.

And now Winegard has let himself get butt-fucked by Abe Stern.

And this guy Ryan.

Licata knows a little about Ryan by reputation. Was a soldier for the Irish back in the days when they were fighting the Italians for control of New England. Lost the war, but came out of it okay, turned up in L.A. banging some movie star. Got into some kind of beef out there with Angelo Petrelli. Word was that Petrelli put out a contract on him, but it didn't work out. No surprise there, Petrelli was always a limp dick and the L.A. family a joke, not so much a family as a colony of Chicago and Detroit. But it also means that this Ryan can take care of himself.

Word also is that Ryan has a long relationship with old Pasco Ferri.

Ferri is no joke, a very heavy guy who has the ear of all the big families. Supposed to be retired now but sticks his beak into just about everything.

So is he running Ryan?

And through Ryan, Stern?

Wouldn't be a surprise, Licata thinks. Abe was tight with the Irish back in the day, with old John Murphy and Marty Ryan. I wonder if this Ryan is anything like his old man, who was one tough fuck in his time, before he fell into the bottle and couldn't climb out.

Fucking Irish.

Old joke, "This Irish guy walks past a bar . . ."

That's it, that's the joke.

Speaking of jokes, the feds think they chased OC out of Vegas, think it's run by corporations now. They don't even see that those corporations still have connections with the likes of Pasco Ferri and Danny Ryan.

Nothing has changed except the names.

A joke.

And Winegard?

Vern's a good guy, a smart guy, but not a tough guy. Not tough like Pasco Ferri. And he's up against it now.

Licata looks out the window at the snow coming down.

Sometimes people ask him if he misses Vegas.

Do I miss Vegas? Do I miss ninety-five and sunny? Broads dressed in next to nothing? Skim coming off the top like cream? Blow jobs on the cuff? Why would I miss all of that? I got Detroit. Filthy, run-down, all-the-jobs-have-gone-to-Japan, the-women-screw-in-down-vests Motown.

Fuck that.

# FORTY-TWO

CAMMY *IS* AS CLEAN AS she looks.

Hard to believe but apparently true, because no one—not Fahey, not Josh's people—can find a speck of dirt on Camilla Cooper's white jumpsuits. Her finances are immaculate, she pays her taxes, her afternoon tennis lessons are really tennis lessons.

Her past seems as pure as her present.

No teenage pregnancy, no abortions, no affairs, no drunken party indiscretions. Coop was her college sweetheart (she was of course a cheerleader), they got engaged, they got married, they started having kids.

They attend church on Sundays, they go to their children's sports and school events. Cammy has a glass of wine on Saturday nights, Coop a beer at Sunday barbecues. That's it—no prescriptions for Valium, antianxiety drugs, herpes medication . . .

"How do you get this information?" Danny asks.

"You don't want to know," Josh says.

No, I guess I don't, Danny thinks.

He feels dirty. Has to remind himself that Cooper is trying to destroy him, that she's digging into *his* past, but he still has misgivings.

Doesn't matter, anyway.

There's no dirt to dig.

The shovels come up clean.

Fahey delivers worse news.

"Cooper has your meeting with Ferri," he tells Danny. "She's also looking into a Kevin Coombs? There was some sort of scene at a party of yours, something he might have said about you fleeing Rhode Island? She's also asking questions about a Sean South, James MacNeese and an Edmund Egan. Egan has a record?"

"Yeah."

"She's trying to connect you not only with the Mafia, via Ferri," Fahey says, "but also with an old Providence crew the feds list as the Murphy Organization."

It's like being in the ocean in a heavy undertow, Danny thinks. You try to walk out, but the ocean pulls at your legs, and if you can't keep your footing, it sucks you back out. You think you're on shore and the next thing you know, you're drowning.

"Apparently she's also trying to get the file on an old homicide," Fahey says. "A cold case—Phillip Jardine. An FBI agent."

And Fahey's giving him a hard, inquiring look, like: *Are you a cop killer, Dan? Did you kill a cop?*

"The tabloids were printing that shit years ago," Danny says. "There was nothing to it then and there's nothing to it now."

"It's a bad look, Dan."

Danny knows this. Cooper doesn't have to actually prove anything—just the *appearance* of a connection with OC is enough to get his license revoked. The board isn't a court of law—it can convict you on a rumor.

Except in this case it isn't a rumor.

He had shot Jardine.

Only after Jardine tried to shoot him first, but he had still pulled the trigger and killed the man.

"The word is that this Jardine was dirty," Fahey says. "He was involved in heroin trafficking. It's a double-edged sword—it makes him less sympathetic, but it also links you to drugs."

Also true, Danny thinks.

The mistake of my life, and it won't let go.

The pull of the ocean.

He'd heard it a hundred times from the old fishermen back in another life: If the sea wants you, she gets you. Maybe she gives you back, sometimes alive, more often dead. A lot of the fishermen he knew couldn't even swim. They'd just shrug and say—

If the sea wants you, she gets you.

There's nothing you can do.

A WEEK LATER Danny gets a certified letter demanding his appearance at a board hearing at which it will be determined if he can retain his license.

It's a foregone conclusion.

Cammy tells him so personally.

They run into each other in one of the Shores restaurants, Cammy coming out of the ladies' room as Danny is going to check on things in the kitchen.

"Mr. Ryan."

"Mrs. Cooper," Danny says. "I'm a little surprised to see you here."

"Oh, I have nothing against the Shores," Cammy says. "It's you I object to."

"How much is Winegard paying you?"

"See, there you go," Cammy says. "The corrupt see only corruption."

"I see what's in front of me, Mrs. Cooper."

"Please, call me Cammy, everyone does," she says. "I'm going to destroy you, Dan. I'm going to run you out of Las Vegas, out of Nevada. We don't want your kind here."

"My kind?"

"Please, you know exactly what I mean."

"Enjoy your dinner," Danny says. "It's on the house."

"Oh, I couldn't," Cammy says. "That would be corrupt."

He watches her walk away.

If the sea wants you . . .

# FORTY-THREE

RON FAHEY DRIVES NORTH ON I-15, careful to stay well behind Coop's Ford Bronco.

Coop is on one of his weekend hunting trips. Fahey had watched him load his guns into the car, kiss his wife and kids and head out, ostensibly toward the Dixie National Forest in southern Utah, where he has a cabin.

Fahey drives across the desert flats north of Las Vegas, past the little border town of Mesquite, then nicks the northwesternmost corner of Arizona before hitting the red rock canyons in Utah along the Virgin River.

Coop stops for gas in St. George and Fahey keeps driving, confident that he will pick him up again in Cedar City, where he'll turn off on Route 14 to head for Duck Creek Village, an appropriate enough place, Fahey figures, to hunt ducks. So Fahey pulls over near the exit to the 14, and sure enough, a few minutes later the Bronco comes by. Letting another car get in between, Fahey pulls back on the road. He knows the address of Coop's cabin, so even if he loses him he'll find him again.

Fahey's playing a long shot.

One of those Hail Mary throws you loft up in an investigation that's going nowhere.

Cammy Cooper's clean.

She actually hits balls instead of the instructor during her tennis lessons, but maybe Coop is hunting pussy instead of ducks.

Fahey doubts it (why would a guy store his mistress three hours away?), but he's desperate. The hearing on Ryan's license is just a week away, and at that hearing Cammy's going to fuck Dan Ryan six ways to Sunday. And Fahey likes Ryan.

He's a good guy, he pays good money.

Did he kill a cop?

Maybe, but it was a fed and he was dirty. So maybe he had it coming.

He follows Coop into Duck Creek Village, a tiny resort town with a couple of lodges and a number of vacation cottages. Coop drives through town, then turns north on a dirt road and drives far out into the country.

Fahey pulls over. He can see the road goes to only one cabin, on top of a low knoll that he can see through binoculars.

Coop's cabin is a modest place, a log cabin with a steeply pitched roof for the snow. Fahey watches Coop get out, off-load his bag and guns and go into the cabin.

And now we wait, Fahey thinks.

He sits there for two hours and then another car, a Land Rover, comes up the road. Pulls into the driveway and parks behind Coop's car. A man gets out and goes in. Doesn't knock, Fahey notices, so he must be a friend and an expected guest.

Looks to be about Coop's age.

Tall, well built.

Coop's hunting buddy, probably.

Fahey sits in his car and waits.

A big part of police work, waiting. Waiting on stakeouts, waiting for forensic results, waiting for warrants to be issued, waiting for trials . . . waiting now for dark, because he wants to get closer to the cabin.

He's not sure why. It's more a question of why not, because he's come all this way so he might as well check it out, even if it's just to see Coop and his buddy having a beer and a steak, turning in early to be up before dawn to slaughter some unsuspecting ducks. At least he can report the disappointing but not unexpected news that Coop is as vanilla as his wife.

So when it gets dark he grabs his camera, gets out of the car and approaches the cabin. A light is on, the blinds are open, so he makes careful approach, presses against the wall and peeks in.

What he sees is Coop, naked and on his knees in front of the sofa, going down on the other guy.

Jesus, he thinks as he snaps photos, Cammy is his beard.

He takes more pictures—Coop on all fours, Coop lying with his head in his lover's lap on the sofa, gazing into the fire.

Looks like love to me, Fahey thinks.

He gets what he needs—well, what Ryan needs—heads back to the car and drives back to Las Vegas.

# FORTY-FOUR

IT'S DIFFICULT, BRINGING THIS UP to Josh.

That the only way to get to Cammy Cooper is through her husband's gay relationship.

Danny doesn't know how Josh is going to react to that, and wouldn't blame him if he doesn't want to go there. He and Danny are sitting in Madeleine's living room. Ron Fahey just left, leaving behind a file folder of the photos.

Josh is looking at the photos.

"If you don't want us to use this," Danny says, "it ends here."

"You mean because I'm gay?" Josh asks.

"Yeah."

"So I'd have some sympathy with Coop."

"I could understand it," Danny says.

"I don't have any sympathy at all," Josh says. "If he were just a closeted gay man, okay, maybe. It's sad. But the Coopers have been aggressively vocal opponents of gay rights. The harm they do, the pain they cause . . . this is justice, karma."

"I wonder if Cammy even knows."

"If she doesn't, she should," Josh says. "She deserves to know. On the other hand, if she does, fuck her, the hypocrisy is mind-boggling."

"Still . . ."

"Still nothing," Josh says. "Danny, when you really look at it, you have no choice."

"They have kids," Danny says. "What about them?"

"You have a kid," Josh says. "What about Ian? This is his future, too. If you don't use this—"

"You will?"

"No," Josh says. "I'll respect your decision. But I wouldn't let my conscience bother me about a sanctimonious hypocrite like Cammy Cooper."


DANNY CALLS CAMMY personally. "I'd like to meet with you before the formal meeting."

"I think that would be highly inappropriate."

"You'll find that it's in your best interest."

"If you're going to offer me a bribe—"

Danny says, "No, I just want to talk about duck hunting."

Silence.

Danny knows that she knows. "Piero's? One o'clock?"

He chose the location deliberately.

So that she understands the symmetry.


CAMMY SITS DOWN.

"Would you like something?" Danny asks. "A drink?"

"Why are we here?"

Danny slides the folder across the table. "Be careful how you open that."

He watches her look at the photos. Her face flushes. She closes the folder, slides it back to him and says, "You're filth. Human garbage."

Danny doesn't say anything.

"My husband is a good man," Cammy says. "A wonderful father . . . He has needs, he's discreet, we have an understanding."

Danny's grateful for that. At least, he thinks, I didn't destroy her world out of nowhere.

"Have you thought about what this will do to my children?" Cammy asks. "It will destroy them. The other man is a father, too, he has a family—"

"So do I."

Cammy looks at him, startled, as if this never occurred to her.

"None of this has to go any further," Danny says. "Nobody's family has to get hurt."

"How is that?"

Danny says, "At the hearing, you'll lead the board to find that there's no truth in the allegations against me or my company."

Cammy doesn't hesitate. "I can do that."

"If it goes any other way—"

"It won't."

Danny gets up.

"I love him, you know," Cammy says.

Danny does feel filthy.

Not like human garbage, but still dirty.

# FORTY-FIVE

MADELEINE WALKS TO THE BAR in her suite at the Willard Hotel in Washington, DC, and pours three brandies.

One for herself, one for Evan Penner, one for Reggie Moneta.

She hands out the drinks and says, "Thank you both for coming. Let's get right to it—I want to know why my son is being persecuted."

"Because your son is a murderer," Moneta says.

"Easy, Reggie," says Penner. The former director of CIA, Penner is retired but nevertheless still a power in Washington, a sort of éminence grise with enormous influence and the power that comes from knowing where all the bodies, literal and figurative, are buried.

"No, she wants to get to it," Moneta says, "let's get to it. Ms. McKay, your son murdered an FBI agent named Phillip Jardine. But you already know this."

"I know no such thing," Madeleine says. "I know that there have been allegations and rumors. I know that he has not been prosecuted because there is no evidence."

"He hasn't been prosecuted," Moneta says, "because people like Mr. Penner here have shielded him. But you already know that, too."

"What I know," Madeleine says, "is that you have pursued, and continue to pursue, a vendetta against Danny. You have manipulated investigations against him and exacerbated the conflict between him and Vernon Wine-gard. Please don't attempt to deny it."

"I wasn't going to," Moneta says. "Why should I be the only one to play by the rules?"

"I want it to stop," Madeleine says.

"Believe it or not," Moneta says, "your wants don't drive the world. I don't care what you want. I care about justice."

"Because Jardine was your lover."

"That's irrelevant."

"Lie to yourself," Madeleine says. "Don't lie to me."

"Your *life* is a lie," Moneta says. "You slept your way into wealth and now you act like Maggie Smith in some BBC production. To me, you're nothing but a jumped-up whore from Barstow."

"That's enough," Penner says.

"No," Moneta says, "what's enough is this constant cover-up of Danny Boy Ryan. Every time he gets in trouble, he goes running to his mommy."

"Actually, he doesn't know I'm here," Madeleine says.

"*Actually*, what difference does it make?" Moneta asks. She turns to Penner. "I know that Ryan did some dirty work for you back in the day. The key phrase here is 'back in the day.' Your party isn't in power anymore, Evan. And I doubt that the current administration is going to ride to his rescue, despite what contributions Danny has made. Vern Winegard has made contributions himself."

"And you're on Winegard's side," Madeleine says.

"If someone is trying to take Danny Ryan down," Moneta says, "that's the side I'm on."

"Despite the fact that Winegard has deep connections to mobsters like Allie Licata," Madeleine says. "Your hypocrisy is mind-boggling."

Penner leans forward. It's enough to get their attention, stop the dialogue. "I have a summer house in Chilmark. I have grandchildren, *great*-grandchildren, actually. I should be there with them, on the Vineyard, instead of here with you adjudicating a dispute that should have ended years ago.

"Reggie, the facts are that there is not enough evidence to indict, much less convict, Ryan for the murder of Phillip Jardine. That is a dead letter.

"In regard to what you think you know about something that Ryan may have done for a previous administration, I assure you that is also a dead end. The current office-holders do not want to know about these things, because if they did they would have to take action, action that would be politically perilous at a time of extremely narrow congressional margins. So the down card you think that you are holding adds nothing to your actual hand."

Moneta's jaw looks like it's been wired shut.

"But in this regard you are correct—this administration will not lift a finger to help Danny Ryan in a conflict with Vern Winegard. Or for that matter, to help Winegard. It is a matter of total indifference to them. If you are, as Madeleine alleges, behind Winegard's attacks on Ryan, no one wants to know.

"But I will tell you this, Reggie," Penner says as he sets his brandy glass on the side table, "you have now taken two swings at Ryan—one through a hostile takeover, another through the gaming commission. You have missed on both. I don't know if you intend a third swing, or what it might be, but banks, corporations and hedge funds have billions of dollars invested in the gaming industry and they want peace and stability. If you do anything further to disrupt that, your head will be on the chopping block. Now I wish to speak with Madeleine alone, please."

Moneta gets up and leaves.

Madeleine looks at Penner.

Once, in their younger days, she thought him leonine—a full mane, a big jaw, his eyes bright with both humor and threat. Now he looks elderly and she wonders if he's sick.

"I'm getting old, Evan," she says.

"Not you. You're ageless."

"And you're ever the gentleman," she says. "A gallant liar. You were bluffing that horrible woman."

"I bought you some time," Penner says, "nothing more. She won't stop, you know."

Madeleine nods.

She knows.

REGGIE MONETA HITS the street.

Furious.

She's tried everything.

Everything legal.

But the law won't give her justice.

So it's time to go outside.

# FORTY-SIX

THEY MEET IN THE ENORMOUS parking lot out at the Speedway.

A little power contest at first, then Vern gets out of his car and into Licata's. "Shut the dome light off."

"Long time no see," Licata says. "What's it been? Fifteen years?"

"You get your money," Vern says.

"Don't be so defensive. I'm just saying."

Vern's in no mood. "Why are we here?"

"I understand you have problems," Licata says. "I'm here to help."

"I don't need your help."

"Well, you keep losing to Danny Ryan," Licata says. "It's embarrassing. And expensive. When you lose points, I lose money."

"I've made you more goddamn money—"

"You know what's better than more money?" Licata asks. "*More* money. I'm not here to bust balls, I'm here to help. You have a Danny Ryan problem. I can make that problem go away."

"How?"

"I gotta spell it out for you?"

"No," Vern says. "Absolutely not. Buying your linens and shit is one thing, giving you a couple of points . . . but murder? No. *No.* Don't you even *think* about it, Allie."

"You telling me you haven't thought about it?"

"That's right," Vern says. "I'm getting out of the car now."

Licata leans across him and holds the door shut. "Ryan is connected with Pasco Ferri. You really believe they won't do you if they think it's necessary?"

"I'm taking measures."

"Fuck your measures," Licata says. "You're outgunned. I can have a crew out here *tomorrow*. And I promise you, I can get Chicago, Detroit and L.A. lined up behind you."

"I don't want them behind me," Vern says.

"Careful what you say, now."

"Are you threatening me?"

"I'm protecting you."

Vern gets out, then leans back through the door. "You leave Ryan alone, or my hand to God, I'll—"

"You'll what?"

"Just do what I say."

Licata throws his hands up, like, sure, whatever.


LICATA CALLS A service and is glad it's still in operation. They send a special girl and it *costs*.

A lot more.

"They tell you what we're doing here?" Licata asks.

She nods.

"Take your clothes off and bend over the bed."

When she does, he slides the belt out of its loops.

Just the sound gets him hard.

# FORTY-SEVEN

**D**ANNY RINGS EDEN'S DOORBELL.

"A rare nocturnal appearance," she says, surprised, a little concerned.

"Ian has a sleepover at a friend's."

Eden can tell something's wrong. She waves him in. "You could have used your key."

"I didn't want to scare you," Danny says.

"You want a drink?" Eden asks.

The bar is stocked with his favorites—Samuel Adams beer, Johnnie Walker Black, Coke, and lately, Diet Coke. "Scotch if you're joining me. Otherwise, a stinking Diet Coke."

"I could go for a whiskey." She pours two glasses and hands him one.

"Slainte."

"Slainte," Eden says. "So?"

"So?"

"What's going on?" she asks. "You're the world's most polite, most scheduled man. You don't just show up. Not at night, not without calling first."

"I did something terrible."

"And you're coming to confess?" Eden asks.

Once an Irish Catholic boy, always an Irish Catholic boy, she thinks. Although Dan has joked about it—"I come from a town where guys go to confession and take the Fifth. 'Forgive me, Father, for I have sinned. And I believe you know my attorney, Mr. O'Neill?'"

"Sort of, I guess," Danny says.

Her phone rings. She looks at the caller ID and says, "Hold that thought."

She goes into the bedroom. Danny turns on the television and finds a Red Sox game.

Eden comes out a few minutes later and looks shaken.

"What is it?" Danny asks.

"One of my patients," she says. "A sex worker. She had a 'special' tonight. The guy got out of hand and beat the hell out of her. She's in the emergency room."

"Christ."

"She was at the Shores, Dan."

"At one of *my* hotels?"

"Room 234B," she says. "Dan, I'm sorry, I know you wanted to talk, but I should—"

"No, it can wait," Danny says. "Go to her."

Eden leaves.

Danny's at the Shores in ten minutes, standing with the night security director, looking at videotape.

"The guy already checked out," the security director said. "A Bob Harris. I logged back to when he checked in . . . here it is . . ."

"That's him?" Danny asks, looking at a sixtyish guy. Average height, average weight, sunglasses. "Run his card, find out about him. He's banned for life from any of our properties. He doesn't stay, he doesn't play."

Then Danny goes to the hospital.

The doctors admitted Eden's patient, a young woman named Su Lin. She looks bad—her face bruised, one eye swollen shut. Eden tells Danny that the girl has two cracked ribs and multiple lacerations, welts on her back and buttocks.

She'd been whipped with a belt.

And yet now she's swearing that she fell down the stairs.

"I can't arrest this guy if she won't file charges," Fahey says. He came to the hospital when Danny called.

"She's afraid," Eden says.

"Who sent her on the call?" Fahey asks.

Eden hesitates. "That's client privilege."

"You want to tell that to the next girl?" Danny asks. "Because there will be a next one."

Eden looks at Fahey. "You said you couldn't do anything."

"I said I couldn't arrest the guy."

"What does that mean?" Eden asks. "What are you thinking about doing, Danny?"

"Who sent her?"

"She's talked about a woman named Monica."

"Monica Sayer," Fahey says.

DANNY AND FAHEY go to Sayer's penthouse condo. One look around the place, Danny thinks, and you know the high-price call-girl trade in Las Vegas is lucrative and that Monica Sayer has made a good dollar on other women's backs.

"To what do I owe this nice surprise?" Monica asks.

Danny says, "You sent one of your girls out on a 'special' tonight."

Sayer tilts her head, like, *So?*

"He beat her up," Danny says. "Put her in the hospital."

"Su Lin is a professional submissive," Sayer says. "She knew the risks. Shall we call it an occupational hazard?"

"I have an occupational hazard for you," Danny says. "You send another girl, you send *any* girl out to get beaten—I'll make you persona non grata in every hotel on the Strip. You call to reserve a table, the restaurant will be booked; you want a ticket to a show, it's sold out; you go to any social event in the city, everyone turns their backs."

"Because you're the all-powerful Dan Ryan?" Sayer asks. "I'm not without connections myself, Mr. Ryan."

Danny looks to Fahey.

"I'm a lieutenant in the Criminal Intelligence Section," Fahey says. "Do you know what that means?"

"Why don't you enlighten me?"

"It means I have swag," Fahey says. "You drive twenty-six in a twenty-five-mile zone, we'll pull you over. You spit on the sidewalk, we'll haul you in."

"That's harassment," Monica says.

"No, that's just annoyance," Fahey says. "*This* is the harassment—I'll find out who your girls are. Every one of them. And then I'll bust them and bust them and bust them until they speak your name. And then I'll arrest *you*—pandering, sex trafficking, I'll bring the feds in for income tax evasion. When you get out of prison, it'll be on a walker."

"Do we have an understanding?" Danny asks her.

They have an understanding.


"WHAT DID YOU do?" Eden asks.

They're sitting in the living room of her condo.

"What do you mean?"

"About this Monica person."

"We talked to her."

"Just talked?"

Danny glares at her. "Don't let your imagination run away with you. Jesus, Eden, what do you think? She's in a hole out in the desert somewhere? We *talked* to her."

"You threatened her."

"With legal consequences," Danny says.

"Okay."

"Okay?" Danny says. "Big of you."

"I'm sorry," she says. "Maybe I'm afraid I'm being dragged into your world."

"No more than it's your world," Danny says. "She's *your* patient."

"She got hurt at *your* hotel."

"Which is why I did something about it," Danny says. "Did you want me to do nothing?"

"I don't know," she says. "I guess I was scared about what you'd do."

"Because I'm Danny Ryan the gangster," he says.

"That's unfair."

"*That's* unfair?" Danny asks. "Tell me you're not a little relieved, a little grateful, maybe even a little excited that I took care of this."

"You're right," Eden says. "I'm conflicted."

"Save the therapy speak for your patients."

"Now you're angry."

"Damn right I'm angry," Danny says. "You asked me to help you—"

"Actually I didn't—"

"—and I did, and now you're accusing me of God knows what."

"I'm not accusing you of anything," Eden says. "I'm only saying that I'm starting to ask myself if our two . . . very different lives . . . can mesh."

Danny gets up. "I've taken care of the girl's medical bills. You can blame me for that, too."

"Dan—"

"Let me know what you decide," Danny says, "about our very different lives."

He closes the door quietly behind him.

# FORTY-EIGHT

DANNY MEETS FAHEY AT A Subway off the Strip.

"What did you find out?" Danny asks.

"We matched your security footage to the time that Harris checked in," Fahey said, "and got a facial image. I ran it against known sexual assault offenders."

"And?"

"Nothing," Fahey says. "But then I played a hunch and ran it against the wiseguy files. It's not good news."

"Hit me."

"He's an old Detroit wiseguy," Fahey says. "Allie Licata. He used to own a piece of Winegard's first hotel and is a silent partner in the company that does the Winegard linen supplies, but we can't find any direct contact between them."

"Okay."

"Licata's been spotted in town. So have a couple of his crew, including his son, Charles, aka Chucky. I'm guessing the apple doesn't fall far from the tree."

"What are they doing here?"

"I don't know," Fahey says, "but I doubt it's a bachelor party. Be careful, Dan. In a world of sick fucks, even the sick fucks think Licata's a sick fuck."

"Keep me informed, huh?"

Licata was hooked up with Winegard, Danny thinks.

I fight off Winegard's takeover.

Then Licata shows up.

How far is Vern going to take this?


NED EGAN IS frying bacon when Danny knocks on his door.

Every morning, seven days a week, Danny thinks, Ned Egan makes bacon and eggs. Christ, the place *smells* like a coronary. Danny turns down the offer of breakfast but sits at the little kitchen table. "You ever hear of a guy out of Detroit named Allie Licata?"

"I met him once with your father," Ned says.

"And?"

"Your father didn't like him," Ned says. "Didn't want anything to do with him."

That would be it for Ned, Danny thinks. If Marty Ryan didn't like someone, Ned didn't like him either. "He's in town. With a crew."

"I'll take care of it," Ned says.

"No," Danny says. "I just want you to keep an extra-close eye on Madeleine and Ian."

Danny leaves, drives to a phone booth, and gets Pasco on the horn. A phone booth, Danny thinks. Christ, it's like the old days.

"Licata's a piece of work," Pasco says. "He's bad business. The kid, Chucky? All his father's meanness with none of his brains."

"You think it's just Licata or is Detroit backing him?" Danny asks.

"Licata won't take a dump that Detroit doesn't okay," Pasco says. "You got Detroit, maybe Chicago, too. This Winegard has heavy artillery coming at you."

"No, he's not that guy," Danny says.

"You want that carved on your headstone?" Pasco asks. "Wise up, buddy boy. Take precautions."

Yeah, Danny thinks.

I will.

SEAN SOUTH SETS the phone down, looks over at Kevin Coombs and asks, "You know who that was?"

"A Nigerian prince? Owns a gold mine?"

"Danny."

"No shit."

"No shit."

No shit, no shit. They've been exiled to Reno since Kevin's drunken faux pas at Ian's party. Sean's been running his business mostly from there, and Kevin . . .

Kevin did a stint in rehab and now he hits AA meetings, sometimes two or three a day.

Amazingly, he's stayed sober.

And become a spurting fountain of bromides: "one day at a time"; "let go and let God"; "it's not the last drink that gets you drunk, it's the first." If Kevin says, "Don't drink, go to meetings" one more time, Sean might shoot him in the face.

Kevin had a little stumble over Step 5: "Admitted to God, to ourselves, and to another human being the exact nature of our wrongs."

"The *exact* nature of your wrongs?" Sean asked. "That could be problematic."

Seeing as how the exact nature of those wrongs included multiple homicides and armed robberies, the kind of things that it's unwise to admit in even a less-than-exact nature.

"You can tell God," Sean said, "you can tell yourself, but another human being? Like who, a D.A.?"

"I could tell *you*," Kevin said.

"But I already know."

"Good point."

So Kevin decided to skip that step. Likewise the ones about making a list of all the people he'd harmed and then making amends.

"You're not making any list, Kev," Sean said. "That's called evidence."

As far as making amends, Sean pointed out that in a number of cases making amends was impossible, as the harm Kevin had done was terminal, and as far as the ones who are still alive, they'd probably respond to such a gracious overture by killing *him*.

Kevin found a loophole, though. You were supposed to make amends "except when to do so would harm them or others."

"I guess I could be considered an other," Kevin said.

"Absolutely."

"I should apologize to Danny, though," Kevin said, "for wrecking Ian's party."

"I'd let that lie, I were you."

"What does Danny want?" Kevin asks.

"He wants us to come back," Sean says.

"They have Alcoholics Anonymous in Vegas, right?" Kevin asks.

They have *everything* anonymous in Vegas, Sean thinks.

JIMMY MAC GETS the call.

Sitting in the office of his car dealership in Mira Mesa, he hears Danny ask, "You want to open a dealership in the new hotel?"

"Maybe," Jimmy says.

"I need you here," Danny says.

# FORTY-NINE

CONNELLY BRIEFS VERN. "OUR GUY in Metro says Ryan has brought his old crew back. Jimmy MacNeese, Sean South, Kevin Coombs . . ."

Vern remembers the drunk who ran his mouth at Ryan's party. His name was Kevin.

"I told you he was a thug," Connelly says. "It was just a matter of time."

Ryan didn't bring his crew in for a class reunion, Connelly tells him. He brought them in for a reason—intimidate or even murder potential board witnesses, maybe go after Jay Cooper.

"*You* could even be the target, boss," Connelly says.

"You watch too many movies," Vern says.

"It's not a movie," Connelly says. "They're really here."

"I'll beef up security."

"That's all well and good," Connelly says. "But security isn't going to do it. You have to think about getting proactive here."

He waits for a second, then says, "Metro also says that Allie Licata is in town."

"So?" It makes Vern feel sick. It's all getting out of hand, he thinks. We threaten Ryan with his Ferri connection, what happens if he connects me to Licata?

Mutually assured destruction.

We take each other down, hands on each other's throats while throwing ourselves off a cliff.

Connelly's aware of this dynamic, too. He doesn't give a shit—Reggie Moneta wants Ryan taken down. If that means Vern goes down the drain, it's too bad, but that's the way it is. "Come on, you and Licata have an old relationship. Has he reached out to you? It might not be the worst idea in the world to reach back."

"We're not going to do that," Vern says. "You said yourself we're trying to keep the mob out, not invite them back in."

"Fire with fire. I'm just saying."

"Don't," Vern says. He doesn't tell Connelly that he already said no to Licata—absolutely no violence against Dan Ryan or anyone else. Except now Ryan's brought in a crew.

For what?

I told the mob no—did Ryan say yes?

This has to end, Vern thinks.


DANNY LOOKS AT his people.

"We do *not* make the first move," he says. "Hopefully, Licata's presence is just a coincidence."

"You don't really believe that," Sean says. "If Licata is as bad as everyone says, we should hit him first."

"A preemptive strike," Kevin says.

"No," Danny says.

"What?" Kevin asks. "We're going to wait for him to whack you and then get revenge? Fuck that."

"Settle down," Jimmy Mac says.

Danny's phone rings.

He glances at it. It's Winegard. Danny holds his hand up for quiet and puts the phone on speaker. "Vern."

"We need to talk."

"I agree."

"No lawyers, no boards," Vern says. "Just you and me."

"I'm all for it."

"Tomorrow morning?" Vern says. "Someplace quiet, away from eyes and ears. I don't want to read about it in *Casino Executive*."

"Where do you have in mind?"

"The parking lot at Desert Pines?" Vern says. "I know you're an early riser. Six thirty?"

"See you there and then."

He clicks off.

"It's a hit," Kevin says. "A setup."

"I have to agree," Jimmy says.

"Licata could have a shooter anywhere," Sean says. "The second you step out of the car, maybe even before."

"No, I think he really wants to talk," Danny says. "This could be peace."

"Serenity," Kevin says.

Sean wants to shoot him.

"You can't go to this meeting," Jimmy says.

If Vern wants to talk face-to-face, Danny thinks, maybe we can end this thing, come to some sort of arrangement.

It's well worth the risk.

"I'm going," he says.

Jimmy Mac turns to the others. "Okay, we go there now, check it out. Fire angles, sniper positions. In the morning, we'll be there and ready."

"He said alone," Danny says.

"You think *he'll* be alone?" Jimmy asks. "Don't be crazy, Danny. We'll be invisible, no one will see us."

"All right," Danny says. "But no one gets trigger-happy, no one shoots first."

"Danny—"

"Did you hear what I just said?"

"We heard," Jimmy says.

He don't like it, though.

NEITHER DOES JIM Connelly.

"You can't go by yourself," he says. "What if he brings his crew?"

"This was my idea," Vern says.

"Which he might see as an opportunity," Connelly says.

"This shit has gone far enough," Vern says. "I'm meeting with Ryan, I'm going alone, like I said I would."

Connelly knows better than to try to argue with him. Once Vern has made up his mind, that's it.

But he can't let him walk into what could very well turn into a trap.

"WHY A GOLF course, before the sun comes up?" Madeleine asks. "You could just as easily talk over the phone."

"It's not the same."

"You're walking into an ambush."

"I don't think so," Danny says. "Say what you want about Winegard, he's not a killer."

"You don't know what he's capable of."

"I can have an army down here tonight," Josh says. "Former Mossad people—"

"No."

"Why not?"

"Because I don't want a freakin' war," Danny says.

"These people are the best," Josh says. "They'll make an accurate threat assessment and act accordingly."

"I have my own people."

"No offense," Josh says. "But they're not as good."

"I know them and I trust them."

"I'm going with you," Josh says.

"The hell you are," Danny says. "I promised your grandfather I'd take care of you, not expose you to risk."

"So you *do* think there's a risk," Josh says.

"There's always a risk," Danny says. "There's a risk driving to the office in the morning."

"Oh, please," Madeleine says.

"This is a chance," Danny says, "to make peace with Winegard. I'm not going to throw away that opportunity. Now does anyone mind if I spend a little time with my son?"

He finds Ian in his room playing video games. "You want to go out and shoot a few hoops?"

"Sure," Ian says. "But you kind of suck."

"Should be easy to beat me, then."

They go outside to the court Madeleine had built and play some one-on-one.

"We should do another bike trip soon," Danny says.

"We should."

Danny tries a hook shot. "Kareem Abdul-Jabbar!"

"Who?"

"Oh, my god."

"You played in high school, right?" Ian asks.

"I did."

"Were you any good?"

"I was a little less terrible than I am now."

"So pretty bad." Ian laughs. He does a crossover dribble, steps around Danny and makes a layup. "That's how it's done."

"Do I give you an allowance?" Danny asks. "And why?"

They play for a little while and then Danny says it's time for a shower and then bed. "School night. I won't see you in the morning. I have an early meeting."

"Okay."

"Dinner, though."

"Could we do takeout?" Ian asks. "Like Popeyes?"

"It's okay with me," Danny says. "But ask your grandmother."

They go into the house and Danny hugs him good night. "Love you, kid."

"Love *you*."

Maybe there is a God, Danny thinks.

He showers and gets into bed.

Morning will come early.

# FIFTY

HIS WIFE'S SCREAMS ARE LIKE nothing Vern has ever heard.
They seem to rip out her throat.

He runs down the stairs, almost falling, to find her in the kitchen still screaming, the phone on the floor.

Her eyes bulge, a vein throbs in her forehead.

The screams tear at his ears. He grabs her by the shoulders. "What is it? Dawn, what is it?!"

"It's Bryce, it's Bryce."

She collapses.

Slips from his hands like dust.

# FIFTY-ONE

DANNY PULLS INTO THE PARKING lot just as the sun is coming up.

He almost laughs—isn't this the time of day when they used to fight duels? Maybe Vern has a flair for the dramatic after all.

But no one is there. Danny's is the only car.

Good as his word, Jimmy and the crew—if they're here, Danny thinks—are invisible.

Danny parks, turns off the engine and waits.

Six twenty-five.

Six thirty.

Nothing.

It's unlike Vern, who's famous for being punctual, if not early, for all his meetings.

Six thirty-five.

Something's wrong.

Danny starts to feel paranoid, starts to imagine the crosshairs on the back of his skull, on his forehead. Feels the creeping fear—or is it instinct, good sense?—come over him. He slides down in the seat, opens the glove compartment and takes out the Sig Sauer 380.

Maybe Jimmy was right.

Maybe all of them were right.

This was a setup.

The best thing I can do, he thinks, is hit the gas and race out of here.

But it's hard to sit up to get behind the wheel. Hard to make that move that could mean meeting a bullet square on. If there is a shooter, maybe Kevin or Jimmy or Sean has a bead on him, will take him out before he can squeeze the trigger.

But maybe not.

Suck it up, Danny tells himself. Do what you need to do.

The phone rings.

Danny grabs it. "Yeah?"

"Sorry to wake you," Fahey says, "but I thought you should know right away."

It's Bryce Winegard.

Vern's kid.

He's in the ICU at Sunrise on life support.

# FIFTY-TWO

DANNY HATES HOSPITALS.

He's spent too much time in them. Weeks when he was recuperating from getting shot, more weeks in rehab.

Months when his wife was dying.

But he goes to Sunrise, because it seems like the right thing to do. Madeleine comes with him, because "Dawn will need another woman there, another mother."

It's a horror show.

When they get up to the ICU floor, Dawn is sobbing and pounding on Vern's chest. "No! No! *NOOOO!!!*"

Madeleine steps in, takes Dawn and holds her tight against her chest.

"Jesus, Vern," Danny says. "What happened?"

"He went into the garage," Vern says. "Took the Maserati out for a joy ride. Lost it on a curve and rolled it in a ditch."

"My God."

"He's brain dead," Vern says. "They're just keeping him alive on the machines. I have to decide . . ."

His face is twisted with grief.

Anguish.

". . . whether to pull . . ." He drops his face into his hands. "They say he'll be a vegetable. There's no brain activity. For all intents and purposes, he's already gone."

Dawn wrenches herself free and launches at Vern. "You're not going to kill my son! You're not going to kill my *baby*!"

He grabs her wrist to keep her long nails from his face. "Dawn. Dawn. Dawn."

*"Don't kill him! Please!"*

Vern wrestles her into a chair. A nurse comes with a syringe. Madeleine sits beside her, touches her arm, but doesn't say anything.

There are no words.

Danny says, "If there's anything I can do . . ."

"Just leave. Get out."

"Vern—"

"*Your* boy is alive."

Madeleine gets up, takes Danny by the arm and walks him out.

"It was a mistake to come," Danny says.

"No, it was the right thing to do," Madeleine says. "Let's go home. I need to hug Ian."

So does Danny.

But he feels bad.

That he's grateful.

That it was somebody else's child and not his.

# FIFTY-THREE

"THEY WERE THERE!" KEVIN SAYS. "At the freakin' golf course!"

Jimmy Mac nods his agreement.

"I didn't see anyone," Danny says.

"We made them in two cars on the street," Sean says.

"How do you know they were Licata's guys?" Danny asks.

Sean lays photos out on the table. They're grainy through the telephoto lens, but Danny can make out faces, and they sure as shit look like wiseguys. He'll run the photos past Fahey later, see if they match with any ISC pictures.

"Who else do you think is out there before dawn, parked along the street?" Jimmy asks. "You gotta face facts here—Winegard set you up for a hit."

"Then why didn't they shoot?" Danny asks. "Why didn't they move in?"

"Maybe they didn't have a good angle," Jimmy says. "Maybe they didn't have the shot. Maybe they were waiting for an order and it didn't come. What freakin' difference does it make? Are you going to wait for the next time, when they *do* have a shot?"

"We need to move now," Kevin says. "Track them down and take them off the count."

Danny says, "That's always your answer."

"Because it always *is* the answer," Kevin says.

"Danny," Jimmy says, "I know how bad you wanna be legit. I know you want all this mob shit to be in the past. But it isn't. It's right here, right now, and you gotta deal with it."

He's right, Danny thinks.

If we let Licata run over us, we lose everything. But if we're involved in a gang war in Las Vegas, even if we win, we lose everything.

"We double down on our security," Danny says. "Find these guys, keep our eyes on them. But we do not make the first move. Under no circumstances do we fire the first shot."

"It's a mistake," Kevin says.

"If you can't live with it, leave," Danny says. "If you stay, you do what I tell you."

"I'm staying," Kevin says.

# FIFTY-FOUR

VERN HAS HEARD IT MANY times.

No man should have to bury his own child.

But until this moment, standing at the grave site, watching them get ready to shovel dirt on his son, he had no idea what it really meant.

Had no idea what pain was.

Now he knows.

Beside him, Dawn is catatonic on pills. He doubts that she's ever coming back.

I'm not, either, he thinks.

Vern refused the medication because it somehow felt disloyal to Bryce not to feel the pain. Now he *breathes* pain, breathes it in but doesn't breathe it out. It swirls in and around him, like an invisible chain that makes it hard to move his arms and legs, makes it hard to think. It's like walking underwater, like he's at the bottom of a pool, looking up at the rest of the world.

He's aware that the funeral was packed and that most of the mourners have also come to Eden Vale cemetery. Knows that the "anyone who's anyone" crowd is here—some out of genuine sympathy, others from respect, others from fear of not attending the funeral of the powerful Vern Winegard's son.

Vern doesn't give a shit.

Not about anything.

Not about who's there or who's not, not even that he spotted Dan Ryan standing at the back of the crowd.

Dan Ryan.

Connelly had been yapping about him just that morning as they were getting ready to go to the church.

"His crew was out there," Connelly said. "It was an ambush."

"You bring this to me on the morning of my son's funeral?" Vern asked.

"It can't wait, Vern." Like he's standing at the edge of the pool, talking to him through the water. His voice is dull, muted, distorted. "It can't wait."

"It can wait."

"We need to act."

"Do what you want," Vern said. "Do what you think you need to do."

Vern didn't give a shit.

They're tossing dirt on his son.

His wife wails.

No man should have to bury his own child.

BLACK CARS LINE up like crows on a telephone line.

Dan watches Vern shuffle to the waiting limousine. He wonders if he's tranquilized. I would be, Danny thinks.

If I hadn't swallowed a gun already.

His mother didn't want him to go to the funeral. "He tried to kill you."

"We don't know that."

"Maybe *you* don't," Madeleine said. "In any case, he'll misinterpret your presence. He'll think you're gloating."

"That's ridiculous."

"Is it?" Madeleine asked. "*I'm* glad Bryce was killed."

"That's a terrible thing to say."

"I'm glad," Madeleine said, "because if the accident hadn't happened, Winegard would have gone to your meeting, and you'd have been assassinated when you stepped out of the car. And your son would be without his father."

"Again—"

"I know it," Madeleine says. "I know this world in ways that you don't."

Maybe, Danny thought.

He'd taken the photos to Fahey and gotten confirmation that they were from Licata's Detroit crew. His son Chucky and three others, all hitters.

Now he watches Vern help Dawn into the limo.

Was he going to have me killed? Danny wonders.

Is he still?

Or does the death of a child change your thinking, make you realize what's important in this world? Maybe it goes the other way, though. Maybe it makes a man angry, makes him hate, makes him willing to do anything.


DANNY TAKES JIMMY Mac aside and tells him to leave.

"You have a family in San Diego," Danny says. "You have your business, a life. It wasn't fair to get you involved with this."

"We've been friends since, what, kindergarten?" Jimmy says. "My business, every material thing I have in this world, I owe to our friendship. I ain't goin' nowhere, Danny."

It's old-school, Danny knows.

It's Irish, it's New England.

It's Providence.

# PART THREE

# The Rules
# of Justice

## Providence, RI
## 1998

. . . you know the rules of justice, know them well.

Now learn compassion, too.

Aeschylus
*The Eumenides*

# FIFTY-FIVE

**H**EATHER MORETTI IS DEFIANT ON the stand.

Marie takes her through all the foundational stuff, that she met her brother, Peter Jr., at the cemetery the day of the murders, visiting their father's grave; that she then met him and Timothy Shea at a bar for drinks; that Shea left and that she had a subsequent conversation with her brother.

"Did you discuss your father's murder?" Marie asks.

"Yes."

"Did you give your brother an opinion as to who might have killed your father?"

"I told him I thought Vinnie Calfo had done it."

"And on what did you base this opinion?"

Heather almost sneers. "Common knowledge."

"What does *that* mean?" Marie asks.

"Come on," Heather says. "Can we get real here? You know what I'm talking about."

"Edify me."

"The way we grew up," Heather says. "The people we grew up around. Everyone in Rhode Island knows what I'm talking about. And all those people talk. Blah blah blah, they can't help themselves. So, yes, I heard it whispered, I don't know how many times, that Vinnie killed my dad. That girl, too. Cassandra Murphy."

"And you shared this opinion with your brother."

"Like I said."

"Is that a yes?" Marie asks.

"Yes, that's a yes."

"Did you also express your thoughts about your mother's involvement in your father's murder?"

"I think I said that she practically pushed Vinnie through the door."

"And on what do you base that?"

"She as much as told me," Heather said. "Drunk one night."

"What night would that have been?"

"I don't know," Heather said. "There were a lot to choose from."

"What exactly did she tell you?"

"That she blamed my father for my sister's suicide."

Marie asks a question lawyers rarely ask of a hostile witness. "Why?"

"She said that she begged him to send her to a mental facility and that he refused," Heather said.

"Was that because he didn't want to spend the money?"

"That's what she said."

"What else did your mother say?"

"That she didn't know if Vinnie killed my father," Heather says, "but that she gave her okay for it."

"And you expressed this to your brother also."

"I did."

"Did you tell him anything else?"

"I wasn't sure he believed me, so I told him to go talk to Pasco Ferri," Heather says.

"Why?"

"Because Pasco knows everything."

"Did you encourage your brother to kill Vincent Calfo and Celia Moretti?" Marie asks.

"No."

"Did you hear from your brother at a later date?"

"Yes."

"What did he tell you?"

"That he didn't know what happened," Heather says. "That he didn't know what to do. He wanted me to come pick him up."

"Did you?"

"No."

"No further questions."

Bruce Bascombe gets up. "It's your belief that Vincent Calfo and Celia Moretti were responsible for your father's murder, is that right?"

"It is."

"But you never went to the police with that information, did you?"

Heather smirks. "No."

"What's funny?" Bruce asks.

"I'm a Moretti."

"You testified that you didn't encourage your brother to kill Vincent or Celia, is that correct?"

"Yes."

"Did he tell you he was going to kill them?"

"No."

"Did he tell you that he *wanted* to kill them?"

"No."

"So Peter Jr. did not tell you that he wanted to kill either Vinnie Calfo or Celia Moretti."

"No, he didn't."

"Was there any discussion about killing *anyone*?"

"No."

"You testified that you spoke with Peter after the killings, is that correct?" Bruce asks.

"On the phone, yes," Heather says. "He called me."

"And he said that he 'didn't know what happened, and that 'he didn't know what to do,'" Bruce says. "Did he say anything else?"

"Yes."

"What was that?"

"'She came at me,'" Heather says.

"I'm sorry, I didn't quite hear."

"'She came at me.'"

Bruce looks at the jury. "No further questions."

That little bitch set me up, Marie thinks.

# FIFTY-SIX

THE JURY VIRTUALLY HUMS WITH anticipation when Marie calls Pasco Ferri to the stand.

The old mob boss might be the most famous guy in New England who doesn't play for the Red Sox or the Patriots.

Marie's disgusted with it, the deference Ferri has been shown by the cops, the guards, even the judge, like he's some distinguished elder statesman or community father instead of the vicious killer he is.

It makes her want to puke. But she plays nice. "What is your relationship to the defendant?"

"I'm his godfather." It gets a soft titter from the courtroom. Even Pasco breaks a small smile.

"So when he refers to you as Uncle Pasco, you're not really his uncle."

"It's an Italian thing."

"Did he come to see you on the day of the killings?" Marie asks.

"Twice," Pasco says.

"Let's talk about the first time," Marie says. "What did he talk about?"

"He asked if I knew anything about his father's murder," Pasco says.

"Did you?"

"Only the rumors everyone else heard," Pasco says.

"Which were what?"

"That Vinnie Calfo did it," Pasco says.

"Did you believe that?"

Pasco shrugs. "I thought it was within the realm of possibility."

"Did Peter say where he had heard this rumor?"

"From his sister," Pasco says.

"Heather Moretti."

"That's what he said."

"What else did you and Peter talk about?" Marie asks.

"He asked if I thought his mother was involved in his father's murder."

"What did you tell him?"

"That his parents had a complicated relationship," Pasco says. "A troubled marriage."

"To your knowledge," Marie says, "did Celia Moretti blame her husband for their daughter's suicide?"

"I don't know anything about that."

"Why else would she want him killed?"

"I don't know," Pasco says. "I only know that Peter Junior suspected she did."

"What else did Peter talk about?"

"He asked me what I thought he should do," Pasco says.

"What did you tell him?"

"I told him to let it be," Pasco says. "Not to do anything stupid."

"Did you encourage him to get revenge?"

"No."

Marie lets that hang for a few seconds, and then asks, "Did Peter come see you again?"

"Yes," Pasco says. "It was about one o'clock the next morning."

"What did he tell you?"

"He asked for my help."

"To do what?"

"I don't know," Pasco says, "because I refused to help him."

"Did you know what had happened?" Marie asks.

"Yes."

"How?"

"A cop called and told me," Pasco says.

"Why would a police officer call you?"

"If a wiseguy is killed anywhere in New England," Pasco says, "I might not be the first person the police call, but I'll be high on the list."

Marie lets it go.

"So you knew that Mr. Moretti had killed his stepfather and mother," Marie says.

"Objection."

"Sustained."

"When Peter arrived at your house," Marie says, "you had already been told that Peter had allegedly killed his stepfather and mother. Is that right?"

"That's right."

"How would you describe his emotional state?"

"He was very upset," Pasco says. "Crying. He asked me what he should do."

"What did you tell him?"

"To turn himself in."

"What happened next?" Marie asks.

"I threw him out of the house," Pasco says.

"Did he go willingly?"

"Yes."

Another small laugh. Everyone knows that if Pasco Ferri asks you to leave, you're going to leave.

"No further questions."

Bruce gets up. "Mr. Ferri, at any time prior to the murder, did Peter tell you he was intending to kill Vincent Calfo or Celia Moretti?"

"No."

"At any time *after* the murder," Bruce says, "did Peter tell you that he *had* killed Vincent Calfo or Celia Moretti?"

"No."

"So all you know," Bruce says, "is that someone in law enforcement told you that he had."

"Right."

"And you based your treatment of him on that," Bruce says. "Is that correct?"

"That's correct."

"So you don't know to this day what he was asking your help *for*, do you?" Bruce asks.

"I don't."

"Thank you."

"Redirect?" Faella asks Marie.

"You bet." Marie stands up. "Isn't it true that Peter Moretti Jr. came to you—not as his uncle, not as his godfather, but as *the* godfather—to get your permission to kill Vincent Calfo?"

"Objection!"

"Overruled."

"No, that's not true," Pasco says.

"But that's the way it works, isn't it?" Marie asks.

"Objection!"

"Overruled."

"I don't know anything about any of that."

Marie asks, "And isn't it true that you gave that permission?"

Pasco's eyes start to get angry. "No."

"And isn't it true," Marie says, "that after Peter Moretti Jr. did kill Vinnie Calfo, that he came to you to help him get away?"

Pasco looks murder at her. "Not true."

"And that you threw him out because he got carried away and murdered his own mother?" Marie asks.

"I was disgusted when I heard that."

"Because you thought it was true?" Marie asks. "Because you knew that he was going there intent on murder?"

"Because the cops told me that's what he did."

"You didn't call Calfo to warn him, did you?" Marie asks.

"No."

"You didn't call Celia, either, did you?"

"No."

"The police?" Marie asks. "Did you call the police to inform them of the potential threat?"

"No."

"You didn't do anything, did you?" Marie asks. "You didn't lift a finger to stop it. Sit down, Bruce, I withdraw the question. That's all. Mr. Ferri can be escorted from the courtroom with due deference."

So much for being governor, she thinks.

But it scored, she saw it on the jurors' faces.

Maybe Pasco Ferri doesn't know anything about how it works, but people in Rhode Island know *exactly* how it works.

# FIFTY-SEVEN

IT'S FOGGY IN RHODE ISLAND.

The gray, soup-like fog is common on the coast, but it's something that Chris Palumbo hasn't experienced in years, and so thick that he can't see past the little patio outside his motel room.

The room is nice but basic. A bed, a bathroom with a shower, a sofa, a table, a coffee maker with cellophane pouches of sugar, creamer and a stir stick. A television with basic cable.

The location of the Pig and Whistle (the owner had the conceit of an old New England tavern, even though the motel is a series of mid-century guest cabins stitched together) works for Chris, off the highway in a small town on the south shore. Out of the way, inconspicuous except for the name.

Chris isn't quite ready to announce his return to Rhode Island.

It's going to be tricky.

Peter and Vinnie are dead, Paulie's down in Florida, but there are still guys who remember what Chris did and would gladly kill him for it. *After they squeeze every penny out of me first, though,* he thinks as he opens the side-table drawer and puts his 9mm Glock in.

*It's their greed that just might keep me alive.*

*Long enough.*

He thinks about calling Cathy but chickens out. His wife is going to be angry, and Cathy's anger is something you don't mess with. And he doesn't know what she's been up to the past few years—she could have someone, she could even be remarried.

Better to find out first.

Suddenly tired from the long drive, he falls into bed and sleeps the sleep of the dead.

It's sunny when he wakes up, and now he can see the view of the salt pond that leads out to the ocean. Two large willow trees stand on the long, well-tended lawn that slopes down to the water. A small motorboat bobs at a wooden dock; a teenage kid in a ball cap stands in the boat, wiping it down with a rag.

Chris makes a cup of the terrible coffee and walks down to the dock.

Now he sees it isn't a boy cleaning the boat, but a girl.

Eighteen? Nineteen? A face so pure and innocent you can't believe a bad thought ever went through her head.

"Good morning," she says.

"Beautiful morning."

"Are you a guest at the motel?"

"Yeah," Chris says. "I'm from New York."

"What brings you here?"

"I heard about Rhode Island," Chris says. "Thought I'd check it out."

"Do you like it?" she asks.

"So far."

She stops wiping the boat and looks at him. "May I ask you something?"

"Shoot."

"Have you found Jesus?"

Chris is about to give some smart-ass answer like "Is he missing?" but the girl looks so sincere he doesn't have the heart. "I grew up Catholic."

"I mean the real Jesus," she says. "In the Bible. I'm a Jehovah's Witness."

Again, Chris almost answers with some crack about being in the Jehovah's Witness Protection Program, but he doesn't. "How's that working out?"

"I know where I'm going to spend eternity."

Yeah, the DMV, Chris thinks, like everyone else. But he says, "Jesus and I, we give each other a wide berth."

"He loves you."

"Not so you'd notice."

"Really?" she asks. "You said yourself it's a beautiful morning. And we're here."

She has a point, Chris thinks. "Okay."

"He's always looking out for you," she says. "You just don't always see it."

I have been pretty lucky, Chris thinks. A lot of guys in this life are already gone, and I'm still here. For how long is another question, but today I'm still here.

"Think about eternity," she says. "This life is just a blink in time."

"You have a great day," Chris says.

"I will," she says. "You too."

He wanders up to the office. The old guy behind the desk turns out to be the owner, a guy named Browning.

"Nice place," Chris says.

"Glad you like it," Browning says.

"The Pig and Whistle, though?"

"There used to be a tavern on this site."

I don't remember a tavern here, Chris thinks. "When was that?"

"In the 1790s," Browning says. "Burned down in 1811."

Like it was yesterday, Chris thinks.

Freakin' New England.

"I saw you talking with Gina down there," Browning says. "Was she driving you crazy with the God talk?"

"She's a good kid."

"It's the Bible with her all the time," Browning says. "But she's a worker. You getting breakfast? Any table, any seat, we're not busy."

Chris goes into the dining room and takes a seat by the window. He's surprised that they have linen napkins at breakfast service and says so to Browning when he comes to pour his coffee.

"I hate paper napkins and plastic utensils," Browning says. "Wasteful."

"Who does your laundry?"

Browning looks at him for a long moment and then smiles. "I thought you looked familiar."

"Me? No. Never been here before."

"It's funny," Browning says. "You look a lot like the man who used to do our linen. Now it's that kid, sometimes the mother, who delivers."

Goddamn Rhode Island, Chris thinks. Everyone knows everyone or knows someone who knows someone.

"You're thinking of somebody else," he says.

"My mistake," Browning says.

But from the look on his face, Chris can see that he doesn't think he's made a mistake at all, and that he knows the whole story, at least the part about Chris Palumbo disappearing.

"Cream and sugar there on the table," Browning says. "The girl will be right here to take your order. And Mr. . . . . Patterson, isn't it . . . here at the Pig and Whistle, we respect our guests' privacy."

Browning looks him square in the eye.

"That's good to know," Chris says.

"The person I mistook you for," Browning says, "was always very good to us. Good service, on time, fair prices. We're loyal customers."

"Loyalty is everything," Chris says.

After a big breakfast of eggs (over easy), bacon and pancakes, Chris stops by the desk.

"All to your satisfaction?" Browning asks.

"It was great," Chris says. "Hey, when does your linen service do pick-ups? The kid you mentioned . . ."

"Jake," Browning says. "Thursday mornings."

It's Tuesday.

Chris takes a hundred-dollar bill out of his pocket and slides it onto the counter. "Do you think maybe you could call and ask them to come early? You were really busy or something, need a supply . . ."

"I guess I could do that. Loyalty *is* everything."

He slides the bill back.

WHEN JAKE GETS out of the panel truck, he sees a man standing in the driveway looking at him.

The man walks up to him. "Jake."

Jake doesn't know what to do.

Maybe punch him in the mouth. That's his fantasy, what he imagines— rearing back and blasting his old man in the grill. Watch him tumble back, hit the deck. Then say, "Fuck you," and walk away.

Jake grabs him and hugs him.

Chris kisses him on the forehead. "Christ, you've grown up. I left a boy, I come back to a young man."

They both cry.

CHRIS SITS ON the bed in his motel room.

"I'm sorry," he says. "I had no clue it was that bad."

Jake has just told him about what's been happening. The guys harassing them, abusing Cathy, milking the businesses.

About John Giglione getting more and more aggressive.

"I searched for you," Jake said. "I couldn't find you."

"I'm sorry," Chris said.

Now he looks across the room at his son—his grown son—and knows he has to do something. Pasco said so; now Jake is saying so; Cathy will say so, if she even speaks to him.

"Mom's missed you," Jake says.

"I thought she'd find someone else," Chris says.

"She claims she's too busy," Jake says. Then he adds, "And I think she still loves you. I don't know why."

"I don't know why, either," Chris says. "Jake, you know I had to leave."

"You could have called," Jake says. "You could have written. We'd have come to where you were."

"It wasn't safe," Chris says. "It's not safe now."

"What are you going to do?"

"Put a stop to this bullshit," Chris says. "But, Jake, it's going to take a little time. I'm going to have to go hat in hand, eat a boatload of shit. So are you. Can you handle that?"

"I can handle whatever I have to," Jake says. Then, "We should tell Mom you're back."

"Not yet," Chris says. "If she knows, she won't be able to hide it, and I need to stay on the down-low a little bit longer."

"Okay."

"You're a good kid," Chris says. "I'm proud of you."

# FIFTY-EIGHT

**M**ARIE PUTS TIM SHEA ON the stand.

She sees several jurors literally lean forward. They heard about Shea's testimony in her opening statement, so they know he's key to the case. They're already angry, upset. They've seen the bloody photos—Calfo's virtually decapitated body, Celia's disemboweled trunk, her unrecognizable face. Marie made a point to introduce those early in the trial to make the jurors want to hold someone responsible.

They've heard the testimony of the security guard at the gate, putting Peter Jr. and Timothy Shea at the scene at the time of the murder. They've heard his further testimony about the car rushing out ten minutes later.

Now they're going to hear from Shea himself, an eyewitness to Calfo's murder.

It's a moment.

Peter Jr. knows it, too.

His friend, his marine buddy who fought alongside him in Kuwait, the guy who drove him to and from the murder scene, can now put him away for life.

When Tim walked to the stand, he couldn't look at Peter.

Still can't—he keeps his eyes fixed on Marie Bouchard as she asks her questions.

It goes just like they rehearsed it.

Marie had worked with Shea, walking him through his testimony again and again, making sure his answers were consistent, and also consistent with the forensic evidence.

So now it goes smoothly. She starts by first establishing that he was at the Moretti residence the night and time of the murders, then asks, "Why were you there?"

"I drove Peter Moretti there," Tim says.

"That's Peter Moretti Junior, correct?"

"That's right."

"Can you identify Peter Moretti Junior?" Marie asks. "Can you point him out in this room?"

Tim points at Peter Jr. Their eyes meet just for a second. "That's him."

"Let the record reflect that the witness identified the defendant," Marie says. "Why did you take Mr. Moretti to the house?"

"To kill Vinnie Calfo and Celia Moretti."

Peter Jr. expects Bascombe to object, but he just sits there.

"How do you know that?" Marie asks.

"Peter told me."

"In fact, you supplied Peter with the weapon, isn't that right?"

"I gave him my shotgun."

Marie looks at the jury. "A twelve-gauge."

"Yes."

"Tell the jury what happened when you arrived at the house," Marie says.

As coached, Tim looks directly at the jury as he recounts the events. They got out of the car and opened the trunk. Peter Jr. took the shotgun, held it behind his back, walked to the door and rang the bell.

Calfo opened the door in a robe.

"Did you hear him say anything?" Marie asks.

"He said, 'Peter Jr., we didn't know you were here.'"

"Then what happened?"

Peter Jr. swung the shotgun up, Tim tells the jury. Calfo turned to run. Peter shot him.

"You saw this," Marie says.

"Yes."

"Then what happened?"

"Peter Jr. ran inside," Tim says.

He kicked the door shut. A minute later, Tim heard another shotgun blast, then another. A few seconds later, Peter ran out the door.

"Did he say anything to you?" Marie asks.

"Not then."

"Did you say anything?" Marie asks.

"I said we had to get out of there."

"And did you?"

"Yes."

"Where did you go?" Marie asks.

"We drove to Goshen," Tim says.

"Did Mr. Moretti say anything on the way there?"

"Yes," Tim says. "He said, 'What did I do? What did I do?'"

"What did you do when you got to Goshen?"

"We busted the shotgun up and threw the pieces into the harbor," Tim says.

"What happened next?"

"I drove Peter to Mr. Ferri's house," Tim says.

"Why?"

"Peter wanted to talk to him."

"Did he?" Marie asks.

"I guess so," Tim says. "He rang the bell, Mr. Ferri opened the door, and I drove away."

"Why?" Marie asks.

"I was scared," Tim says. "I was freaked out."

"When's the next time you saw Mr. Moretti?" Marie asks.

"Just now."

"Here in court," Marie says. "Today."

"Yes."

"Have you spoken with him or communicated with him in any way?" Marie asks.

"No."

"Thank you, that's all."

She knows it was deadly.

The nail in Moretti's coffin.

Bruce Bascombe gets up, walks slowly to the witness stand. "Mr. Shea, in exchange for your testimony, the state offered you a deal, isn't that right? Early release from prison?"

"Yes."

"And they told you that you could walk away a free man," Bruce says, "never spend another day in jail, if you'd testify against your friend."

"Yes."

"And you took that deal, is that correct?"

"Yes."

"Sure, who wouldn't?" Bruce asks. "Peter Moretti was your friend, is that right?"

"Yes."

"You served in the Marines together?"

"Yes."

"In Kuwait?"

"Yes."

Marie knows what Bruce is doing—stringing together a series of short questions, the answers to which are always yes. It does two things: gets the witness into the habit of answering yes and gives the jurors the impression that the lawyer is always right.

"In combat together?" Bruce asks.

I have to break this up, Marie thinks. "Objection. Relevance."

"I'm establishing their relationship," Bascombe says. He knows Marie objected only to break his rhythm.

"Overruled."

"In combat together?" Bruce repeats.

"Yes."

"Forms a bond, doesn't it?"

"Yes."

"Which you've now broken," Bruce says.

Tim looks stricken. Again, Marie knows what Bruce is doing—making the witness look bad. Untrustworthy. "Objection."

"Sustained."

Bruce smiles. Too late. The damage is done. He moves on. "You testified that you drove Peter to his house for the express purpose of killing his stepfather and mother. Is that right?"

"Yes."

"But that's not true, is it?" Bruce asks. "Peter never told you that, did he?"

"Not in those exact words," Tim says.

What? Marie thinks. What the hell?

"In fact," Bruce says, "what Peter said to you was 'I have to do something. I have to do something.' Isn't that right?"

"Yes."

"But he never said what that something was, did he?" Bruce asks.

"It was pretty clear." Tim looks at Marie. "I mean, he said that he found out that his stepfather and his mother killed his father and that he had to do something."

"Did he say he was going to kill them?"

"He asked if I had a gun he could use."

"To do what?" Bruce asks. "Maybe defend himself while confronting Vincent Calfo, a known mob hit man?"

"Objection!"

"Sustained."

"Your Honor," Bruce says, "I can bring in witnesses that would testify to Calfo's reputation. In fact, I could call Ms. Bouchard herself for that purpose and have her testify to Calfo's convictions and prison sentences. She prosecuted one of them."

"Your Honor, could we have this discussion in chambers?" Marie asks. Bruce wants to do it in front of the jury—have them hear how dangerous a guy Calfo was, how Peter Jr. might have felt threatened.

In chambers, Marie says, "Vinnie Calfo was never arrested, indicted, charged or much less convicted of murder."

"But he had that *reputation*," Bruce says, "and it's the reputation that matters, as it goes to my client's state of mind. If he believed that Calfo was a hit man, if he believed that Calfo murdered his father, he would feel that he needed a weapon. He wouldn't be alone in that, Your Honor, a lot of people believe it. Marie here believes it. Ask her. As to his criminal record and potential for violence, I can cite the state's own sentencing memoranda on his previous racketeering convictions."

Marie has to walk through the raindrops on this issue. On the one hand, she can't have Calfo viewed as an immediate threat to Peter; on the other, she needs to establish Peter's motive—Calfo's alleged murder of his father.

"I'm going to allow questioning that goes to Moretti's state of mind," Faella says. "But I'm cautioning you, Bruce, we're not going to put the victim on trial here. At that point, I shut you down."

They go back in.

The question is read back to Tim: *Maybe defend himself while confronting Vincent Calfo, a known mob hit man?*

"Peter never said anything about that," Tim says.

But the damage has been done, Marie thinks. Bruce has introduced an ambiguity about the shotgun.

Bruce moves on. "You testified that you saw Peter raise the shotgun, is that right?"

"Yes."

"But you didn't see him pull the trigger, did you?"

"Yes, I did."

"But you testified that Peter's back was to you, isn't that right?"

"Yes."

"So you couldn't have seen his hand on the trigger, could you?"

Tim stumbles. "No, I guess not."

"Well, we don't want you to guess," Bruce says. "The fact is that you couldn't have seen him pull the trigger, right?"

Tim gets stubborn. "I saw the blast."

"Right," Bruce says. "You testified that Calfo turned and ran first, correct?"

"Correct."

"Could you see his hands?"

"No."

"So you couldn't see if he was holding a weapon, could you?" Bruce asks. "Isn't that right?"

"I guess so."

"This isn't a multiple-choice exam," Bruce says. "The fact is, you couldn't see Calfo's hands, so as far as you know, he might have been holding a gun, a knife, anything."

"Objection," Marie says. "Lacks foundation. No weapon was found in the victim's hand or anywhere near his person."

Bruce shrugs, like, *So what?* He moves ahead. "You say Calfo ran. But you don't know what he was running toward, isn't that right?"

"Yes."

"As far as you know," Bruce says, "he could have been lunging for a gun, right?"

"Objection!"

"I'm examining the witness's state of knowledge," Bruce says. "If counsel wants to introduce evidence that there were no firearms in the house, she's free to attempt that, although the evidence will show that the place was a virtual armory. Do you want me to run down the inventory?"

"Judge, this is just speculation—"

"I'm going to allow."

Bruce turns back to Tim. "So as far as you know, Calfo could have been going for a gun."

"I guess so."

"Again, I don't want you to guess," Bruce says. "As far as you know, Calfo could have been going for a gun."

"As far as I know, yes."

"You testified that you didn't go into the house, is that correct?"

"Yes."

"But that's not true, is it?" Bruce asks. "You did go in, didn't you? You went in and you shut the door behind you."

"No, that's not true."

Bruce smiles like he knows something. But he lets it sit with the jury. "You testified that you heard two shotgun blasts."

"Yes."

"From outside the house?" Bruce asks. "Really?"

"Yes."

"Now, you also testified that you didn't go upstairs, didn't you?" Bruce asks.

"Yes."

"So you didn't see anything, did you?"

"No, I didn't."

"You didn't see what happened in the upstairs bedroom, did you?"

"No."

"All you saw was Peter run down the stairs, isn't that right?" Bruce asks. "Or, sorry, 'run out of the house.'"

"Yes."

"And it was you who said, 'We have to get out of here,' isn't that right?" Bruce asks.

"Yes."

"Peter never suggested that, did he?"

"No."

Bruce picks up the pace. "You testified that Peter said—or rather, asked—'What did I do? What did I do?' Is that right?"

"Yes."

"But he didn't tell you what he did, did he?"

"No."

"He didn't tell you that he murdered Calfo, did he?" Bruce asks.

"No."

"He didn't tell you that he murdered his mother, did he?"

"No."

"You testified that you busted up the shotgun and threw it in the harbor, is that right?" Bruce asks.

"Yes."

"That wasn't Peter's idea, was it?" Bruce asks.

Tim hesitates.

What the hell? Marie thinks. He told us it *was* Peter's idea.

Then Tim says, "No."

"It was your idea, wasn't it?" Bruce asks.

"Yes."

Jesus Christ, Marie thinks. She knows what's coming next.

"But in a sworn statement to the prosecutors," Bruce says, "you testified that it was Peter's idea. Would you read page 124, please? Second line from the top?"

He hands Tim the sworn affidavit.

Tim reads: "'Peter said we had to get rid of the shotgun. Break it up and throw the pieces into the harbor. So I drove him there.'"

"That was your sworn statement, is that right?" Bruce asks.

"Yes."

"So you lied."

"Yes."

Bruce moves in for the kill. "You're a liar."

"I lied when I said *that*, yes."

Great, Marie thinks. Our key witness is now an admitted liar. And the jurors will wonder: If he lied about that, what else is he lying about? Is he lying about not being in the house? Lying about not going upstairs?

She could kill Shea.

Bruce walks right through that open door. "And was that the only time that night you handled the shotgun?"

"Yes!"

"Are you sure?"

"Objection!"

"Sustained."

"No further questions," Bruce says.

He turns, smiles at Marie, and walks back to his table.

Shit, Marie thinks. Bruce just introduced the possibility that Timothy Shea shot Celia Moretti.

# FIFTY-NINE

**B**RUCE'S DEFENSE CASE IS PRETTY much what Marie expected.

He made most of his case cross-examining the prosecution witnesses, so it's short and to the point. He does the usual defense thing of calling the detectives and pissing on their investigation, making them admit to the little things that they didn't do.

It's pro forma and trivial, she knows.

There's really only one more question the jury has on its mind, and it's a big one.

Will Peter Jr. take the stand?

He's the only other person the jury wants to hear from.

She allows herself a rare second Scotch (two fingers), puts a Chopin nocturne on the stereo and sits down to contemplate the issue.

Bruce would be insane to put Peter on the stand.

What could he say? "I didn't do it"? He's already pleaded not guilty. He can't deny being there—in fact, he hasn't—so he can only make a shaky case for self-defense as regards Calfo. That doesn't help him on Celia. He proactively went upstairs to her bedroom and he shot her.

Not that Bruce might not try a self-defense strategy.

A dresser drawer was open in the bedroom and there was a gun in the drawer. Bruce has already had a detective testify to that. But Celia didn't have the gun in her hand. She was shot from the front, so she must have turned around without the gun.

The jury will believe that.

So Bruce might be tempted to put Peter on to say that he was afraid she was going to shoot him.

Marie doubts it will work.

Once, maybe, but not twice. The jury isn't going to buy a story that Peter shot Calfo because he was going for a gun and then shot his mother for the same reason.

So what else could Peter say? Marie asks herself.

He can say that Shea shot Celia.

In some ways, it's a distinction without a difference. From a strict legal standpoint, it doesn't matter which of them pulled the trigger. They're both guilty of homicide.

But juries don't always decide from strict legalism, regardless of the judge's instructions. They decide from emotion, and if they like Peter, if they find him sympathetic—and he looks sympathetic now, the clean-cut marine combat veteran—they might find him guilty of one of the lesser charges.

They might, she thinks with a shudder, even acquit.

And Bruce knows as well as anyone that juries want the defendant to testify on his own behalf, they want him to declare his innocence, and they think it's suspicious when he won't, despite the judge telling them that they can't take it into account.

So there's a downside for Bruce holding him back.

But it's extremely risky.

For one thing, Peter is likely to be a terrible liar. He simply doesn't possess the feral cunning that career criminals have to lie convincingly on the stand. Second, the story he would have to carry is a tough sell.

And third, and most important, she thinks, there's me.

Bruce won't want to expose his client to my cross-examination.

Rightfully.

Not to put too fine a point on it, I'd tear him a new one.

I'd expose him to the jury for what he is—a liar, a double murderer and a matricide.

So please, Bruce, please.

Put him on the stand.

PETER JR. WANTS to testify.

Bruce tells him that he's out of his mind.

"How many assholes are you sitting on right now?" he asks. "I'm guessing one, but however many, there'll be one more after Marie Bouchard is through with you."

"I want to testify."

"To say what?" Bruce asks. "Are you willing to say that Tim Shea pulled the trigger on your mother?"

"I won't do that."

No, Bruce thinks, because you let me do it for you. "Then you have nothing to say that can help you."

"I can say I acted out of self-defense," Peter Jr. says.

Bruce never ceases to wonder at the ability of guilty defendants to start believing the rationales that he puts out. At this point, the kid actually believes he shot two people out of fear for his life.

"You could," Bruce says. "But I've already done a better job of it than you can. Do you want to know why? Because Marie can't cross-examine me."

"I can stand up to her."

"No, you can't," Bruce says. "You want to play it out right now? I'll be Marie? You be you? 'Mr. Moretti, you testify that you shot Vincent Calfo out of fear for your life, is that right?'"

"Yes."

"But he was running away from you when you shot him," Bruce says. "You shot him in the back, didn't you?"

"Yes, but—"

"And you further testified that you shot your mother out of the same fear, do I have that right?"

"Yes."

"But you went upstairs, didn't you?"

"Yes, but—"

"In order to kill her, right?"

"No, to talk with her."

"With a shotgun in your hands," Bruce says.

"Yes, but—"

"She saw you kill Vincent Calfo, didn't she?" This is a guess on Bruce's part, but seeing the expression on Peter Junior's face, he knows he guessed right.

"Yes."

"She was a witness."

"I guess. I—"

"And you didn't want to leave a witness, did you?" Bruce asks. "So you killed her."

"No, that's not why—"

"Or was it because you believed that she conspired in murdering your father?" Bruce says.

"No."

"You did believe that, didn't you?"

"I didn't know—"

"Your sister told you that, didn't she?" Bruce asks. "You heard her testimony."

"Yes."

"So you went up the stairs into the bedroom," Bruce says. "She was terrified, she went to get a gun to defend herself, but you pulled her away, turned her around and shot her."

"No, I—"

"You shot her twice," Bruce says, "out of self-defense? After you shot her in the stomach with a twelve-gauge shotgun, did you then shoot her in the head out of fear for your life, too?'"

"No."

"Wasn't she helpless by then?" Bruce asks. "Dying, in fact? Were you afraid of her at that point?"

"No."

"Because *you* pulled the trigger, didn't you? *You*, not Tim Shea, isn't that right?"

"Yes, it was me."

"'You murdered your own mother, didn't you?'" Bruce asks. "'Strike that, no further questions.' And that's how it will go, Peter, if you insist on taking the stand. Worse, in fact, because you'll have a woman asking you about killing a woman in front of five women jurors."

"But won't the jury hold it against me . . ." Peter Jr. asks, "if I don't testify?"

"That's a risk," Bruce says. "It's a worse risk to put you on."

# SIXTY

CHRIS WATCHES THE DANCER WHIRL on the pole, her red hair whipping her shoulders.

It's funny, he thinks, this sort of thing used to turn me on; now it does nothing for me. It does something for other guys, though. Four thirty on a Thursday afternoon and the place is busy.

And my family is struggling, Chris thinks.

These motherless fucks are robbing us blind.

He signals the topless waitress, but she blows him off. Dressed as he is, holey jeans and an old shirt, she's already made him as a guy who's not going to do her a lot of good. When she finally condescends to acknowledge him, he asks, "Is John around?"

"John who?"

Like she doesn't know, Chris thinks. "John Giglione. He hangs out here."

"Who's asking?"

"Tell him Chris Palumbo would like a word."

It takes ten seconds for Giglione to come out of the back room. He spreads his arms wide. "As I live and fucking breathe. The prodigal son."

"We need to talk, John."

"I should think so," Giglione says. "Let's go in back. It's more private."

"I go in the back," Chris says, "I leave via the dumpster in the alley."

"No, come on."

Chris follows John back into the office, a tight, windowless room that's seen more women on their knees than the Vatican.

Giglione gestures Chris to an old couch and then sits behind the desk. Nice, Chris thinks, he welcomes me to my own office.

"Where the fuck have you been all this time?" Giglione asks.

"Here and there."

"Mostly there," Giglione says, "because no one's seen you here. I gotta pat you down for a wire, Chris?"

"Be my guest."

Giglione pats him down, finds nothing. "So when did you get back?"

"Yesterday."

"Why?' Giglione asks. "*Why'd* you come back?"

"I missed Dunkin'."

"Same old Chris," Giglione says. "Always a comedian. You left a lot of people holding the bag, my friend."

"I didn't take that heroin," Chris said. "Your problem is with Danny Ryan. All these years, I notice nobody's taken it up with him."

"Don't worry about Ryan," Giglione says. "I've got that handled. You wanted a word?"

"Listen, John," Chris says. "I didn't come back to stir onions. You want to be boss, *a salud*, be boss. I have no ambitions."

"No shit. You're shoot on sight."

"I can't pay you guys back if I'm dead," Chris says.

"For some of the guys, that might be payback enough."

"How about for you?"

Giglione doesn't answer for a second. Then he says, "Me, I like money. How are you going to get me mine?"

"Let me earn," Chris says. "You've been soaking my businesses. You're going to run them into bankruptcy. Lay off a little. Let me get them back in shape, put some money on the street, make a score or two, I'll pay you back."

"I dunno, Chris," Giglione says. "I can't issue you a pass on my own. I'll have to talk to some people. If we summon you to a sit-down, will you come?"

"If you guarantee I'll walk out of it."

"No guarantees," Giglione says. "Beggars can't be choosers."

"I guess that's what I am now, huh?" Chris asks. You have to eat shit, though. "Okay."

"Come back in a day or so," Giglione says. "I'll let you know."

"Thank you, John." Eat shit, eat shit, eat shit.

Giglione nods.

Like he's Brando, Chris thinks.

Like he's got a fucking kitten on his lap.

# SIXTY-ONE

DANNY MEETS FAHEY AT THEIR usual spot.

"Licata's moving around from hotel to hotel," Fahey says. "But he has a crew, with Chucky, situated at a cabin out in the desert southwest of town."

"Where exactly?"

Fahey gives Danny the location, then says, "Dan—"

"Don't worry," Danny says, "we'll just keep an eye on them. We won't take any action."

Fahey's relieved to hear it. He's not about to be an accomplice to a hit. But as long as Ryan stays strictly on the defensive, it's all right. And Fahey believes him—he's good people. "Dan, if you want us to run these guys out of town . . ."

"No," Danny says. "They'd just send someone else. At least we know who we're dealing with, and we have eyes on him. Thanks, Ron, huh?"

"You got it."

Fahey leaves the meet and goes to get a Snapple.

That's it, just a Snapple, because it's his routine, his habit, in the hot midafternoons.

Sometimes that's all it takes, a mundane decision to do a simple thing.

He swings into the little strip mall, walks into the convenience store to the back where the coolers are with the beers, the sodas and the iced teas. Chooses a peach-flavored over a plain, goes to the counter to pay for it, and then he sees it.

The little branch bank across the parking lot.

That weird cop sense, the one you never lose, tells him something is wrong.

So he takes a closer look.

Through the big plate-glass window he spots the guy with the gun. Classic black ski mask over his face.

Shit, Fahey thinks.

What he could do, what he should do, is go back to his car, call it in and wait for backup. This is none of his business—it's a job for the uniforms, for SWAT.

But all he sees is the one guy, backing out of the bank now, one of those Lone Ranger robberies that have become common at branch banks. And Fahey isn't that guy—the "it ain't my job" guy. He's a cop, this is a robbery, so he's going to be a cop.

Fahey draws his weapon, holds it low by his waist, and walks out into the parking lot.

The robber sees him.

Grabs a woman just getting out of her car, wraps his forearm around her throat and uses her for a shield as he sticks his pistol into the side of her head. "Back off! I'll kill her!"

Fahey keeps walking toward him, slow but inexorable. Lifts his weapon into a shooting position and says, "Go ahead, she's nothing to me! And the second you do, I blow you away!"

Gives the robber something to think about. He hesitates, then yells, "I ain't goin' back to prison!"

True, Fahey thinks.

He squeezes off a double tap.

Two shots through the ski mask.

The woman faints, crumples to the ground as the robber drops.

Fahey lowers his gun. Never hears, never sees the getaway driver walk up behind him.

Never hears the shot.

# SIXTY-TWO

*READY . . . AIM . . .*
        *"Fire!"*

The rifles crack.

The honor guard lower their rifles to their waists, bolt in another round, raise them again.

*"Ready . . . aim . . .*

*"Fire!"*

Danny stands bareheaded in the rain.

A rare rainy day in the desert.

Eden stands beside him. She insisted on coming to Fahey's funeral, despite the expected heavy media presence. And the reporters are out there, cameras clicking, taking pictures of Danny and her.

He warned her. "They won't stop with photos. They'll find out who you are. They'll link you to me."

"Ron was a good person," Eden said. "He tried to help. I want to show him respect."

That's true, but she knows it's more than that.

Her presence here is also an answer to Dan.

About their lives.

It's a step that neither of them thought they'd take, a step beyond their easy, convenient, comfortable arrangement. She knows that taking their relationship outside the doors of her condo sets it on a whole new path.

If you were your own patient, Eden thinks, you'd tell yourself that you hide behind your work and your books, that you shrink from life (pun intended) because you're afraid of it. You'd also tell yourself that you may love this man, that exploring that love is terrifying, and that you should do it anyway.

Her answer to Danny isn't yes, our lives mesh together, but instead is let's see if they do. Let's set out on that road and see where it takes us.

So now she stands beside Danny, dignified, ignoring the cameras and the rain.

For Danny, her presence isn't any kind of victory, more like the possibility of a redemption. He didn't want to lose her, even if it was just the same arrangement they've had. He has to admit that she wasn't entirely wrong in the argument—they do live in different worlds, and his is, to say the least, morally compromised.

So he's glad she's there, glad that she's willing to take a chance on them, to move things forward.

Glad and scared shitless.

His first great love died of cancer, his second at her own hand. Sometimes he feels like he's cursed, or that women who get involved with him are cursed, that he's the curse.

It's superstitious, it's stupid, but it's a feeling he can't shake.

And will we work out together? he wonders. Can she handle the notoriety, the exposure?

A police officer's funeral is impressive and sad, solemn with the knowledge that it's happened before and will happen again, awesome with the rituals that such knowledge begets.

A motorcycle coterie led the cortege, followed by patrol cars with flashers lit but sirens silent. Then came the hearse, followed by the cars of mourners.

Now Danny stands and looks at Fahey's widow and his two teenage kids, a boy and a girl.

It's heartbreaking.

The widow will get death benefits and Fahey's full pension, but Danny will see that an envelope of cash will appear at her door once a month, and that the forthcoming college bills will be delivered directly to him.

He's aware that it's not an even trade for the loss of a husband and a father.

Nothing can make up for that.

So many funerals, Danny thinks.

"The longer you live," his old man said, "the more funerals you go to. You live long enough, you go to your own."

Marty's sense of humor.

*"Ready . . . aim . . .*

*"Fire!"*

The rifle cracks echo.

A bagpipe plays.

The rain comes down harder.

# SIXTY-THREE

HE'S BLIND NOW," CONNELLY SAYS.

"Who is?" Licata asks.

"Ryan," Connelly says. "Fahey was his eyes and ears in Metro. Did you have something to do with it? Killing Fahey?"

Like I'd tell you if I did, Licata thinks. "It was a bank robbery gone bad, right? They find the shooter yet?"

"Not yet," Connelly says. "They will."

"I hope they do," Licata says. "Stupid, bad thing to do, killing a cop. You're dumb enough to get caught robbing a bank, what you do is lay your gun down, do your time like a man."

"Anyway, Ryan's blind now."

"What are you saying?"

Connelly shrugs.

Like, *It's not obvious?*

LICATA GETS ON the phone.

To Providence.

John Giglione.

# SIXTY-FOUR

**A**LL I'M SAYING IS IT'S a hell of a coincidence," Josh says.

"You're being paranoid," Danny says.

They're driving together from the Strip out to the office where Il Sogno is under design.

"Is it?" Josh says. "Fahey gets the goods on the Coopers, Licata comes to town with a crew, and then Fahey gets killed in a random bank robbery?"

"'Random' is the operative word," Danny says. Cammy Cooper is a lot of things, he thinks, but a murderer?

No.

Or Vern a cop killer?

No.

"And listen to you," Danny says. "Crew."

"I was on crew at Wharton," Josh says.

"You rowed boats."

"Still," Josh says. Then he gets serious. "So what are we going to do now, Dan?"

We're in bad shape, Danny thinks.

He doubts that Licata killed Ron, but what if he did? Killing a cop is serious business, and Licata wouldn't have dared do it without support from his bosses in Detroit. They in turn would have been unlikely to give their okay without the assent of Chicago and New York.

Pasco says that Licata has their support anyway.

So whether he killed Ron or not, Licata is coming with the big families behind him.

And it looks like Winegard has stepped aside, is going to let him do whatever he wants.

I can't go up against that, Danny thinks.

So what's my move?

"We make peace," Danny says.

"How?"

Danny blows out a deep breath. Then he says, "We offer to let Vern buy a share of the Lavinia property. Equal to ours. He becomes a full partner in Il Sogno."

"Are you serious?"

"Serious as a midnight phone call," Danny says. "Are you good with it?"

"I'm not crazy about it," Josh says. "But yes, if that's what it takes."

It's the only way, Danny thinks. And I should have thought of it sooner. A lot sooner.

"But will he go for it?" Josh asks.

Vern hates me, Danny thinks. "I don't even know if he'll take my call."

"Let me make the approach," Josh says.

"No, it should come from me."

"Dan," Josh says, "this is a guy who very likely tried to have you murdered."

"You don't make peace with your friends," Danny says.

When Danny goes to the Winegard Group offices, Jim Connelly comes down to the lobby to meet him. "What the hell are you doing here?"

"I want to see Vern."

"He doesn't want to see you."

"This has gone too far."

"You took it here," Connelly says.

Danny keeps his temper. "I didn't come with empty hands."

"You got nothing in your hand besides your dick," Connelly says.

Danny pushes past him.

"You can't go up there!" Connelly yells.

"Shoot me."

Danny gets into the elevator and rides it to the top floor. Connelly must have called ahead, because Vern is already out of his office and striding toward the elevator bank when the doors slide open.

"We need to talk," Danny says.

"We have nothing to talk about."

"We just going to start killing each other?" Danny asks. "At least hear me out first."

Vern glares at him but doesn't say anything.

"I was wrong to take the Lavinia the way I did," Danny says. "But I'm inviting you in now. We'll set up a new company, we'll share it."

"You take something from me and then offer me half of it back?" Vern asks. "That makes you, what, some kind of hero?"

"It's fair, Vern, and you know it."

"Is Stern on board with this?"

"Enthusiastically," Danny says. He senses that Vern is on the edge. He needs a nudge. "Vern, we both have our pasts. But we don't have to be chained to them. This is a chance to leave them behind. I'll send my guys away, you send yours."

Another elevator opens.

Connelly gets out. "Vern, I'm sorry, I'll—"

"Shut up." Vern hasn't taken his eyes off Danny. "You think there are fresh starts. There are no fresh starts. My son is gone and he's not coming back."

"I know. I'm so sorry. I can't imagine—"

"No, you can't."

Danny keeps his mouth shut. Anything he says now can only hurt, not help. Vern needs to work this out for himself.

"You and me partners . . ."

"We'd shock the world," Danny says.

Connelly says, "Vern, let me—"

"Did you hear me tell you to shut up?" He stares Connelly down and then turns back to Danny. "I need to think about this."

"Of course," Danny says. "There's no clock on the offer."

"No, I'll get back to you first thing in the morning," Vern says. "I just want to sleep on it."

"I look forward to hearing from you." Danny knows it's time to leave.

Outside, he calls Josh.

"How did it go?" Josh asks.

"I'm not sure," Danny says, "but I think we have a deal."

I think we have peace.

Finally, finally, we've left our pasts behind.

# SIXTY-FIVE

LICATA DRIVES OUT TO THE cabin.

He's got his guys on ice there and wants to make sure they stay cool. Waiting around for the action.

Which should come soon, because Connelly did everything but give him the green light on Ryan.

And so did that fed. If Danny Ryan was to go, the FBI would go on a search-and-avoid mission for his killers. Something about Ryan killing an agent back in the day.

So Licata walks in and tells them.

Chucky gets up from the card table and goes to the fridge for another beer. He's a big fucking guy, takes after his mother. Raw-boned. His son isn't the brightest bulb on the Christmas tree, but Licata loves him anyway. He's tough, brave, has a good heart, he does what he's told.

"When exactly?" Chucky asks.

"The sooner the better, far as I'm concerned."

"Far as we're all concerned," Chucky says. "I'm tired of hanging out in Rancho Sand and Gravel out here. Let's clip this leprechaun and get back to civilization."

"I like it here," DeStefano says. "Quiet."

"Quiet," Chucky says. "Fucking coyotes at night. *Coyotes.*"

DeStefano looks over his shoulder at Licata. "Deal you in, boss?"

"No, I got a piece of ass booked," Licata says. Nice one, too. Chinese. Those Asians know how to take a little beating. He had to go to a new service because the old one cut him off. That's loyalty for you, huh?

"Why don't you send some girls out here?" Chucky asks.

"Why don't I just take an ad out saying where you are?" Licata says. "A couple more days, you can fuck every whore in Detroit."

"That would take some time," DeStefano says.

"What do I have but time?" Chucky asks.

"Enjoy your party," Licata says. "Don't get too drunk, we got work to do tomorrow."

Not easy work, either, because this can't look like what it is, a mob hit. It has to look like some kind of tragic accident.

At the very least, a hit-and-run.

It'll work—he has some good people coming in.

Specialists.

Licata goes out and gets in the car. He's eager to get to his Chinese girl.

He loves that little way they whimper.

# SIXTY-SIX

I'M SICK OF BEING IN Danny's shithouse," Kevin says.

"*Dog*house."

"Huh?"

"The expression is *dog*house," Sean says. "Not *shit*house."

"Dog," Kevin says. "Shit. Dog shit. I'm sick of it. It makes me want to drink."

They're sitting in the apartment out in Winchester that Danny rented for them. The TV is on, some dumb show about cops in Miami or somewhere.

"Go to a meeting," Sean says.

"*You* go to a meeting," Kevin says. "I want to get back in his good graces."

"And how are you going to do that?" Sean asks. On the TV, the cops, who are all good-looking, are doing shit that cops never do.

"Trimming the Licata crew might be a start," Kevin says.

"Are you crazy?" Sean asks. "Danny specifically said that's what he *doesn't* want."

"Danny doesn't know what's best for him anymore," Kevin says. "He's lived too long among the suits, he doesn't know what's what."

"And you do."

"I know there's a crew of Detroit hitters looking to take him out,"

Kevin says. "Probably us with him. I know that the guy who throws the first punch usually wins the fight. I know it's better to ask for forgiveness than permission."

"What are you trying to say?"

"I'm not trying to say anything," Kevin says. "I'm *saying* it. You and me should go out on a little snipe hunt. Like the old days."

Sean isn't so sure. He doesn't miss the old days. He likes being a businessman, making legit money, not having his head on a swivel all the time. Still and all, it's hard to argue with what Kev is saying. Licata's crew is probably tracking them down right now, and it's always better to be the hunter instead of the hunted.

And it won't take much of a hunt. They already know where the Licata crew is holed up.

Jimmy Mac is on surveillance there now.

"Believe me, this is what Danny really wants," Kevin says. "He just doesn't want to give the order. He'll be grateful when we present him with a fate incomplete."

Sean doesn't bother to correct him, even though it means exactly the opposite of what was intended.

# SIXTY-SEVEN

"Y OU JUST MISSED LICATA SENIOR," Jimmy says. "Came, stayed a few minutes, left."

It's too bad, Kevin thinks, but not so bad. They know Licata is spending the night at Circus Circus. All the major gaming operators have spies in each other's hotels—no one can go anywhere without being seen and reported.

Apparently Allie Boy don't care. He wants to hide his crew so it ain't obvious, but he knows he's safe on the Strip. It's always been a no-fly zone.

But maybe tonight's different, Kevin thinks.

Maybe after we finish here, we pay him a visit.

He don't let nothing show on his face, though, because if Jimmy gets a sense of what they're up to, he'll have a conniption fit and rat them to Danny. So he says, "You're relieved. We got the watch now."

They're parked off the side of the dirt road on a little hill above the old ranch house, the only road in or out.

Jimmy hands Kevin the infrared binoculars. "There's nothing happening. Six of them in there, drinking and playing cards. They're not going anywhere tonight."

That's for fucking sure, Kevin thinks. "Just to be safe, though, we'll hang out."

"I'll come back at six," Jimmy says.

"Bring donuts or something?" Sean asks. "Coffee?"

"You got it." Jimmy takes off.

"Time for the snipe hunt," Kevin says. They walk to the crest of the hill and look down at the house, see lights through the window, guys sitting at a table. A rickety front porch, a dirt yard, two cars parked out in front.

"I'll go around back," Sean says. "You take the front. Whoever gets a target starts the party."

Kevin smiles. This is the Sean South he remembers from the days when they were the Altar Boys.

Let the mass begin.


DESTEFANO STEPS OUTSIDE to puke.

Seems like the polite thing to do.

He staggers down the two steps of the porch onto the dirt yard and then makes a weaving course toward the brush, bends over to let fly and then sees a pair of eyes looking up at him.

At first he thinks it's a coyote.

The bullet hits him square in the forehead.

Well, that was easy, Kevin thinks.

Sean hears the shot.

So do the guys inside. One's drinking straight from a wine bottle, stands up and looks out the back window.

Sean has the shot and takes it.

Blood and wine spew from the guy's mouth before he crashes on the table, scattering cards, poker chips, bottles and cans.

The others dive for the floor.

Two of them crawl to the front window and start shooting out.

Kevin aims for the muzzle flashes and shoots.

He can't tell if he hit anyone or not, but he belly-crawls toward the house to get closer. He hears Sean firing from behind, wonders how long it will take these fuckwits to figure out they're getting it from both sides.

Two down, though—only four to go.

The Altar Boys, serving Last Communion.

Sean shifts position, moves left toward the corner of the house so he can get to the wall and use it as cover to edge in toward the back door. One of the guys inside has moved to the back window and is firing out into the dark where Sean used to be.

Good, Sean thinks.

Shoot me where I was, not where I am.

He makes it to the corner and presses himself against the wall.

Kevin's only twenty yards from the house when the night lights up.

*What the fuck?!*

Headlights hit the porch and the front of the house, and Kevin is exposed on the bare ground like a convict in a prison break gone bad. He looks over his shoulder and sees the car coming, some kind of fucking SUV bearing straight at him. He rolls to the side and keeps rolling, trying to make it back into the brush before they see him.

He makes it.

Breathing heavy—Christ, it's loud, can they hear me?—he watches four people get out of the car, guns out, scanning.

The front door opens.

A big guy steps out and yells, "Two shooters! One in front, one in back!"

Kevin crouches and runs.


SEAN HEARS THE voices, the footsteps. He'd heard the car engine, the car doors, knows that the fucking cavalry came.

Bad timing, worse luck.

Then he hears shots.

Did they get Kev?

He backs away, still pressing against the wall. His best chance is to get to the corner, press against the side wall of the house and make a break for the brush. If he can get there, maybe he can make it to his car.

Unless Kev is lying out there wounded; then it's going to be even harder.

Or if the newcomers spotted the car already.

Then we're totally fucked.

Why did I do this? he asks himself. Why did I let Kev talk me into this? I had a perfectly good, boring life. Nice house, nice car, money in the bank, and I have to throw it away to play cowboy.

He starts making promises to God.

Let me get out of this, God, and I'll never do it again. I'll live right, give money to the church, go to mass every Sunday and Holy Day of Obligation, just let me get out of this one.

Sean makes it to the side wall, stays tight against it and eases to the corner.

He can see the front now—shooters are spread out in an arc ahead of him and to the right—doubtless looking for Kevin.

Is he wounded? Sean wonders. Lying in the brush like some gutted animal?

Kevin runs.

He was always fucking fast, but now he's fucking faster as he races up the hill. Bullets zip past his head, he doesn't give a shit, he's not stopping until he gets to the car, and please Jesus, Mary and Joseph, let their backs be to me, Sean thinks.

Let them move a few feet farther away and then that's the time to break for it. Get into the brush and make it up to the car.

There's what, thirty yards between you and the brush? You can do it. Even if they hear you, by the time they spot you and get it together to shoot, you'll be in cover.

He takes a deep breath and goes.

Crouches forward and dashes.

The bullet from the house hits him in the back and he goes down, sprawling forward into the dirt.

Kevin sees the car in front of him.

Thank freakin' God.

He turns back and sees—

Two guys dragging Sean toward the house.

Oh, God, no.

No, no, no, no . . .

There's nothing you can do for him, Kevin thinks. There's too many of them. All you could do is die with him.

He gets into the car, starts the engine and backs out.

Gotta get going before they hear me, he thinks. Send cars chasing me down. He does a K-turn and heads out.

Sorry, Sean.

There's nothing I can do for you.

Sorry, buddy.


SEAN WRITHES ON the floor.

Chucky steps on his back like he's some fish flopping on the dock. "You're going to die, my friend."

He kicks Sean over onto his back. "But not yet."

Kevin hits the brakes.

Can't do it.

Can't leave his friend behind.

He turns around, stomps on the gas and races back toward the house, the car fishtailing on the dirt road.

Kevin doesn't stop at the hill but charges down the road into the yard. Sticking the MAC-10 out the window, he lets loose at the house and screams, "Motherfuckers! Motherfuckers! *Motherfuckers!*"

He crashes into the porch, wrenches the door open, gets out and keeps shooting.

A volley of gunfire comes back, blows him back into the open door.

# SIXTY-EIGHT

ALLIE LICATA WALKS INTO A scene.

The house shot to shit, table smashed, broken glass and drying blood everywhere, three of his people dead.

Thank God, thank the Blessed Virgin Mary, his son isn't one of them.

Both shooters are still alive.

Barely.

Tied up and lying on the floor.

Why did Chucky bother to tie them up? Licata wonders. They weren't going anywhere.

"This one," Chucky says, "was clean away and came back. Blasting. Lucky shot got Tony."

"Not lucky for Tony," Licata says. He looks down at Kevin. "Why did you come back? He your boyfriend or something?"

Kevin's in agony. "Mom . . ."

"They all ask for their mamas," Licata says.

"We'll start digging the hole," Chucky says.

"No," Licata says. "I got a better idea."

JIMMY MAC DOESN'T see the car.

Did those lazy bastards get tired and go home? I'll give them such a rafter of shit . . .

He walks ahead and looks down at the house.

No cars.

Shit, did Sean and Kevin desert their posts and these guys slipped out? Now what are we going to—

Then he sees it.

Can't believe what he's looking at.

Kevin and Sean stare back at him.

Their two heads stuck on branches jammed into the ground.

Eyes and mouths open, flies dancing on their tongues.

# SIXTY-NINE

THE CHARRED, HEADLESS BODIES OF the Altar Boys, chained together, lie in the dirt.

"Let's dig the graves," Danny says to Jimmy. "Get them buried."

Danny's seen a lot of violence in his life. A lot of killing, a lot of death, a lot of corpses.

But he's never seen anything as bad as this.

This, he thinks, is what comes of going clean?

They find shovels and bury the bodies.

Walking back, Jimmy looks at the tire tracks.

"What?" Danny asks.

"There were two cars parked here when I left," Jimmy says. "Now I'm looking at four: the two that were here, Kevin's, and a fourth . . ."

It tells a story.

There are two Licata crews, not one.

One for me, Danny thinks, another for . . .

Jesus, no, please, he thinks.

They race to Josh's condo.

On the way, they call again and again.

It goes straight to voice mail.

*"You've reached Josh Stern. It's another* beautiful *day. You know what to do."*

# SEVENTY

RYAN PLAYED ME. VERN THINKS.

Again.

While I was mulling his offer, he attacked.

Killed three of Licata's people.

"I know you're all eaten up with sympathy," Licata says. "But don't worry. We got the guys who did it, took care of them good."

"Then it's over," Vern says.

"Fuck that!" Licata yells. "It ain't over till Danny Boy Ryan is over! And don't give me any of that peace-and-love kumbaya shit. Ryan is a dead man. You want to join him, get in my way. I'll take the both of youse out."

Fuck Dan Ryan.

Fuck everything.

"Do what you need to do," Vern says.

"I did," Licata says.


THE DOOR IS unlocked.

They find Josh slumped over his desk, a bottle of vodka and an empty vial of pills beside his left hand.

Danny feels for the pulse at his neck.

There isn't one.

# SEVENTY-ONE

CATHY DOESN'T KNOW WHAT ELSE to do.

She's out of choices.

She's going to lose her businesses, her house, whatever money she has left. So now she sits in front of a mirror and does her makeup carefully, in ways she hasn't for years.

Sexy.

Face it, she thinks—seductive. John Giglione isn't going to give you something for nothing. He'll have expectations you'll have to meet.

You use, she thinks, the resources you have.

Your body is still a resource.

But for how long?

The dress she's chosen emphasizes her legs—always, she's thought, her best feature. Flat-chested, she can't do the cleavage thing these goombahs seem to like, so the dress shows a lot of thigh to make up for it. And she lays the mascara on heavy, smoky, because these guys can't seem to get enough of that.

Her lipstick is an almost violent red.

Unsubtle, she thinks, slutty.

Almost as slutty as meeting a man in a strip club.

But that's where I'm likely to find him, in my own goddamn club. She had barely ever gone there when Chris was still around—why would she—

and now, when she has to, she usually goes during the day, when the place is relatively quiet, with a few sad losers attracted as much by the cheap lunch buffet as the girls.

But now she's going at night, because that's when John is usually there and to send a message.

I'm here.

I've softened.

I might be available.

Her reasons aren't only financial, although the money situation is bad, but also to pull Jake out of the trouble he's gotten himself into, going around stirring up questions about his dad.

Giglione and the rest don't like it, wonder what he's up to.

She's terrified they might do something.

Jake is home now, back from Florida, back at work, and she hopes he's given up this foolishness about finding Chris.

Chris—if he's even alive—doesn't want to be found. And she knows from experience that if her husband doesn't want to be found, he isn't going to be.

So now she's going to go to John Giglione and flirt.

Maybe more than flirt, maybe she'll have to blow the guy, sleep with the guy, who knows what it's going to take?

You do what you have to do.

You play the cards you're dealt.

All the goddamn clichés.

She checks her makeup one more time and leaves the house.


WHEN AN ATTRACTIVE, well-dressed woman who isn't a stripper comes into a club alone, it's a moment.

Cathy feels the eyes on her as she walks in.

Customers at the bar, guys at tables, even the dancers on the stage sneak looks at her as she stands scanning the room, obviously searching for someone. Their assumption is that she's a pissed-off wife looking for a husband. Even the few—the bartender, the bouncer, John Giglione—who recognize her are surprised to see her come in at night, and looking like that.

The hair, the makeup, the dress.

The fuck-me shoes.

Howie Morisi, Giglione's flunky and driver, spots her first.

"I'm here to see John," Cathy tells him.

"Is he expecting you?"

"I think he'll be happy to see me," she says. "Don't you?"

Morisi leads her to a banquette along the back wall, and she slides in beside Giglione.

"To what do I owe the pleasure?" he asks.

"A girl can't go out on a night?" she asks.

Girl, she thinks. Jesus.

"Sure, but to a strip club?"

"It's my club," Cathy says.

"Yeah, but—"

"Maybe I wanted to see you."

"What for?"

"You have to give me a break," she says. "I'm about to go bust, you have to let me make some money. You and the others. I know you can persuade them."

"What makes you think that?"

"Because you're going to be the boss," Cathy says. "Everyone knows it."

It hits. She sees it in his eyes, the way his posture straightens.

"I give you this," Giglione says, "what do you give me?"

"You know."

"I do?"

"I know you want it. And it's good in there, John. Even better than you think." She lets this sit with him for a second, and then says, "I want it, too. It's been a long time since I've had a man. A girl gets lonely, you know. We get horny, too."

Then she sees him.

Walk through the door.

Chris.

"Oh, didn't I tell you?" Giglione says. "Your hubby's home."

He lifts his hand, waves for Chris to come over.

Like a dog, Cathy notices, Chris comes. Doesn't sit, but waits for Giglione to gesture him to a chair.

Chris being Chris, he makes a joke of it. "John, what are you doing with my wife?"

"I'm not your wife," Cathy says. "I divorced you three years ago."

"No one told me," Chris says.

"No one knew where you were," Cathy says.

Her mind is reeling. She barely recognizes him. His hair is long, his face fuller. And he isn't the arrogant man she was married to, but acting like Giglione's butt boy.

"How long have you been back?" she asks.

"A few days."

"Does Jake know?"

"Yeah, I saw him," Chris says.

"But you don't bother to tell me."

"I didn't know what kind of reception I'd get," Chris says. "Sure enough, I find you with another guy. No offense, John."

John holds up his hand, like, *None taken.* He seems to be enjoying the shit out of this scene.

Cathy says, "You thought, what, I was going to wait forever?"

"No," Chris says. He turns to Giglione. "John, about what we talked about yesterday—"

"I told you I'd have a decision when I have a decision," Giglione says.

"Of course." Chris slides an envelope out of his jacket pocket. "But I realized I came empty-handed. I don't know what I was thinking. I made a little money while I was . . . away . . . This is your taste. The first, I hope, of many."

Cathy watches Giglione take the envelope.

Chris Palumbo kicking up to John Giglione?! A freakin' giant paying tribute to a pygmy?!

She can't believe it.

Giglione, he's as puffed up as a pigeon. He puts the money into his own pocket and gets up. With this freakin' leer on his face. "You two lovebirds probably have a few things to work out. Chris, stay in touch. Cathy, about your offer . . . I'm sure we can work something out. I'll call."

He virtually struts across the room.

# SEVENTY-TWO

THEY TAKE IT OUT TO her car.

"You fucking him?" Chris asks.

"Like you have any business asking."

"You're still my wife."

"Bullshit I am," Cathy says. "You leave without as much as a call? Stay away what, ten years, without a word? Where the fuck have you been?"

"Surviving."

"Well, good for you," she says. Looks out the window and then asks, "Were you in the program?"

"You know me better than that."

"So . . ."

"Cathy," he says, "you know I had to run and you know why."

"Oh, I know why," Cathy says. "They've been taking it out of my flesh."

"I'm sorry."

"Fuck your sorries."

"I deserve that," Chris says.

"No shit, ace."

"So *are* you?"

"Am I what?"

"Fucking him," Chris says. "What's the 'offer'?"

"What was that act in there?" Cathy asks. "You kissing John Giglione's ass. Who *are* you now?"

"Ask me anything but that," Chris says.

"No, that's what I'm asking," she says. "I don't know you anymore."

"*I* don't know me anymore!" Chris says, punching the ceiling. "All right?! I don't know that I've ever known who I am!"

Cathy starts to cry.

It's been building for years, so it lasts awhile. When she finally stops, Chris says, "I need to suck up to Giglione. To all of them. They still might not let me live, but if they do, I'll pay off the debt, I swear. What's the offer he was talking about?"

"He lays off if I sleep with him."

"Do it." He sees the hurt in her eyes.

"You *want* me to fuck him."

"I *need* you to fuck him," Chris says. "It might keep me alive. It's no fun for him cuckolding a dead man."

"Jesus, Chris," she says, "just when I think you can't get any lower, you surprise me. You should enter one of them limbo contests, you'd win."

"Will you do it?"

The hurt turns to rage. "Get out of my car."

"Will you?"

"Get out."

"Will—"

"Yes!" she yells. "I'll fuck his brains out! Just get out of my car and stay out of my life! I hate you!"

Chris gets out of the car.

Hears her crying inside.

# SEVENTY-THREE

CHRIS GETS HIS SIT-DOWN.

Except they don't let him sit down.

They make him stand at the end of a table in the back room of the restaurant.

Six guys sit and stare at him.

John Giglione, of course.

Then Angelo Vacca, Gerry La Favre, Jacky Marco, Tony Iofrate and Bobo Marraganza.

Of them, Giglione's the smartest. The talker, the dealmaker.

Marco is the toughest—the muscle, the killer, the one most likely to take Giglione out and seize the throne for himself. It's also Marco who'll do the job on me, Chris thinks, if that's how the decision goes.

And it won't go quick or easy.

"You wanted a hearing," Marraganza says. "We're listening."

Chris goes with his opening gambit. Starts taking envelopes out of his pockets and tossing them in front of the guys—money he had left from his heroin deal. "I come bearing gifts. A little cash I made while I was away. A goodwill gesture."

"It's going to take more than this," Marco says. But he takes the money. They all do.

"Of course," Chris says. "This is just the start. I know I left you in the lurch, I know I cost you money. I lost it to Danny Ryan. But you all know me, you all know I've always been an earner. And one thing I know for sure, I can make you more money alive than I can dead."

Nobody laughs.

Chris starts to sweat. "I know these are different times. Peter Moretti is gone, *buonanima*, Paulie's playing shuffleboard. I'm not looking for my old place back, I'm not looking for power. I just want to earn, take care of my family."

"How do we know we can trust you?" Marraganza asks.

"I'm here," Chris says. "Let's face it, you can pull the trigger on me any time. Now or later. So why not wait and see?"

No one says shit.

Finally, Giglione says, "Go wait outside. The men need to talk. We'll call you in when we're ready."

Chris nods his head and goes out.

"Fucking kill this fucking fuck," Marco says.

"Concur," Marraganza says.

"I agree," Giglione says. "But not yet. What's the hurry? The wife's about tapped out. Let *him* make some money for us now."

"He gave us each twenty g's," La Favre says, "so there's probably more where that came from."

"Chris could always make," Vacca says.

"You think he means it about not wanting power?" Marraganza asks.

"That's a beaten man," Giglione says.

"You think?" asks Marco.

"I'll prove it," says Giglione. "Bring him back in."

Chris comes in.

They still don't offer him a seat, still make him stand.

It means something, he knows.

"Chris," Giglione says, "if we give you another chance, there's a few things we need to get straight first. You're *our* boy, our bitch. We say jump, you ask how high. We say kiss our asses, you pucker up. Do we understand each other?"

"We do. Absolutely."

Giglione looks over at Marco. See?

"Oh, one more thing," Giglione says. "I'm going to be seeing your ex-wife. That's not going to be a problem, is it?"

"She's my *ex*-wife," Chris says.

"Still and all," Giglione says, "you being a made guy . . ."

"I appreciate the courtesy, John," Chris says. "But it's not a problem."

Giglione pushes it. Looking around at the guys, he asks, "You got any tips for me? You know, in the sack. What gets her off."

It's humiliating. They all know it.

"Well, it's been a while," Chris says.

"Yeah, but you must remember."

"She's not complicated," Chris says. "Not a lot of bells and whistles, you know what I mean."

"Okay, thanks. You can go," Giglione says. "When you come back, come back with money in your hands."

"Thank you," Chris says. "*Thank you.* I won't let you down."

He backs out the door.

"Jesus fuck," Marco says.

"Like I told you," Giglione says.

A beaten man.

# SEVENTY-FOUR

DANNY WATCHES THE COFFIN BEING unloaded from the plane.

Sitting at the window, he sees the hearse and several cars parked along the runway. A driver opens one of the car doors and Danny sees Abe Stern get out—slowly, feebly—and two of the grandchildren walk him toward the coffin.

The cops called it a suicide, of course.

Danny knows better.

Josh loved life too much, would never do that.

What happened was that Licata's crew came in, put a gun to his head, made him guzzle the vodka and swallow the pills. Made it look like a suicide so there'd be no headlines about a "gangland slaying" in Las Vegas.

He knows why, too.

Josh could bring in a freakin' army, so Licata figured if he got rid of Josh Stern, the army would go away.

And he was right.

Goddamn Kevin and Sean, Danny thinks. Disobeying his direct order and attacking Licata's safe house. He knows what they were thinking, that they were doing him a favor.

But we were that close to peace, Danny thinks.

So close to putting it all behind us.

And they had to go off the reservation and wreck it.

But they didn't deserve to die that way. Tied together, burned, decapitated, their heads jammed on sticks as a message.

Freakin' sick.

And Josh?

He didn't deserve what happened to him, either. And it's my fault, Danny thinks. I got Josh murdered. A truly good, truly decent, truly clean young man is dead because he sided with me and I didn't handle my business.

Everyone pays for my sins except me.

He gets out of the plane.

Abe doesn't see him but continues shuffling toward Josh's coffin. He stands there for a second and then collapses on top of it, crying and wailing. The grandchildren try to lift him, but he wraps his arms around the coffin and won't let go.

Danny walks over and gently picks him up. The old man has become ancient. His cheeks are drawn, his eyes mere slits; he's unshaven. He looks at Danny and says, "I blame you for this."

You should, Danny thinks.

"You promised to take care of him," Abe says.

"I know."

"You didn't."

"I know."

Abe turns and with the help of the grandchildren walks alongside the coffin as it's carried to the hearse and loaded inside.

> "Yitgaddal veyitqaddash shmeh rabba
> Be'alma di vra khir'uteh
> veyamlikh malkhuteh . . ."

Danny sits and listens to the kaddish, the Jewish prayer of mourning recited at the Stern house.

He wasn't sure he'd be welcome there, but came anyway after the burial at the cemetery to show respect. Josh's mother had opened the door and let him in. All she said was "Please take your shoes off," as the wearing of leather shoes is prohibited during the shiva. She handed him a yarmulke to cover his head and then went back to her seat.

Now he sits on one of the low stools that are traditional for shiva and listens to the ancient Hebrew words without understanding their meaning.

> *"Yehe shmeh rabba mevarakh*
> *le'alam ul'alme 'almaya*
> *Yitbarakh veyishtabbah veyitpaar veyitromam*
> *veyitnasse veyithaddar veyit'alleh veyithallal . . ."*

Danny looks across the room, lit by a candle, at Abe. He looks worse than before. Still unshaven—as tradition demands, he won't shave or cut his hair for thirty days—he seems exhausted as he rocks back and forth.

The prayer ends and Abe sees Danny. He gets up, cocks his head for Danny to follow him, and walks into his study.

Neither of them sits down.

He's quiet for a moment, then says, "Vernon Winegard."

"I don't think he had anything to do with Josh's murder."

"He invited the monster in," Abe says. "He bears responsibility. I want him destroyed. Not dead—destroyed."

After the thirty days of mourning, Abe tells him, Stern will buy up Winegard stock. It will take over his company, drive him out, and put him out of business wherever he goes.

Danny nods.

"Allie Licata," Abe says, "I want him dead."

"I'll do it myself."

"One more thing," Abe says. "You'll resign from Tara. You'll sell your shares and leave. We'll build your hotel, your Dream, but you'll have nothing to do with it. I will never see or speak with you again. Now please leave us to our mourning."

Danny leaves.

He understands.

A price must be paid.

# SEVENTY-FIVE

**M**ARIE STANDS IN FRONT OF the jury and makes her closing argument. "You've heard the testimony," she says. "You've seen the physical evidence, the photographs, the blood spatters, the diagrams. They're all consistent. It's clear beyond a reasonable doubt that Peter Moretti Jr. went to that house that night with the intent to murder Vincent Calfo and Celia Moretti, and that's exactly what he did.

"Ladies and gentlemen, the classic test is whether the defendant had motive, means and opportunity. The answer in all three cases is clearly yes. Opportunity? Yes, he was at the murder site—he doesn't dispute that. There were two and only two people who had the opportunity to commit these murders: Timothy Shea and the defendant. Whether or not Mr. Shea was lying about being in the house, the testimony is clear that he never went upstairs. Only the defendant did. Only the defendant had the opportunity to kill Celia Moretti.

"Means? You heard Timothy Shea testify that he provided the defendant with a twelve-gauge shotgun and you heard forensic experts testify that the victims were killed with a twelve-gauge shotgun. The defense doesn't dispute that, either. There is some dispute over who suggested destroying the murder weapon. What does it matter? Regardless, the defendant had the means to commit these murders.

"Now let's talk about motive. Did the defendant have a reason to kill Vincent Calfo and Celia Moretti? Again, the answer is clearly yes. You heard Mr. Shea's testimony that they drove to the house with the specific purpose of exacting revenge for the victims' alleged roles in the murder of Peter Moretti Sr., the defendant's father. You heard that they drove there directly from Pasquale Ferri's house after the defendant and Mr. Ferri had a conversation about the murder of the defendant's father and that the defendant asked Mr. Ferri what he should do about it. I guess the answer to that question is now pretty clear.

"Whether Vincent Calfo and Celia Moretti actually had anything to do with that murder is irrelevant. The only issue is whether the defendant believed that they did, and you heard testimony that he heard it from his own sister, who said she got it directly from her mother's lips.

"The defendant believed it."

Marie pauses, takes a sip of water.

Then she says, "Peter Moretti Jr. grew up with a certain moral code. This moral code taught him that he should not seek justice through the legal system or through the police, but that he had the right—no, the *duty*—to extract revenge personally, even if it meant that he had to murder his own mother.

"This warped code has corrupted this state—this entire nation—for too long, and you have the opportunity—the responsibility—to clearly state that no person, no group, no culture, is above the law.

"You have received evidence of the brutal and grisly murders of two human beings. The evidence is overwhelming. The defendant committed the premeditated murder of Vincent Calfo and then committed the murder of Celia Moretti, his mother. His mother.

"I ask you to find the defendant guilty on all counts.

"Thank you."

She sits down.

•   •   •

BRUCE PACES IN front of the jury.

"My client, Peter Moretti Jr., was present at the scene. Ms. Bouchard is correct about that much—we don't deny it. A twelve-gauge shotgun, which was the property of Timothy Shea, was the murder weapon. She's right about that, too.

"Beyond that . . . nothing she has told you is beyond a reasonable doubt. And that is the standard here, ladies and gentlemen. For you to send that young man to prison for the rest of his life, you must believe that there is *no reasonable doubt* about the story that the prosecution has woven for you.

"And I put it to you that there is not just one reasonable doubt, but that there are many.

"Opportunity? Peter Moretti Jr. had the opportunity to commit the murder of Celia Moretti, his mother. But he was not the only one. For you to believe that, you have to take the word of a convicted felon, Timothy Shea, who has accepted a deal, a get-out-of-jail-free card, from the prosecution. Let me ask you this—do you have no reasonable doubt that it was not Shea who pulled the trigger on Celia? You have only his word. He literally drove my client to the scene. How do we know that he didn't drive the rest of the action? We don't. That is reasonable doubt.

"Means. My client had the means, we agree that he was in the presence of a shotgun—Mr. Shea's shotgun—but he was not the only one. Again, all we have is Shea's story. Timothy Shea, a self-confessed liar and perjurer. And that is also reasonable doubt.

"Motive. We have sat here and heard a tale that my client was motivated to murder by a rumor about his father's death. But there has been no testimony—other than Mr. Shea's—that Peter was motivated to kill. His sister didn't say it, Mr. Ferri didn't say it. The only people who have said it are the liar Timothy Shea and the prosecutor, Ms. Bouchard. And I need to remind you that Ms. Bouchard's closing argument is not testimony, it is not evidence, it is only her opinion. Based on what? Not on the evidence, not on the testimony, but in her belief that there is some fanciful 'moral code' about which you were given no evidence.

"No one in this trial—except for Timothy Shea—has stated directly that Peter Moretti went to the house that night with the intent to kill. He might have gone just to talk; he might have gone, yes, to confront his stepfather and mother with what he had heard. He might have carried a gun—if in fact he did—because he was afraid of Vincent Calfo, who was a dangerous member of organized crime as my client certainly knew, having grown up in it.

"And that is reasonable doubt.

"About motive, there is also—clearly—reasonable doubt.

"Yes, Vincent Calfo was shot in the back. But I presented to you multiple cases of police shootings of persons in the back that were ruled justifiable for self-defense. It happens. You heard testimony from investigating detectives that the house contained multiple firearms, that there was in fact a gun in a closet not five feet from Mr. Calfo when he was shot.

"Reasonable doubt? I think so.

"Now let's talk about Celia.

"It's horrific, I agree. Those photographs that you were shown are deeply disturbing.

"But was it murder? Premeditated murder?

"Celia was reaching for a gun. The drawer that contained the gun was open. There was some kind of struggle. But whoever shot Celia Moretti—and we are not conceding that it was the defendant—could very well have acted out of self-defense. Could it happen twice in the same house during the same event? In a house full of firearms, yes! You bet! Can you honestly say that it didn't? Can you honestly say that you have no reasonable doubt?

"The simple fact of the matter is that we don't know what happened in that bedroom. We don't know who did what to whom. The prosecution hasn't proved its version beyond a reasonable doubt.

"We do know that it was Timothy Shea, not Peter, who said they had to get out of there. We do know that it was Timothy Shea, not Peter, who said that they had to destroy the murder weapon. We know that—he admitted as much, when pressed to finally tell the truth. Or, at least, *some* of the truth. He originally lied about those facts. What else did he lie about?

"We don't know. And *that* is reasonable doubt. When we don't know something, there is perforce reasonable doubt.

"We don't know that Peter went to the house with the intent to murder. We don't know if he felt fear when he was there. We don't know it was he who fired the shot that killed Vincent Calfo. We don't know that it was he who fired the shots that killed Celia Moretti. And if it was, we don't why.

"We don't know, we don't know, we don't know, we don't know, we don't know. Reasonable doubt, reasonable doubt, reasonable doubt, reasonable doubt, reasonable doubt.

"Two more issues and I'll stop.

"The Mafia is not on trial here. Peter Moretti Jr. is. Ms. Bouchard has tried to make him responsible for an entire criminal history, which is of course ridiculous. He is only answerable for the specific charges he faces. Ms. Bouchard has indicated to you that by convicting him, you will put an end to organized crime. Peter, whatever family he came from, is not responsible for all that. He has never been a member of organized crime. He has no criminal record. He is in fact a decorated marine, a war veteran.

"Now, the judge in his instructions will admonish you that you must take no negative inferences from the fact that Peter didn't testify in his own defense. He will tell you that this is Peter's constitutional right, and that you must not take it into account when making your decision.

"I know juries—this isn't my first rodeo. I know it's on your minds, that you wonder why he didn't, that you feel that if it were you, you'd want to take that stand, take that oath and proclaim your innocence to the heavens. I understand, I get it.

"But Peter Moretti Jr. is not capable of doing that. That's my judgment, not his. It's on me. Peter suffers from post-traumatic stress disorder, a history of drug addiction, and the additional psychic burdens of having a sister who committed suicide and a father who was murdered. He is simply not capable of withstanding the kind of vicious interrogation that you have seen Ms. Bouchard conduct during the course of this trial.

"You must take the judge's admonition to heart. It is the law, it is your duty.

"When you consider all these issues, when you consider the evidence and the testimony, I know that you will do that duty and find my client not guilty.

"Thank you."

Bruce sits down.

# SEVENTY-SIX

IT WAS GOOD. MARIE THINKS.

It was damn good.

Bruce has landed some punches.

But she has one more crack at the jury in her rebuttal.

"With all respect to Mr. Bascombe," she says, "he is a master of deflection. 'Look here!' 'Look there!' Look anywhere but at what's right in front of your nose, what you can all see.

"So . . . his deflections . . .

"Did we make a deal for Timothy Shea's testimony? Darn right we did. Was Shea always honest? Apparently not, but guess what, ladies and gentlemen, in this kind of case we rarely get to put saints on the stand.

"Mr. Bascombe lofted a ball up there that it was possibly Shea who committed the murders. There is no evidence of this. At all. And I ask you, what possible motive would he have? He didn't even know Peter Moretti Sr. Or for that matter, Cassandra Murphy. Had never met them. But the defense wants you to go running after this decoy.

"Self-defense? Please.

"Vincent Calfo was shot in the back. Running away.

"Celia Moretti? Was she reaching for a gun? Maybe. But here is what totally demolishes any self-defense argument: the defendant didn't shoot her once, he shot her *twice*.

"*BAM!* The first shotgun blast hits her in the stomach at close range. It eviscerates her. You saw the photos. She slides against the dresser; you saw the smears of blood. She sits down with her intestines spilling out and then . . ."

She pauses for maximum dramatic effect, lets the jury feel it coming.

"*BAM!* He shoots her again. Sorry, ladies and gentlemen, but he blew his mother's face off. That wasn't self-defense, that was *rage*."

THERE ARE RAGES that are loud—shouting, yelling spit-flecked barrages. There are rages that are quiet—whispered threats, hissed invective. There are rages that are silent—no sound at all, fury swallowed into the gut.

These are the killing rages.

There is nothing to say, there is only killing to do.

This is Danny's rage now.

He's going to kill Allie Licata. Not going to farm it out, let other people do it for him. Danny wants to do it himself, needs to do it himself.

The silent, killing rage.

Jimmy tries to talk him down. "We don't even know where Licata is now. He's probably back in Detroit by now."

"No," Danny says. "He's here."

He has unfinished business.

Killing me.

"Then he's here with two crews," Jimmy says. "We got you, me and Ned."

"I don't need a crew," Danny says.

"Danny—"

"They killed that kid," Danny says. "They didn't have to do that. I promised I'd take care of him. I didn't."

"So getting yourself killed is going to make up for that?"

Maybe, Danny thinks.

But Jimmy's right about one thing, we don't know where Licata is. And you can't kill someone you can't find.

# SEVENTY-SEVEN

ALLIE LICATA HAS THE SAME problem.

He can't locate Danny Ryan.

He knows Ryan went up to Reno to put the Stern kid in the dirt, but after that, Danny Boy has gone off the radar.

But he knows who he *can* find.

# SEVENTY-EIGHT

H E'S COMING OVER TONIGHT," JAKE tells his dad.

"Giglione?" Chris asks. "To our house?"

"Yup."

The balls on this one, Chris thinks. He's not only going to fuck my wife, he has to do it in my house.

But okay, okay.

"What time?" Chris asks.

"Ten thirty."

"That's a booty call," Chris says.

"This is my mother we're talking about," Jake says.

"Sorry," says Chris. "Okay, here's what I need you to do."

He lays it out for the kid. Well, as much as the kid needs to know.

Then just hopes he'll do it.

# SEVENTY-NINE

THE WAITING WAS THE WORST.

Waiting for the jury to come in.

For Bruce Bascombe, it wasn't so bad. As the old saying goes, in a ham and cheese omelet, the chicken is involved, the pig is committed. Bruce is the hen in this thing; he doesn't want a loss, he cares about his client, but either way the verdict goes, he walks away from the courtroom and lives his life.

It should have been the same for Marie Bouchard. Either way it goes, she also walks away, but she's not sure she can get on with her life if Peter Moretti Jr. just gets on with his.

She has too much invested in this—too much time, too much effort, too much energy. Too much belief in justice. Marie truly believes that she is Celia Moretti's voice in this world, her last and only chance to be heard. So for her, the wait was terrible.

For Peter Jr. it was excruciating.

He is the ham in the omelet. If the verdict is guilty, he's not walking out of the courthouse. He's going to be taken in cuffs to a back room and then put on a bus to the Adult Correctional Institutions, for maybe the rest of his life.

Certainly for decades.

So the waiting was horrific.

A day went by, then another.

Bruce told Peter that this was a good sign, because a quick jury deliberation usually means a conviction.

Marie worried the same.

Most of her verdicts have been fast. Basically the juries have waited to get the free lunch, then come back with the conviction.

Not this one.

Three days, four.

Peter Jr. felt like he was going to break.

Just crack.

But now, five days in, the clerk has let them know that the jury has reached a verdict.

Now they sit in the courtroom and watch the jury file in.

Marie looks at the foreman, trying to get a clue, but he doesn't look back and he's poker-faced.

She can hardly breathe.

Judge Faella comes in and they stand.

Bruce puts his hand on Peter Jr.'s shoulder.

The kid looks like he's about to cry.

The clerk reads from the verdict form.

"On the charge of first-degree murder of Vincent Calfo, have you reached a verdict?"

"We have," the foreman says.

"How do you find?"

Marie swallows.

Peter Jr. grips the edge of the defense table.

The foreman says, "We find the defendant not guilty."

Marie feels her heart drop in her chest.

Listens as they go through second-degree murder, voluntary manslaughter, involuntary manslaughter . . . not guilty, not guilty, not guilty. So either they bought the self-defense argument or they thought Peter was justified in killing Calfo, and to hell with the judge's instructions.

Now Peter Jr. is crying.

Shoulders shaking, crying in relief.

Yeah, well, hold on, Junior, Marie thinks. The jury might not be okay with your killing your mother.

"On the charge of first-degree murder of Celia Moretti, have you reached a verdict?"

Here it comes, Marie thinks.

The foreman says, "We have not."

*What?*

"Your Honor," the foreman says, "we can't reach a verdict."

Marie is stunned.

More stunned when Peter Jr. loses it.

Breaks down.

Sobbing.

Then he lifts his head, looks up and over at the jury.

"I did it," he says. "I killed her."

Bruce grabs him. "Peter, you don't—"

Peter Jr. rips his arm free. "I did it! I killed her! I meant to! I'm sorry! I'm so sorry!"

The packed courtroom goes nuts.

Reporters push their way out to phone their editors.

Faella gavels for order.

Bruce looks over to Marie and shrugs.

Like, *Now what?*

Marie shrugs back. Now what, indeed?

# EIGHTY

FAELLA TAKES OFF HIS ROBE, drapes it over his chair and sits down. "Jesus, Bruce, a little client control?"

"I'm sorry, Your Honor."

"This is uncharted territory," Faella says. "I've never been here before."

"None of us have," Bruce says.

It's a mess, Marie thinks. The Calfo verdict was a case of jury nullification if ever she saw one, and she says so.

Faella says, "The verdict was filed. It's over."

"But they clearly disregarded your instructions, Your Honor."

"And I'm going to let it go," Faella says. "Our problem is the Celia Moretti verdict. We have a hung jury."

"The defendant confessed in open court," Marie says.

"He wasn't sworn in," Bruce says. "Technically, it's hearsay. It's certainly not testimony. I'd move to strike, but in reality, there is nothing to strike."

"He's right, Marie," Faella says.

She knows it. But she also knows that Faella is in a difficult position. By the evening television news, certainly by the morning newspaper, everyone in Rhode Island will know that Peter Moretti Jr. confessed to killing his mother. So what's he supposed to do, cut the kid loose? But if he sends the jury back for more deliberation, they come back in ten minutes with a guilty verdict prompted by "evidence" they should never have heard.

As usual, Bruce is ahead of the curve. "You can't send the jury back. They heard what they heard and you can't un-ring that bell."

"That 'bell' was an open admission," Marie says, arguing even though she knows she's wrong. "It wasn't coerced, it wasn't manipulated, it was voluntary."

"Made by a clearly unstable defendant," Bruce says. "Five more minutes, that wackadoo would have confessed to the Lincoln assassination. The only option here is a mistrial."

"Will you move for mistrial?" Faella asks.

"I move for a mistrial, Your Honor."

"For Chrissakes," Marie says.

"Marie . . ."

"Well, do we really want to do this all over again?"

"That will be up to you, Marie," Bruce says. "You can opt not to retry."

"What," she says, "we're supposed to say it's okay that he disembowels and decapitates his own mother because it's too much trouble for us to go through another trial? That's who we are now?"

"Again," Bruce says, looking at Marie.

"Okay, here's what I'm going to do," Marie says. "Peter Jr. repeats his confession in writing, I come back with an offer of a second-degree murder plea. Does that work for you, Bruce?"

"I won't allow him to repeat that outburst."

"Oh, *now* you have client control," Marie says.

"It's a reasonable solution, Bruce," Faella says.

"Unless you're Peter Moretti," Bruce says. "Sure, it works for us, cleans up a messy problem. But I can't in good conscience recommend it to my client because a retrial is his best option."

"Oh, Bruce . . ." Marie is disgusted because she knows what his next move is. "Then you're going to argue that he can't get a fair trial because the potential jury pool has all heard his inadmissible confession."

Bruce shrugs, like, *Yeah.*

"Your Honor," Marie says, "if we accept that premise, any defendant could stand up in court, blurt out that yes, he did it, and then argue that he can't get a fair trial based on his own confession! We're in cloud-cuckoo-land here!"

Faella sighs. "I have no choice but to declare a mistrial. Marie, if you want to reprosecute, that's up to you. I suspect that a new trial would go forward because you can probably find twelve people who don't watch television or read newspapers. Good luck with *them*, by the way. But it will be with another judge, because I will be down in Delray Beach trying to forget this case or that I know either of you."

"I want the jury polled, Your Honor," Marie says. It would be good to know how close it was, it could inform her decision to retry.

"You're a pain in the ass, Marie," Faella says.

"It's not a hung jury, it's a mistrial," Bruce says. "There's no requirement to poll."

"Thanks for instructing me in the law," Faella says. "There will be no poll. Now let's go tell the happy jurors that they can go home."

He gets up.

Bruce smiles at Marie. "The ball's in your court."

She knows what he's saying.

Go play with yourself.

# EIGHTY-ONE

"JOHN GIGLIONE'S COMING OVER," CATHY says.

"When?" asks Jake.

"In a few minutes," she says. "And don't give me that look."

"What look?" Jake asks. "I'm not giving you any look."

"That disgusted 'my mom is a slut' look," Cathy says. "What do you want me to do, Jake, wait for your father forever?"

The secrets stand between them like a wall. Him not telling her that his dad is home, her not telling him that she knows.

"You've waited this long," he says.

"And it's long enough."

He's that close, that close to telling her. She knows her boy, can see him struggling to hold back.

"So you want me to go," Jake says.

"What, did you want to be here to say hello?"

"Hell no."

"Then you'd better go."

"I'll go out the back," Jake says, getting up. "I don't want to bump into him."

He goes out through the kitchen and the back door.

He leaves it unlocked.

# EIGHTY-TWO

**D**ANNY RINGS THE BELL AT Eden's.

No one comes to the door.

He rings again, waits, then uses his key to let himself in. "Eden?!"

Nothing. No answer.

Then he sees the note on the table.

*YOU WANT HER? WE GOT HER.*

There's an address.

# EIGHTY-THREE

JOHN GIGLIONE ALREADY HAS A boner you could hang a coat on.

What's the word? he thinks.

Anticipation.

He's been waiting years—*years*—to bang this broad, and tonight she's finally going to give it up. Fucking woman thinks her cooch is like gold or something, platinum, whatever, the keyhole to the kingdom.

Hasn't had a man in years? She's going to be *creaming*.

Anticipation.

He pulls up outside Cathy Moretti's house.

Morisi is already parked just down the block. He rolls down the car window. "The kid just left. A few minutes ago. She's alone."

"You're sure?"

"Nobody else has come or gone."

"Keep an eye," Giglione says.

He goes up and rings the doorbell.

# EIGHTY-FOUR

CATHY HAD GONE UP AND changed, "slipped into something more comfortable," like they say in the movies, not some negligee or anything blatant, but a green silk robe that highlights her eyes. She dabbed perfume on her neck and her stomach, which should leave John in no doubt as to what's going to happen.

"You look great," he says when she opens the door.

"Don't I just," she says. "Come on in."

She walks over to the little bar in the living room. "You want something to drink? A glass of wine?"

"What are you having?"

"A glass of wine."

"I'll have a glass of wine, then."

"Red or white?"

"Red."

"Red it is." She pours a glass for herself, one for him, and hands it to him as she sits down next to him on the sofa. "This has been a long time coming."

"What took you so long?"

"I was waiting," she says. "I wanted to see . . ."

"What?"

"Which of you guys would finally seize the reins," Cathy says. "Looks like it's you."

"So that's it?" John says. "You're going to bed with me because I'm going to be the boss?"

"Show me the woman who isn't attracted to power," Cathy says. "It's an aphrodisiac."

She figures that's one of the only polysyllabic words he might know.

He does. "Like Spanish fly."

"There you go."

"Or oysters."

"Even better," Cathy says. "So let's finish our wine and take this to the bedroom."

Get it over with.

That's when Chris walks in.

# EIGHTY-FIVE

IT'S A WAREHOUSE IN THE eastern part of town.

Danny pulls up and gets out of the car. He knows they're not just going to shoot him on sight—Licata wants more than that. They're not going to kill him here, they're going to take him to Licata, somewhere he can die at the mobster's leisure. Then he'll just vanish. "Danny Ryan disappears again."

That's okay.

But that doesn't matter. All that matters is Eden.

A guy gets out of a van.

Nods at Danny, then juts his chin at the van.

Like, *She's in there.*

Danny says, "If you hurt her in any way, I'll kill all of you."

The guy grins. "Nah, you'll be dead."

"My people will come after you," Danny says. "It will never stop."

"Relax, chief," the guy says. "She's fine, just scared is all."

"Let her go."

"It's simple," the guy says. "You get in, she gets out. I'm going to pat you down. You know I'm not alone. You try anything, she gets her face blown off first, then you. You got it?"

Danny raises his arms.

The guy comes over, pats him down, takes his Heckler & Koch P30. "Nice piece."

He walks Danny to the van and slides the door open.

Danny gets in.

Eden's hands are tied behind her back. She's blindfolded, with a gag in her mouth.

A guy sits beside her, another in the front behind the wheel.

"It's going to be okay," Danny says to her. "You're going to be okay."

She's been crying, mascara has run down her cheeks. But she doesn't look hurt, it doesn't look like they hit her.

"Take the gag out," Danny says.

"She'll scream."

"She won't."

He reaches over and takes the gag out.

Danny says, "They're going to release you. Then I'm going to go with them. What I need you to do is forget this happened. You don't go to the police, you don't try to help, you just get on with your life. Do you understand?"

Eden nods. She's terrified.

"I love you," Danny says. He takes Eden by the elbow, helps her out of the van and unties her hands.

"You're going to count to a hundred," the guy says, "just like hide-and-go-seek, and then you can take the blindfold off. You do it before that, the last thing you hear is *bang*. Okay?"

Eden nods.

The guy slides the door shut, goes around and gets into the passenger seat.

The van takes off.

Danny looks at Eden standing there.

The guy points a gun at his head. "Lie down on the floor."

Danny does.

The guy asks, "You're going to make this easy on everyone, right?"

Yeah, Danny thinks.

# EIGHTY-SIX

**C**HRIS CAME IN THROUGH THE kitchen, the unlocked door.

Pointing the silenced .38 at Giglione's head, he says, "Set the glass down, John. Keep your hands where I can see them."

"You're making a mistake here," John says. "I got a guy right outside."

"You got a *dead* guy right outside," Chris says. "I put two in his stupid head. Cathy, you need to get out of here."

"I'm in a *robe*."

"Go," Chris says. "Out the back. Drive somewhere. Stay in the car."

She gets up and walks out.

Chris hears the kitchen door close behind her.

"You bust out my businesses and you were going to fuck my wife?" Chris asks.

"Chris—"

"Chris, nothin'."

"Don't do this," Giglione says. "The other guys will come after you."

"Vacca?" Chris asks. "Dead. La Favre? Dead. Iofrate dead, Marraganza dead. Jacky Marco will be dead by morning."

"Then Pasco—"

"Pasco gave the order," Chris says. "Did you think him and the big families were going to let this clown car spin around forever? Did you really think they were going to let a small-change fuckwit like you be boss?"

The big families sent crews.

Real hitters.

It's over already.

But Chris wanted to do this one personally.

# EIGHTY-SEVEN

DANNY LIES ON THE FLOOR in the back of the van, a gun pointed down at his head. They didn't bother to blindfold him, so Danny knows he isn't coming back. They're not worried about him testifying.

"I'm still going to kill your boss," Danny says.

"Yeah, how you gonna do that?" the guy asks. "From the grave?"

"If that's what it takes."

The guy laughs.

Danny says, "Hey, you'd be up for a promotion."

"Chucky's next in line."

"He's going, too," Danny says.

# EIGHTY-EIGHT

CHRIS POINTS HIS GUN.

"Upstairs," he says. "That's where you were headed, wasn't it? With my wife. Go on, bring your wine."

He holds the gun on Giglione and walks him up to the bedroom, then into the bathroom. "Get in the shower."

"What?"

"Get in the shower," Chris says. "You think I'm going to spray you all over Cathy's nice clean carpet? She's a neat freak, man."

Gig steps into the shower. "Chris, please. I have money, it's all yours, all of it, just *please*—"

"Have a drink, John. It'll calm you down."

"I'm begging you—"

"Have a drink."

John lifts his glass. He needs two hands to get it to his lips, and even then he slobbers it. He manages a swallow before Chris shoots him in the throat.

# EIGHTY-NINE

THE VAN STOPS.

Danny hears a gate creak open, the car move forward and then stop again.

"We're here," the guy says.

Danny sits up a little and looks out.

It's a salvage yard out in Rulon Earl.

A concrete and gravel yard surrounded by a chain-link fence topped with coiled barbed wire. A dozen old cars sit outside a corrugated iron building, which is where Danny figures Licata is waiting to torture him.

Probably looking out the broken window behind the metal screen.

They haul him out of the car and drag him toward the door, open it, and toss him inside.

It looks like a chop shop.

A couple of cars up on hydraulic lifts, another on a jack, acetylene torches, metal saws and sanders.

Plenty of tools for Licata, Danny thinks.

"Danny Ryan," Licata says. "I'd make this quick, but some friends of ours in Providence want you to suffer. John Giglione sends his regards. He asked me to hurt you bad."

Chucky giggles. It's not a laugh, it's a freakin' giggle, like a little girl's. A strange sound from a big man.

Licata watches for Danny's reaction.

Danny doesn't give him one.

# NINETY

CHRIS GOES OUT TO THE shed, gets a mop, a bucket, a pair of rubber gloves and a hacksaw.

He goes back upstairs and cuts Giglione up. Puts his pieces in several black plastic garbage bags, mops up the shower and scrubs it down with Lysol. Then he drives off and dumps Giglione all over Narragansett Bay.

He calls Jake to meet him at the house.

When he gets there, the kid looks shaken. "Is Giglione—"

"He was never here."

Jake turns white. "Did I—"

"You didn't do nothing wrong," Chris says. "You did good. You're a good son, Jake. You're a better son than I am a father."

"So now what . . ."

"I'm boss now," Chris says. "Someday it'll be you, if you want it. But I hope you don't. It comes with a price."

"I understand."

"I think you do," Chris says.

# NINETY-ONE

LICATA JUTS HIS CHIN AT a steel post. "Chain him up. Let's get started."

The two guys who brought Danny in bolt toward the door.

Licata's eyes get big. "What the—"

Danny pulls the gun out, aims it at Licata's head. "You know what someone once told me about you? That even the sick fucks think you're a sick fuck. Your own people want you dead."

Licata doesn't blink. "You think I'm stupid? Careless? I borrowed a page from the Danny Ryan playbook. I got people by your house. I don't come out of here, make a call, your kid—Ian, right?—goes where Bryce Winegard went."

Danny lowers the gun.

# NINETY-TWO

THE SOX ARE AHEAD FOR a change.

Up two runs against the Angels.

Bottom of the seventh.

But it won't last, Ian thinks. Not when the gas cans come in for deep relief. There isn't a lead big enough.

"You want more popcorn?" Ned asks. "Another soda?"

"I could go for a Coke," Ian says. "You want a beer?"

"Bear shit in the woods?"

Ian gets up and goes to the fridge. Grabs himself a Coke, Uncle Ned a Sammy. His grandmother would kill him if she knew what he had for dinner tonight—burgers topped with bacon, potato chips, then ice cream. Now popcorn, pretzels and several Cokes.

But Madeleine's out of town, won't be back until later, and what she doesn't know . . .

He hands Uncle Ned the beer. "Are two runs enough?"

"Six outs? On the road?" Ned says. "Twenty runs ain't enough."

Sure enough, two pitches in comes a hanging curve that goes the other way, over the Green Monster.

"Shit," Ian says.

"Language," says Ned.

"Sorry."

"I can't watch this," Ned says. "Again. I'm going out for a smoke."

"You can smoke in here."

"I promised your grandmother."

Ned gets up and goes out.

# NINETY-THREE

LICATA RAISES HIS GUN.

Danny's younger and faster. It's a reflex action—his hand comes up and he pulls the trigger.

Chucky jumps in front of his dad. The shot hits him in the chest, knocks him down.

Licata dives for the floor, then belly-crawls backward, shooting up.

Danny spins behind the post. Bullets ricochet inside the metal building.

Chucky gasps for air.

Licata calls out, "Chucky! Chucky!"

Danny looks out toward his voice.

Licata fires again. The bullets hiss past Danny's nose and he ducks behind the post.

Quiet now, except for Chucky's rasping breath.

Danny turns to the other side of the post and looks.

Licata is behind one of the jacked-up cars.

Danny shoots.

Licata crouches down.

Chucky crawls toward the car, blood streaking behind him. "Dad . . . Dad . . . Daddy, please. Help me."

Licata won't come out from behind the car. Instead he crawls under it, reaches for his son's hand. "Chucky . . ."

Danny rushes out.

Licata shoots again but has no angle.

Danny steps to the side of the car and . . .

. . . releases the jack.

The car comes down on Licata's legs.

He screams, he twists, he squirms.

But he's trapped.

Blood bubbles out of Chucky's mouth.

He's gone.

Licata sees it.

He presses the gun to the side of his own head.

Danny kicks it out of his hand.

Licata looks up at him. "Your kid is *dead*."

# NINETY-FOUR

LICATA'S SHOOTER, A DETROIT HITTER named Dave Meegan, checks his watch.

Ten o'clock.

Licata's orders were firm—if he hasn't called by ten, Meegan should go in. But Jesus, killing a *kid*? That ain't never been their way.

Families have always been out of bounds.

Meegan don't like it. But what he does like is breathing, and if he don't do what Licata tells him—

# NINETY-FIVE

LICATA SHRIEKS.

*"Oh, God, it hurts! I hurt! Get it off me!!! Get it off!!! I hurt!!!"*

Danny squats beside him.

*"Please . . . please . . . Oh, God! Mama!"*

Licata howls, then moans, then grunts.

His bladder gives out, then his bowels.

He sighs.

His mouth opens.

Danny finds a rag and shoves it into the gas tank.

Lights it and walks away.

He has to get to Ian.

It's only then he feels the blood flowing down his leg and realizes he's been shot.

He doesn't care.

He has to save his son.

God, Danny thinks, please let him be alive.

# NINETY-SIX

THE ARM SQUEEZES MEEGAN'S NECK like a vise.

He tries to turn his head to relieve the pressure, but he can't. Then he tries to reach the gun at his hip, but he can't do that, either.

Ned, he just holds on—his forearms are strong, much stronger than the guy who twists and squirms, then kicks spasmodically.

Then Ned smells the shit.

He holds on for another second, lets go, and the would-be killer slides to the ground. Ned grabs his feet and drags him to the back of the house, out by the garbage cans.

It's a lot of work.

He's breathing heavy as he goes back into the house. "What's the score?"

"We're down a run," Ian says.

"Figures. I gotta make a call."

Ned goes into the bedroom and dials Jimmy Mac. "Have you seen Danny?"

"No. He went to see that woman. Why?"

"Get over here," Ned says. "I need you to take some garbage out."

Ned hangs up.

Then he collapses.

Ian hears the crash.

Runs into the bedroom and sees Uncle Ned on the floor.

"Uncle Ned! Uncle Ned!"

He's scared, but he picks up the phone and dials 911.

Then he kneels beside Uncle Ned and tries to remember what he learned about feeling for a pulse.

# NINETY-SEVEN

THEY'RE STANDING IN THEIR BEDROOM.

"I'm looking at this room," Chris says. "I'm thinking this bed should be on the other wall, so you wake up, you're looking at the sun."

"Oh, that's what you think?" Cathy asks.

"Which is why I said it."

"What happened to Giglione?" Cathy asks.

"John?" Chris says. "He won't be bothering you no more."

"There are others."

He looks straight at her. "No. There aren't."

She gets it.

"So what do you think about the bed?" Chris asks.

"You think it's going to be that goddamn easy?" Cathy asks. "You show up, practically pimp me out, and now I'm just supposed to jump in the sack with you?"

"Yeah, pretty much."

"We missed years together, Chris," she says.

"I know," he says. "I'm sorry."

"Some of the *best* years."

"So we shouldn't lose any more," Chris says. "Come on, help me with this bed."

They move the bed.

Then they use it.

Again and again.

When the sun comes up in Chris's eyes, it warms his face.

# NINETY-EIGHT

DANNY HUGS IAN.
Tight.

"Thank God, thank God."

"You're hurt," Ian says.

"I'm okay."

But it took everything he had to get into the van and drive to his house. Scared the shit out of him when he saw the flashers, then the ambulance.

His heart stopped.

But then he saw Ian standing out there with Madeleine. He jumped out of the van and grabbed his son. "Thank God, thank God."

"It's Ned," Madeleine said. "Heart attack."

"I was with him," Ian says. "I didn't know what to do. I called 911."

"You did good."

"You're bleeding," Madeleine says. "Let's take care of that."

"What happened?" Ian asks.

"I got stupid," Danny says as they help him into the house. "Fell asleep at the wheel, ran off the road."

"Whose van is that?"

"Belongs to some friends," Danny says. "Buddy, do me a favor? Go make some coffee? You know how to do that?"

"Sure."

"Good man."

Madeleine takes him into a downstairs bathroom. She lowers his pants and looks at his leg.

"You've been shot," she says.

"I think it went straight through," Danny says. "You got any Tampax?"

"Those days are over."

"Bandages, then."

She opens the medicine cabinet, finds two large compression bandages. "But you need to get to the hospital."

"No," Danny says. "I'll get to one of our doctors later, but right now I need to go see Winegard."

"Danny, why?"

"To settle things." Danny struggles to his feet and pulls his pants up. "Ned?"

"He's gone. The EMTs told me."

"You'll break it to Ian?"

"Of course, but I think he already knows," Madeleine says. "What are you going to do with Winegard?"

"I don't know."

Jimmy's standing in the living room. "You good?"

"I'm good."

"Detroit?"

"That's over."

Jimmy nods. "Ned left a package behind his house. I took care of it."

Jesus, Danny thinks. Licata did have a shooter here. To kill Ian. Ned saved my son's life.

He protected three generations of Ryans.

God bless him.

"I'm going to see Winegard," Danny says.

"I'll drive you."

"No," Danny says. "What you're going to do is drive back to San Diego, run your business, be with your family. Goodbye, Jimmy."

"Goodbye, Danny."

They hug quickly.

Danny breaks it off when Ian comes in with a cup of coffee.

"Oh, man, thanks," Danny says. "I need this."

"Dad, is Ned . . ."

"Yeah, Ian. I'm sorry."

Ian tries to hold the tears back, but they spill from his eyes and down his face.

"He was a good guy," Danny says.

Ian nods.

Danny puts his hands on Ian's shoulders. "Ian, I have to go do something—"

"But you're hurt!"

"I'm okay," Danny says. "I'll be back in a little while. We'll start planning another bike trip, okay?"

"Okay."

"I love you, kid," Danny says. "You know that, right?"

"I know," Ian says. "I love you, too."

"I'm a lucky man," Danny says. "You go to bed now, get some sleep. When you wake up, I'll be home."

# NINETY-NINE

THEY MEET OUT IN THE desert.

Away from eyes and ears, off a dirt road east of town, along a steep bluff. Now they sit in the dirt at the edge and look out at the full moon over the desert.

"Jesus, Vern," Danny says. "How did we let it get to this?"

"I don't know," Vern says. "Licata—"

"Is dead," Danny says.

Vern barely reacts. Then he says, "Good. That's good."

"Did you send him after me, Vern?"

"I thought your guys were coming after *me*."

"We both fucked up," Danny said. "If we had talked . . ."

"That morning . . . Bryce . . ."

"I know," Danny says. He looks out at the desert, a sheet of silver now under the full moon. "You need to know, Stern's going to destroy you."

"I don't care," Vern says. "You lose a child, the rest of it . . ."

"I'm out, too, if it matters," Danny says.

"You still have your son."

Vern slowly pulls a pistol from his waistband.

Points it at Danny.

"Vern—"

"Walk," Vern says. "Get up and walk."

"You don't want to—"

"Get up and walk, Ryan," Vern says, "or I swear to God I'll shoot you in the fucking face."

Danny pushes himself to his feet. His leg throbs, it's weak under him, but he manages to walk.

Vern says, "You have your son."

Danny hears the hammer click back.

"Hold on to that," Vern says.

The shot echoes through the canyon.

# ONE HUNDRED

EDEN OPENS THE DOOR.

Sees Danny.

He's pale.

White.

She takes him by the arm. "Come in."

"No," Danny says, "I just came to say I'm sorry. To say goodbye. I know you can't be with me."

"I can't, Danny. I love you, but I can't."

"You shouldn't."

"Those people—"

"You don't have to worry about them anymore," Danny says. "They'll never bother you again. No one will."

"What did you do?" she asks. "No, never mind, I don't want to know."

Eden looks down, sees his leg.

"You're bleeding," she says. "You'd better come in, sit down."

"I don't want to get blood on your furniture."

"Fuck that." She pulls him in, leads him to the couch and sits him down. "Dan, I'm calling—"

He's unconscious.

# ONE HUNDRED ONE

TO RETRY OR NOT TO retry, Marie thinks.

That is the question.

Of course, Bruce didn't allow Peter Jr. to repeat, much less write, his confession, and Peter took his counsel's advice. The young man's conscience has whipsawed back and forth between guilt, responsibility and a natural desire to avoid spending his life in prison—Marie understands that.

He's a basket case. The word from ACI is that he swings between near-catatonic silence and manic outbursts, from crying jags to nonsensical soliloquies, proclaiming his guilt, proclaiming his innocence, cursing the world, cursing himself, cursing God.

She's gone through all the technical issues—the cost to the state, the possibility of finding unbiased jurors, the availability of witnesses, the odds of a guilty verdict.

All of them tell her to retry, that she simply can't allow a man to get away with slaughtering his mother.

The practical issues are one thing, the moral issues another.

So now Marie is stuck on a basic question, all the more difficult for its simplicity.

What's the right thing to do?

On the one hand, the right thing is to do everything she can to get justice for Celia Moretti. That's my sworn duty, Marie thinks, as well as my natural inclination.

Celia Moretti deserves justice.

But what is justice for her? Marie wonders.

Is it putting her son in prison for the rest of her life?

Would she have wanted that?

It doesn't matter what she might have wanted, Marie tells herself.

It's the law.

But can the law show mercy?

(What mercy did Peter show his mother? Marie asks herself.)

She remembers her early training, her biblical education. To wit, James 2:13: *"for judgment shall be without mercy to anyone who has shown no mercy; mercy triumphs over judgment."*

She picks up the phone.

Punches in Bruce's number.

"Marie," he says, "are you calling to tell me that we're going to square off against each other again? I can hardly wait."

"I'll accept an insanity plea," Marie says.

A long silence.

Then Bruce says, "Why this change of mind, may I ask?"

"Because it's the right thing to do," Marie says. "I'm not sure that your client is mentally capable of understanding the charges against him or participating meaningfully in his own defense."

"I agree."

"And maybe he can get the help he needs."

"Marie, you do have a heart. What a pleasant surprise."

"But it has to be a locked facility," Marie says. "And we have to have a private understanding that he's there for at least ten years."

"Why don't we leave that to the psychiatrists?"

"Why don't we not," Marie says. "That's my offer, Bruce. You know it's a good one. Take it or we go to trial and you roll the dice on Peter getting life. Talk to your client."

"Actually, I'll talk to Heather."

"Heather? Why?"

"Because I got the courts to appoint his sister as his trustee," Bruce says. "As you're aware, he doesn't have any other family."

"Will Heather take the deal?"

"I'll see that she does," Bruce says. "Because it *is* the right thing to do. Thank you, Marie."

Marie hangs up.

"Mercy triumphs over judgment," she thinks.

Mercy over judgment.

# ONE HUNDRED TWO

**D**ANNY RYAN WATCHES THE BUILDING come down.

It seems to shiver like a shot animal, then is perfectly still for just an instant, as if it can't bring itself to acknowledge its death, and then falls down on itself. All that's left where the old casino once stood is a tower of dust rising into the air, like a cheesy trick from some lounge-act magician writ large.

"Implosion" they call it, Danny thinks.

Collapse from the inside.

Aren't they all, Danny thinks.

Most of them, anyway.

The cancer that killed his wife, the depression that destroyed his love, the moral rot that took his soul.

All implosion, all from the inside.

He leans on the cane because his leg is still weak, still stiff, still throbs as a reminder of . . .

Collapse.

He watches the dust rise, a mushroom cloud, a dirty gray-brown against the clear blue desert sky.

Slowly it fades and then disappears.

Nothing now.

How I fought, he thinks, what I gave for this . . .
Nothing.
This dust.
He turns away and limps through his city.
His city in ruins.

# Home

## Rhode Island
## 2023

What is left at the last?

Virgil
*The Aeneid*
(Book 12, Line 818)

AN WALKS ALONG THE BEACH.

Save for him and the small film crew, it's deserted on this November morning. The wind blows from the northeast, the ocean is the bottle-green of late fall.

"This is where it all started," the interviewer, Jeff Gold, says.

He's doing a story for CBS about Ian Ryan, the newest gambling mogul, who has built an empire, and this location is important background for the piece.

"So I'm told," Ian says. "I wasn't born, but, yes, my understanding is that the war between the Irish and the Italians started after a clambake right about here."

Jeff points to a house a few feet above the high-tide line. The cameraman swings his camera to follow his prompt. "That was Pasco Ferri's house."

"It was," Ian says.

"And now you've bought it," Jeff says.

The camera swings back for a close-up on Ian's face.

"I did," Ian says. He points to the two houses to the east of it. "And that one and that one."

It had cost him eight mil and change to buy the three modest beach cottages, but it's worth it.

His wife, Amy, likes it more than the Vegas estate, more than the ski chalet in Park City, even the cottage in Aix-en-Provence. She likes its simplicity, its ease, that the kids can spend the summer on the beach, boogie-boarding, swimming, building sandcastles, digging holes.

Ian has three kids of his own now—Theresa is ten; the twins, James and Ned, are seven. He looks at them now, totally absorbed in building a big sandcastle, a veritable city of towers, walls, even bridges made from small pieces of driftwood. It's too close to the high-tide line, but he doesn't say anything. It's a lesson they'll learn—castles of sand don't last.

So Ian bought the houses for them, but also for Amy's family—her parents, siblings and cousins. What he envisions is an extended family compound where people can come for the summer, or a week, or a few days to escape the brutal Las Vegas heat.

And be together.

Which is important to Ian. His own nuclear family was small—his dad, his grandmother and him, basically—and now he loves having a lot of relatives around. He knows that he's way ahead of himself, too, imagining his kids bringing their kids here, to hang out with Grandpa and Grandma.

The real estate agents tried to steer him to the tonier areas of Narragansett and Watch Hill, with their coastal mansions, but Ian wanted to be here. This was his old man's place, his favorite place in the world, a place from which he was exiled.

And now I'm bringing him home, Ian thinks.

He feels a little guilty, combining his last obligation to his dad with a publicity piece, but his father would understand. The company's next big hotel, the Neptune, opens New Year's Eve, and the profile on the popular Sunday-morning TV show will be a big boost.

"Why?" Jeff asks. "Why did you buy three houses, and why here?"

He knows the answers, he's cuing Ian. Tossing softballs.

"My dad loved it here," Ian says. "It meant something to him. I want my kids to spend time in a place that means something."

"There's a story," Jeff says, "that your father . . . well, fled . . . from here with you, just a baby, in the back seat."

"That's true."

"So this is a homecoming for you, too."

"Also true," Ian says.

"Maybe even a little revenge?" Jeff asks. "I mean, you buy a place you were basically thrown out of."

Ian feels the camera focus on him. He makes a point to look Jeff straight in the eye. "I'd say more redemption than revenge."

"This would have made your dad happy."

"I like to think so," Ian says. "He was a good guy, my dad. He had a past he wasn't proud of, but he did his best to live decently in an indecent world. He was a great father."

"And now you're the wunderkind of the gaming industry," Jeff says.

Ian laughs. "Is that what I am?"

"Well," Jeff says, "you combined the Tara Group and the Stern Company and built an empire, the largest gaming conglomerate in the world. Casinos and hotels on five continents. And you're thirty-six. What would you call yourself?"

"Lucky," Ian says.

"Come on, it's more than that."

"It is," Ian says. "My dad taught me to treat people decently, fairly and honestly. That's been a big part of our success."

"You must feel gratified that your father lived to see it," Jeff says.

"Sure."

His dad left the business so abruptly, after all the trouble with Winegard, which Ian didn't understand then and barely understands even now. He had the feeling then that his father had been forced out, perhaps not entirely unwillingly. After that, Dad was home a lot more, spent time with Ian—biking, going to soccer games, playing tennis, watching movies . . .

Ian remembers him as a little sad, a little lonely. But not depressed, certainly not depressing. He was relatively young, still had a lot of energy, and he put most of it into his son.

Ian remembers the conversation about their wealth.

He was sixteen, a typical teenager, and his dad sat him down out by the pool and asked, "What do you think you want to do with your life?"

"I dunno," Ian said. "I mean, we're rich."

"*I'm* rich," his dad said. "You're a pauper."

Ian remembers feeling stunned.

"I'm going to give you enough money to do something," his dad said, "but not enough to do nothing. So what do you think you want to do?"

"I want to go into the family business."

"You don't have to," Danny said. "You can do anything you want, be anything you want."

"I want this."

"Okay," Danny said. "You can always change your mind, but that means college, business school . . . In the meantime, you start as a dishwasher in one of our restaurants."

Ian went and told his grandmother what his dad had told him.

"Good," Madeleine said. "We have too many entitled little twits running around as it is."

Ian still misses his grandmother.

For all intents and purposes, she was his mother. Took care of him when his dad was off doing . . . whatever it was he did. Ian is grateful that she got to meet Amy, that she liked her, got to come to the wedding. When Madeleine passed, he cried like a baby.

Resented his father for being dry-eyed at the funeral.

"Your grandmother and I had a complicated relationship," Danny said.

"Did you love her?" he asked.

"Eventually," Danny said. "Yes, I did."

Anyway, it was Madeleine who advised Ian to do what his father said, learn the business from the bottom up.

Ian did.

Worked his ass off washing dishes.

Hated it and loved it. Loved the camaraderie, the sense of accomplishment, the satisfaction of putting in a good hard shift. Worked his way to busboy and eventually to server.

He stayed in town for undergraduate, working as a room cleaner and a bellman and as a parking valet on the side and during the summers. Took a psych class from a woman professor who looked at him a little intensely, and he found out later that she had once been involved with his father.

He and his dad were walking down the Strip one day when they bumped into Dr. Landau, and Ian was surprised when she greeted his dad first.

"Dan," she said, "how nice to see you."

Ian was more surprised when she kissed his dad on the cheek.

"Eden," Danny said. He took her hands, both of them. They looked at each other for a couple of long moments, and Ian felt like he was intruding on something, something intimate.

Danny smiled. "You're good?"

She nodded. "I am. And you?"

"This is my son, Ian."

"I know Ian," Eden said. "He's in one of my classes."

"Ah."

"Well . . ."

"Yeah, it's . . . hot out here."

Then Ian saw his dad lift her hands to his lips and gently kiss them. Then he let her go. "It's great to see you."

"Wonderful to see you."

And that was it. They walked away in different directions. Ian wanted to ask about her, but there was a sadness in his father's eyes that stopped him.

By the time he was ready for graduate school, Ian knew the hotel business from the kitchen to the front desk to the boiler room, and he went to Wharton with a practical hands-on knowledge that most of his colleagues didn't possess. He came home between semesters and worked as a bartender, later as a blackjack dealer, still later in security and the counting room.

He had his MBA and had been working at the company headquarters for three years when his father sat him down again. "Do you still want to be in the business?"

"Very much."

"Okay," Danny said. "Over the past few years I've been transferring shares of Tara to you in trust, kept by the Stern management. In two years, the trust will be transferred to you."

Again, Ian was stunned. "How many shares?"

"In two years," Danny said, "you'll own 51 percent of Tara. Do something with it."

Ian did.

Controlling the Strip was fine, but Ian and the younger generation at Stern—Joshua's cousins—agreed that the world was bigger than Las Vegas, that taking it to the next level meant going international. Over the next few years they bought or built hotels in Rio, Dubai, Macau, Mexico City.

And it was Ian who put together the deal with Barry Levine, a merger that created the largest gaming conglomerate the world had ever seen.

But always, *always*, his focus was on customer service, creating and maintaining customer loyalty.

Ian knew his dad was proud.

Proud, too, and happy about Ian's marriage to Amy. When he came to the hospital at Theresa's birth and heard her name, it was the first and only time Ian saw his dad come close to tears.

"Your mom would . . ."

"I know."

When the twins came along, Danny was over the moon, and he became *that* grandpa. He played hide-and-go-seek and had tea parties with Theresa. One Easter he strung lollipop chains from the trees, hid eggs and led a kids-only search.

He loved being with his grandkids.

He didn't have enough time with them.

It started innocuously at a Memorial Day family cookout when Danny started slurring words. Ian wrote it off as maybe one beer too many, but a few days later Danny was forgetting words altogether. Then he got dizzy and fell. The brain scan that Ian forced him to undergo showed the tumor.

Malignant, hostile, aggressive.

Inoperable.

The doctors, the best that a billion dollars could afford, wanted him to undergo radiation, laser, chemotherapy to buy him some time. Danny cooperated for a few weeks, then basically told them to go fuck themselves.

"You went all Marty on them," Ian told him, referring to his grandfather.

"Marty wasn't *all* bad," Danny said. "Just mostly bad."

Danny's passing wasn't easy, quick or noble. He was mostly out of it on morphine.

He had no coherent last words.

Ian was with him at the last, the next September, holding his hand when he stopped breathing.

When it was over, it was just over.

Now Jeff is looking at him curiously. "Where did you go just then?"

"Into the past, I guess," Ian says.

"Your father."

Ian nods.

"This place is evocative."

"It is," Ian says.

He sees Amy walking down from the house.

Ian watches her, never tires of it. That strong, beautiful face, long blond hair disheveled in the wind, blowing across her black cable-knit sweater. Under her left arm, she cradles a brass urn.

She walks up and kisses him on the cheek. "Do you want to do this now?"

"Yeah."

Amy hands him the urn.

His dad was clear about his wishes—no funeral, no burial, no memorial service, no "celebration of life." All he wanted, *all* he wanted, was for his ashes to be thrown into the ocean here.

Amy takes him by the elbow and they walk to the edge of the water, where the kids are still playing.

Spindrift dances across the tops of the waves.

Ian's aware of the cameras behind him, and then he forgets about them as he realizes that his cheeks are wet with tears.

Amy's hand tightens on his arm. "He was a good guy."

"It's funny," Ian says. "Given his history, the stories that I've heard about him—I don't know how true they are—that can be hard to explain sometimes, even to myself. But he took care of his friends, he took care of his family, and I think that makes him, yeah, a good guy."

He opens the urn.

Tips it upside down and pours the ashes into the sea.

A strong wave crashes, breaks into white water, rushes in and hits the sandcastle, wiping it out.

The kids moan and then laugh.

They'll build another one tomorrow.

Or the next day.

The same wave rushes back out and takes the ashes with it.

Danny Ryan is home.

# ACKNOWLEDGMENTS

S O. HOW?

How, after a long and happy career, can I even *begin* to thank all the people who contributed to that life of writing, without whom, in fact, it could never have happened?

It's impossible, yet I have to try.

Start with my parents, Don and Ottis Winslow, bibliophiles both, who always made sure there were books around the house and who allowed my sister, Kristine Rolofson—also a novelist with a fine career of her own—and me to read anything we wanted at any age.

Then there are the teachers and librarians, those unsung, underpaid and oft-abused heroes and heroines who taught me to read and write and who provided a world of wonder and imagination to a kid in a small town. I thank them all, but particularly the late Winthrop Richardson and Josephine Gernsheimer and my dear friend Bill McEneaney, who taught me, among many others things, to love and appreciate jazz.

Later there are the professors at the University of Nebraska. Again, I thank them all, but particularly: James Neal, who in his "basic reporting" class taught me to write a basic declarative sentence; Leslie C. Duly, who brought me to African history; Martin Q. Peterson, for believing in me; Roberto Esquenazi-Mayo, for all his support; and, especially the great military historian Peter Maslowski, who taught me how to work, teach, research and so much more, and who has been a treasured friend for over forty years.

Later still comes Professor James G. Basker, who turned me on to picaresque literature (the progenitors of my beloved noir fiction) and brought me to Oxford for those years directing Shakespeare productions that were so formative to my career. Again, he remains a dear friend.

Then there is my great mentor, the late, legendary Sonny Mehta. One of the great moments of my life was sitting with him at his kitchen table as we went over his careful, handwritten marginal notes of my manuscript for *The Power of the Dog*. It was the sort of thing I dreamed about as an aspiring author, and there were many such moments with Sonny. I miss and mourn him.

Then again, I have been blessed with editors, from Reagan Arthur (my first book was her first as well) to my current wonderful editor, Jennifer Brehl, whose careful and thoughtful work has made this trilogy much better than it would otherwise have been.

And to my poor, long-suffering copy editors, I express both my apologies for all my mistakes and my appreciation for your redeeming them.

I have been likewise lucky with publishers, and want to express my deep gratitude to Liate Stehlik at William Morrow for her trust and enthusiasm, and to Brian Murray for all his support.

There are so many people at William Morrow to whom I owe my appreciation: Andy LeCount, Julianna Wojcik, Kaitlin Harri, Danielle Bartlett, Jennifer Hart, Christine Edwards, Andrea Molitor, Ben Steinberg, Chantal Restivo-Alessi, Frank Albanese, Nate Lanman and Juliette Shapland. Thank you for all your fine efforts on my behalf.

To all the marketing and publicity staff at HarperCollins/William Morrow, I know that you have a tough and demanding job, and I'm so appreciative that you do it so well.

And a big thank-you to my lawyer, Richard Heller.

To my followers on social media, @donwinslow on Twitter, the #DonWinslowBookClub, and the troops of the #WinslowDigitalArmy, I can't thank you enough for all the support. The fight goes on; thank you for marching with me.

How do I thank The Story Factory (more about which below)? To Deb Randall and Ryan Coleman, thank you so much for everything that you do for me and a whole bunch of other authors. I'm so lucky to have you.

I've also been blessed with the support and friendship of so many authors over the years, colleagues and heroes of mine who have been so generous to me—Michael Connelly, Robert Parker, Elmore Leonard, Lawrence Block, James Ellroy, T. Jefferson Parker, Adrian McKinty, Steve Hamilton, Lee Child, Lou Berney, Anthony Bourdain, Ian Rankin, John Katzenbach, John Sandford, Joseph Wambaugh, Gregg Hurwitz, David Corbett, TJ Newman, Mark Rubenstein, Jon Land, Richard Ford, Pico Iyer, Meg Gardiner, Dervla McTiernan, Reed Farrel Coleman, Ken Bruen, Jake Tapper, John Grisham, David Baldacci and so many others. The crime fiction community is truly a family, and I've been so honored to be one of them.

My special thanks, of course, to the great Stephen King. How kind, gracious and generous you have been to me.

To the journalists, reviewers and radio, television and podcast hosts who have done so much to get the word out about my work, I am truly appreciative of all your hard work and support.

And to the booksellers, all over the world—without you I would not have had this career. You have been so supportive, so warm and hospitable, and stuck with me through events that have been both great and not so great. I owe you all so much, but I want to give a special thanks to Barbara Peters at the iconic Poisoned Pen, where, at my first signing, I sold exactly one book—because Barbara bought it.

To my readers—again, all over the world—how do I begin to thank you? How do I even begin to express how much you mean to me? I owe you all the good material things I have in life, and, more than that, I thank you for all the support, appreciation, for all the warmth you have shown me at readings and other events. It's meant the world. I've tried to do my best for you, and my greatest hope is that I've never let you down.

I've often said that you'll know your true friends on two occasions, when you've had a great success and a great failure, because they'll be the same people. I have been so blessed with so many friends—David Nedwidek and Katy Allen, Pete and Linda Maslowski, Jim Basker and Angela Vallot, Teressa Palozzi, Drew Goodwin, Tony and Kathy Sousa, John and Theresa Culver, Scott and Jan Svoboda, Jim and Melinda Fuller, Ted Tarbet, Thom Walla, Mark Clodfelter, Roger Barbee, Donna Sutton, Virginia and Bob Hilton, Bill and Ruth McEneaney, Andrew Walsh, Nehru King, Wayne Worcester, Jeff and Rita Parker, Bruce Riordan, Jeff and Michelle Weber, Don Young, Mark Rubinsky, Cameron Pierce Hughes, Rob Jones, David and Tammy Tanner, Ty and Dani Jones, Deron and Becky Bisset, "Cousin" Pam Matteson, David Schniepp . . . so many. I treasure you.

And how do I thank Shane Salerno, my agent and dear, dear friend? You took over my career when it was in the ditch, turned it around and set it on the high road, where it would never have gone without you. You have been tireless, brave, creative and ferocious on my behalf. I truly don't know how to thank you, except to have tried to give you the best work I could. Thank you, brother.

To my son, Thomas, and his bride, Brenna: you have given me so much joy and pride over these years. I know, Thomas, that being your father has been my best and happiest work.

To my wife, Jean: What can I say? How can I thank you? You have literally given blood, sweat and tears, cheerfully stuck with me through some very thin years, been so patient, warm, supportive, enthusiastic and energetic, been both a wonderful mother and a wonderful partner as we struggled to build a life. I have loved every moment of it, because it was with you. I love you madly.

Goodbyes are hard.

After a long and wonderful career—much more than I ever dreamed—I can only say a simple and sincere "thank you" to all of you.

Thank you so, so much.